JACK MURPHY

AND THE TRIALS OF TITANS

BOOK 1

WRITTEN BY

RICHARD A. DANIELS

Special Thanks

I would like thank my parents, family, friends, students, wife, and children for sharing in the beginning this journey. Without your ears allowing me to ramble for hours, none of this would be possible.

Thank you all.

Dedication

Special dedication to my grandparents Al and Ann Thoren, aka Papaw and Mammy. You both have supported me every step of the way and always believed I could achieve anything. You used to say, dynamite comes in small packages and it's time now to blow up. ;-)

Much love,

CAL

Oh, I like to acknowledge all the OG students who listened and motivated me to start this journey. From 1st period APHUG, the real Jack Murphy, Sam and Max Duval. Thank you students for being the best part of teaching.

Stay up to date on series news, signings, promotions, etc.

Visit official website with QR code

Editor and Proofing - Paige Lawson @paigelawson216

Cover Art - Razia Naveed @razia_naveed

Staten House

CONTENTS

CHAPTERS

"Thank you for your support. Please recommend to friends and family. The more books in this series sell, the more can be donated to SynGAP1 research, Cerebral Palsy research, and various local charities supported throughout the year. Every bit helps, many voices are heard together, and you can make the difference. Happy reading and enjoy the story. Sincerely thank you!"

- Richard A. Daniels

CHAPTER ONE

A BOY NAMED JACK

The crack of twigs and crunch of crisp leaves fades, softly giving way to laughter innocently inoculating the woods. Friends frolic foolishly, tagging each other. A sun-kissed canopy warming all below, filling the air with life's simplest joys. To play, to laugh, to bond.

"Jack, where are you? None of that Ninja Warrior stuff you're always pulling." A rather out-of-place-looking girl with faded pink dirty-blonde hair flowing behind awkwardly jogs down a leaf-covered path amongst randomly arranged trees.

"Tag, you're it, Ari!" A voice calls from behind.

The athletically challenged teen spins stiffly, finding only an empty path. "Jack, no fair; I said no MacGryber Ninja warrior stuff! Com'n, I'm serious, Jack!" Ari stamps her foot.

"It's MacGyver, Ari . . . you're still it." The voice emanating from thin air breaks through the ambient sounds of nature.

Spinning slowly, Ari's eyes dart in all directions. "Every time. . ." she mutters, assuming her companion's concealed close enough to hear anything above a whisper.

7

"ARI, JACK, WHERE YA'LL AT?!? IT'S HOT, huh . . . huh hot out here! Can we go inside now? Got Dekken Dragons boaster packs comin' today! Can we go home!?!" A third voice gasps.

Ari heads towards her less spectral sidekick. Winding through an aging forest, locating her friend.

"Do you always have to shout, Reggie?" Still glancing over her shoulder for a hint to Jack's location.

"JACK COME OUT! IT'S HOTTER THAN VENUS's. . ."

"Shhhhh, don't be gross. Shh . . . he's near." Pressing a finger to faded pink and blue lips, Ari instructs her portly pal silently around a large Oak.

Pausing, the pair navigate each side of the ancient Oak. Moss dances from every passing breeze. Ari points to herself, then to Reggie, who uncomfortably steadies himself. Ari gestures quietly, beginning her countdown.

"One, two, threeeee!" Ari lunges awkwardly, Reggie tripping on a root and falling off balance. Colliding unavoidably from their collective clumsiness. "Ouwwwaaa, Reggie, you big galoot, I said on three!" Ari shrieks angrily.

"Me? You're da one who counts like they're tryin' to beat Dale Earnhardt in a race!" Reggie moans, brushing bark from his arms.

"Dale, who?" Ari rubs feeling into her legs, brushing bits of bark and dirt from her clothing.

"WHAT DO YOU MEAN, DALE WHO? He's only da greatest driver EVER! Number 3? THE INTIMIDATOR?"

8

Reggie frantically points to his faded black hat displaying a dingy silver red trimmed number three.

"More like THE IMPALER!" Ari rises gingerly to her feet, still reeling from their collision.

"Ooo, don't have that card, think it will come today?" Reggie asks ridiculously, brushing bark from his back.

"C'mon, guys, one's supposed to go high, one low. Jeeze, you guys are a mess." A victorious voice chuckles, emanating from above.

"Hey, no fair, Jack! You know we ain't no good at climbing trees." Reggie scrambles to his feet.

"Yeah, Jack, no fair! The rules of tag clearly state . . ." Ari begins to protest, cut off by her clearly superior opponent.

"Oh, c'mon, guys, just havin a bit of fun!" Jack exclaims, executing an agile landing from his perch above. Flipping luscious locks from his eyes. "More importantly, you two gonna survive?" He consoles, attempting to brush debris from Reggie's back.

"No, no, I can do it myself, mister climby, climby, flippy, flippy." Reggie pushes him off. "Oh, c'mon, Reg, don't be like that, betcha pull Impaler today." Jack catches his friend with ease.

"Jack, you always do this!" Ari retorts.

"Do what?" Jack's mood turns from jest to genuine concern.

"You know what! You play too hard, and we can't keep up. Besides, Reggie is right; it's hot out here. Can we go inside now?"

Much to his dismay, Jack yields to his friend's request, following them down a leafy path.

"Jack . . . ya really think I'll pull Impaler today? . . ." Reggie confides, concealing concern.

"No Reg . . . nobody pulls Impaler." Jack pats Reggie's back, using his best funeral voice.

"Not funny, Jack . . . not funny." Reggie swats Jack's final flick, sending bark from his back.

The three walk silently for a minute, and Jack's face lights up with excitement.

"Hey, I know what will make ya'll feel better. Aunt Anna's makin' apple cobbler tonight. She wouldn't mind the company. I wouldn't." Hustling ahead of his companions, he stretches his arm out invitingly.

"Um, you're gonna have to do better than apple cobbler." Ari playfully scoffs, feigning discontent for her friend's early actions.

"Just bought nilla bean ice cream. Whatcha say, Reg?" Jack playfully nudges Reggie.

"Well, don't think cobbler and nilla bean ice cream will do anything for these scrapes, but might do somethin bout my bruised ego." Reggie produces poorly, trying to mimic Ari's fraudulent discontent.

"Pff, why does cobbler always work? Apple cobbler on a Thursday? Always!" Ari says slapping her thighs, stifling a smile.

"Always works because Aunt Anna's cobbler is the best in the county five years runnin. Guys, don't look now, JACK ATTACK!" Jack swiftly jabs both friend's ribs, simultaneously sprinting a safe pace ahead.

"G'back here, ya dirtbag!!!" Ari shrieks, sprinting stiffly. "I hope you trip and fall inna ditch full of poison iv, iv, iveeehooo!" Reggie sprints after their friend, quickly running out of breath.

The two stumble pathetically, arms flapping awkwardly in another vain attempt to catch Jack on their way to Aunt Anna's house.

CHAPTER TWO

"THAT'S SUM GOOD COBBLER!"

Leaves rustle, giving way to the familiar crunch of clay and occasional gravel underfoot. Weathered wooden fencing lines the roads along their path.

"Walking everywhere sucks. Why can't we stay inside?" Reggie protests, kicking a small rock into a nearby ditch.

"Well, if someone had put our bikes in their Daddy's shed, our chains wouldn't be all rusted." Ari retorts, shooting Reggie a disapproving stare.

"Oh, okay, like it's Daddy's fault we live in the hurricane capital of the world! Shed's good enough." Reggie exclaims.

"Oh, you mean the one that always leaks? Damn, if your parents could put down a bottle every now and then, they could afford such luxuries!" Ari snaps.

"That's cap and you know it! How am I supposed to know it had another hole in da roof? We've replaced them tarps like four times this year." Grabbing a rock and throwing it hard into the woods, Reggie walks ahead dejectedly.

"Kinda harsh, dontcha think, Ari?" Jack interjects. "Besides, Ari your uh, parents aren't exactly. . ."

"Exactly what Jack? Like Aunt Anna, all perfect little miss stick around for your child homemaker?" Ari scoffs dismissively.

"Look, we all have issues, Ari, issues we can't control, is all I'm sayin. Give Reg a break. He made a mistake. It's not his fault his old man can't hold down a job in this town." Jack offers attempting to make peace.

"Oh, and I'm supposed to just forgive him for ruining a perfectly good bike?" Ari hisses.

"Chain, a bike chain, that's all. I'm sure there are a few chores Aunt Anna will let me do to earn a little extra to replace all our chains." Jack offers Ari an olive branch.

"Whatever, my brakes and springy things are shot because of that stunt ya'll pulled at Devil's Dip last weekend!" Ari fumes.

"Shocks. I can replace those, too. No biggie. Look, we're almost to Aunt Anna's. We can revel in our misery later, c'mon." Jack sprints off as he often does, passing Reggie.

"Pffff. This is stupid . . . Reggie, I'm sorry. Shouldn't have said those things about your folks." Ari sprints to catch up to her disgruntled friend.

"It's okay, Ari, it's not like any of us are ever gonna get out of this wasteland anyways." Reggie responds, cracking a halfhearted smile. "Also, I'm sorry for telling Crissy Freeman you use ashtray-scented Axe." Ari's voice trails off as she gallops ahead, hoping Reggie didn't hear her confession.

13

"CRISSY FREEMAN, YOU TOLD CRISSY FREEMAN WHAT?!? I'm gonna kill . . . ya. . . ya. . . hff not made for all this runnin'!" Rumbling ridiculously after Ari, Reggie attempts to catch her before Aunt Anna's front door, failing miserably.

Ari bursts through the door with Reggie on her tail.

"Ari you assh. . ." Reggie shouts, flinging the door open. "shole, uh, uh Miss Anna, so good to see ya." Reggie stutters sucking wind, eyes darting around the room.

"Welcome, Reginald, shoes, please. Thank you. Now go wash up, supper will be ready in a few. Jack, set the table, please! Correctly, this time, forks go. ."

"I know, I know, forks to the left, knives, spoons on the right. Yeah, yeah, I got it, Aunt Anna. Where does the glassware go again? Tiny forks, right?" Jack jests playfully anticipating her response.

"Jack! We're having grilled chicken, greens, seared corn on the cob, and mashed potatoes." Aunt Anna raises her volume only slightly, maintaining her usual calm composure.

"Okay, okay, I kid. Where are those napkins?" Jack's voice trails off, attending to his task.

"Scorched corn? Ewg, what's the burnt stuff?" Reggie wrinkles his face.

"Seared corned buttered with lime and paprika, Reginald. Snff, snff. Reginald Anthony Alton, when's the last time you showered?" Aunt Anna's tone turns from diner dictator to concerned mother.

14

"Um, um, Sund . . . yesterday!" Reggie roguishly replies.

"Reginald, there are extra clothes in the spare room. Please go shower, oatmeal soap and use shampoo this time, please. You have time before supper." Lowering her voice and nearing her pungent patron. "Leave your clothes, hat, and all in the hamper; I'll wash them after supper."

"My, my hat, what's wrong with Pop's hat? Snff, snff. I don't smell like an ashtray." Reggie shrugs sheepishly, sniffing the faded number three as he goes about Aunt Anna's wishes.

From the dining room, Jack interjects, aiding his friend. "No, Aunt Anna, not the Earnhardt!"

"Quiet in there, or you're getting a haircut tomorrow!" Returning a jest of her own.

"No, not my lovely locks!" Jack runs his fingers through his heavenly hair.

"You could use a trim, Jack, no those on the left, give me those, and go wash your hands." Ari arrives, helping Jack complete his task.

The warmth of a home may start in the kitchen, but it burns brightest at suppertime. Many hands helping to place the meticulously prepared meal on the table. The trio sit, eating with greedy bellies and grateful hearts.

"Nom, nom, this scorched pamprikar'd corn is scrumptilious, Aunt Anna. What's in these greens?" Reggie shovels a melody of mouthfuls. His table manners leave room for much improvement, but Anna offers no correction to her hungry guest.

15

"It's paprika Reggie, wipe your mouth, you slob," Ari starts up, delicately cut off by her hostess.

"Nice try, Reginald, my greens are a secret recipe, I haven't perfected them yet, but I do believe I will enter them in the county fair coming up." Aunt Anna expertly averts negativity otherwise detracting from a peaceful moment in the lives of those without much.

A hot meal made with care and love can warm all hearts. Grabbing his glass in a grand display to capture the seemingly meager moment, Jack rises from the table, trying his best to orchestrate a speech.

"As you should, Aunt Anna, your greens are the best in the county, no, the state, the whole dang world. Your cobbler, well, we already know at county, it's a wrap!" Jack exudes a confidence of one destined for more than his humble beginnings would bestow.

"Nom, num, I second that, Miss Anna," Reggie pipes up, licking his plate clean.

"Ugh, gross. . . Miss Anna. Your cobbler is divine, but this chicken, Nana would love this. What's your secret? I'd. . . if I could? Would love to try it myself." Ari struggles to break her gaze from Reggie's grotesque table manners.

"Oh, this is nothing special, really. It's all about seasoning the protein first," Anna adds, hiding behind her humility.

"Arianna, I'd be more than happy to share the recipe with you. Who wants cobbler? Jack, bowls if you would please. Don't

16

forget the ice cream; vanilla bean should be in the freezer." Aunt Anna politely excuses herself, collecting empty plates before setting off to retrieve her locally acclaimed masterpiece.

Warmth dominates the dining room with grateful sounds of gleeful munching on hearty portions of warm apple cobbler and vanilla bean ice cream.

"Mmm, that's, mmm, some good cobbler Miss Anna." Ari looks up from her bowl.

"Well, thank you, Arianna. Glad you appreciate it." Aunt Anna responds with a warm smile, caressing kind creases.

"Yeah, mmm, perf, mmmm, nilla ice cream is mmm, perfect," Reggie adds between large mouthfuls.

"Thank you, Reginald. Please feel free to help yourself. Reginald, use a napkin, here, let me," she responds, dabbing morsels of flaky goodness from his messy mouth.

"I, I got it, Miss Anna." He leans away into Ari's personal space.

"Get off you oaf, missed a spot!" Ari mashes clean linen in his face.

"Yeah? Where? Here?" Pursing his lips leaning closer.

"Eww, gross. Not even if you were the last breathing mammal on Earth. May I please be excused, Miss Anna? I really must be going." Rising quickly from her seat, Ari gathers her bowl and utensils, pausing for Aunt Anna's response.

"Of course, Arianna. Would you like a ride home?"

"Yes, please, that'd be great, Miss Anna."

"It's settled then . . ."

"Shotgun!!!" Jack shouts from the kitchen.

"Aww, man. . ." Ari exclaims, catching Reggie smiling devilishly, wiggling his eyebrows at her suggestively.

"Is the trunk available?" She continues, proceeding to the kitchen with dishes in tow.

"Reginald, how do perfect gentlemen act?" Aunt Anna calls from the kitchen.

"Oh come on Ari, I'm juss playin. Yes, ma'am, gentlemen must always . . . shut up, Jack, it's not that funny," Reggie quips playfully, throwing crumpled linen at his friend, silently mouthing his rehearsed response.

Given the hour, all place their wares in the sink before heading out. The drive to Ari and Reggie's houses takes only a few minutes.

"So, ninth grade, finally in high school. Ya'll ready to get back to school?" Anna asks, anticipating their individual responses.

"No, I mean, ready for it to be over with already," Ari responds first, followed by Reggie, who has strategically seated himself as close to her as his seatbelt permits.

"Yeah, I guess. Why do we have to do so much school anyway? It's not like we are going to learn anything useful. There's literally an app for everything these days. Who needs driver's ED?" he quips, tapping tranquility from his window worriedly.

"Well, there's always something new to learn, and you never know when it may come in handy," Aunt Anna responds gently, glancing in the rearview mirror. Turning her attention to an unusually quiet Jack. "Jack, what are you looking forward to this year?"

Before Jack can gather his thoughts, Reggie offers his opinion. "Kattie Thompson, that's what!" Making kissing noises in the general direction of the front passenger seat's occupant.

"Stop it, Reggie. Do you always have to be so inappropriate?" Ari speaks up, mushing her hand in Reggie's face.

"Kaitlyn Thompson, she's a nice girl, Jack, very pretty. Coach Steph said she made varsity cheer, happy for you. . ." Anna continues before her co-pilot interrupts her.

"It's, it's not like that, Aunt Anna, she's just a classmate. Shut up, Reg, not now." His usual congenial disposition gives way to potential social embarrassment and fear of uncertainty driving most teenage angst.

"Yeah, shut up, Reggie, not like she'll ever break up with Chip Eckles anyways. He gave her a promise ring back in sixth grade." Ari shoots him a disapproving look, furrowing her brow.

"Can we please change the subject? It's gonna be like every school year. I'll make good grades because schools isn't hard, and with any luck, nothing exciting will happen because nothing ever does in this town," Jack states, shifting sharply and staring into the same nothing pierced by porch lights glowing in the distance.

"It's ok to have a crush. Do the kids still call it that these days?" Anna attempts to comfort her young ward.

"Does it matter? It's not like a girl like Kattie Thompson will ever see me more than an orphan." Jack spits sharply, burying deeper against the glass.

"That's not true, Jack, and you know it." Ari comes to the defense of her friend. "Kattie is stupid anyway. She only cares bout impressing Crissy Freeman and the rest of those planks of wood she calls friends!"

"Take that back. Crissy Freeman is the most beautiful creature on this planet, and you're just jealous because she can do a back-to-front handspring flip frop, and you'd break your neck just thinking bout it." Reggie comes to her unattainable love aide.

"You're an idiot. It's called a flip flop, and so what? She should be an expert flip-flopper given all the boyfriends she's had since the sixth grade." Ari expounds, staring defiantly into Reggie's eyes, challenging his next response.

"Okay, okay, sorry I asked, Arianna, we're here. Would you like me to get out and speak with your Nana?" Aunt Anna attempts to break the mounting tension among the vehicle's inhabitants.

"No, Ma'am, won't be necessary; she barely knows I exist these days. Thank you for supper and dessert, Miss Anna. Text you later, Jack. g'night." Ari unbuckles her seat belt and makes her way down the darkened path.

"What about me?" Reggie makes texting motions with his thumbs to a door slammed swiftly without response. She turns politely, waving at Jack and Aunt Anna before heading up rickety steps into her dilapidated dwelling.

"Wow that ended expectedly!" Reggie exclaims, absorbing the entirety of the back seat.

"Reg, don't know why you just won't tell Ari how you feel and get it over with." Jack turns to his friend, attempting to elicit a response.

"I don't know, man. I just get nervous around her and say all the wrong things. Besides, she likes Suki Fujisaki, who is like the best Dekken Dragons player at school. How am I supposed to compete with her?"

"Oh, I heard Akasuki was going to stay another year with the Phillips. How nice." Anna attempts to change the tone of the conversation, playfully tapping Jack's shoulder.

"Yeah, that's great. She's stuck here another year to suffer like the rest of us," He quips, absorbing another bump from the rough road below. Shaking her head, Anna refocuses her attention on the other reeling member in her back seat.

"So Reginald, you like Cristina, what's your plan, Casanova?"

"Given I don't know who Casanova is, I suppose I'll impress her by beating Suki in a Dekken Dragons death match. If I only had The Impaler . . . Suki would be toast." Reggie sheepishly responds, unaware that his quarry cares nothing about the internationally acclaimed children's game.

21

The conversation continues for a few more brief moments as loose gravel and sand crunch beneath Aunt Anna's car, when Jack makes a suggestion.

"Regs' got clothes at the house he stay the night and we can ride to school together? Please Aunt Anna please can Reg?" Clasping his hands together Jack begs.

"I'd have to speak with Ms. Alton first, Reginald what's the matter dear?" Her sweet voice cracking with concern.

"Well, today was fun, but I gotta make sure Isaac gets bathed and in clean clothes. Parents were probably too toasted to feed him either. Snff." Reggie pauses kicking open the door to conceal his emotions.

"Maybe next time Bro, for now I must retire to my humble abode to plan Suki's demise. Alas, I will claim my queen. I bid you both adieu and to all a good night." Reggie exits the vehicle, scurrying energetically up the dilapidated wood structure posing as a porch, barely clinging to the front door of his parent's ramshackle mobile home. Turning to wave, fidgeting with an almost inoperable doorknob, fighting off the least agreeable storm door in existence. Reggie disappears into accepted misery.

CHAPTER THREE

GREAT AND UNEXPECTED THINGS

As the vehicle rumbles down the winding dirt road, darkness has firmly settled upon all below the chalky night sky. Anna clearly concerned for her young companion, attempts to break the tension building in her front passenger seat.

"Should've sent Reginald home with leftovers for Isaac and his folks." Anna sighs at the missed opportunity, her attempt failing to break the ice.

"Well you're friends are home safe and that's important. Would you like to share what's really going on, Sweetie?" Smiling warmly, Aunt Anna's voice is soft and inviting.

"Please don't call me that in front of Reg . . . It's nothing, just tired."

"I know when you're tired, sweet Jack. All those post-wrestling practices are tiring, this isn't that." Returning her eyes to the darkness surrounding them. The tires sending sand and rocks sailing into shadows.

"Well, I find it sweet that Arianna and Reginald like each other. They just don't know how to tell each other." Chuckling to herself quietly.

"It's weird, honestly, like ugh I don't wanna . . . wish we could do more to help Reg's little brother." Jack's shudders as his voice trails off staring into darkness.

"It's not weird for two young people to like each other and not know it. Many people chase relationships they think will make them happy, always overlooking obvious obstacles. I agree we can do more for little Isaac. The Altons must be terribly overwhelmed between doctor visits and bills. I know, we'll bake extra cobblers and donate some of the proceeds to the Altons and some to that research fund Mrs. Alton was telling me about the other day." Adjusting excitedly in her seat Anna notices little change in Jack's disposition.

"Jack, Sweetie! What's that enigma of a mind gotten you so worried?" Anna presses.

"Nothin' . . . I mean, it all gets old. It's the same old thing around here." Warming to Aunt Anna's charm and persistence, hesitating his thought.

"What do you mean "it" gets old?" She presses.

"It, you know, the whole same old, small-town stuff, it just gets old. I love my friends, but I don't understand why people complicate things. Reg is always taking care of Isaac, that's his parent's job. We're just kids, I mean fourteen isn't grown yet. I know his parents are struggling with Isaac's condition, but some days I feel like they've just giving up. They both can still work and do better for their kids. I don't get it Aunt Anna." Pulling away from the window, Jack settles comfortably in his seat, eyes darting around the dashboard seeking answers.

"Heavy stuff Sweetie. Having a child with Syngap is scary Jack. Don't be too harsh on the Altons, they don't have the best healthcare and it covers very little therapy they need for Isaac. We can help in small ways Sweetie, but don't want to embarrass them." Her sweet voice offering an adult's perspective.

"Well it's all dumb! Insurance companies are dumb, neuro conditions are dumb, pff growing up in this dump is dumb. . ." Jack rants before hearing the sound of his words retiring his tirade.

"Tell me how you really feel sweet boy." Anna's attempt at humor does little to lighten the mood. Pausing for a second she shifts tactics.

"So what is it that you really want, Jack? I used to know whether it was that Red Ryder or that set of Legos. Oh shoot, what were they called again? Power Pirates, no, that wasn't it. . ." Anna ponders.

"Ultra-Agents, they're alright. Can't beat a tote of random Lego sets, none of em complete, but they were the best." Jack's eyes glimmer from each passing porch light.

"You would play for hours, just tickled me to death to see you so happy." Sniffing away deeper emotions, she wishes she could afford him the new versions of everything.

Always aware of their situation, Jack places his hand gently on her shoulder, speaking softly. "It didn't matter. Using my

25

imagination was the best part. I could build whatever. Remember that big mech I built, joints moved and everything."

"Yeah, I remember; it even had a hatch thingy for your little guys to get in and out." Choking back a tear, grateful their struggle didn't matter and what mattered, mattered.

"That hatch took me forever to get just right, and those shoulder lasers, really shot those missiles. I must have lost every one of them at least twenty times." Turning to an emotional Anna beaming ear to ear.

"Pfff. More than that, it had to be at least a thousand times." She smiles. Both share a laugh, one that truly heals the heart.

"Don't know how to say it, Aunt Anna, but I feel trapped, not trapped . . . wrong word, like school isn't hard. Heck, I'm sure I'll like high school, I just feel like I can't help anyone the way I'd . . . never feel like I'm doing enough."

Gathering his thoughts, silence fills the vehicle again.

"Take your time, Sweetie. I'm here for you." Anna smiles, eyes buzzing between the road and her conflicted companion.

"Aunt Anna, have you ever felt like, like you were in the wrong place? Like there's something out there calling you, but you don't know what it is? Like I'm not supposed to be here. Like I'm . . . I'm . . ." Searching her eyes for answers, his dart nervously.

Anna realizes the little orphan boy she raised for nearly fourteen years is gone. Replaced not by an angst-filled teen but a resilient youth seeking purpose. Hastily struggling to gather her

thoughts, sighing deeply, she begins. "Huuhh, here goes."
Speaking under her breath. "Jack, I don't know exactly what that
is, but some of us are called for great and unexpected things.
Years ago, I thought I was going to be a paralegal, maybe a
lawyer even. Thought I'd have a long career in and everything . . .
doesn't matter now. Jack, you are my great and unexpected
thing." She continues gaining confidence.

"The day I took you in changed my life for the better. I don't
know what path calls you . . . unfortunately, sometimes we have
to wait for its reveal. Be patient, you don't have to make any
decisions right now. Just enjoy being a kid for a little while
longer. Please, for me? Snff . . ." Anna pauses, poorly concealing
a sniffle.

"Ok, Aunt Anna, missed our turn back there?" His mood
quickly changes as he gently wipes a single tear from her cheek.

"Snff, I know. Figured we'd get some ice cream at Hoot Owls
like old times, Snff."

"But, we had ice cream already?"

"Ehh, nothing like a lil Hoot Owls and a late night drive to get
our minds off life, you buying?" She winks.

"Hell yeah, sorry, I mean heck yeah!" Jack winks, poking
around for loose change.

"Right on, so what will it be, Jack?" *Lost behind the Wall*?
Thunder in Your Heart? Oh, oh, I know, *Dream On*! Wait
Whitesnake; *Children of the Night*."

27

"Wait? What? No, no *Children of the Night*, that's about. Mff .
. . mff" Jack fails miserably to speak, Anna cupping a hand
covering his mouth.

"Thpt, thpt, who does that?" Jack mumbles through fumbling
fingers, wiping his mouth comically. "*Lost Behind the Wall*?
Classic, big time pass, little close to home right . . ." His feeble
attempts are eclipsed by Anna's sporadic and unexpected
behavior.

"What was that? *Home sweet Home*? Ooo, love that one."

Unable and unwilling to stop her playful chaos, Jack settles in
comfortably, letting the moment live. Moments pass faster than
blurs blowing past his window. Muggy midnight air filled with
epic soundtracks birthed from the greatest era in music, the sweet
taste of mint and chocolate on his tongue stealing precious
memories before the world awakens to its usual business.

CHAPTER FOUR

BACK TO THE GRIND

As with all things, summer ends for Jack and his friends. As the inevitable return to school looms large, the three friends spend their last days of freedom hanging out, allowing the freedom of their youth to steal away every productive moment. Trips to the swimming hole, tag in the woods, and supper at Aunt Anna's will soon become weekend rarities as the new school year begins.

"Packed your gym clothes in the second front pocket. Your schedule front pocket. Sit up straight, Jack. Let's see, what did I forget? Classroom map? No, yes?"

"Got it; I got it, Aunt Anna. Besides, they send us our schedules through Focal Point these days. Schedule's on my phone and it's a junior, senior high. Already been here for two years. It's not like the classrooms moved over break." Playfully flicking his phone back and forth, Jack exits before she can try to kiss him goodbye.

"Jack, oh, I remember now. Don't forget I can't leave the library until 2:30, so just feel free to stop by and hangout if you want." She yells through the open passenger window at a now mortified Jack, who is amongst an ever-growing crowd of peers. Attempting to cover his face, Jack sprints off to first period.

As expected, the halls are filled with the lively hustle and bustle, consumed by first day confusion when Jack spots Reggie in the distance.

"Sup Reg!" the two dab it up.

"Sup Jack, hey, seen Ari?" Reggie responds.

"Ari? Nah, bro, I haven't seen her. Dontcha ride the same bus?" Jack inquires, adjusting his pack.

"Yeah, what? Why? No, I was gonna say, did you see Crissy Freedman's fit today? So fye bruh!" Reggie nervously looks over Jack's shoulder as he adjusts his pants, tugging at his wrinkled shirt.

"Today's the day. I'm finally gonna tell Crissy how I feel. How do I look?" Reggie asks nervously adjusting the dirty number three hat on his head.

Perplexed at his friend's lack of tact, Jack shakes his head while attempting to wipe the last bit of sleep from his eyes.

"Today's the first day of school bro, what are you talking about "tell Crissy Freedman how you feel"? Stop that noise, man. C'mon, we got to get to first period. You can tell her how you feel later." Turning away in the direction of their classroom, still shaking his head.

"Later? Like in 5th? I mean I guess anatomy would be more appropriate." Before Reggie can rub his chest and nod suggestively, Jack cuts him off with a disgusted look dominating his face.

"What, eww bro, 5th's biology. Come on, stop doing that!" Jack corrects as the pair slide and shoulder through the crowded halls in a vain attempt to avoid being tardy, a familiar voice rings out.

"Jack! Reggie! Wait up! They got the roompff." Her books and supplies are spilling onto the ground, as Ari hits the floor.

"Watch it, noob!" A tall, fit young specimen says, standing over her.

"Thanks for nothing, jerk!" Ari hisses gather her things.

"What was that, Chumbalious?" The young braggadocios bro responds.

"Hey bro, uncalled for! Ari, you alright?" Knifing through the crowd, Jack kneels, helping his friend gather her supplies.

"Hey, man, not cool!" Reggie pipes up, rushing in awkwardly.

"Well, look who it is, it's Ashtray Alton! Hey, smoker's express is down the road bro!" The villainous voice howls pointing towards the closest exit sign. The braggadocios bro begins laughing amongst an awkwardly growing crowd. With negativity nearing napalm, Jack steps between the two.

"Sup Chip, not cool bro, not cool. Long time no see. How'd that summer wrestling camp go?" Jack cuts coolly.

The perennial pest, Chip flips his near perfect blonde locks before responding.

"Yeah it was pretty lit. I'm ranked second in the state; no worries. I'm gonna pin that kid from Trinity Catholic at states, so basically state Champ little bro." Chip dismissively eyes Ari's hair color choice as he high-fives one of his usual cronies, Dale.

"Shame you ain't on the team no more, Jack, could have used a one thirty-six in Louisville, but I understand you gotta make sure the Rainbow Smoker's Express isn't running into. . ." Before Chip can finish his thought, Ari cuts loose, obviously fed up with his antics.

"Hey, you ran into me, douc. . ." She shouts, before Jack interrupts.

"No harm, no foul, Chip. glad ya'll bumped into each other. Gave us a chance to catch up with Ari. One thirty-six, you said? I'll think about it. Have a good one, bro." Jack shoots his friends a quick glance in the direction of class as the three hurry off.

The bell blares well before the trio makes it to their first period, the companions are late for their first official day of high school.

"Hurry up, Reggie!" Ari insists as she turns to give him a hard jerk toward class.

"Hol, ho, hold up guys. He, hey now, Ari! At least take me to the cafeteria before you get all handsy!" As usual, Reggie huffs, never in running shape.

"Come on, guys, or we won't be able to sit near each other." Jack gives them a friendly push toward the door.

32

"Hey! Hey, Jack, that's double nuggies from you, man!" Reggie stumbles into class when an unfamiliar face halts them in their tracks.

"Late on the first day, Mr. Murphy? I was told to expect more punctual behavior. As for you, Mr. Alton and Ms. Dennis, good morning. Your seats are as directed on page four of the syllabus. Please take your seats now so we can begin introductions." The crisply dressed man states moving from the doorway, handing each student a syllabus.

With an inviting arm motioning in the general direction of their seats, he shuts the door behind them, checking its security. The trio frantically rifle through the absurd amount of pages saturating the syllabus, finding their pre-selected seats.

"Good morning, class. My name is Mr. Wiley. I am aware that some of you had last-minute schedule changes and that tardiness is an excepted practice on the first day of school, however as indicated on page two labeled "Rules and Procedures", rule two, sub-article one, all students tardy after the first day of scheduled class will be referred to the tardy office immediately." The oddly well-dressed instructor indicates.

Mr. Wiley continues to elaborate on various rules and procedures. Jack's eyes shift between the syllabus and random objects in the room. He notices an interesting quote on the wall behind Mr. Wiley's desk, referencing fearlessness and those with power. His mind quickly begins to ponder on his teacher's earlier enigmatic comment.

"What did he mean by "told to expect"? What's punctual mean again? Sir!" His thoughts broken by a sharp rise in Mr. Wiley's voice.

"Mr. Murphy, good you're still with us!" The prepared professor-like postulates.

Jack responds, "Yes, Sir. Tardies don't count on the first day, phones are to be in our backpacks unless instructed for academic purposes, students are to stay . . ."

"Okay, okay, Mr. Murphy, point taken." Mr. Wiley quickly changes gears. "Okay, class, let's leave the rest of the rules and procedures for tomorrow. Take out a sheet of paper. I want you to tell me something about yourselves. I'll model what this exercise looks like on the board. Let's begin." As the dry-erase marker squeaks, Wiley writes his name in the center of the board, writing randomly calculated details about himself surrounding it.

Like many others, the rest of the first day is filled with a mixture of baited excitement to see old friends, making new ones, and the various assortment of school and classroom policies selectively adhered to when convenient for the overseeing authorities. Later at lunch, amidst random conversations that pervade every lunchroom around the world, Jack finds himself still pondering Mr. Wiley's earlier comment when Reggie breaks his thoughts.

"Hey, slide over, bud. You gonna eat that? So you're saying I should wait to tell Crissy how I feel? Mmm, mummm."

"No, he's saying that you have a better chance at two sharks breaking into this cafeteria and eating you alive then Crissy Freeman reviving you with mouth to mouth!" Ari sharply adds before returning to her school-sanctioned meal.

"Wait, so she'd have to revive me mouth to mouth twice? Dude, that's freakin awesome. Jack, do that chicken thing hold that you almost killed Danny Gather with that one time. That's sure to work."

"It's actually an inverted armbar, no, Reg. I'm not gonna choke you out so Crissy Freeman can walk past your corpse and take a selfie for the gram. Come on, get serious for like two seconds. What did Mr. Wiley mean he "was told to expect more punctual behavior?" I mean, remember he said he was from Michigan? Who would he possibly know that would make him say something like that?" Jack's usually quick nature is clearly perplexed by this comment.

"Well, just because this is his first year here doesn't take away the years he taught in Michigan. Maybe he's one of those weirdos that moved down here for the beaches, we're a peninsula. Kinda have a lot of beaches around here." Ari offers her suggestion, trying hard not to look at the carnage between Reggie and his lunch.

"Yeah, maybe, but that doesn't explain the comment," Jack replies, still perplexed.

"Maybe he like talked to other teachers here and asked which students suck and which ones don't. He seems like the over-prepared type." Reggie's response drawing a momentary silence from his friends.

"You know what, Reggie? Every now and then, you say something that isn't completely stupid. Jack, Reggie's probably right. You know how new teachers always either try to be our friends or do a bunch of asking around to figure us out. That's probably all it is." Ari and Reggie share a rare nod of agreement.

Jack nods too. "You may be right, guys. I guess."

"Speaking of teachers, did you see Mrs. Callaway's fit today? So hot. I'm tellin' ya, she had to be a . . ." Reggie returns to form before Ari can escape the quickly decaying conversation.

"Yes, we did and she looked very nice, professional, and very nice. Geeze, Reggie, do you hear yourself sometimes? And besides, she's married with like three kids," Ari retorts, secretly always willing to argue with her misguided friend.

"Yeah, so? Married women with careers are hot as hell. They make their own money, understand commitment, and know how to you know?" Suggestively nudging Jack while wiggling his eyebrows towards his clearly disagreeing friend.

"Reg, we have gym class with her twins, dude, no, yes, she's attractive, but have some respect, bro. Dude, you know I love yah, but just cuz your Dad jokes about that noise all the time, doesn't make it true." The disapproving level of Jack's eyebrows tells Reggie to drop it.

"I'm sorry, I get it. You know, ever since you and Ari took that social consciousness class last year, you two have been acting

36

more woke every day." A frustrated Reggie quickly grabs his empty plate, returning to the free and reduced lunch line.

"Now who was being a little harsh?" Ari quips at her friend, who is now hanging his head. "You know he's sensitive about his dad since Pops passed."

"I know, Ari, I know. Damn, I should go talk to him."

"It's alright, Jack, I'll do it. Your next class is all the way on the other side of campus. Besides, this takes a women's touch, I think?"

CHAPTER FIVE

POWER FEARS THE FEARLESS

On his way to class, Jack is consumed with the happenings and emotions of the day when he pauses at a random locker. Filled with regret at his actions towards his friend, Jack strikes the locker three times rapidly. As the blood surges to his now throbbing hand, an authoritative voice echoes from down the hall.

"Young man, we don't do that here. No Sir. Your I.D. badge!" The sharply dressed man demands assertively. Jack, still reeling from his regretful comment and the fresh wound on his hand, digs frantically into his pocket. As the man nears, Jack becomes increasingly nervous as the menace nears, Principal Dodger Reilly.

While not tall; the physically fit, self-absorbed, arrogant man always impeccably dressed, displaying authority through tailored suits steps into Jack's personal space. Few teachers respect him, and even fewer students as well. The perception of tailored three-piece suits in a low-income school is completely lost on the man clutching Jack's school I.D.

"So, Jack Murphy, do you think that destruction of school property is fitting of a student so highly thought of by his teachers? Listen, I understand. I've been there. Your girlfriend had a summer away and developed a relationship with someone else or whatever the case may be. I get it, but that doesn't give you the right to destroy school property. Shall I say, my property?"

"Your, your property? This is school district property." Jack suddenly adopts a defiant stance on the subject.

"Typical of you people, well either way, this locker, these teachers, this school, and everything contained within is under my supervision. This means, Mr. Murphy, you have just earned yourself a week's detention on the first day of school. As much as I'd like to look the other way on this one, what would faculty and your peers think if I allowed such dissidence to pervade my campus? Regardless of how trivial the infraction may seem, what would they think? What would they say, Mr. Murphy? They'd say. . ."

The pompous principal seeking to continue his preposterous pontification suddenly cut off by a voice emanating from behind them.

"If well read, they'd say; "Fearlessness in those without power is maddening to those who have it."

Principal Reilly turns swiftly to address his literary adversary. Taking a step back, the pompous principal is confronted by Mr. Wiley, who stands mere feet from Mr. Reilly and his quarry.

"Mi, mis, mister Willis?" The great pontificator stammers.

"It's Wiley, Mr. Wiley. What egregious action has Mr. Murphy coalesced to occur such an uncordial and unprofessional conference?" Mr. Wiley, while not tall himself, presses looking down his nose at Mr. Reilly.

"Mister Wiley, I do not believe we have had the pleasure of professionally getting to understand each other."

"Admittedly the brevity of our initial interview was concerning. However, upon accepting the position, I was not under the impression that faculty could resort to such boorish tactics to illicit desired behaviors from our student population." Mr. Wiley states, intimidatingly entering Principal Reilly's personal space.

Taking a step back, Principal Reilly clears his throat, but Mr. Wiley is well-versed in these encounters.

"Mr. Murphy, do you recall the quote written on my board this morning?" Turning to address Jack as if Reilly had simply vanished.

"Um, it was something about power and fearlessness if I recall."

"Very good, Mr. Murphy. The quote is "Fearlessness in those without power is maddening to those who have it." by the esteemed American writer Tobias Wolfe's from his 1989 work *This Boy's Life*. I have a few spare copies if you're interested. I'll lend one to you tomorrow after class. Turning to address their unwanted third wheel, Mr. Wiley presses Principal Reilly's perturbed disposition.

"Mr. Reilly, Sir, I apologize for my lack of discretion. However, I noticed that something had upset Mr. Murphy earlier in lunch period and decided to pursue a resolution. I didn't expect him to take his grievances out on school property, a behavior I'm sure he will soon correct." Wiley nods at Jack, who nods in return.

"Well, this has been all too convenient, Mr. Wiley. However, I still expect Mr. Murphy to report to detention tomorrow after school. As I recall, another convenience, given you have signed up for after-school detention the entire first semester." Shooting a quick glance at the unlikely pair, still unsure of the nature of the whole situation, Principal Reilly combs his roman styled hair nervously excusing himself as the bell rings filling the halls.

"I'm sure I'll be in the Principal's office before you, Mr. Murphy. Those emotions of yours must be sequestered for now. That means hidden for now." Mr. Wiley humorously scoffs.

"Yes Sir, thanks for the save. See you tomorrow." Jack rushes off, confused more than ever.

"Kids these days." Wiley chuckles to himself before heading back to his classroom.

The rest of the day goes by without much incident.

"Jack! Jack! We've been DM'ing you since lunch. Where you going, dude? I thought we were gonna meet up at the usual spot?" Ari insists, hurrying to catch up with him.

"Oh, hey, Ari. Did ya talk to Reg?" Jack responding attempting to calm her rising disposition.

"Yeah, I did. He's at ole Shades McTree like always. What's going on with you?" Grabbing his arm to halt Jack's progress.

"I was mad at myself for what I said to Reg and punched a locker. Principal Reilly saw me and, BAM, now I have after-school detention probably till forever."

"Damn dude, well that sucks, anything Miss Anna can do about it?" Ari's concerning comment strikes deeper unresolved thoughts weighing heavy on her friend.

"Ari? She's the school librarian. What's she gonna do?" Jack pulls away a growing list of concerns filling his thoughts.

"I'm sorry, Jack, I didn't mean to." She persists, noting his dwindling demeanor.

"Don't worry about it, Ari. Is Reg still mad at me?" Jack redirecting to current concerns.

"Yeah, he's good, swears Crissy Freedman smiled at him in the hallway, and now he's all good. He was droning on about showing you some Dekken Dragon card move thingy Dexter told him about today." Withholding her true thoughts, Ari says the only thing she feels most helps the situation.

"Ok, Jack, everything will work itself out. Guess no bus ride convo? Call me later, K?" She presses playfully.

Jack nods assuredly. "Yeah, of course, it's only detention. Not like I'm going anywhere anytime soon." He jests sprinting off.

"Ari, you're a good friend for calling Reg. Call ya later." Before she can return the pleasantries, he sprints off to serve his time, the questions of the day searing his brain like a cattle brand.

42

CHAPTER SIX

A NEW DEAL

As the first week of school comes to a much-anticipated end for all, Jack finds himself serving the last day of detention. Looking around a room more fitting a prison than a space found on a school campus, Jack leans deeply in his seat, noting the time.

"Good afternoon, Mr. Murphy, apologies for my tardiness; I was in an IEP meeting for another student. What homework from the week have you completed?" Mr. Wiley rushes to his seat, placing his unusually expensive briefcase on the desk at the front of the room.

"Yes, Sir. There's usually not much homework the first week of school, well outside of yours." Jack poorly concealing his tone, reaching into his backpack, temporary Warden opens an equally expensive laptop.

"Mr. Murphy, how far into This Boy's Life did you get yesterday?" Wiley asks, looking over his laptop.

"Um, like chapter one, I guess. The book doesn't have chapter numbers, just a title for parts of his story. I got a few pages into the part titled, A Whole New Deal." At this, Wiley smiles, clearly no longer interested in his laptop. Given Jack is barely a third of the way through, Wiley thinks it best to be outwardly supportive of his progress.

"That far, eh? What parts of the first portion of the book did you like the best so far?"

"Um, there's a lot that happens. Toby is on a trip with his mother across country. He seems to get into a lot of trouble. His father doesn't like that he became a Catholic. It's kinda odd, really. Oh, I like Sister James. She seems nice, kinda reminds me of Aunt Anna." Jack responds, looking up at nothing in particular to remember what he had read the previous few nights.

"I can see that. She speaks very highly of you, Jack. What's kinda odd?" Wiley asks, leaning in attentively.

Jack thinks this over for a moment. "It's just that I don't get it. Why does someone's faith make others so mad?"

Mr. Wiley chuckles and then quickly stifles it. "Well, young man, people have all types of beliefs, and religion helps clarify those beliefs. Many people choose to pass those on to their children, thinking of it as a living memory or a legacy of sorts. For many people, that's all they can really pass on to their children. Take your friend Reginald, for example. What do his parents have to pass on to him but bad habits and broken promises? Respectfully I mean."

A crease forming between the boy's brow, tilting his head perplexed at Mr. Wiley's acute assessment of his friend.

"How do you know that about Reg? It's not exactly something we discuss in class?"

"You don't have to teach thirty years to point out those who never had a chance. When you're older, you will meet enough people to make the most unfortunate read of them. That and in a family, secrets rarely stay secret. I hope this is not a sore subject."

Leaning forward in his chair, breaking his usually proper posture. Leaning forward as well, the young conversationalist responds. "No, no, it just feels like that stuff like that is so common here, that nobody really cares to do anything about it. Why is that?"

"Hm, a penny's worth answer for a million-dollar question. Because fixing a problem takes more energy than preventing it, and it takes no energy at all to do nothing." Wiley sits back deeply in his chair, allowing the comment to manifest in his protégé's young mind.

"I see, so how does someone like Reg get out of a situation like that? I mean, there's college, but there's lots of people who left for college but came right back a few semesters later." Jack presses.

"Well, that's a conversation for another time, but simply, it isn't just about changing one's environment. One has to change their mentality as well. Millions travel to new places every day, few change who they are when they get there, and fewer change when they return to their beginning. Back to the book, what's another part that stood out?" Wiley leans deeply back into the conversation and waits patiently.

45

"Let's see, the character wanted to change his name to Jack. That was pretty cool. I mean, who wouldn't want to be a Jack?" Pointing to himself arrogantly.

"Hm, yes, who wouldn't, but why do you think he wanted to change his name?" Knifing through the little display with a deeper purpose.

"I suppose he did it to make his dad mad because his loser dad got awful mad at it."

"Maybe, or maybe in the opening of the section, the author talks about transformations having more merit than you think. What better way to transform yourself than to change your name? By claiming a new identity, you can be whoever you decide you want to be, not what you're expected to be. As a young person, the character is trying to figure out who he is as a person. He doesn't want to be his father for sure. Why do you think that is?" Wiley pivots the conversation to test its depth.

"Um, I'm not sure. His Dad stepped out on him when he was young, and I guess with the other guy, Ron or Ray, whatever his name was, is like a father figure he never had."

"Correct, very perceptive, Jack, and it was Roy." Wiley confirms. "So, Jack, I noticed that all the records indicate that you have always lived with Anna. What happened to your parents? If I may ask?"

Jack shrugged. "What's there to know? I was young when they gave me up for adoption. Aunt Anna took me in shortly before moving here, and I never really ask about them."

46

"I'm sorry if that's not a subject you're willing to discuss, and I understand. Parents indelibly impact a young person's identity, as you can tell from the character's journey to find who he is. Even the absence of said parents conjures a potent impact on identity. In some cases, this void leaves a young person searching. Some search for closure, some for identity. In your case, it seems your identity may explain your withdrawn posture." Pointing calmly to Jack's arms folded tightly around himself.

Unfolding his arms rapidly and leaning again towards his interlocutor. "It's not that I miss them. You can't miss something you never had. It's not even like I think of them often. There's nothing to think about."

"I see; the logic is there. You paused deep in thought a second ago, and I was curious about that. That is all. I apologize for assuming it was about your parents." A gentile and caring look comfortably etches itself across Wiley's face.

"It's ok. I don't get emotional about them because I have no memory of them. I was thinking about a story Toby tells about getting that rifle from Roy." Pausing to gather his thoughts, Jack shifts in his seat to gain some semblance of comfortability.

"Yes, the Winchester .22, if I remember correctly. Did that story speak to you in some way?" His momentarily ridged frame relaxes greatly as the topic shifts. "I don't remember everything about that part, but when he gets the gun and is pointing at people walking by his apartment window, acting like he is shooting people. That part was crazy. Do people really think about that

47

kinda stuff? I mean, Aunt Anna hated the idea of me having that BB gun a few summers ago, but I never thought about doing something like that. I could never."

"Well, I think what the author was trying to communicate was that because he didn't really have proper direction, those thoughts, while odd, are not all that unexplainable. Growing up, he had no proper figure to help navigate to less aggressive thoughts. So those thoughts are just generated in a mind that lacks direction. To his credit, he doesn't actually shoot anyone outside his apartment window."

"Yeah, but he does shoot the squirrel!" Jack expresses his confusion.

"Ah, yes, so he does. And it had an effect on him, given that he and his Mother loved animals." Wiley continues before he is abruptly halted.

"But we still did it?" Jack interrupts, pausing to look down at his worn shoes.

"We? I'm afraid I do not follow?" Remaining gentle in tone, Wiley presses.

"I, I once. . ." He pauses, still looking at his feet,

"So you, too, share something more than just an affinity for a name?" Careful not to provoke more sensitive feelings, the wily conversationalist attempts to change the subject, but his companion presses on, bravely swallowing his gilt.

"No, it's ok. That summer, I had that BB gun. I also shot a living thing. It was no different. I just did it. I can't explain why I did it." Looking up from his misery eyes reddening from the swell of emotions.

"Have you told anyone this story before?" The intuitive inquiry hitting its mark.

"Not really." The young lad kicks his feet.

"It's not healthy to harbor feelings of guilt. The burden of remorse is a heavy one. One that many shoulders can help carry to some semblance of absolution Jack. So what happened?" Mr. Wiley sits on the corner of his desk now, removing the physical barrier between them.

"Snff, I was in the woods just shooting cans when I heard the chirping. It was a small brown sparrow with a white speckled chest. HE was just sitting there on his perch when I . . . I sighted him up. I honestly thought I'd miss. The quiet release of one too many pumps, and it fell from its perch. The instant rush of excitement, the feeling of achievement, all of it hit me at once. I ran over to about where it fell. I searched for a couple of minutes to claim my prize, but when I saw it." He pauses, his thoughts riddled with guilt. "It was just lying there, its little chest moving up and down. Its eyelids opened and closed weakly, and in that, one moment I realized what I did. I, uh, couldn't take it back. I wasn't even afraid of what Aunt Anna would say because I already knew." Lowering his head near touching his desk.

"What did you do from there?" Wiley asks.

"I, I watched him or her. I didn't know. I watched it die. That's when the guilt hit me. So I dug a hole with my bare hands nearby

49

and buried it. But I was also burying my guilt. I sat there numb for at least an hour or so. Then I went inside, hid the gun under my bed, and never used it again." He returns to a much-warranted silence when Wiley speaks.

"Beautiful."

"What's beautiful about murder?" He looks up, perplexed, with tears swimming in his eyes.

"Empathy, empathy is beautiful. You know the difference between empathy and apathy, Jack?" Wiley takes a defensible tone.

"No, not really. I've heard the words before, but. . ." he begins, but his older companion finds the words for him.

"Empathy, simply put, is the ability to sympathize without someone else's pain, emotions, situation. It comes in different forms, and even though you don't know what it feels like to die. The remorse for your actions, so that you can feel other's pain." Thinking deeply, the young teen asks sheepishly.

"And apathy, is that the opposite?"

"Very astute, more or less, apathy is the lack of care. Which is why many your age feel like no one cares about them, because these moments, while they should be occurring with some frequency with young people, don't. The best lessons are sometimes not found in a common textbook, but I digress. You have a good heart, Jack. Own it. Let it be part of your identity. Feeling remorse is a way we allow ourselves to connect and care for each other." Before another word can be said, a late bell for on-campus activities rings out.

Jack gathers his things as the two exchange a silent nod. "Mr. Wiley?"

"Yes, Mr. Murphy, something on your mind?" Returning to his seat, never breaking his focus on the young man's needs.

"Outside of the million questions, one still bugs me."

"And that is?"

"In the hallway on the first day, why did you stop and speak to Principal Reilly like that? Are you not afraid of losing your job?" Of all the burning questions running through his brain, he chooses the most basic.

"Simple, Mr. Murphy, I don't like bullies." Mr. Wiley says without breaking his serious gaze. Nodding in agreeance, Jack concludes the same.

"Neither do I."

"Tell you what, Jack, since you have to stay after hours until Miss Anna's day concludes, you are more than welcome to stop by my classroom and discuss whatever is on your mind. Also, keep reading the book. I'm sure we'll find something to talk about. Deal?"

A smile creases Jack's face. "Bet, I mean deal. Good day, Sir."

"You as well. See you on Monday in class. Have a great weekend."

Jack waves, leaving to meet up with Aunt Anna. The conversation in the car ride home is a simple one centers around first-week library happenings. Aunt Anna prods Jack about his time in detention however he decides to conceal much of what was discussed. Mostly, because Jack knows her focus will be on the sparrow, and he has now moved past the event. Over the weekend, he focuses on his schoolwork and reading more of the book, thirsting for future discussions with Mr. Wiley.

CHAPTER SEVEN

BIGGER THEY ARE

As the school year settles deeper into fall, leaves turning a bright array of oranges and reds smattered with various browns, days and ideas blur together as deep conversations with Mr. Wiley and helping Aunt Anna in the school's library occupy Jack's time after school. Caregivers of teenagers become accustomed to changes in their teens. Although she notices the changes, Aunt Anna patiently waits for Jack to open up in his time and in his own way. Unfortunately, teenage friends don't handle metamorphic changes in their close childhood friends well.

Bells blare flooding halls with excited students eager to see their friends when Ari catches up to Jack between classes.

"Hey man, it's been like two days since you've said anything to us. What's going on?"

"I'm sorry, just have had a lot on my mind the last few months. Is Reg's b-day party this weekend?"

"Were you not listening to him today at lunch? His parents canceled, because it doesn't matter. Hey, let's do something for him anyway. Do you think Miss Anna would be cool with a surprise party at ya'lls place? I finally found that first edition Emperor Dragon Supreme he's been on about it for ages."

"Yes, no problem, I'll text her in a minute. Can we get to gym already?"

"Okay, okay. It's only dodgeball day, yet another humiliation. What's with you lately? Man, you've changed." Leaving him behind, Ari enters the girl's locker room to prepare for her inevitable demise. Jack changes quickly while in the locker room, looking past what used to be one of his favorite events in gym class, when a familiar voice breaks his thoughts.

"Hey bro, ready to get our asses handed to us again?" Turning swiftly to Reggie standing in just comic book boxers. Shaking his head mockingly.

"We will see. You never know, bro. It could be our day. Get dressed. I'm going all out today."

Stumbling into his school-approved gym shorts, Reggie comically dresses quickly to catch up with Jack. "You always go all out on D-ball day."

As Jack makes his way from the locker room, Chip catches him in the hallway. "Bro, bro. Hey, Jack. If you want, I'll tell Coach Melly to put us on the same team this time."

"Yeah, and why would you do that?" Jack retorts, not wanting to engage in Chip's weak mind games.

"Well, you know. It hurts me to see you lose all the time. Teaming up with those, um, you know." Chip's usual arrogance is stifled by the seriousness of Jack's gaze.

54

"Don't bother bro. It's only D-ball, ya'll got this."

After stretches, lines, and warmups, teams are selected to maximize the entertainment of the gym Coaches. The monotony and boredom frequently devolves into some sort of sadistic game orchestrated by those whose best athletic days are firmly behind them.

"Of course, every freakin' time! All the athletes on the other team, Jack." Reggie pointing to two particularly tall and lean volleyball players.

"It's gonna be another slaughter. Let's see what injury I'll fake today. Hmm, think I'll go with asthma today." Ari adjusts her shorts that are a size too small.

"You used asthma yesterday. I want asthma today. Ari, please, it's my birthday, please?" Reggie nervously hiding behind her.

"What? No, your birthday is Friday, and I "rolled" an ankle yesterday." Using air quotes as she dismisses his request.

"Oh, great, Chip and that goon Dale are finally doin' something. Figures they choose to participate today. Shouldn't have given Crissy that letter in anatomy yesterday. He freaked out about it on snapgram." Reggie begins to crouch deeper behind Ari.

"Stop that, this is happening. I told' ya not to mess with one of Chip's girls."

The scene of his friend's usual apprehension in athletic endeavors is nothing new to Jack; however, today, it is different. As he surveys the mounting odds staring across from him and his

55

team of misfits, he notices the gym Coaches snickering in the corner. Pointing at their knee and then at one of his teammates, Jodie's knee brace. An injury sustained at a recent band competition. Suddenly a feeling he has never felt before washes over Jack. A rush of renewed enthusiasm, but this not the usual thirst for competition, but a sense of justice.

"I'll show them jerks. The bigger they are . . ." Jack whispers under his breathe.

Looking across the court, Jack's thoughts are clear. The smallest of details become as large as mountains. A football player's loosely tied shoes, the Volleyball player's height an initial hindrance, Chip's habitual use of his dominant hand, and Dale's overconfidence in Chip's presence.

As both sides ready, the final ball is placed in the middle of the court. A rather portly coach holds up his hand, whistle in the other.

"Ok, quickly, as most of you know, the rules are simple. If an opposing player's ball contacts any part of your body, you're out." Audible laughter resonates quietly from both sides.

"Har, har. If a teammate catches the opposing team's ball throw. The thrower is out, and one player from the catcher's team can return. If a Coach calls you out, you're out. No arguments this time, Dale. Players may use a ball to shield a throw. The ball must be the deflecting object, not your face or other part of the body. In the event that one player finds themselves alone against three or more opposing players and catches a ball, the entire team is allowed to return to the field of play."

With his hand still raised, the Coach shuffles awkwardly to the sideline. For the briefest of moments, Jack closes his eyes as images of how his victims will fall plays through his mind. The piercing sound of the whistle initiates the ensuing carnage as both teams rush frantically to center court. Many attempts are in vain, as the first volley cost both teams a handful of victims. Jack's agility and low center of gravity are to his advantage. Grabbing a ball, deflecting a failed attempt by Dale, lumbers to the pack's safety. Knocking a ball backward to a teammate, Jack sees a chance to eliminate the football player with the untied shoes.

Nimbly avoiding two miscalculated throws, he throws a nifty head fake to his left. Reversing to his right as the footballer loses his footing, one shoe flying away toward the bleachers. In the player's desperate attempt to avoid being hit, his sock causes him to perform a split, compromising his footing. Jack pegs him easily, then dashes to grab a loose ball, avoiding another volley.

As players are eliminated and reinstated, it becomes clear that Jack is a man possessed. Downing both tall volleyball players, striking them below their knees. Jack's daily bike rides and youth pay dividends as he skillfully navigates through barrage after barrage of dodgeballs. As the brutish game wears on and egos begin to fray, Jack racks up kills left and right. Fatigue begins to set in with most of the players from both sides as the adrenaline resides, but as the game labors on, Jack seems to be getting stronger with each passing elimination. A deliberate throw at Ari's face from Dale draws the ire of the dodgeball demon.

Losing his focus for an instant and with the energy of ten wild broncos coursing through his veins. Jack chases Dale into the opposing team's side of the court. In a cowardly effort to avoid being pegged, Dale runs to a corner of the gymnasium with Jack in hot pursuit. Holding his arms protecting his face, wheezing heavily, the oversized teen cowers in the corner. For a moment, Jack pauses, not to assess his encroachment but to revel in the pathetic scene before him. Rearing back to blast the large coward, Jack restrains himself. Instead, a simple tap on the shoulder sends the big boy crumpling to the ground to sulk in his public shame.

"Murphy, offside, you're out, take a seat!" The portly Coach yells from across the gym. "Dale, get up ya big baby, you're out too."

Chip runs over to the Coach to argue the call in vain. "What do you mean he's out?

"Murphy was clearly offside when he tagged him. They're both out!" Coach insists, finding a deep satisfaction in his call.

Enraged by such an atrocity, Chip takes his place back in center formation as Jack trots past, clearly content with his decision. As the two competitor's eyes lock, a childish arrogance boils over inside Chip. As play resumes, Chip grabs a ball chasing down an actually hobbled Reggie, who is toughing it out for once. Faking a throw below the knees, Reggie's hands react, expecting the low throw, only to receive a crushing blow to his face, sending him crashing to the floor. Smashing Reggie's glasses hard into his face. As Reggie falls, clutching his broken glasses, another ball strikes him against the side of his head. The pain of embarrassment cutting deeper than the frames of his glasses ever could. A sinister smirk shooting across Chip's face as he gleefully eliminates his courting rival.

"You're out, Biggum!" A coach shouts as Chip jogs past Jack, who is forced to watch helplessly from the sideline.

"Get your friend, bruh. Think I broke his face." As the sinister look of cruel satisfaction settles comfortably on Chip's face. Jack surges to his feet, seething with anger and thirsting for a chance, as his teammates restrain him. It isn't hatred or ego that drives the feeling in the young lad's chest. A deeper realization has set in, bullies if left unchallenged, will never stop exacting their tyranny upon others. He is forced to wait patiently as the odds mount against his team.

The opposing team surgically dissects Jack's. As the numbers whittle down, Ari and one other clumsy student remain. Ari huddles nervously against the wall. Chip's team gathers all available balls and begins to target the only viable threat, a computer enthusiast named Dennis. Much to his credit, the skinny young man dodges more than five different volleys before being mercilessly pegged twice, one on the knee, and the other under the chin also knocking him to the hardwood below. Coughing from the blow, Dennis is helped off the court, leaving only one. Six players, including Chip remain for his team. All locked and loaded, setting their sights on the unlikely Valkyrie. Pausing his team before their inevitable victory, Chip takes a step ahead of his fellow arbiters of pain.

"Make her dance first. Then I'll finish this!" He spits viciously. The others nod in agreement and begin throwing wildly at her feet.

Clasping her hands over her face, Ari leans heavily against the wall, kicking her feet up. Twisting and turning against the wall, she spins uncontrollably, dodging each throw, until only one stands before her still armed. Breathing heavily, sweat perspires, streaking down her brow into her eyes. Ari's cotton candy-colored hair finally settles on her damp shirt. Fatigue sets in as she wipes the salty solution from her eyes. Chip eying his opportunity with her hands breaking their guard and unloads his volley maliciously.

Closing her eyes and turning her face away from impending doom, Ari squeals as the ball rockets towards her face. By some chance of fate, the Gym Gods deter from their usual course of humiliation of those less worthy. The entire gym is silent as a ball, once destined for certain destruction, is caught. Peeking through one eye, Ari sees the gift of life she now holds. Her hands still shaking, Jack and the rest of her comrades explode onto the court. Rushing excitedly towards the treasure trove of gifts lying at her feet.

Chip and his team of popularity vacuums scurry helplessly from the middle of the court as they're picked off in their retreat. Momentum firmly swinging in Jack's team's favor. The young hero makes the most of the opportunity. Downing two baseball players, eliminating the two best arms, sending another volley through the chest of Dale, who crashes hard to the floor, comically sliding like a hockey puck.

"Stay down Dale da snail!" With a ball in hand, Jack deflects a ball high into the air after leaping over a downed Dale, sending a return shot of his own, eliminating the remaining volleyball player. With his rival defenseless midflight, Chip hurls an errand volley at Jack, who lands quickly, exploding again, catching the skyward ball and dodging Chip's throw simultaneously.

In retaliation for his recent transgressions, Jack pursues Chip, who has been kicked out of play by one of the coaches. Chip gathers the instrument of elimination, sending a desperate heave as hard as he can at Jack's feet. Dodging Chip's hardest throw, he pivots hard on the balls of his feet, thrusting with greater intensity than his shooting technique, which Chip reveres and fears. Chasing Chip to his impending demise, the young predator sprints hard towards his prey.

Chip runs cowardly toward of coaches, staring blankly at the incredible turn of events. Looking over his shoulder, Chip seeing Jack uncork his payload with deadly intent, he screams slamming hard into the corner of the retracted bleacher. As the ball careens harmlessly past its target, Chip writhes in pain on the glossy hardwood floor, clutching his shoulder.

What should have been the comeback for the ages turns into a scene of chaos and accusations. Dale, who has now made it to his feet, dashes over to Chip's side.

"Jack, you did that on purpose!" He shrieks. As coaches spill onto the court, sending students to the locker room, one radios for the school nurse. Jack is grabbed roughly by the portly coach, who is yelling at the shocked crowd gathered over Chip.

"Get outta here, go to the lockers, and get changed for class! You! Murphy! You just cost us State, you piece of garbage." The stench of cheap coffee and stale donuts masked by convenience store mints fill Jack's nostrils.

"If Anna had a man around, you wouldn't pull stunts like this boy!" Licking his lips, breathing harshly into Jack's ear, who he roughly escorts to the front office. Careful not to make things worse Jack remains silent, absorbing stench and stupidity.

CHAPTER EIGHT

THINGS BETTER LEFT UNSAID

Sitting alone, his head hanging low, Jack is solemn and quiet. He can hear two of the present coaches excitedly explaining their erroneous version of events to Principal Reilly behind closed doors when the school's nurse, Mrs. Nelson, strides past him. The usually kind woman glares at Jack, clutching a document proceeds into Principal Reilly's office, closing the door behind.

"What will Aunt Anna think? Jack, why? You're an idiot, why?" Burying his face deep into his hands, his fingers tug roughly, pulling the follicles of his hair taunt. With the excitement dying down in the office, the door opens. Mrs. Nelson exits first, followed by the two coaches, who don't even acknowledge his existence.

"Mr. Murphy, come in here young man. Help me understand your actions." Principal Reilly's voice is shrill but firm. Uneasy, Jack rises from his seat.

"Shut the door behind you and take a seat, Mr. Murphy," Reilly demands sternly.

"Do you even understand the trouble you're in, Mr. Murphy?" The assertive fool begins.

"Sir, sir, I . . ." Jack stammers before he is abruptly interrupted.

"Mr. Murphy, these are serious accusations I have been presented. Not only did you cause a disturbance during instructional time, but your actions led to the serious injury of one of this school's distinguished athletes. What do you have to say for yourself?"

Gathering his words, Jack attempts a response, but the pontificating pundit cuts him short of a response. "Instructional time, it was gym class. . ."

"Your actions were utterly belligerent, reckless, and without question, motivated by a hatred that has never once occurred under my administrative guidance. Your actions, if left unchecked, could cause further erosion to the law and order that I've meticulously established over the last three years. Actions I will not allow. I have here a written statement by Coach Meltzer that you intended to cause bodily harm to Mr. Eckles. In my best estimate of the information afforded to me, you have been jealous of Mr. Eckles' considerable talent for some time. You, Mr. Murphy, have proceeded past a line that even I, with my substantial pull in the county, cannot abscond you from. As much as it pains me. . ."

If not for the sudden ring of the phone, the perpetual pontificator with the hairstyle of a Roman emperor would have assuredly continued with his expatiating explanation. Answering the call, turning in his chair, the Napoleonic narcissist listens attentively to the voice on the phone.

"Yes, Ma'am, yes, yes. Yes, Ma'am, I understand. I will, yes, Ma'am. I will, to the letter. Thank you for your call. I will convey the, yes, Ma'am, I will. Yes, Ma'am, you have a wonderful day as well."

Hanging up the phone roughly, the pious Principal turns to his pre-maturely selected prey, visibly shaken from the phone transmission.

"It would seem that I am not the only one with friends in high places. That was Superintendent Collins, and she said . . . she is abreast of our situation and that a week's suspension should suffice. Mr. Murphy, you are getting off lightly, but let me be frank. You and the plethora of mobile home marauding miscreants may win a battle here and there, but you will not win this war! Let me delineate something to you, Mr. Murphy. I am the supreme authority here. I may have to answer to a higher power, but all those under my regime answer to me. That means you're precious Ms. Huxley. So be warned, Mr. Murphy, no little orphaned brat such as yourself will ever get one over on me. Kids like you don't make it out, and do you know why? I'll tell you why, because delinquents like you don't understand your place in this world. Your type always bites the hands that feed you. Let me warn you now, Mr. Murphy. If this behavior continues, you will never be successful at anything!"

65

Menacingly leaning over his superfluously oversized desk, he attempts to continue when a commotion on the other side of the door sounds.

Bursting into the office, Aunt Anna pushes past the Principal's secretary to Jack's side.

"What is going on here, Dodger? As his legal guardian, I have every right to be here. Come on, Jack, we are leaving. I will be taking a few day's leave, which you will approve, or I'll make another phone call." Her usual gentile demeanor dissolved the moment she walked through the door.

"Ms. Huxley, Ms. Huxl. . ."

"No, you have said enough. Let's go." Glaring through the well-tailored man, she turns and leaves. Rising from his seat, Jack leaves, catching a glimpse of his Principal's dogged face still flush from their brief confrontation.

CHAPTER NINE

DAYS LIKE THESE

The first few minutes of the car ride were silent ones. Aunt Anna gathering her words, fighting back frustrated tears. Jack looking out the window, searches passing trees for words to break the silence.

"I'm sorry. I don't know what came over me." He timidly utters.

She glances over at him. "Sorry? Sorry for what? That Charles Eckles has been a spoiled bully his whole life. Serves him right to pick on students in a gym class game. I never understood why you wanted to be on the wrestling team with jerks like him. But, like always, I've supported as many activities as we could afford. Charles is the least of your worries, Jack. It's that boar Reilly. He is a spiteful and jealous man." Pausing to gather her composure, loosening her grip on the wheel. With color returning to her knuckles, the gentle woman continues.

"Look, Jack, I love you with everything I have, but you must understand that this situation affects more than just you."

Turning from the window, he responds.

"I wasn't thinking. I wasn't thinking about the backlash this would cause you at work. Honestly, it's just he. . . they were picking on Ari and Reg, and I just snapped. I got caught in the moment. It won't happen again. I promise."

"Backlash? I'm not talking about retribution towards me. I'm an adult, and any retaliation in a professional setting has later legal ramifications. I am worried about Arianna and Reginald. Did you see Reginald's face? His glasses were in pieces."

A perplexed look draws itself swiftly on his face to her deeper concerns.

"How did you hear about it anyway?"

"Arianna called me, and I instructed her to FaceTime me on their way to my office. Just to be safe. Jack, in a small town like this, you cannot just defend yourself against their false hopes for success and not expect some retaliation."

"I don't care. Bring them on. I'll kick all their asses if I have to!" His temper flares at her insinuation.

"I know, I know. You were never one for running from a situation like this, but Jack, my dear, you must understand there will always be days like this. There will always be Chips and Reilly's of the world, looking to force their personal agendas on others. You have to learn to walk away. What gets me is that one day, you are punching lockers, then for months, your grades improve, and there is no issues. Then BAM! You are trying to send a message to the most popular jock this community has produced this century. Care to explain?"

The sudden directness of her question causes his frustration to dissolve instantaneously.

"I, I... I don't know. I feel different than before. Before, I just wanted to make it through school and get on with it."

"Different? What do you mean different?"

"I mean, I don't know. I've been reading these books about others like me or kinda like me and. . . ."

"And what, Dear? You know you can tell me anything. What is it?" Her inquisition quickly turns to concern.

"Like, who am I? I don't really fit in with one click like the others do. I don't have anything against classmates or athletes, but I don't like how they treat others. I get along fine with techies, I guess. It's super interesting, but I like being outside too. I don't like hunting because it's kinda boring, just sitting around with Reg and his Dad just waiting to shoot something that doesn't have a high-powered rifle. I don't want to wear crazy clothes that hide my deeper emotional needs for acceptance, feeding my infantile need for attention. I just don't feel like I fit in, like I'm an alien. I used to imagine what it would be like to just run away, but where would I go? What's so funny? Ain't I in trouble? What's so funny?" Creasing his brow, confused at her uncharacteristic response.

"Um, I think we need to turn around. I must have kidnapped the wrong student. Hold on one sec, young man, do you need to call your parents?" Poorly stifling her laughter as she mockingly hands Jack her phone.

"Har, har, don't got parents anyways!" Pushing away the device, Jack turns scowling out the window.

69

Composing herself, somewhat she responds. "Deeper emotional needs for acceptance? Feeding my infantile need for attention? I didn't know you were taking Psychology this year. Doesn't Mr. Shoemaker teach that? I don't remember him on your schedule." She snickers trying to lighten the mode in the car.

"I'm not in Psych, and it's not that funny. These are thoughts I've been having for a while now, for years. I just didn't know how to say them or what they meant. I still don't know what they mean, but I want to." Returning to his thoughts, Jack adjusts in his seat.

"I'm sorry, dear. I guess I didn't expect those thoughts from my fourteen-year-old. But I think I understand where you're coming from. These years are the toughest because you're constantly questioning who you are because you don't know who that person will be in ten minutes, more or less ten years. You don't have to know who you are right now. Some just find their click or niche earlier, for whatever reason. Your path may just be more complicated than those who choose the simple life." Anna offers in her typical comforting voice.

"Ha, there's nothing but the simple life around here." Laughing to himself. "I just can't escape this feeling of being more than I am, like there's something out there for me. Something that's not here. Why here anyways?"

"You know I worked in the city before adopting you and wanted a quieter life. I know this disagrees with you now, but it's for the best. So, can I guess where some of these ideas are coming from?" She rhetorically asks, already suspecting their origin.

"Well, you know Mr. Wiley? The new teacher? I've told you that he's been tutoring me. I really enjoy our conversations. He's been helping me as he says, "Create a framework of understanding" to better understand my thoughts. I wish there were more teachers like him in schools."

"I figured Mr. Wiley had something to do with all the different books you have been bringing home. There are plenty of teachers like Wiley who care, just wish there were more youths like you who cared. Takes two to tango ya know?"

"Yeah, those. They really help me. Too much social media got my generation thinking life's some party. Should spend more time understanding ourselves before we care so much about what others think. My generation just seems lost in boredom, why don't they just read or learn something useful?" Eagerly awaiting her response, Jack pulls on the seatbelt strap shifting in seat.

"I suppose that's a billion-dollar question my sweet Jack. Older generations always struggle to understand younger ones. Wish I knew kiddo!" Looking out her window now, searching for answers.

"More like a priceless one. I mean, why can't we just learn who we are, then let that be our path? Math is important, sure, science, duh, no-brainer, but to learn them in such a stiff system that passes judgment year after year seems kinda dumb. We live

71

in the internet age; if we don't know something, then let us just look it up, and now we know it."

"But, how well do you know it? Education isn't a string of superficial Google searches. That's surviving the moment, not learning to thrive with the information, transform it into something that creates deeper understanding." Aunt Anna now playing devil's advocate while still allowing the proper space for her young ward to explore the conversation at length.

"Well, I mean, I guess that's true. Don't want Doctor's Googling open heart surgery before they scrub up." With that, they both share a laugh, melting the tension away.

"Point is, Jack, it's difficult to have a system with structure while allowing complete creative exploration at the same time. Those are competing forces. Creativity drives the exploration of new adventures, ideas, or discoveries. A system focuses on what has already been explored, an established order of sorts." Her best attempts to answer his questions only serve to generate a deluge of more.

The car gently rumbles to a halt as Jack and Aunt Anna arrive home. The pair continue their cavernous conversation for hours. Conversation traveling from the car, the front porch, to the kitchen, and long into the night.

"Jack, tea?" Anna asks shuffling through the dishwasher seeking her favorite mug.

"Yes Ma'am, I'll grab the honey." Jack responds helping gather necessities from the pantry as the conversation continues, only broken by a whistling kettle.

"So then I jumped up real high, like the highest I've ever jumped and caught the ball. Then I chased Chip. He ran squealing like a pig from Ole Rhett's farm." They both laugh uncontrollably at the thought.

"Is that when Charles ran into the bleachers?" Anna asks, sipping an aromatic lavender tea. Her usual ritual before going to bed. "Basically, too bad nobody had their phones to record it, or it'd be all over socials." Jack's enthusiasm in the retelling swells his ego even in the late hour. Quick to check such impulses Anna is quick to respond.

"Convenient for his sake, but Jack we mustn't revel in others humiliation. He got what he deserved, but for his long-term health, hopefully he makes a full recovery."

"Sure, I guess. But you should've seen Ari's face when she caught that ball, she couldn't believe it, it was dope. Still bummed about Reg's glasses." Returning to teenage normalcy as Aunt Anna emits an audible yawn, signaling her readiness for bed.

"Don't you worry about Reginald's glasses, you both go to the same Optometrist. I've already spoken to Reginald's mother, Mrs. Alton, about replacements. With all the doctor visits little Isaac's Syngap, it's the least we can do. I'll take it out of savings." Elated at the news, Jack springs up from the couch.

"Really, that's awesome! You're the best!"

"Alright, alright, Jack, settle down. It's partly coming from your allowance."

"I don't care. Maybe he can get those really cool transition ones he's been eyeing for a few years." Leaping from the couch and folding his hands, groveling on his friend's behalf.

"We will see, but in the next few days, you will have to complete extra chores to ensure you learn your lesson."

The two share a warm hug. "I do ninety percent of the chores as is. What more could I possibly do around here?"

She tilts her head back and laughs.

"Ninety percent, more like nine. I'm going to bed. G'night." Taking a few steps down the hall, she pauses.

"Oh yeah, by the way . . . you're out." She squeals playfully pelting him with a sock left on the floor.

"Hey, no fair." He begins as Aunt Anna's voice echoes down the hall.

"Dodgeball Champ!" On that note, Jack clears the dining room, placing dishes into the washer, and making the proper adjustments before heading off to his room as well.

CHAPTER TEN

WITHIN SILENT SCARS

"Sure, bro, I bet you're enjoying it. A week's suspension, you're like Lord of the Losers here, bro," Reggie states confidently, walking the halls, serving as Jack's un-anointed second lieutenant Face Timing Jack on his way to first period.

"Dude, even Crissy Freeman speaks to me in science . . ."

"Because she has to." Ari interrupts pushing her face into focus. "C'mon, Ari, don't listen to her. I."

"Stop that. Since your suspension and Chip's medical absence, Mr. Lewis had to change some teams around. Crissy is partnered with Reggie, given that both of their partners are disposed of now. If I didn't hate her over-use of foundation, I'd feel bad right now, but I'm kinda enjoying the slow, agonizing death of Reggie's chances right now."

Breaking into the conversation with a slight lag, Jack's broken laughter can be heard through the device. "I figured it went that bad!"

"Oh, screw the both of you with a two by four!!!" Reggie argues, adjusting his surgically repaired with duct-taped glasses. "I'm going to class. I'll catch you later, J-Dawg. Big Reg out. Ari, give me my phone Ari."

"Who's J-Dawg? Big Reg? Ari, what's going on?" Before Reggie can reclaim his property, Ari runs ahead, quickly explaining Reggie's new monikers for them.

"He thinks Crissy's impressed with ya'll's ridiculous nicknames, and he also. ." Before she can finish her thought, Reggie grabs his phone, lumbering a few paces ahead.

"Not today, Sista." Suddenly he runs into Dale, standing with a group of unfriendly goons.

"Watch where you're goin simp." He spits.

"Oh, I, I'm sor" Reggie stumbling to find his wording and footing at the same time.

"You must think you run this yard now, don't you?" Shoving Reggie hard against the wall, his head cracking dangerously against the painted cinderblock wall.

"Na, no, I just." Reggie stutters trembling with fear.

"You just what simp?" Dale retorts, striking Reggie's stomach as the group surrounds their prey. An individual pulls out his phone, giving Dale a nod as the big goof hits the floor, holding his stomach writhing from the counterfeit contact. Another voice begins screaming convincingly;

"Whoa, Bro, what the hell, man, that's not cool! Not cool, bro!"

Acting fast, Ari rushes into action and places her body in front of the camera, attempting to get between her faltering friend and the gaggle of goons. Her fast action saves Reggie for the

76

moment as a familiar voice breaks through the amassing murder of crows looking to pick the bones of their unsuspecting victims.

"Hey, HEY ENOUGH!!!" A voice rings out sternly, scattering those bred from the loins of cowardice and mediocracy. Grabbing two of Dale's goons, Mr. Wiley pins the two teens effortlessly, for a man's strength comes from a quiet reservoir to preserve the innocent.

"Bro, bro, get your hands. . ."

"Shut your mouth, you fraudulent excuse of a human being." Dale's teenage courage disappears as his eyes cross those of the enigmatic educator.

"What is going on? Mr. Wiley, that is more than necessary. Release those young men now!" An inferior but authoritative voice rings from down the hall. Principal Reilly enters the fray, pulling Ari roughly from the testosterone stew.

"Go to class Arianna, now. I will speak with you later." His tone causing much trepidation in the young Valkyrie.

Leaving hastily, turning, she sees the numbers advantage clearly shifting.

"Unhand those young men, Mr. Wiley. What are you thinking placing your hands on students?" Principal Reilly demands. Loosening his grip on the two goons, Mr. Wiley helps a wheezing Reggie to his feet.

"Mr. Alton, I should have known you'd be in the middle of this skirmish. Come with me. Dale, gentlemen, get to class." Reilly demands grabbing Reggie roughly.

"He's not going anywhere with you!" Wiley grabbing his superior only in title, by the wrist, roughly ripping his hand from the young man.

"Ahh . . . I knew you were bad apples, Wiley. Always taking up for . . . sfff" Reilly winces as Wiley's grip tightens informing him of his physical inferiority. Halting himself from further indictment and pain, the postulating principal pauses, controlling his contempt.

"Mr. Wiley, thank you for your due diligence in this egregious event. I will escort Mr. Alton to the front office for further questioning. Would you be so kind as to do the same for Dale and these fine young Gentlemen to their classes? That will be all." The pretentious Principal nods cynically as Wiley releases his grip. Still rubbing his wrist, Reilly escorts Reggie to his office. Gritting his teeth, Mr. Wiley acquiesces to his fictitious superior's requests, leading the classless classmates to their respective classrooms.

Unbeknownst to all, Reggie is questioned and insulted mercilessly by the charismatic cretin. After being mentally and emotionally battered, Reggie is allowed to return to class. Many suffer retaliation's cruel compulsion to forever speak in sanctuaries of silence. Never to see redemption from their tormentors, thus removing the soul from joyous continuation. Only when the courageous, immune to such contemptuous consolations, resisting such assaults, do the protagonist amend the actions of the antagonistic.

CHAPTER ELEVEN

SOMETHING'S GOTTA GIVE

The final bell blares sending students excitedly mingling with friends as they make their way to pick up or bus. Reggie quietly trudges to his bus, sitting to himself pulling his worn Earnhardt hat over welling eyes. Ari attempting to console him sits quietly after multiple failed attempts. Several bumps and minutes pass when her frustration boils over.

"Listen Reg, Dale and those guys are jerks! They don't know how much fun you are, most of the time. They don't know how much you help your parents, with Isaac and his Syn, um Syn something condition." Ari stutters feeling foolish, realizing she's mostly ignores Reggie when he talks.

"It's Syngap Ari, I help because my parents just don't know how to deal with him or are too drunk to care. . . snff thanks Ari." Reggie's tones lowers, sniffing away deeper emotions rising.

"Just tryin' to help Reg. Sorry to bother." Ari apologizes noting his uncharacteristically negative mood.

"We're good Ari. Thanks for stepping in today. Means a lot. Snff. I'll facechat Jack when I get off. Let me be for a bit. Snff." Reggie sniffs wiping a tear away, pressing his head heavily against the window.

79

"Ok Reg." Ari replies turning her attention to her phone. "PSSssssss!" Whistling brakes puncture the silence of woods as Reggie and Ari's bus comes to a stop. The pair and a few other students quickly exit making their way home.

"Catch'ya later Reggie. Tell Jack to call me after ya'll talk." Ari says with a half-hearted smile making her way down a dusty driveway.

"k!" Reggie murmurs kicking loose rocks down the dirt road he's walked so many times before. Reaching into his pocket, Reggie dials Jack's surprised he's got signal. C'mon pick up, pick up." Reggie taps its sides nervously, when a familiar face pops up on his screen.

"Sup Dude?" Jack answers, his voice sending confidence into his companion.

"Sup Bro, so today was interesting . . ." Reggie begins, telling Jack his tale. Minutes and steps pass without notice as the two friends' converse.

"Reg, then he said what? When I get back, it's on." An exasperated Jack sits back in his desk chair, the glow of his phone illuminating his face.

"Jack, you can't say or do anything, bro, he's serious this time. Can't we just change the subject? I'm in enough trouble as it is. Dad's probably gonna kick the crap outta me when I get home."

"Look, I'm home Bud. Gotta find my charger, help out with Isaac, clean up the house kinda stuff. I'll facechat ya tomorrow after school. Whatever you do, Jack, do not say anything to Ari.

She's worried for the both of us, and right I just want to get through freshman year so I can drop out next year."

"Wait, what? Reg, you can't be serious!"

"Bro, this ain't for me, man. I'm barely passing half my classes as it is. My parents need the money, its ok Bud. School's just not my thing. I've gotta go. Talk to you tomorrow."

A sense of desperation hangs heavy as Jack stares helplessly at his phone. The glow of his screen fading quickly as numbness settles in. His friend's sad words hanging heavy in his thoughts.

"It's all your fault, Jack. You gotta make things right. Something's gotta give." Tossing his phone on the desk, Jack buries his face into his hands, running them through the length of his hair, tugging roughly at their ends.

"Something's gotta give." Repeating to himself when a gentle knock raps his door.

"Jack, Sweetie is everything ok?" Anna asks noting his face as she enters the room, settling softly on the corner of his bed.

"Something's the matter. Was that Ari?"

"Nah, I mean no, Ma'am. It was Reg. His parents are gonna probably come down hard on him. I'm sure that rat faced Reilly already called home."

"Is Reginald ok? Should I be concerned?"

"It's my fault, I shouldn't have. . ."

"No, Jack, you did what most don't. From the coaches to Charles, to Principal Reilly. None of them has the right to act the way they did. It's all ridiculous and wrong. Come'on, I need help

81

in the kitchen. The fair is in a couple of weeks, and I need help with a new cobbler recipe."

"I'm sorry, Aunt Anna. I just do not feel up to it tonight."

"Oh, come on sourpuss. All things pass. Besides, this new recipe is a sure winner, and you could use the distraction. We have the next few days off, so let's not waste them." Rising from the edge of his bed, shaking him lovingly on the foot.

"Not, not tonight. I just need to think. I'll clean up in the morning, promise."

"Ok sweet boy, I understand, but the mixer will need some serious scrubbing in the morning." The loving lady exits, leaving the door ajar.

Jack waits a few minutes to ensure her departure before venturing to the bathroom to splash water on his face. Returning swiftly to his room, Jack retrieves a book borrowed from Mr. Wiley and begins to read. *"The Old Man and the Sea.* Ernest Hemingway? Jeeze Wiley, always with these old books. Well, let's see what this old dude has to say about the sea."

Hours pass as Jack reads voraciously through the nautical novella. His pace slows by the frequency of researching unknown words. Reading until his eyelids are heavy with sleep and emotional depletion, Jack places the old book on his desk, settling in for much-needed sleep. With visions of massive marlins, the scent of salt and sweat populating his dreams, the youngster drifts deeper into his own ambitious adventure upon the high seas.

The sun beams between the cracks of his binds, warming his face and inviting him to a new day. Stretching out on his bed, Jack rises, rubbing sleep from his eyes. A burning sensation radiates from his hands, observing tightly pulled wrinkles taunt into his sheets.

"What the?" He shuffles to the bathroom, running water to cool his hands. Redness and pain radiating from hands subsiding, Jack makes his way to the kitchen. The morning sun chases away shadows to the corners of the house.

"Good morning, sleepyhead." Anna's voice floats softly from across the small breakfast table in the kitchen.

"G'mornin. What time is it?" He responds, using the palms of his hands, rubbing reminisce of sleep from his eyes.

"It's eleven fortyish. You looked so peaceful this morning, and I thought it best to let you sleep. There's some eggs, ham, and toast from breakfast. I ran by the store for some things. There's OJ in the fridge. The kind with the orange cap you like so much."

"Thanks, I had the weirdest dream last night. I was fighting a big fish for what seemed like forever." Sauntering over to gather the cooled remainder of breakfast, eating greedily.

"It was so odd." He pauses between large bites.

"Yeah, were you in the water punching this fish?" She responds, smothering a soft laugh behind her phone.

"No, no, I was like in a boat, and it kept taking me further out to sea. You know, fishing like normal people would. No, I wasn't in the ocean boxing this thing. I was reading a book Wiley gave

83

me about some old desperate dude fishing. Anyway, it was intense. Here, let me get that for you." Jack collects her plate and utensils from breakfast and makes his way to the sink.

"Oh, no, you don't, well, if you insist. So tell me about this dream." Placing her phone face down on the small table, giving him her undivided attention.

As he goes about cleaning the few items in the sink, Jack rocks between his dream and the book, a masterpiece she was familiar with.

"And then I was fighting off sharks with an oar or was it a knife? Either way, they still ate the big fish. It was crazy."

"Sounds like it, then what happened?" She asks, placing the last dry dish away.

"Then I woke up, so weird."

"It's not weird. You got pretty far in *The Old Man and the Sea*." Anna turns, anticipating the tone of his response.

"Wait, what? How didgya?" Jack throwing his hands up at her apparent invasion.

"Well, I know you don't like me checking in on you, but well, Jack, you weren't even covered up. I noticed you got rather far in the book. Pretty impressive for one night's reading." Sheepishly, Jack places his hand on her shoulder to comfort and condone her actions.

"Well, I kinda skipped around here and there, but I got the gist." He reveals boyishly.

"So do you want to "spoiler" it?" Aunt Anna uses air quotes.

"No, no. I'll finish it tonight. I'm good, that's not how those work. Anyways, do you still need help with your recipe?" He swats playfully at her continued incorrect use. "Stop that. Don't you have some all-world masterpiece to create?"

Halting her childish gesture, she hurries to a thick, dated recipe book. "Check this one out. I wrote this a few days ago. It's gonna kill."

After a few more playful exchanges, the two work in a culinary concert in preparation for the rapidly approaching event. In small towns that dot many a landscape, county fairs afford the unassumingly quiet to speak aloud with earnest and joyful intent.

CHAPTER TWELVE

ALL'S FAIR IN LOVE AND WAR!

Jack and Aunt Anna return to school, and the next few weeks pass without incident. Although the tension between all concerning parties remains, Jack consumes his time after school resuming conversations with Mr. Wiley, who quietly shares Aunt Anna's concerns about the unresolved issues pervading the campus, continues to challenge and expand Jack's understanding of the world outside of his small town.

"So you see, Jack, Santiago respected the big marlin. He respected the fight the great fish put up. The story may seem to focus on his need to make a catch, but it, in many senses, focuses on the determination of mankind and the fight we have to survive."

Pondering for only a second, Jack responds to his mentor. "Towards the end, when he says *I went too far*. What did he mean, it can't mean that he sailed too far from shore?"

Sighing deeply, Wiley gathers his thoughts. "Well, that is up to the reader to determine. That's what makes this a masterpiece. Santiago is possibly admitting his fault or maybe simply implying he knew sailing with such a large catch he couldn't defend the fish back to shore. It has been suggested that this is an allegory for life. If we go too far beyond our station, those sharks or events will destroy any gains we made before we see their fruits bared. Simply put, when we reach beyond our abilities and understanding, others will always be there to destroy what they were too afraid to attempt or accomplish without taking from others with more obvious talent. Envy, Jack, is one of the greatest sins of humanity."

Wiley pauses, allowing Jack to absorb his wisdom.

"So what you're saying is that it doesn't matter how far we reach. Others will always be there to take what they didn't earn?"

Leaning deeper on the desk, the young literate waits eagerly. "One could surmise that, however, Jack, what if Santiago made it back with his catch? We mustn't lose hope. Hope that for every failure, there is a chance for success. If we are assured there is darkness, we are also assured there must be light. One cannot exist without the other. Your story is yet revealed; therefore, do not assume failure because an old man didn't make it back with his quarry. He made it back with his dignity and respect. A quarry some never venture far enough to hunt."

Before another word can be exchanged, Jack's phone begins buzzing. Swiping his finger across Aunt Anna's face. "I'm on my way. No, no, we just finishing up for the day. Meet yah at the car. Okay, I mean, yes, Ma'am. See yah in a sec."

Stuffing notes into his backpack, he politely excuses himself.

"I'm sorry to cut our conversation short today. Got to go, Sir. Hafta help Aunt Anna with her fair stuff, I mean. . ."

87

Before the young pupil can finish his explanation, Wiley interjects. "No need to apologize. Going to the fair tonight? This wouldn't have anything to do with that award-winning cobbler I've heard so much about, would it?"

"Yes, Sir, it's won first in the county every year since I can remember. Chip and some of the other boys in elementary school used to call me the cobbler kid. It's pretty good, and judging is tonight. I can bring you some tomorrow if you want."

"I may make a brief appearance. How could I pass up Miss Anna's county-famous cobbler?" Wiley settles behind his laptop to finish up a few items before leaving himself. The two share a cordial nod as Jack exits the room.

"One last thing, Jack, don't let Chip take up any more of your mental space. He'll get his. Bullies always do! Try to have some fun tonight. It's the county fair. Never know what could happen."

"Yes, Sir, see you later."

"What took you so long? We have to hurry." Anna adjusts the mirror as Jack enters the poor excuse for a vehicle.

"It's only two thirty. We have plenty of time to get home, get the stuff and get to our booth." The younger retorts, shutting the door and tossing his pack onto the back seat.

"Speak for yourself. We still have to pick up Arianna and Reginald on our way and you know I don't like driving fast on Reginald's dirt road." She gestures hurriedly for him to buckle his seatbelt.

88

"Go, GO!!! Jeeze, you always get like this. You know that recipe is gonna kill." Fighting off her attempts to back up and buckle his seatbelt simultaneously.

"Well, it's a good thing we stayed late last night and set up the booth. You know I get nervous like this every year."

"Come on, Reg, yeah just put a shirt on. What do you mean you don't want to go? Crissy? I don't have GPS on her. Maybe she'll be there. No, I'm not checking her location on snapgram. Why? Because it's creepy. Let's go." Jack yells standing on the collection of dilapidated wood posing as a front porch to Reggie's home.

"Come on, Bro! No, Mrs. Alton, he doesn't need any money. We'll get in for free because of Aunt Anna. Food? Got that covered, too, no worries. Yes, Ma'am. I'm sure a Lincoln would help, but we're good." Jack taps impatiently on the dirty doorframe. The two head down the deteriorated steps.

"What's the rush all about anyways? I've been on Devil's Drop twice, and I've had Aunt Anna's cobbler a thousand times." Reggie fluffs his hair before settling ole Earnhardt back on top.

"Snff. When's the last time? Never mind. I've never ridden Devil's Drop, so maybe this is the year you finally get me on that death trap. No, no shotgun!" Jack hurries past Reggie, who is making his way to the front seat.

"You always get shotgun, and I'm not sitting next to Ari!" Reggie expresses.

"Com'n get in. You two can make out, I mean makeup on the way there." Jack slaps the door, but not before rapping his friend roughly on the chest.

"Eww, I mean I would, but she couldn't handle all this."

Reggie pauses to rub his chest as the passenger door becomes slightly ajar. "Yeah, when all life as we know it has died, maybe you and that water buffalo Crissy can repopulate the world."

Ari pulls herself back to her side of the back seat, obviously hearing the boys' earlier comments.

"Hey, that's a double no, no. How dare you talk about water buffaloes like that! They're the most crucial piece of the food chain in the Sahara!"

Reggie scoffs, buckling his seatbelt.

"You mean Serengeti? Idiot, shut your door!" Ari demands, smacking Reggie's attempt to unbuckle hers.

"Glad you could join us, Reginald. Everyone set? Let's go." Aunt Anna's delivery is more uncharacteristically exasperated than normal. In the unison, the three companions answer.

"Yes, Ma'am." With all parties secure, the quartet quickly makes haste to their collective destination.

Arriving to a side parking lot designated for special entries, the group work like a well-oiled machine to complete final prep.

"Well, that should be it. With minutes to spare. Thanks ya'll. Now, gang, be back by ten for cleanup. We've got to be out of here by ten thirty. Most importantly, go have fun. You three deserve it."

As the smell of fresh cobbler permeates the air, Aunt Anna mentally prepares for the next few hours. Her usually unassuming demeanor giving way to the charismatic creator of cobblers.

"Yes, Ma'am, ten thirty, got it. Good luck, know you got that blue ribbon already, Aunt Anna." Jack and company stride off to enjoy their freedom, taking advantage of every fleeting second.

Kicking up a mixture of clay and gravel underfoot, the three companions hurry off, childish exuberance filling their imaginations. Armed with a pocketful of cash and wristbands for unlimited rides; they rush to all their favorite. Taking in the gleeful squeals of joyous children whizzing by on rides of every imaginable color, the smells of deep-fried foods hang low, tempting every nostril in attendance.

The trio leaves a few rides unexplored. Even the innocence of children's rides isn't off limits. Leaving Ari to the mercy of her boyish companions, who spin the worn green frog on its lily pad till the bolts rattle menacingly. Whether it's her terrified begging for mercy or the sight of her now lime green and jet black hair tossing uncontrollably about the unintentional device of dread. Like sharks with the scent of blood in the water, the two dynamos of devastation carry on.

"What was that Ari? Faster? She wants it faster, Reg! Faster Reg! Faster!" Jack gleefully commands his companion.

"I'M GIVIN EM ALL I GOT, CAPTAIN!" Reggie shouts over her audible screams of terror in his best Scottish accent. "I'M GONNA KILL YOU TWOOO, AAAAAHHH!!!"

Contraptions of terror terrifically designed to both delight and demoralize dot the lively landscape. With the sun setting in the backdrop, rides dazzle the imagination. From the Ring of Fire, whose lighted flames lick the sides of the ride, emitting an auburn glow upon the faces of passerby's and riders alike to the famous Pharaoh's Fury. A longboat lit up from bow to stern. Gems gleaming golden topaz, ruby, and sapphire, contrasting the royalty of amethyst, twinkle playfully as the ride whizzes by. After some convincing, the boys coax Ari on a ride shaped like a large starship.

"Oh, come on, Ari, you've never rode this ride. Com'n." Jack prods. The glimmer of glittered paint sparkles more amid the generously sequenced lights, creating a dazzling display. With music blaring loudly from inside, Ari makes a concerning observation upon entry.

"What? No seat belts? Harnesses? No, no, I want off." She protests as the operator shuts the hatch behind her.

"Ok, everyone please take a place against the walls. Only two things to discuss first before the Starfire 5000 takes flight. Whatever song you choose determines the speed and duration of the ride. Taking suggestions now."

The operator dressed like an extra in a Space Odyssey looks around the craft daringly.

"Oh, OH! PICK ME!" Reggie stepping up to the challenge.

"Ok, my young cadet, what would you like me to play?"

92

"Oh, um. Can you play Through the Fire and Flames by Dragonforce? Um, Sir." Reggie salutes, also getting into character. Checking the time on his watch, chuckling to himself.

"Oh a long one, what the hell? I'm about to go on break." Momentarily breaking character, the Starfire Commander quickly regains form, selects Reggie's desired track, pressing a large red button and slapping the blue-tinted visor down over his eyes.

"Buckle up, Cadets; it's gonna be a long ride to Terra Nova Prime."

The ride begins with a slow creak as the engine below comes to life. Suddenly, the lights go out, blackening the cabin as it begins to rotate. Gaining speed, power metal blasts, filling the cabin with the rapid intro the song is famously known for. As the song aggressively accelerates, so does the craft. Lights explode, beaming around the craft, moving melodically as if designed for the song. Spinning faster and faster, Jack feels his body pull into the wall behind, and his limbs become heavy as the centrifugal force intensifies.

"WWWWOOOO! NOT FUNNY GUYS, not. . ."

A combination of music and force exerted, extracting Ari's.

"I KNOW RIGHT! THIS IS SOOO METALLL!!!" Reggie responds, looking in her direction. With the music filling their bodies with increased adrenaline, Jack and a few others begin climbing the walls. Crouching low, driving hard through his heels, Jack attempts to stand but is pulled repeatedly back to a crouch. With his legs shaking under the sheer force upon him, Jack gives

93

it one last attempt to raise his hands to the heavens above, but without wings, his dream is so far beyond reality. Collapsing roughly to the wall, chest heaving, turning, noticing Reggie applauding his attempt.

Moments later, the music fades as the ride gently slows to a halt.

"THAT WAS AWESOME!!!" Reggie expounds, failing to adjust his volume.

"I hate you guys. Oompf. I really hate you both right now." Ari stumbles uneasily down the exit steps.

"Great ride! WOOOO!!!" Jack shouts, breathing heavily.

"What's next?" Ari wobbles, pressing past her companions.

"Oh com'n, Ari, that was fun. How about it, Reg? Reg?" Turning, Jack sees his friend leaning behind the ride almost out of sight.

"You ok, Bro? Get it out." Slapping his friend on the back playfully.

"Ugh, Jack, you think. Hmpf. You think that's what cheerios feel when it gets sucked up into a vacuum?" Reggie gulps fighting through his own dizziness.

"I don't know about that, but food doesn't sound bad right about now." Jack says, taking a few paces to get his baring on the food vendors.

"You two are awful. How could you think of food after that?"
Ari strides over next to Jack, glancing over her shoulder at
Reggie.

"Uggh, that's better. I could eat, I'm running on empty."
Reggie wipes his mouth with the back of both hands.

"Eww, gross." Ari heads in the direction of the vendors.

The group passes more rides on their way to the food court,
and a familiar glow licks viciously against the group as they pass.

"Jack, Bro, this is the year! We ain't no middle schoolers
anymore. Ari, you down?" Reggie clasps Jack's shoulders
roughly, shaking confidence in his friend.

"Hell Yeah! Jack, we got to! Jack? Jack?" Snapping her
fingers in his face. Jack stands petrified, staring up at a sinister
apparatus of aggression.

"JACK!" Ari's voice heightens over the ambient abundant
noise surrounding the trio.

"What? Who?" Snapping out of his trance, Jack stares blankly
at them.

"Bro, you like looked up and went full re . . . oof!" Reggie
begins before Ari cuts him off.

"Shut up, you oaf." Shoving Reggie aside, coming face to face
with Jack.

"We don't have to ride Devil's Drop this year if you don't
want. Is everything ok?"

"Yeah, yes. I, I just don't know. It's like I just freeze when I see the lights. I don't know, it's nothing. Can we get something to eat now?"

"Lights? It's red, orange and yellow. What's so scary about, oaf!"

"Come on, Reggie, we will figure it out later!" Ari turns, sprinting in Jack's direction.

"My man, Jack, it's just a stupid ride. Ugh, all this running, why? Why always with the running guys?" Reggie slogs after his companions.

"Hooff, can we hoof. . . can we promise to hoof, to not run so much? Walking is... is. . . yeah, walking is fine, guys." Reggie leans heavily against catching his breath while eying all the desires of his heaving heart.

"You should take gym class more seriously, Reggie!" Ari ever ready to belittle.

"It's not the running, it's the wedgies. You know those gym shorts like to travel to parts unknown." Reggie reaches behind to readjust himself.

"You're gross, wash your hands before you, stop that you. . ." Ari responds.

"Alright, alright, guys, let's find something to eat." Jack injects, shooting Reggie a disapproving nod.

"So what will it be? Classic Conies? The Trough? Oh, Kluckin Kenny's is here. I could go for a couple turkey legs." Reggie stumbles on shaky legs wide-eyed towards a green-trimmed truck adorned with two giant fried chicken legs atop.

"Reggie, where are you going?" Ari interjects before noticing Jack staring through the hungry horde surrounding them.

"What's up, Jack?" She begins.

"Hey, I'll get ya'll get something. Text you in a minute." Jack hands Ari two twenties without looking, slipping off into the crowd.

"Jack? Jack? Boys!" Ari protests pathetically before losing sight of him.

"Where did Jack go? Hello Hamilton and Hamilton!" Reggie snatches at the currency in her hand.

"Boys. Come on, Reggie, stop that. Let's feed the beast." Ari says, catching sight of Jack's quarry, shaking her head disapprovingly as Reggie gyrates his girth.

"Jack, why do you always have to get involved?" she whispers to herself.

Knifing expertly through the crowd, Jack moves methodically sneaking into the shadows of a cart selling an assortment of fried Oreos and other sugared confections. Observing a familiar scene between Chip and Kattie, Jack noting Chip's advantage, waits patiently.

"Whatchu mean I'm good?" Arrogance stares menacingly into a face caressed by cascading sunshine auburn hair.

"I, I don't want to do this anymore, Chip." The homespun heroin responds.

"What do you mean this? I'm Chip Eckles, and you're Kattie Thompson. Future Prom King and Queen. We are this!" Chip hovers over Kattie aggressively pinning her against a cart. Alternative avenues of escape cut off by his cronies.

"C'mon, Babe. We've been it since sixth grade and everyone knows it! What's it this time? Criss . . . I mean, Brittany? I have like only third period with her, and she's like smart and shit, so I just copy her work, that's it!" Chip moves in for a kiss as Kattie dives, slipping his grip.

"Chip, I need space, time to think. You get it, right?" Her attempt at escape slowed by Chip's cronies, who surround her immediately.

"Get what? What's there to get? You're mine. I'm like the wrestling team captain. Only freshman captain in the history of ever ya'know!"

Chip high-fives one of his four cronies as patrons pass by without noticing.

"Hand off creep! So I've heard, over and over and over again. Chip, you don't get it." Kattie, failing to storm off surrounded from escape Chip, whips around angrily.

"I get it, I get it all. It's him? I saw how you looked at him, how you asked about him all the freakin time." Chip spits, striking a nearby cart.

"Think what you want, Chip, I'm outta here." Kattie noting his rising aggression, pushes past her oppressors.

"Let her go, she'll be back. I'm Chip freaking Eckles! She'll be back. They all come back! C'mon, boys, let's go hit up sum toothless hobo games." He sniffs with a flick of his finger.

As the goons head off towards precarious carnies, Jack emerges from concealment. Stifling a boyish smile, he follows Kattie into the thicket traversing the assortment of frivolous foods. Moving quickly but cautiously to not reveal his pursuit Jack follows his quarry's golden auburn hair barely able to peek over the masses milling about. Occasionally ducking behind a cart moving closer when he notices Kattie standing in front of a generic cart selling an assortment of deep-fried foods.

Patiently, Jack observes Kattie contemplating drowning her sadness in funnel cake when another patron pushes roughly past him, knocking Jack into her.

"Ja-Jack Murphy. I thought I saw you earlier. Here for the funnel cake?"

Unprepared Jack jokes. "Not the worst choice, but hollow deep-fried dough covered in sugar, doesn't seem like your thing."

"Is that so? So what do you suggest then, blue ribbon cobbler?" A twinkle dances flirtatiously in her eyes.

"Uh, uh yeah, we could, I know a spot." He chuckles sheepishly.

"Well, the cobbler will have to wait. I'm hungry for real food, but what's good around here?" Kattie grabs his hand, directing Jack away from the delectable desserts. Stunned, he follows.

"Well, what does Jack Murphy like to eat?"

"Um, um, well, I always go for the Atomic slaw dogs at Nuclear Nancy's, but not everyone likes. . ." He stutters before she cuts him short.

"OMG! Nuclear Nancy's is the best! Heard they use that new Cripplin' Hot Sauce! C'mon!" Tugging him roughly, they make their way through the crowd. Surprised by her enthusiasm, Jack's legs move without conscience thought.

"Yes, there isn't a line!" Kattie squeals excitedly, golden hair bounces as she bounds towards a cart adorned with an atomic bomb atop it. "I'm so excited, Chip never, oh never mind . . . what do you want, my treat!"

"No, no, I got it, but I have to warn you, I like it hot, like hot Cheetos have nothing on The Destroyer Dog hot!" Jack responds, cracking a devious smile.

"Ha, we will see, tough guy!" Kattie playfully flips Jack's hair from his eyes as they make their way to the window.

A sweet-looking woman adorned in military fatigues slides the window open. "Welcome to Nuclear Nancy's home of the world-famous Destroyer Dog and other assorted assets waiting to punish the palate. What can I get started for you two daring desperados?"

"We will take four Destroyers and one large Coke, please." Jack, surprised by her audaciousness, nods in approval.

"Would you like Half-life, Atomic, or Nuclear for the slaw?" The sweet arbiter of atomic wares asks.

"Nuclear!" Jack and Kattie answer.

"You got it, that'll be. . ." Before she can confirm the order, Jack interrupts.

"Oh, can we get an order of Fallout Fries? Nuke em Please."

"Roger that, it'll be $26.75." Jack hands her two twenties, receiving his change before turning to Kattie.

"I hope you're down? These Fallouts are no joke." Kattie playfully pushes him aside, retrieving the large drink and straw.

"Hmm. I live for them Fallout Fries, boi!" A few minutes pass as the two wait in the glimmering ambiance surrounding them.

"Order up! Some tissues for ya known. Enjoy!" The sweet woman's eyebrows raise as she nods suggestively at Jack.

"Thank yah!" Jack replies, whisking the tray of delicious destruction to a nearby bench.

The two eat greedily to their delicious demise. "Snff, snff. That, that hit the snff spot." Kattie wipes her nose aggressively to conceal the molten mess.

"Snff. Those, snff Fallout Fries are where it's at!" Jack says, stuffing the last bit of his dog with fiery fries.

"Uhh, snff, snff." He sniffs, eyes watering.

"Hey. I've got…" Jack protests mockingly as Kattie wipes nimbly under his nose. Kattie scoots hip-to-hip, completing her task. Jack's warming cheeks perfectly concealed by heat of downed dogs.

"So, Jack Murphy, what next?" Brushing golden locks her ear, eager eyes glimmering from illuminations above.

"Do'you like pigs?" Jack gulps nervously.

"Pot-bellies?" She replies, a smile reciprocating his.

"Races start in like ten. We can still get good seats, c'mon!" Jack tosses their trash expertly into a nearby trashcan. Grabbing his freehand, Kattie wraps it around her shoulder.

"Lead the way, Jack Murphy!" The two stride off in the direction of a well-lit area.

With dusk setting in the background, the crowd roars with excitement, sending energy through all in attendance as Jack and Kattie arrive.

"There!" Jack yells, pulling Kattie to open seats near the finish line.

"Here?" Looking up, she responds inquisitively.

"Of course, best seats in the house. My money's on Kevin Bacin. He always wins!" Jack's reassuring nature brimming with newfound confidence. The festivities kick off with introductions to all the competitors, Hamhock, Babyback, Wilbur, Babe, HogHeaven, Kevin Bacin, and the list goes on. Cheers from the crowd encourage the proceeding events. Multiple elimination-style events entertain all. After each victory, Jack's confidence grows.

"I told you Bacin was the best. He always runs the last third the fastest!" Jack howls, rooting on his pig of choice.

"And this year's Grand Champion is. . . Kevin Bacin!!!" A voice shouts to the excitement of the crowd.

"We won! We Won!" Kattie jumps up and down grasping an obviously ecstatic Jack.

"I told you, Bacin for the bag!" The two embrace, staring deeply into each other's eyes, anticipating the night ahead. Jack, Kattie, and a few other winners collect random memorabilia before exiting.

"Wow, I've never won a pig race. That was amazing, Jack! How'dyu know?" Her eyes gleaming with excitement.

"Eh, I've been to every state fair since I was five, and Bacin wins almost every year, so you know." He replies, sauntering ahead coolly.

"C'mon, let's hit up some rides." The pair ride an assortment of contraptions, cultivating a connection compared to none before.

"Oh, oh. This one, Jack, I've never been on Devil's Drop!" Kattie tugs tantalizingly towards the demonic device.

Necks craned peer into the night sky at the menacing machine before them.

"Yes! Yes! Whooo! This is the year, Jack, ain't it?" Staring frozen in time, Jack stares upward.

"Yea, Yeah. Let's do it." His voice cracking, burrowing themselves in line.

"I've always wanted to, but I never had the nerve . . . what's the matter, Jack?" Her eyes sparkle with anticipation.

"Oh, nothing. I've nev. . .I've ridin this a dozen times, no biggie." Jack coughs, turning to conceal a sudden shutter.

"Super!!! Get your wristband ready Jack Murphy. OMG this is really happening!" Kattie bounces, hair shifting from golden auburn to a sinister collage of red and orange.

"Yay, super stoked." Jack says, displaying a faux expression of excitement.

"Oh, com'n, the lines moving quicker than usual, how lucky." She gallops giddily forward, grabbing Jack by the arm.

"Okay, okay. Lines moving." Stuffing sweaty hands into his pockets. Each step forward accompanied by the tormented screams of preceding participants.

"I can't believe I waited this long, com'n Jack Murphy, we're next. Get them wristbands ready. Ooo!! Ooo smile!" Before Jack can react, Kattie snaps a selfie, eyes radiating with youthful expectancy. Teeth clinched tightly, half stumbling up the final step, his face a portrait of pending punishment as he humors his heroin.

"Didya get it?" the jostled juvenile asks.

"Ohhmm, you're not smiling." Before the hyped heroin can snap another, a gruff voice rings out.

"Next riders, please!"

Kattie steps confidently forward, tugging Jack excitedly.

"Place all valuables securely in pockets before seating. Welcome ta Devil's Drop. Next!" The smell of cigarettes and cheap whisky permeating the air.

"Pretty Lass ya got there." The crusty carnie smacks, poorly puckering his protruding peckers in Jack's direction. Smiling uncomfortably, Jack shudders, saved only by Kattie's impatience. Hopping in, pulling roughly, the harness creaks as it clicks.

"Come on, Jack, you have to. . ." Reaching over to assist.

"I got, got it." Jack pulls roughly against the resisting restraint. His heart racing as if clawing its way to the safety below.

"Com'n, you stupid thing." Muttering under his breath, when a forceful hand thrusts the decrepit device downward.

"Gotcha, little buddy." The gruff voice breathes, roughly tugging the restraint. Gripping worn padding tightly the sound of the menacing machine coming to life rattling Jack to his core.

With each click, the vile vehicle ascends to its apex. Squeezing his eyes tighter, Jack senses the merry mob below deafly drifting into the distance. The sinister sound of a voice demonically describing the devilish descent deafens the ear when a warmth wrapping his hand pulls Jack back to the moment. Peering past her restraint, a face of fascination, framed in auburn golden hair, forgetting all fear, a second of clarity capturing Jack, a world of worries washing away. Jack smiles in the silence surrounding them.

In an instant, a perfect moment ripped away by rapid rotation, the demonic device spins sinisterly into darkness. Hearts heaving for heaven, panicked patrons squeal in surprise as the cruel contraption swiftly spins southward. Jack's dread dissipates during the diabolical descent. A rush of reverence readies him for any evil epilogue enveloping all fear.

"Whoaaa! That was awesome! Again, again, again!!!" Kattie kicks with surging serendipity.

"Hell yeah!!!" Jack jigs jovially. The pair ride Devil's Drop three more times before moving on.

105

"It's only 8:13, Jack Murphy. I wanna go dancing." Kattie jerks Jack towards a makeshift building, blaring bars boisterously.

"Com'n, Jack, it's Eighties night!" The vivacious vixen ventures through an open door. Lights strobe splashing those swaying back and forth, intoxicating individuals in dance. The crowd explodes with elation as Starship's, *We built this City* surges. The earlier events evaporate as Jack and Kattie dance. Between the Bon Jovi blaring, Mötley Crüe crushing, and Poison permeating, the two dance losing track of time and themselves in a gluttony of glam metal. Kattie, placing Jack's arms around her waist and reaching hands towards the Gods of Glam, spins seductively. Thankful for the litany of illuminations, concealing his cheeks blushing bashfully.

"Alright, party people!" A voice rips over, resonating rifts of RATT fading into the raucous crowd.

"For all the old and new couples out there. This isn't an oldie, but give it up for. . ." The enthralling intro to Bonfire's *Crazy Over You* sending synchronized spirits frenzying further. Kattie grabs Jack, exploding with excitement.

"Whoa, it's a long way that we have come! I've given my heart to a love. . ." Her voice melding into musing masses moving around them.

Her eyes sparkle Jack catching glimpses of excitement and intrigue. Only time will tell if it's Heaven or Hell that awaits him. The two dance and dance, their bodies filling with energy not their own, harnessed wholeheartedly, stealing precious moments from the precarious mundane that awaits all when the melody melts away.

"Hhff. Hhff! That was heavy!" Jack exudes, catching his breathe.

"Dam . . . damn, didn't think you could dance like that." Kattie pants pathetically. Simultaneous smiles connecting; only separated by a gentle breeze blowing between them, tethering two tense souls.

"Hff, what next? hff," The depleted dame directs.

"Um, Aunt Anna. . . shoot. It's fu. . ." Jack fumbling his phone astonished at the time.

"It's only 10:12. What's up?" Pushing auburn golden locks bchind one ear, lights from distant distractions defining her every feature.

"Oh, um, I mean, I gotta." Jack stutters.

"I get it, forever an enigma wrapped in a mystery." Taking a few paces from him, Kattie saunters off.

"No, no. I have to help my Aunt Anna clean up her booth at 10:30!" Jack spits out.

"10:30, you say?" Her voice hails hotly over one shoulder.

"Then there's still time. Com'n, I'm no good at games. Maybe you can win something softer than my heart." Flaring her eyebrows, sending further flirtations, she heads off in the directions of the game alley.

"Oh, boy. What are you doing, Jack?" rifling through his pockets, checking his account.

107

"Fifteen bucks. Pff. Plenty, com'n Jack, you got this."

"Now that's a winner!" She exclaims ecstatically. Pointing at an enormous yellow Pikachu.

"Pokémon, really?" Jack looking at the sizable stuffy.

"Gotta catch'em all, go I choose you, Jack Murphy!" Pushing him closer to a strong stench of smoke with a whiff of whiskey.

"Step right up. Everyone's a winner at Billy's Bullseye!" The jovial Joint jests.

"That'll be five bucks per round. . .twenty for five because I likes the look of yah, kid!"

Stepping up to the calculating carnie, Jack readies himself. "I only got ten, but I tell ya, if I hit bullseye first shot, how'bout five rounds for fifteen?"

"Oh, big cojones on this one. Deal, first shot'sa bullseye or it's twenty." The Joint jests. Suspecting the stray sight, Jack shoulders the wayward weapon.

"Expert, we have a marksman on our hands!"

The Joint jokes mockingly. Jack rattles off his first shot, breathing in slowly and tightening his core.

"MISS! Ooooo! Better get that Hami ready, little man!" Licking his decaying dentals deliciously, the Joint jabs. Looking over his shoulder, cracking a smile.

"How many for the yellow rat?" Pointing the barrel at the popular Pokémon.

"Uh, uh. Two, Uh, three bullseyes." The jesting joker responds.

"Three in a row or just three with the four shots I have left?" Jack returns.

"Just tw, uhh three. Yeah three." The musky miscreant counters capriciously.

"Hmm." Turning the rifle sideways, using his middle finger as the sight, rattles off three consecutive shots. Each shredding skillfully the fictitious fixed fabrication's red center. Stunned in disbelief, the disjointed Joint jolting to his cunning contraption. Poking his finger through the paper, hanging his head.

"Well, we have a winner! What it'll be, young man?" The dejected derelict decries.

"You already know, bruh!" Pointing at the prized Pokémon, Jack peeks over his shoulder mockingly. Jack hands the disjointed Joint a five-dollar bill, taking the handpicked prize.

"Here you go, one prized Pokémon."

"Hehe! Thankya." The gleaming girl giggles.

"OMG, I can't believe you actually, how'dyou?" Clutching the considerable cuddly, the curious cutie questions.

"Well, I've played that game a million times. They always mess with the sights. Err, u they mess with the aiming thingy, you gotta adjust ya know." Jack quips.

"Honestly, all these games are rigged. I just know how not to get took." Jack's confidence cascading over his homely humility.

"Oh, I'm sure. I bet Adrianna has six of these in her room. Would you care to explain?" She jokingly jabs.

"Whaat? Ari, she's just a friend. She's bi, lez. She really likes Reg but doesn't know what she wants. I don't know, it's complicated." Jack sputters.

"Doesn't sound complicated. Sounds like she needs get off the internet, just live, and go after what she wants." Kattie suggestively nudging Jack, caressing his chest before bolting off. "Thanks Jack, see ya at school!"

"Hey, hey, what?" Jack steps in her direction perplexed.

"Don't you have to get back to Ms. Anna's . . .Ooff?" Kattie spilling to the ground roughly.

"Well, well. What do we have here?" Chips spits. "Look boys, ole girl figured out shooters whatever! Com'n, Bae, it's getting late, and I've gotta drive the boys home. Let's go!" Reaching roughly, Chip rips her off the ground, tossing her prize aside.

"Hey, asshole! Hands off!" Jack arrives tense, readying himself.

"Jack Murphy, I should've known. Et tu Brute?"

"Oh, cut the crap, Chip!" Jack responds.

"Figures, my former teammate, my friend Jack Murphy, would move in on my girl." Chip tugs roughly at Kattie's jacket, throwing her to the ground below.

"Well, Jack, you gonna cut her loose?"

"Still butthurt? You always getting caught Chip!" Jack jests.

"Typical Jack, always one to joke." Chip pursues, pushing Kattie roughly downward.

"Stop it!" Jack spits, stepping forward.

110

"Oh, you don't like that? Jack, you were always soft! Tell you what. . ." Chip quips.

"Away with you, you uh uh!" A familiar voice rings out among the crowd. Pushing past a gentile group passing Chip and his populating goons.

"Reg?" perplexed, Jack's confidence quietly grows.

"What the fu. . . Sup Fatso!" Chip quips.

"Shut up, you sisgenhetro!" Ari arriving auspiciously.

"Pff, Ye, Yeah wha, what she said, your sis . . . sister's a generic goblinganger!" Reggie lumbers nodding in support of his friends. Chip continues looking past the pathetic pair.

"What the hell, Jack? Gonna get your ass stomped in and you call the Gaybusters? I mean look, hah, look at these fat fu. . ."

"Shut it, Chip, let Kattie go and I won't have to choke you out like every time since 5th grade!" Jack cuts sharply.

"Pff, never happen'd Jack, cuz you'a bitch like your friends." Chip letting go of Kattie's jacket, a shadow moving into the shadows unbeknownst to the group at large. Chip marshals his goons, ganging up on the fewer numbers. Jack reaching into his intuition calls.

"Reg, Ari RUNNN!!!" Jack urges, calculating the brunt of the brutality. Turning hard, digging deep into the earth below, Jack sprints in the opposite direction, drawing goons from his friends.

"Dale, get Fatso; teach his fat ass a lesson! Ned, ya got the fruity freak!" Chip spits, turning in Jack's direction, grabbing two bumble buffoons in his pursuit.

111

"Um, um, com'n, Ned, you heard Chip. I'll get Ari!" Dale speeds off in Ari's direction, leaving the good-for-nothing Ned to chase Reggie.

"Wha, but Chip said you got the fat one?" Ned nudging Dale. A dangerous look descending on the shorter Ned as Dale heads off in Ari's direction.

"So sorry bout all this, Kattie. Chip will dump me in practice if I don't." Ned sputters as he pursues his person.

"Pff, he's the one dumped! What tools!"

Gathering herself to her feet and already behind, Kattie panics, not knowing what direction to go, racing off in the direction of Aunt Anna's booth.

"Huff, huff, huff." Reggie lumbers, lamenting all the cumbersome calories he'd consumed.

"Gotcha now, fat boy!" Ned's voice rings out, closing hard. Reggie rumbles around an out-of-order ride. Hoping to disappear into darkness but is caught easily falling to the ground.

"Ok, slug, where do you want it?" Ned's voice suddenly turning nefarious, grabbing the good-natured goof.

"Oh crap, Jack, what would you do?" Thinking quietly and quickly to himself, Reggie grabs a fist full of dirt, flinging it into Ned's eyes.

"Ahh! Thppth, thppp! You got it in my mouth, you asshat!" Ned spitting dirt rears back to rap Reggie roughly. Before Ned can rattle off a few good blows, Reggie snaps into action. Raising one arm to block, shooting his other arm, grabbing his attacker between the legs in a lifting motion. Remembering what Jack taught him, Reggie gathers his feet underneath, exploding from the ground, lifting and slamming Ned. The impact driving all breath from his oppressor's chest.

"Whoa! You squeaked like a little mousy! Get up so I can do it again." Reggie rifts. The grounded goon groans when he notices his dirty hat adorned with the number three.

"Ned, you can call me "The Intimidator" now." Patting the pathetic pile of pubescence proudly. Securing the cap of a champion on his crown, Reggie jogs off in search of his own damsel in distress.

Permeating through preoccupied people, Ari pounds the path below. Heart hammering heavily, dashing and dodging her deviant. Seeking a shadow's safety, fumbling frantically, tripping and tumbling from the log fencing of Old Town. Ari slithering silently behind a wooden barrel. Heavy footsteps displacing peaceful pebbles towards their purpose.

"Arianna? C'mon. Ari? I'm not gonna hurt you. I know Chip can be a jerk, but I'm not. Tell ya'a secret? I love your hair. I mean, I don't get it, but's cool!" Dale kicking pebbles childishly.

"Com'n, believe me. I just don't want to be not popular and shit. Ya know, I mean you don't care if ya'll not popular. Tryin to say, I like you, but I can't say it in front of the guys. Remember in the 6th grade, and we had to draw how we felt in art?" Leaning heavy on the barrel, Dale deliberates, chuckling to himself.

113

"I paint'd a rainbow, cause I like rainbows, they remind me of like when nature reminds us that like just one color isn't enough to like. . .you know what I'm sayin." Dale continues kicking pebbles, unable to find words to capture his deeper disposition.

"Anyways, Chip made fun of my paintin, and so I like threw it away. But I remember you painted a dock with a girl sittin on it. It was like sunset, and there was a rainbow in the corner. Her hair was color'd like a rainbow and I figr'd that was lit. I don't know what I'm try'n to say. I'm gonna go now. Sorry bout Chip and for chasin you tonight. Just everything." Leaving, Dale dejectedly muttering to himself.

"Ari, you're my rainbow. Don't say that, you idiot. Chip's not gonna be happy." The conflicted crony trots off.

An astonished Ari rising from behind the old barrel. "What the? Dal. . ." A buzzing from her pocket breaks Ari's bewilderment, she answers her phone.

"Reggie, Reggie, slow down. You're what, headin where? What do you mean you can't get a hold of Jack?" Her voice growing impatient.

"So you're ok, okay, okay. Let me think . . . go to Anna's booth. Why? Maybe Jack's there. I don't know, Reggie, we'll figure this out when we get there. Yeah, yeah."

"C'mon, Jack, be there, be there." She concludes ending the call.

The crunch of gravel gives way to cracking twigs underfoot. The sadistic sounds of steps closing in on him. Hurdling a rusty wire fencing, Jack's heart pounds, demanding his legs to drive deeper into darkness. The moon's sight shielded by the canopy of colossuses, causing other senses to surface. Leaping over logs, roots wickedly reaching woefully at every step. Ducking underneath fallen forestry, making himself small, Jack steadies his nerves.

"Stay calm and look for an opportunity, Jack." Whispering silently, controlling his breathe.

Desperate voices in the distance do little to calm him.

"Chip! Ooff! Chip, he's gone, man. Let's get his ass at school, man!" A voice rings out a few paces from Jack's position.

"Yeah, Bruh, we'll get him Monday. These woods creep me out. There could be spiders and shit, Bruh!" A second voice echoes less than five yards away.

"Shut it, Boys! He didn't get far!"

"Flashlights, boys! Find that little prick!" Chip commands holding up his phone.

"C'mon Chip, my phone got like eleven percent!" One dim deviant complains.

"Shut up and look!" Chip spits sadistically into the silence. Bark digs deeply into his back, sinking lower to conceal himself from spastic searchlights. Jack's eyes dart vigorously.

"Oh, Jack, Jackie Boy! Shhh!" Chip illuminating his irritating features, pressing a finger to his lips. The forest falls silent, Jack's ringtone blares, betraying his burrow. Fumbling frantically into his pocket, bolting bunglingly through the thicket.

"There he is! Get him!" Chip commands. Low-hanging branches batter Jack's face, twisting and turning his escape into torment. "Oof." Tripping and tumbling to the ground.

"Get him up! Ur gonna get it now!" Chip howls with delight. Ruthless hands reaching and ripping, roughly slamming him against a silent sentry.

"Not the face, not the face. Leave that for me!" Chip spits sadistically, striking Jack, driving air from his frame.

"All you had to do was just play nice, Jack!" Taking a few paces away, sniffing the air sinisterly, Chip turning sharply, stalking his victim.

"I tried being your friend and how did you repay me?"

"umppff, uughh." Jack taking multiple shots to the midsection, dropping to his knees. Chip's cronies are lifting his limp form to face his fate.

"You may think this isn't fair, Jack, but guess what? We're at the fair. Kinda iconic ya think? Ha!" Scoffing at his own ignorant humor.

"I tried being your friend, tried taking you under my wing in wrestling. But for some frickin reason, it wasn't enough. You just had to be chill with teachers. You just had to be the "nice guy" and hang with pink-haired freaks." Mocking air quotes thrusting fingers in Jack's face.

"You just had to make a fool of me in the gym and almost cost me State." Rapidly delivering blows to Jack's ribs, the pontificating preacher continues his sadistic sermon.

116

"I'm the guy who wins, Jack, not you! Guys like you should be happy to sit at my table and eat from my success." Pausing Chip's hand quivers with rage.

"All that I can take, no sweat, bump you, but try to take my girl. Stupid Jack, just plain stupid! Kattie's mine, I'm the Prom King, and she's my queen. You just had to go all Lancelot and shit. Stupid!" Grabbing his quarry roughly by the hair, hissing hysterically into his powerless prey's face.

Spitting blood to the earth below, a defiant Jack retorts.

"Iconic? You mean ironic, you moron!" Jack's defiance sends Chip into a rage, pulling Jack roughly, mashing their faces together, Chip wails wildly, slapping his helpless victim.

"You made me look like a fool at school. Sidin with those freaks, those losers, and then attacking me, almost cost me State!"

As the vengeful variant delivers devilish blows, a crack of twigs underfoot go undetected. Refusing further silence, the woods come alive; trees clamor for civility, leaves levy for life, as winds vie for vengeance.

Below hot cheeks, blood trickles from Jack's mouth.

"THEN! THEN!!! You have the balls to show up here to steal my girl! You ass . . . asshat, I'm Chip Eckles and you're Jack "got no family" Murphy!" Repeatedly ramming Jack's face into the dirt.

The sadist signs, squeezing sinisterly securing the chin, digging fingers into Jack's cheeks.

117

"But, I'm your friend, and friends fight from time to time. So, I forgive you. If . . sniff . . if you ghost Kattie, apologize to me and the boys for ruining our fun tonight. How bout it?"

"Pffss. Piss off." Jack creaks, feeling the hands holding him down loosen. Bursting hooking both by the inside leg, throwing them to the ground. Stunned, Chip stumbles backward as the diminutive dynamo deploys a double-leg takedown. Crawling cowardly to escape screaming. Digging deep past the ground, thrusting his forearm under Chip's chin, cinching in a chokehold. "Cuhhkk. Cuhhkk!" Chip thrashes pathetically. Displaying earth and leaves the pair roll, suddenly Jack's feet rip from the ground, releasing his grip. Chip's goons throw him roughly against a tree and begin their work. Faltering from the flurry, Jack struggles to gain footing.

"Enough! Kick his ass!"

The forest, once a sanctuary, transforms into an instrument of torture. Suddenly, one of the derelicts screams, disappearing into darkness. Shrieking sounds silenced by heavy thuds thrashing youthful flesh fade, filling the fiends with fear. Moonlight sheds no solace, shrouding destruction in darkness. A limp form falls from the shadows.

"Wa, What the fu?" Releasing Jack, Chip's remaining ruffian attempts an escape when a branch brandished by darkness sends teeth teeming from mouth. Writhing in pain on the forest floor, mumbling incoherently, a deluge of DNA draining from his newly restructured mouth.

"Kurt! What the hell? Holy sh, sh . . ." Chip turning to aid his fallen comrade. A soulless silhouette surges from the shadows, causing the tyrant's cowardly heart to pound uncontrollably.

"wa, wait. Noo, oompff!" Chip trips, attempting an escape.

Frantically flinging himself upright, Chip scrambles in any direction aimlessly. His escape obstructed by a figure obscured in shadows. Two blows materialize, menacing his midsection.

"Hhhuuuff" Falling to his knees, gasping deeply for breath.

"Pu, pl, plea." Another blow blasting the bully. Spitting leaves and earth, Chip pants as fingers forcefully grip his throat, ripping him from the ground.

Jack weakly winking through a badly bruised eye, blinks Chip's frame dangling like freshly caught fish kicking its last desperate attempts to survive.

"n, n, no. . not worth it" Jack musters, pulling himself up, leaning weakly against a tree. Sounds of desperation gargle, filling the crisp night air.

"Please, st, sto, stop." Jack demands assistance from a nearby tree to make his way to his feet. The shadowy figure sniffs in disapproval, releasing Chip, who collapses almost lifelessly upon leaves below. Jack collapses without assistance, crawls covering Chip's carcass.

"Not ready, willing, but not ready." The phantasmal figure whispers softly before vanishing into darkness. As the sound of faint footsteps fades into the night, as does Jack's consciousness.

CHAPTER THIRTEEN
REST AND RECOVER

Voices and images fade in and out of focus, his head pounding as Jack weakly pushes himself upright.

"Mr. Murphy, please, not too fast." A sweet voice softening the senses.

"Where, where am I?"

"What's going on?" Jack feeling his forearms, exposing intravenous injections, protruding purposely.

"Mr. Murphy, please be still. You are at Morris General. . . Doctor Hardin, paging Doctor Hardin, Patient 4735163 is awake and responsive." The sweet voice says softly, adjusting his pillow.

"Is that better?"

"Ye, yes. Thank you, but how did? Why am I?" Jack begins.

"You experienced trauma and were brought here last night. Still, still. Look straight ahead for me, please." The sweet nurse gently checks his pupils when a knock on the door pauses the pre-med practitioner.

"Yes, nurse Prieto? Oh, good. Mr. Murphy, you are awake. I'm Doctor Hardin. How are you feeling this morning?"

"Doc, what's goin on?"

"Well, young man, I don't know, but as of right now, I do believe you have a concussion." The dutiful Doctor stepping forward to finish where his careful coworker left off.

"Look ahead, now left, and right. Okay, the right one. Good, good. Mmm." A click of his pen, he jots down a few notes. "Not grade 4 or 5, but can't be sure. Mr. Murphy, did you sustain any trauma to the head last night?"

Blinking blurriness, shaking his head Jack responds.

"Um, err, um. I don't remember. Am I in trouble?"

"Oh, no, no. Well, not in as much as the other boys. Can you recall what happened last night?"

"Other boys? Awwouch. Um, Sir, other boys?"

"Still, still, Mr. Murphy. Rest, you are doing great. Nurse Prieto, a word?" The diligent doctor stepping outside the room.

"Nurse, order a CT and call me when the results are in." With a nod leaving her to her duties. Returning to the room, gliding effortlessly.

"Mr. Murphy, get some rest. We will be testing you soon for concussion. No worries, just rest. Is there anything I can get you?" Her bedside manner mastery puts him at ease.

"Um, I dunno, Aunt Anna. Can I talk to Aunt Anna?"

"Ms. Anzalone will be allowed shortly. Try to get some rest, Mr. Murphy." The sweet voice fading into the hall nearby.

"Damn Jack, think, think. The fair, Kattie, Ari, and Reggie were there. Aunt Anna had to be back by, by ten something. Uhg." Throwing himself into the pillow pitifully.

121

"Knock, knock!" Aunt Anna knocks, entering with Ari and Reggie in tow.

"How're you feeling, Jack?" Aunt Anna pats his covered foot faintly.

"Yeah, bro, dude where did you go? It's all over socials that you beat up Chip and his goons! Ooff!" Reggie ramps up receiving a rap from Ari.

"Shut up, you idiot. This is serious. Jack you okay?"

"I'm, I'm okay. The doc thinks I have a concussion. What happened to you guys after, umm, oww."

"Relax, sweet Jack. Arianna and Reginald found you in the woods." Anna begins.

"Yeah, we found you on snapgram just chillin against a tree. Chip and his bros were like right there. Tyler looked pretty messed up, Bro." Reggie rambles before Ari cuts him short.

"Jack, do you remember what happened in the woods? It looks like Chip followed you in there, and well." Ari pauses, concealing further condemnation.

"Well, nothing, you beat them up. Didn't ya Jack?" Reggie says.

"I don't really remember. I remember them chasing me after we separated. I remember the woods, the darkness, and then kinda foggy from there." Jack expresses, pressing his hands to his face.

"Why does my face hurt? The Doc said something about the others, Chip?" He askes feeling dizzy all of a sudden.

"I don't think you have to worry 'bout him anymore. You go em bro. Chip, Tyler, and what's his face." Reggie revving up his revelations.

"Reginald. Let Jack rest; come on Arianna. Jack, Doctor Hardin ordered a CT scan for this afternoon and is hopeful that you can discharge this evening pending results. As for now, get some rest." Aunt Anna ushers an amped Reggie and anxious Ari from the room.

"Aunt Anna?" Pulling himself up.

"I didn't do whatever Reggie said I did, I don't remember who or what, but . . . but, I wasn't alone in the woods. A shadow, I mean someone else must've." A look of innocence etched on his face.

"I know, Jack, I know. My sweet boy, get some rest. See you soon." Laying back, he can hear Reggie arguing his conspiracies with Ari down the hall.

"What did you get yourself into this time, Jack?" Adjusting, Jack drifts off exhaustedly.

"I couldn't have. Did I. . ." murmuring to himself.

CHAPTER FOURTEEN

TOMORROW'S A NEW DAY

"Careful, careful Jack. Baby steps. Ari grab the door." Aunt Anna attempting to support Jack as he stumbles.

"Whoa. Gotcha Bro." Reggie helping him to the couch nearby.

"Thank you, Arianna. Can you get some tea started, please?" Anna closes the door behind them.

'Yes, Ma'am." Hurrying off to her task.

"Now, Jack, Doctor Hardin wants you to take it easy for a couple of days. No phone, no computer games. Just rest, got it?" Anna insists, venturing off to assist Ari.

"Bro, this is nuts. Jack, you like totally whooped them. Tyler had to get his jaw wired shut. Chip wasn't so bad off, but he isn't talkin. So tell me, bro, what happened?"

"Honestly, Reg, I don't know. I remember bits and pieces. I was running in the woods, and then they grabbed me. Hollering and howling like hounds. I tried fighting them off, but they worked me over pretty good. Then, out of nowhere, they just started dropping. I didn't do it, but somebody did. Somebody did." Jack repeats, slumping comfortably onto the couch.

"Yeah, like I'm hearing yah, but that doesn't make sense, Jack. So somebody else was out there in the woods just waiting for three idiots to beat up?" Reggie prods.

124

"Like I said, Reg, they got me and someone got them. I don't know, man. Hopefully, I'll remember soon."

"Well, soon isn't now. Here take these for the pain and drink this." Ari arrives in time to thwart any further interrogation. "Move over, Reggie, you big lummox." Shifting herself between the boys.

"Hey now, you lot lizard, I'm not a paying customer yet. Stop that." Reggie reals as Ari squeezes his chest, twisting hard.

"Oww, that hurts. You know I have sensitive nipples." Reggie resists pitifully. "Okay, okay. I'm movin!"

"That's what I thought." Ari turning away from Reggie.

"Now, Jack, this is important. You have to rest and give yourself time to heal. Everything will be okay. I'm sure of it." The two share a quick, unconvincing smile. Aunt Anna pokes her head into the living room.

"Arianna, Reginald?" The two scramble to attention.

"Yes, Ma'am?" the pair respond in unison.

"Just got off the phone with your parents. You may stay till Sunday; I'll take you back before school on Monday."

"Thank you, Ms. Anna." Ari responds as Reggie fist pumps with one hand, digging feverishly deep into the couch with the other.

"Thanks, Ms. Anna. I know it's here somewhere."

Aunt Anna leaves to prepare supper.

"What are you doing, Reggie?" Ari insists.

"Whatcha mean, a new episode of *Deserted* is on, now where's that remote?" Reggie shuffles around on the couch, pulling out an assortment of unwrapped sweets.

"Ooo, that's where you went off to." Reg downing the combination of candies and crumbs.

"That's frickin disgusting, Reggie!" Ari shakes her head.

"Girl, you don't even know the day I've had, ah, here we go." Reggie continues casually cruising through channels. The three spend the next few nights doing little recovering. Laughing the weekend away, unaware it will be their last.

Light of a new dawn peeks through the curtains, warming three friends sleeping peacefully, randomly arranged along the furniture. The smell of bacon, eggs, and fresh toast traversing the house, filling it with memories of simpler times. Jack, Ari, and Reggie rise and go about setting the table as they've done many times before. The trio spending much of the day as they usually do fishing, playing Dekken Dragons, and enjoying the day. Jack, mostly recovered, still easily outpaces his friends as they play without a care. The events from the fair are barely a topic of discussion as the trio burns the day away.

"It's getting dark, Reggie, we should head back. Where's Jack?" Ari is shoving Reggie playfully, pointing to an inconspicuous construction of branches and leaves.

"Shh." Reggie placing one finger to his lips, directing with the other.

The pair prowl pathetically surrounding the pile. Waving her hands, signaling an attack, they rush the pile.

"Gotcha, wha, what? Ari, it's a trap!!!" Reggie rumbles ridiculously away.

"Reggie, you. Ow, uh, ow, Ow!!!" Ari runs awkwardly, ranting as a barrage of water balloons belt the bygones.

"Ja, ow, Jack! You got us. Reggie, wait up." Both make their way to the dirt road leading to Aunt Anna's, arms flailing frantically.

"Uff, uff. Where is he? Didga see hi, him?" Reggie slowing down to catch his breath.

"Mu, must go faster. Com'n, Reg uff, uff." Ari pulls him roughly by the shirt. The two make it a few paces from the house, silence seizing their senses.

"Thu, thu, there's no birds. Why's there no birds, Ari?" Reggie pants as the pair turn to face their doom.

"Hey guys, had a nice jog, I see!" Jack's voice rings mischievously.

"You two look thirsty!" Standing readying two garden hoses atop Aunt Anna's car.

"Ja, jack, na, no." Reggie begs, moving behind Ari.

"Get, get. I'm not a human shield, you coward. Now, Jack, buddy. Bro, you win!" Cowering behind her hands.

A grin that would tickle the Grinch growing across his face, his thumbs moving toward their drenching desires.

"Jack! What in God's name are you doing? Get down from there. Supper's getting cold. Oh my Gosh. . ." A look of concern giving way to a chuckle at the dripping duo in her driveway.

"Ohh you poor babies. Jack get down from there you scoundrel. Come inside, Arianna, I have a bathrobe you can borrow while your clothes dry." Placing her arm around Ari's soggy shoulder.

"What about me?" Reggie pulls at his shirt.

"Oh, um, Reggie, you can." Mockingly pointing at an old clothesline nearby.

"That's not right, Ms. Anna, that's not right."

"Com'n, Reg, you can take a shower real quick. Got a change of clothes you left here a while back." Jack jokingly jabbing Reggie's rotund ribs.

"Okay, wait, stop that. Better, not eat all the sweet rolls. Not kiddin, Jack." Reggie following right behind.

Supper ending an epic weekend; a necessary distraction, Aunt Anna and Jack drive Ari and Reggie home, returning like many times before. Dirt and gravel crackle under tires as the vehicle comes to a stop.

"Ok, home sweet home. Everything ok, Jack?" Anna reaching softly caressing a still refresh scar about Jack's eye.

"Fine. Aunt Anna, I'm fine. Really." Jack leans away, unbuckling himself before pausing.

"Ok, my sweet Jack. I understand, you've been through a lot, but tomorrow's a new day. Tell me when you're ready."

Unbuckling her own seatbelt, exiting to make her way inside. Jack punches the dashboard alone in the car, wishing he had said something. The dome light clicks off, leaving a lunar luminance on his face. Squeezing eyes tight, trying to remember that fateful night.

"I didn't, but who? What happened, Jack?" The car door shuts, silently sauntering inside he heads to bed. Tomorrows' a new day.

Morning comes quickly as shadows retreat under dew covered trees. The sun climbing higher presiding over a new day. Light peeking through the slightest crack in Jack's curtains gleaming off trophies from days gone by. Medals dangle twisting gently as the fan spins silently above. A quiet hush hums throughout Anna's home, suddenly broken by a reality yet realized.

"Beep! Beep! Beep!" Jack's school alarm jolts him awake. Rubbing sleep from his eyes, stretching breathing deeply. "Ugh, guess it's time to get back to it." He groans, pulling himself upright. He stumbles down the hall and goes about his usual ritual when he hears Aunt Anna's angelic voice emanating from the kitchen. Making his way down the hall, walls adorned with pictures of a life that feels so far away. Careful not to make a sound, he sneaks within earshot.

"Snff, snff. Ye, yes, Sir. I understand. Is there no other way? He's not ready . . . yes, but . . . yes, Sir. Already on your way? But, yes, Sir, I will. I'll let him know. Goodbye." Placing the phone down, wiping away hot tears, Aunt Anna's head hangs low.

Moving cautiously, Jack peers around the corner before making himself known.

"Oh, Jack, you're up, snff. I'll start. I'll start breakfast, go, go get dressed." She sniffs, turning away. Jack's eyes dart uncomfortably around the room searching for words.

"What's going on, Aunt Anna?"

"It's nothing. Go get dressed. We have to get to school." Hiding her face bumbling between cabinets.

"Aunt Anna, com'n tell me. Breakfast can wait. What's up?" Moving to console his champion when her phone begins buzzing on the counter.

"I got it." Moving towards her device, a perplexed look perched upon his face.

"What? Why is Principal Reilly calling you?" Snatching the phone, taking several paces away, Anna answers.

"Hello, Good morning, Mr. Rei . . ." Her voice grows silent for several minutes.

"That's not, no, Sir, but it wasn't . . . yes, yes Sir. Goodbye." Trembling as she sits, Anna hanging her head sobbing softly.

Pulling a seat next to Anna, Jack hugs her tightly.

"What's goin on? Aunt Anna, was it Doctor Hardin?"

"No, Jack, go get dressed. Pl, please."

"Mr. Rei . . . Reilly?"

"Reilly? It was Reilly, wasn't it? What did he want? Aunt Anna, look at me! If he threatened you again, I'm goin to his

130

office right now and beat him right out of that stupid-looking suit! I'm gonna end that idiot right now!"

"No, Jack, you don't. Go get dressed. It's, it's please, Jack."

"I don't know what's goin on. Please, Aunt Anna, tell me." He whispers as she begins sobbing uncontrollably. Kissing her forehead softly, he leaves to do as she says. Returning a few short moments later, Aunt Anna is sitting staring nervously out the window overlooking the driveway.

Two plates of breakfast sit untouched.

"Aunt Anna, eat. Before it gets cold." Jack sits, beginning to eat. Each bite feeling larger at every scoop.

"Aunt Anna, I'm in trouble, ain't I?"

"J, ja, Jack, this life was never meant for you." Sipping cold coffee cryptically.

"This life, what life? I love you, Aunt Anna, Ari, and Reg. What's wrong with this life? I'm happy, Aunt Anna, talk to me. Please." Jack gently placing his hand on hers.

"Hmmphfff. Here we go." Anna takes a big deep breath.

"Jack, I have to tell you something that changes everything. Please, understand. This isn't. I'm not your. Hffff. Jack, no questions, just listen." Anna's energy changes immediately.

"Jack, long ago. I was a young field agent who befriended your mother. We were best friends, but she had her duties and I was looking for a way out. A quiet life. She had a mission and was injured; she was so strong." The mention of her friend causes Anna to quiver with emotion.

131

"She left us, left me her greatest gift, my greatest mission. She left me, you. I was able to get out, but there were strings attached. I was to raise you here quietly until you were ready." Sinking into her hands, Anna sobs.

"Aunt Anna, no, no. My parents died in a car crash, and you were there to take me in. You told me that when I was ten. What do you mean by your greatest mission? I don't understand!" Jack pressing nervously against the edge of the table.

"Snff, I know sweet Jack, it's a lot, but you were never long for this life. I've lived in fear of this day for so long." Composing herself, Anna sips her coffee.

"So what about Ari, Reg, and Kattie? Are they like some part of this coverup? Reilly? Are they acting, and I'm in some sort of bubble?" Jack paces the floor nervously.

"No, no, Arianna, Reginald, and Katherine; they're all real. They don't know anything more than who you are, Jack. Reilly, um, Mr. Reilly he's a jerk, but nothing more than an ambitious asshole that has no knowledge of the world outside his own ambitions. None of them actors save me, I guess." Anna looks away, pushing down years of emotions.

"So, so who am I? Is my name even Jack Murphy?" Jack inquires impatiently.

"Yes, of course, it made no sense to use a code name, because you were a baby and you parent's records; I mean . . . your Mother's records." Anna scrambles to obscure, but she's already said too much.

132

"My parents? Actors, save you?" Jack turns tormented by such revelations.

"Jack, this is by design, not this moment, but this house, this life, was by design until you were ready." Anna sniffs uncomfortably, staring out the driveway window.

"I, I don't understand. I'm just a kid, an average high school nobody, from nowhere. The best I can hope for is maybe a college degree, working a boring job to support a family that's mine. That's it, and that's enough. What do you mean ready for? Ready for what?" Jack's mind racing through a rolodex of memories recalling for any scrap of reality.

Before Anna can respond, the sound of displaced gravel and dirt under heavy tires curbs the conversation.

"Who? Aunt Anna stay here." Jack readies himself, grabbing a knife from the table, he ventures to the door. Peering through the curtains as a clean vantablack SUV settles heavily upon the gravel below. Jack gripping the utensil, body ridged in defense of his home. A rear passenger door bursts open, and then another, as two burly men dressed in sharp black suits exit. Shades obscure their eyes as the front passenger door opens. A figure familiar to Jack steps out, dressed sharply in sequence black attire.

"Mr. . . Mr. Wiley?" Jack whispers.

The two large men in black proceed positioning themselves tactically up the steps looking over each shoulder. Walking with a noticeable limp towards the door, Wiley raps the door authoritatively. Jack's heart races racking his brain, fingers tremble still clutching dinnerware.

"Ding Dong!" The doorbell rings, ushering Anna into action. She races towards the door, unlocking it. Jack jolts to her side, ready to defend as the door creaks open.

"Good morning, Agent Anzalone, Jack, a butter knife?" Mr. Wiley's eyes shift confidently between the brutes behind him.

"Anna, may we talk?" Wiley asks, cracking wolfish smile.

"Would your men care for coffee?" The humble Hostess offers.

"No, no, Anna, that won't be necessary." Wiley steps inside before nodding over his shoulder, silently instructing the two brutes back to the vantablack vehicle. Shutting the door behind the trio to a now thoroughly confused Jack speaks.

"Mr. Wiley, what, what are you doing here? Aunt Anna, your last name is Huxley? What is all this about?" He stammers.

"Anna? How much does the boy know?" Wiley settling comfortably on a nearby sofa.

"Not much, Sir, I, I. . ." She stutters.

"It's ok, Agent Anzalone. Please sit, the both of you. Jack, we have much to discuss."

"No, no. . . I will not. Mr. Agent Wiley or whatever your name is . . . what is this about?"

Sighing heavily, motioning towards a seat adjacent from his own. "Sit, Jack, please." As instructed, Jack sits eyes darting between the two.

"Good. Now, I'm not sure what Agent Anzalone told you, but here goes. Jack, you have been in Agent Anzalone's protective custody for the last thirteen years, seven months, and five days. This arrangement, mind you, was for your protection. However, in light of recent events on and off campus, which has placed you in a compromising position. . ."

"Compromising position, Aunt Anna, what is he talking about?" Jack interrupts. Shaking her head solemnly, he continues.

"So you don't know?" Wiley asks.

"Know what?" The young man shifting uncomfortably.

"Jack, please. Allow Agent Wiley to explain. Please be patient."

"Thank you, Anna, Jack. You are not returning to school. The school board held an emergency meeting this morning to discuss the other night's events. To discuss your involvement that left three of your classmates beaten in the woods. The parents of the three boys all signed statements that you and you alone attacked them that night."

"Beaten? Alone? I didn't. They . . . they chased me into the woods and kicked the crap out of me. I didn't do whatever they said I did! I wasn't alone in those woods! I didn't do it, Mr. Wiley, Aunt Anna, you have to believe me!"

"Jack, Jack, the school board, at Mr. Reilly's approval, motioned to expel you."

"Expelled? I didn't do it! They beat ME up. Where's my statement? Aunt Anna, what's going on?" Jumping off the sofa, his hands reaching towards Anna, now sobbing into her own.

"Aunt Anna, you saw me in the hospital, I . . . I didn't do it." Slumping dejectedly, Jack sits staring at the floor for answers.

Silence seizes the room. Wiley allows the boy a merciful moment.

"Jack, Jack? Look at me." Trembling hands folded, the youth pulling himself tenuously to attention.

"Jack? I know this is a lot, but you can do much more than you even understand." Wiley's voice resembling the mentor he once thought he knew.

"Jack, it's time you know why you are here. I am Agent Wiley of a secret entity known as the Global Advanced Intelligence Agency, GAIA for short. The ancient Greeks believed Gaia to be the primal Mother from which all life sprang. In these more advanced times, Gaia should be viewed as a delicate, interdependent living organism most commonly called Earth. We work with agencies across the globe; CIA, Interpol, Kōanchōsa-chō to name a few. We are the glue that tethers these agencies together. GAIA, in short, works in the shadows to keep the world safe from any and all threats to Earth's inhabitants. At this very moment, world powers brace for the next global conflict. As of right now Jack. . ."

"What does any of this have to do with a high school reject?" Jack murmurs, burying his face into his hands.

136

"Everything, Jack." Wiley retorts.

"GAIA has a training subsidiary, known as Global Youth Advanced Intelligence Agency. A youth developmental program to its parent entity, GAIA. And, Jack, you are not a high school reject. You are GYAIA's newest recruit." Wiley's words washing over Jack, stunning him upright.

"Re, recruit?"

"Aunt Anna, y, you knew about this?" Fighting back tears, Anna nods, sniffing softly. Her eyes are red with the reality.

"Jack Murphy, your Mother was an agent of GAIA, one of our most valuable assets. She gave birth to you, but shortly after, she was lost in action. Agent Anzalone took you in. Her role was to raise you without any knowledge of those events until you were ready. For your protection, this location was specifically selected because of its obscurity, not to draw unwanted attention. I was sent to observe you for a time." Wiley continues.

"Wait, wait, hold on, who is all agents then? Aunt Anna, you, but Ari and Reggie too? Are they all actors in this?" Jack interrupts.

"No, no. They or any outside this room are not illicit or connected to GAIA in any way." Wiley answers coolly.

"Jack, Anna, it's time." Wiley whispers above the silence, rising and buttoning his neatly pressed suit. Without a word, rising from her hurt, hurrying down the hall and returning with a neatly pre-packed backpack,

137

"Aunt Anna, wh, what is all this?" Jack asks sheepishly. Fighting a lifetime of emotions, Anna pulls Jack close, hugging him, suffering silently.

"Snff, snff. Sweet Jack. It's time. I, I." Anna placing a small trinket in Jack's hand, handing Wiley the backpack, sprinting from the room.

"Au, Aunt Anna, wa, wait." Sniffing to himself, Jack still clutching the trinket.

"Jack, it's time." Wiley begins.

"No, no! I haven't said goodbye to Ari and Reg! They need me. They. . ." Jack's voice vaporizes into nothing as Wiley opens the front door.

"Jack, this weekend with your friends and Anna . . . that was goodbye. Come, Jack, GYAIA awaits. This time tomorrow, your real journey begins."

CHAPTER FIFTEEN

LIFE IS A JOURNEY, NOT A DESTINATION

Jack, stepping out on the old wooden porch, a rush of memories mingle with a mind racing for answers. The young man following the muscular men to an open door. Looking over his shoulder, stealing one last look, Jack ventures inside, seated between the two massive men. Doors shut securely as the vantablack SUV rolls off, leaving more than memories behind.

Silent seconds tick from mute minutes turning to hushed hours, the vehicle veering through traffic and tension alike. Turning from more well-traversed paths, trees shoot stoically by. The anxious adolescent's patience grows thin. His brain burning for answers, breaking the silence. "Whe . . . where are you taking me? Mr. Wiley?"

"Hey, I'm talking to you, Sir!"

"Mr., Agent Wiley. . . I don't get it; where are we going? Sir."

"Patience Jack, we are almost, awe, right on time," Wiley speaks as trees clear, giving way to a clearing.

"An airstrip in the middle of nowhere?" Jack presses.

"Nowhere sure, an airstrip, hardly, but it will do." Wiley pauses, reaching for the dash radio.

"Tower, this is Wildwolf. Come in tower."

"This is tower Wildwolf, precede Wildwolf." A voice fills the vehicle.

"Tower, we have the package. Are we ready for lift off?" Wiley responds.

"Tower to Wildwolf, we are a go, sending package now." The voice trailing off, giving way to Wiley's.

"Danzler collect Jack's effects. We are a go. Jack, come with me." Wiley responds, unclicking his seatbelt.

"Come, Jack Murphy, GYAIA awaits!" Wiley's door bursts open to a blast of barreling turbines. Stunned, Jack steps onto the tarmac, his teeth trembling at the sight of the auspicious aircraft. It's silver skin upon first sight, turning translucent at each closing step.

"COME JACK MURPHY!" Wiley motioning toward steps leading Jack into a world, not of his understanding.

Jack is escorted to a seat and strapped in by the other buttoned-up brute. All occupants find their respective seats as the door shuts, sealing all safely within. The perplexed passenger's eyes dart about. Feeling his seat rumble beneath, the ground finding itself further so. The vexing vehicle ascends into the clouds effortlessly toward its destination.

The glow of a reddened light flicks green.

"Wildwolf, all skies ahead clear. You are free to move about the cabin. ETA fifteen hundred." A voice resonates, sending relief racing through the young rogue. "Huuppfff. . ."

"First-time flyer, Jack?" Wiley asks, pouring himself a drink.

"Ye, yeah. Aunt Anna and I usually drove everywhere." Jack replies reluctantly.

"Relax, Jack, won't be long now. The Falcon is the fastest bird in the sky. So you must have a million questions, and given your silence on the ride here, you must have gathered a gluttony of them." The wily Wiley insinuates, returning to his seat.

"Um, I do, but. . ." Jack sputters.

"Take your time. At fifteen hundred, the world as you knew it will change." Wiley comments, checking the contents of his glass. "I feel it already has." Peering out his window, Jack settles, finally pocketing the trinket in his hand.

"So it has. Jack? Remember back in detention, I gave you a book?" Wiley inquires, distracting Jack from the tug of intrigue, drawing him to the item in his pocket.

"Yes Sir, A Boy's Life, Tobias, um. I forget." Jack replies, tapping his forehead.

"Wolfe, Tobias Wolfe. Then we spoke about transformation." Wiley jogging Jack's memory.

"Yeah, the boy changed his name to Jack. What are you getting at? I am no longer Jack?" The distressed youth presses.

"No, no. Your name isn't what must transform. It's you. You must transform into something that you could have never imagined before. At GYAIA, you are no longer Jack Murphy, the boy from nowhere. You must transform into Jack Murphy, the

141

man from wherever you choose to set your feet." Wiley states, striding to pour himself another drink.

"Yeah, well that sounds good, but. . ." Before Jack can finish, the aircraft rocks roughly.

"Wildwolf, we are beginning our descent, ready with the package for transfer." The pilot's voice breaks Jack's train of thought.

"Damn, hate to waste good Gentlemen." Wiley returning to his seat, drinking deeply. Within moments, the craft settles softly.

"Well, Jack, this is your stop." Wiley returning an empty glass, motioning Jack onward.

"Wait, what, my stop? Hey, whatchu doin?" Jack insists, his bag roughly thrust into his arms by the massive mute brute Danzler.

"Alright, alright, I'm goin." Shouldering his pack, Jack makes his way through the opening. Wiley already on solid ground waving his young protégé towards another dark vantablack SUV.

Making his way past Wiley, Jack proceeds without hesitation, Danzler hovering at his backside, limiting all escape options. Wiley's hand resting on the open door as he enters.

"Jack, here, I want you to have this. GYAIA standard issue, read it, become it. . ." Pausing for a second, his mysterious mentor searching deeper thoughts.

"Jack, life's a journey, not a destination, so journey. See you in a few days, young man." Handing the youth a book.

"Oh, Jack, one more thing, when it seems all is lost, remember, when the evil is the loudest, scream louder. When the evil speaks wickedly, speak honestly, and when the evil sees no path, see the path forward." Wiley winks, turning away before Jack can respond. A quick nod in Danzler's direction, the mysterious mister making his way back onboard the Falcon, his limp more noticeable than before.

Seating himself next to Jack, the physically advanced agent Danzler nods, instructing the driver to proceed. Sitting in silence, Jack looks back, catching only a glimpse of the Falcon flying away.

"Okay, Jack, what's next?" Whispering to himself. Trees narrowing along the path, their canopies collecting, concealing any movement below. Jack clutches the book tightly over each bump, feeling his body begin to perspire. Only passing beams of sunlight strobe by illuminating the interior.

"Su . . Sun. . .Tzu's. . . Art of. . .War? Wiley, what is this for?" Bewildered and barely able to make out the title, Jack presses the book deep into his pack.

"Art of War? When the evil sees no path?" Wiley's cryptic words causing his mind to wander. He shutters nervously, feeling his body shift at every curve. The carriage careening faster, disorienting any sense of direction before coming to a halt. Light seeping into a small clearing.

"Hooopff." Jack exhales air exiting his lungs upon the rapid stop. Light blasting the backseat as Agent Danzler deafly departs his side. Struggling to find his senses, his door opens. The massive mound of muscle that is agent Danzler directing his departure, shutting the door behind Jack. The crunch of gravel underfoot sends confusion through the senses.

"Am I dreaming? Art of Evil? Aunt Ann, what's goin on, umpfhh!" Blinking blurriness away, Jack absorbs the scenery surrounding him. Roughly stumbling, the mute brute shoving Jack's things close to his chest.

"Agent Dan. . . Danzler, Sir? We're in the middle of the woods. Where do I go from here?"

Tersely, the muscular man in black points towards an opening in the trees. Wasting not another moment, the mute brute enters the vehicle, leaving Jack alone.

"What the hell? Oh, okay, down the path he points. What kind of super-secret. . ." Jack halting his thoughts, voices in the distance drawing his attention down the path. The voices grow at each passing step until two packs sitting next to each other, causing him to pause. Close enough to decipher the tone of two boys arguing, he estimates around his age. Unable to hear the content of the conversation, Jack places his pack next to the others.

"You're in the woods, think, Jack, think." Surveying his surroundings, noting all distinguishing features above. Sneaking into the thicket, closing distance on the disturbances.

"Just like sneakin up on Ari and Reg, that's it." Instincts taking over every step silencing its predecessor.

"We've been this way, you idiot!" A voice breaking the silence of sentinels overhead.

"Yeah, if you had just listened to me, we wouldn't be lost in the woods. We don't have any signal here." Another subtly similar voice retaliates.

"Shut up! I'm not the one that got us lost, ya dummy!"

"Dummy! Who you callin a dummy, Dummy!?!" Branches break beneath as a chase ensues.

"No, no, don't Aww! You ass. . . ooff!"

"OWWW, you bit me. What the hell, Max?"

"Well, you started it!" a subtly similar voice retorts.

"From the looks of it, the both of you are lost. . ." Jack's voice vaporizes into the canopy above.

"Who was . . . Sam get up! There's someone else." pulling his companion upright. "I heard, let'me go dummy!" Cautiously composing himself.

"Ok, phantom, say you're correct, and my brother is an idiot. We are lost!" One of the young men begins, cut off by the other.

"Hey, now speak for yourself, Sam. We don't know he's a phantom. For all you know, it could be a squirrel?" The other similar voice answers.

"A squirrel, really, Max? Don't be dumb. So, Mr. Squirrel, to what genome of sciuridae do you claim?" Sam inquires, his eyes searching the scenery.

145

"Um, yeah, not a scurida or squirrel. Try again." Jack replies, careful not to reveal himself.

"So where you two headed?"

"Well, if you must know, Mr. Not a squirrel, my brother Sam and I were dropped off here about an hour ago, and" Max begins making his way around an old oak.

"And well, we took the path as instructed, until someone had to go sightseeing." Sam completes Max's statement.

"Okay, so I may have spotted a Spinus tristis and stepped off the path a bit. Don't look at me like that, Sam. It's not illegal to like Goldfinches." Max throwing his hands up in frustration.

"Where is he?"

"I'm near, but far enough away!" Jack says, sneaking silently, snickering to himself, "Birdwatching, oh okay."

"It's the truth, as embarrassing as it sounds, that's the truth, and now we'll probably get in trouble for being late." Sam says, stepping carefully over an exposed root.

"Oh phooey, we ain't getting into any trouble, Sam. We just have to find the path, get our packs and move on. Say, friend, you haven't seen any packs on a path recently?"

"Maybe, maybe not. . . or maybe I've already taken everything of value, and now I'm here to leave no witnesses?" Jack jests.

"You scallywag, you wouldn't, you didn't?" Max exclaims, yelling into the forest surrounding him.

146

"Calm down, Max. So you took everything, you said? Well, you must have found our stash of Sour Patch Kids, then?" Sam says, motioning Max to lower his voice.

"Sour Patch? Eww, gross, more of a Swedish fish kinda guy myself." Jack's voice raises, losing track of its deliberate deception.

"Swedish fish? Those are for old people, dude!" Sam continues, skillfully luring his combatant into conversation.

"Pff, yeah, okay, way better than those overpriced and over-marketed patches of piss." Jack retorts roughly.

"Hmm, well, I have bad news for you, whoever you are!" Sam shouts loudly, obscuring his true intent.

"Bad news? What you like that crummy sour patch cereal too?" Jack scoffs arrogantly.

"No! Neither of us like Sour Patch!" Sam signals for Max to pounce.

"Gotcha! Hhey hey uhhh uhh Sa, Sam he's got me!" Max's excitement turns to terror as Jack reverses Max's hold effortlessly. Sam rushing into the fray grabbing at anything not resembling his brother.

"Max, I gotcha. Oh schnikes, he's got me, he Ackk . . ." Sam gurgles, Jack twisting and squeezing skillfully.

"Ackk, k, ok" Max chokes tapping Jack's shoulder. Shifting his weight, placing one knee on both brothers' chest, Jack gasps with surprise.

"Twins!"

"Huhh, huhh! Yes, twins, dummy" Max retorts, rasping through restricted breath.

"Oh sorry, force of habit. I used to wrestle in school, apologies gents." Jack jumps up, jerking both boys to their feet.

"Sorry bout back there, I hpff, I was just kiddin, I didn't steal anything. Honest!" Catching his own breath, brushing leaves from his locks.

"Ye, yeah, alright, baby Chad Gable, we hear ya." Max rubbing his jaw.

"Hmm, my brother meant to say, he's Maximillian Andrew Duval, and I'm Samuel Antonio Duval. Yes, we know MAD and SAD. The jokes are endless, I assure you." Sam speaks, analyzing their new companion.

"Well good to meet the both of ya, wow twins!" Jack jests, jogging ahead to view the two.

"Take it all in, you freak. Haven't you ever seen twins before?" Max retorts, still rubbing his neck.

"Don't mind him. He's sensitive. So what did you say your name was again?" Sam smartly, cutting off Max.

"I didn't, it's Jack, Jack Murphy. Com'n the path is this way." Jack pats Sam gingerly before jogging off.

"Your new friend is something else, isn't he?" Max smacks Sam soundly on the back, sauntering ahead.

"Our, our new friend, dummy." Sam sprinting after rubbing his shoulder.

"Jerk, Jack, how'd you know the wa, what the fu. . ."
Max' voice lowers, mirroring Jack's.

"shhh." Jack pressing a finger to his lips, pulling the two into
the brush. Dawn settles over the canopy of champions above, Jack
guarding his newfound friends.

"Stay here, stay quiet." His voice low as he slinks off into
shadows.

"Sa, Sam, what's going on?" Max whispers.

"shh, got a good feelin about this one, shhh."

"Boo!" Jack's voice booms behind the pair. "Ahhh, what the
hell, bro?" Max stumbles to the earth below.

"Hehe. Sorry, the coast is clear, I just had to get ya back." Jack
whispers wickedly at his companions.

"Na, no you didn't." Max mulls, stepping onto the path.

"Got him good there, Jack. Haha." Sam smirks, grabbing his
pack.

"Com'n it's almost nightfall. I'm sure GYAIA won't be happy
about our absence." Jack jokes, jogging down the path.

CHAPTER SIXTEEN

"WHAT NEXT?"

The pose' pacing down the path. "Com'n, keep up, guys. I can see something up ahead!"

"Sa, Sam, I'm gonna die, make him stop, make him stop." Max gasps pitifully. "Breath dum, dummy. Com on, we're losing him." Sam replies, sucking in air simultaneously. Stopping placing a fist up, Jack pauses. Eyes searching his surroundings.

"Wha, what, huff, what is it?" Sam stopping mimicking his new friend.

"Da, dam. . ." Max begins, cut off by his twin.

"Shh, what is it Jack?" Sam sneaking behind Jack, lowering his voice.

"The ground it's, it's different," Jack responds, crouching down.

"Different, how?" The duplicated duo ducking as well.

"It's harder than the path, like there's something below us." Jack answers in a hushed tone, probing the ground below his feet.

"Yeah, the earth, that's wha mmm. . ." Max mumbling as Sam covers his mouth.

"Shh, and don't lick me, not the time, Max. Shhh." Taking a few careful paces and tapping his foot, Jack begins digging.

"Hmm, that's not normal" He whispers motioning the twins to his hole.

"It's a hole, Jack. What are we, whoaa!" Max stabs the sturdy surface below. "Sam, it's a bunker of some sort."

"Can't be sure, but it's something that shouldn't be here." Sam stabbing similarly.

"Jack, Jack where you going?" Following their new ally, the pair sneaks carefully behind. He surveys their surroundings when something confirms his suspicions. "Shh, we are being watched." Pointing to a pair of cameras fixed atop of adjacent trees.

"How did you see those, Jack?" Max asks, the gravity of the situation beginning to set in.

"I grew up playing in the woods, climbing trees and such. Hunters use trail cameras all the time where I'm from. These, though these aren't store bought, they have. . ." Max finishing Jack's thought.

"too many lenses. Night vision, high light, low light, and that's gotta be infrared. See Sam, see?" Nudging his brother.

"I wear glasses. I'm not blind, dude, stop that." Sam smacking away Max's attempting to turn his head.

"So what now, Jack?" Sam inquires. "They are facing each other like they are. . ." Jack begins stopping himself to allow Max's interruption.

"Yeah, like they are guarding something." Max.

"Ok, so what's next, Jack where ya goin?" Max interrupting himself this time.

"To see what's in those bushes. Look around you; those bushes between the trees are not indigenous to this area. Not suspicious at all, com'n let's get a closer look." Jack sneaking into the foreign flora, each step more cautious t. "Aha." Knocking softly on against warm metal.

"You shouldn't be here, little guy." Rising slightly halting Sam and Max.

"What is it, Jack?" Mirroring Jack's movements, Sam whispers.

"Manhole of some type." Brushing leaves and earth, revealing a circular surface.

"Damn, that definitely shouldn't be here. We are at least fifty miles from civilization." Sam states, confirming Jack's assessment.

"So let's open it." Max feels for a handle.

"No, Max, don." Sam begins, but a reassuring hand placing gently on his shoulder calming him.

"Max is right. We are in the middle of nowhere, and this leads somewhere." Jack's voice, steady and reassuring, nods for Max to precede.

"Oompff. Just gotta put your back into, damn it's sealed tight." Max attempting to muscle the contraption, throwing himself into the thicket.

"Max, think. We need leverage." Sam surmises searching.

"Wait, wait. Here we go." Grabbing a rusted rail, ramming it into place. Jack, pressing effortlessly, evicting the seal from its setting.

"What, where did you get that?" Max mesmerized by his companion's maneuver. Pointing to brackets meant to house the bar, Jack continues turning.

"That's some MacGyver stuff right there!" Max grabbing to assist.

"Well, well, not quite MacGyver would've used a chopstick or something random, finally someone who understands." Jack jests as he and Max finish their task. The sound of air flooding to the freedom above, the trio lifting the hefty lid.

"Da, damn this thing is heavy." Sam adds, contributing little to the task. His voice echoing into the newly created chasm.

"A ladder, how convenient, ok, since you're the leader, I nominate Jack to go down first." Max leans back, pushing his newfound friend first.

"Ready your packs, boys. We go down together." Jack reaches into his pack, grabbing his phone to light their path.

"Sam after me, Max close the lid behind us would'ya." Jack sinks into the solace of space.

"I'm not. We don't know what's down there?" Max begins finding himself alone as Jack and Sam venture into the unknown.

"Close the lid he says. Let's go into the dark tunnel in the middle of nowhere, he says." Max mules, doing as he's told. The trio trudges downward.

153

"We are here, watch your step." Jack placing feet on solid ground, shining his light, surveying their options.

"This should help." Sam adding his own phone's light to the fray. "Com'n Max, we have to move." Jack insists, pacing down a circular, cemented path. The trio traverse onward.

"So I'm guessing you guys were gathered by GYAIA as well?" Jack breaking the silence.

"Yes, we were first year students at MIT, the youngest in our class to attend. Given fourteen is pretty odd to be college students. Before we were, recruited. . ." Sam stepping up before Max can answer. "MIT? Recruited?" Jack inching forward inquisitively.

"The Massachusetts Institute of Technology, the most prestigious program of study in the country. Where do you hail from?" Max pressing pretentiously.

"Um, Heights Valley high, wha?" Jack begins as Sam comes to his defense.

"Shut up, Max, don't mind him. MIT was his dream, great institution, but it doesn't help us here." His ever-pragmatic pier presses.

"Jack, Max and I are what they would call, "Genius", you'd never know given Max's propensity for stupidity. We got bored one night and may or may not have accidently hacked a secured server with rather sensitive international information." Sam continues conveniently cut off by Max.

"Yeah, we don't do anything by accident. Long story short, we were called down to the dean's office, and there was like a million

154

guys in black suits standing around holding those neuralyzers from that old-ass alien movie, and before you know it BAM! We were dropped in the middle of nowhere by some big dimwit named Danzler." Max maximizing the moment.

"Wasn't a million suits? Just two. But I agree with Max, who knew a little cyber spelunking would lead to some damp sewer in the middle of nowhere." Sam shaking his head at Max.

"Well, every day is a new day. Better to be exact than be lucky, and I think our luck is about to change gentlemen!" Jack pointing in the distance, his reference falling miserably.

"Old Man and the Sea? Ya'know Hemingway?" Jack nods nervously. "Hemingwho?' Max mimicking Jack's awkward mannerisms.

"We know Hemingway, he's being stupid. We're Twain guys, Jack, and you misquoted Hemingway. A tunnel access . . . where do you suppose it leads?" Sam says, slapping silence into Max.

"Not sure, best guess it's an emergency access or ventilation tunnel within this GYAIA." Jack offers, peering into the darkness. "So what you sayin, we don't know?"

"Can't be certain. C'mon use that big brain bro?" Jack jostling Max's hair playfully.

"Stop that dude! It's an auxiliary appendage of sorts." Max mulls feebly, fumbling his hands across slick walls.

"Appendage? Yeah ok! Got an odd feeling this is the spot." Jack shares, staring into the darkness.

"Spot? How do you . . . NOOooo!" Sam shrieks, the ground disappearing underfoot.

The trio tumble into the dark abyss below. "Ma, Max, where are you?" Sam screams into the darkness.

"Sa, Sam here reach for my hand!" Max howls in horror, they bodies twisting and turning in a tube of terror.

"Ooff!" Jack's plummet pausing briefly before being bashed by a bundle of brotherhood.

"Uhhgg, where are we?" Max murmurs.

"Shh, can you guys stand?" Jack whispers.

"Yeah, yes. What are you thinking, Jack?" Sam insists, assisting Max upright.

"I don't know yet, but give me a minute." Jack dispels as he dashes a few paces away. Using his phone's light to investigate their surroundings.

"He's checking the wall, Sam, com'n there's a draft due south. Leave Magellan to his work." Max speaking in hushed tones.

"No, Max. I'm not at a keyboard and you're not in a workshop. This, this is Jack's area of expertise. Besides, there's no way you could know that's "due south," Sam stammers to his sibling.

"So what, we?" Max mumbles. "D'n'D this way." Jack waving his flashlight forward.

"Did he just make a Dungeons an. . . whoa, hands off the merch, Sam!" Max brushes his brother's grip. The trio trotting deeper into darkness.

Each step gripping the group.

"Shh, listen." Jack sinks silently against the wall. Reaching out his free hand towards where the ground meets the wall.

"What is it, Jack?" Sam whispers, Max hovering over his shoulder.

"There's a breeze coming from under this wall." Jack replies in a hushed tone.

"A door, it's not a wall, it's a door." Max adds, his usual playful persona disappearing into the darkness surrounding them.

"Correct, Max, and doors have handles." Jack begins feeling the length and width of the wall.

"Jack, is it possible that this door's handle is on the other side?" Sam surmises, surveying its surface.

"Possible, likely even, but. . ." A quick twist sets off a chain reaction of sounds from within the wall. Jack pushing safely away from the impediment. Creaking open, a stream of air rushing past their feet.

"But not this one, step back, gentlemen." Jack stepping even further, standing between the barrier and his companions.

"Backpacks, boys, kill the lights." Jack commands, crouching to retrieve his belongings, never taking his eyes from what lay ahead. Grabbing their own, the twins do as commanded. Peering cautiously into the suspect space, Jack creeps forward.

"I'll go ahead. Sam, Max, stay close to the wall. Com'n." Placing his hand on Sam, pulling him forward, Sam mimicking the motion, pulling Max behind him.

"Do, do you smell that?" Max adds, sniffing silently.

"Yeah, the air is, is fresh," Jack replies.

"No, not that. Hydraulic fluid is sometimes mixed with propylene glycol. Snff, yeah, that's definitely PG." Max whispers, maintaining one hand on Sam, the other on the wall behind.

"PG? I don't smell anything. What's up, Max?" Jack inquires.

"Max has a sensitive nose. PG is odorless. Unless mixed with hydraulic fluid." Sam turning on his flashlight. The light emanating from his phone, chasing away the darkness, revealing a large chamber.

"Whoaa! It's a hanger. Explains the smell." Max fumbling for his own light.

"Gentleman, I don't think we're supposed to be here. Let's get a move on." Jack insists, waving his companions to him.

"The vehicles in here, they, they shouldn't exist, Jack." Max mutters, mesmerized by the menagerie of mechanical beasts.

"That may be so, but we shouldn't be here, Max, Sam we." Jack insists.

"Got it, Boss. Come on, Max, we have to move." Sam finishing Jack's thought, pulling his dumbfounded duplicate forward.

"Hands off. Boss? When did. . .ooff." Sam muffling Max as footsteps in the distance disturb the silence surrounding them.

"Shit, com'n, gentlemen, there's a door. This way." Jack speeds off in search of sanctuary.

"Damn, it's locked." Jack pulls at the door's handle roughly, pressing buttons profusely.

"Jack. Jack, calm down. We got this." Max moving him aside, digging deep into his pack.

"Sam, shall we?" The twins move, swiftly disassembling the control panel, Max humming to himself.

"Jack? Boss, whatever, a light?" Max motions him near.

"A what?" Curiously investigating their process.

"Your light, here, hold this." Max shoving his phone into Jack's hands.

"Overhead, yeah, like that, thanks." Max commands, continuing his work.

"Setting bypass, Sam, you got the. . . uhhpp, and we're in. Every time, Sam, every time." Max exclaims, rapping his brother's back.

With a beep, the door's lock clicks, opening and spilling light from above upon the trio.

"Finally, alright, gentlemen, let's move." Jack jolting past the twins into the narrow corridor. "Leave it, Sam, it's someone else's problem now." Max pulling Sam roughly away from the outside panel through the doorway slamming the door behind them.

"What the heck? Com'n. This stairway leads to somewhere." Jack jolting up steps with ease.

"Ugh, stairs." Sam rests his foot on the first step.

"Come on, Sam. Boss man says stairs, we take the stairs." Max smacking Sam on his way up.

159

"Okay, okay. Got it." Trudging towards the unknown, Sam hurries upward.

The trio traverse step after step, hearts pounding profusely. "Oh great, another door, Max, the honors." Jack stepping away, allowing Max to catch up. Max jolting the handle down, clicking the door ajar.

"It's just a door, Jack, a regular old door, my dude." Max motioning his companions through arrogantly.

"Ok, okay. You got skill, bro, but now's not time." Jack ushering the trio urgently through.

"This way!" Jack gestures towards a doorway hidden in the shadows. "What, why that one, Boss?" Sam sucking through bated breath.

"Don't know, just feels right." Jack retorts, turning to check behind them.

"All clear, let's move." Jack pausing long enough, allowing the twins into the doorway and securing it behind.

"Now what?" Max shining his light down the tight corridor.

"We move." Jack pressing on. "Oh okay, don't know where we are, but move he says." Max mimics sarcastically.

"Come on, Max. I have a good feeling about this one." Sam stepping by his brother after Jack.

"Got a good feeling, when do you go by feeling?" Max quips falling in line all the same.

160

Lights lowering, the triplet traversing the narrow passage, discovering a small area at its end.

"Dead end, Jack. What noOOWWW!" Max wails wilting where he stood. A painfully piercing siren searing every ear, dropping the trio to their knees.

"Oww, ma, make it stop!" Max succumbing to the sound, screams painfully. An unseen door shuts behind them, cutting off their escape, and reverberations rapidly intensify the sinister siren.

The searing siren separating all sanity from their senses. At every powerful pulse, the pounding in their heads grows more painful. The twins panicked and paralyzed by pain, causing Jack to crawl towards the former entrance. Feeling feverishly for any scrap of solace, unable to detect a handle. Returning clutched hands tightly protecting his ears, Jack crumples to his side. Fading fast, his limbs become heavy as boulders, dropping heavily to ground, further exposing him to the sinister sound.

Laying weakly waning, Jack buries one ear into his armpit when the slightest draft from beneath the door blows across his outstretched arm. The slightness of the sensation snapping back to his senses. Dragging himself to his feet, Jack squats down low, thrusting his fingers into the crease. Willing himself upward, painfully pulling with all his might against the door. The hard unforgiving steel sinking deeply into desperate digits, the young companion driving all his force through his heels into the cold metal below. In a rush of clarity, Wiley's voice ringing in his head. "when the evil is the loudest, scream louder."

161

Jack screams into the heavens above when the door clicks, sliding upward opening in the process. Light dimly creeps in, revealing his prone companions. Turning quickly in the twin's direction, Jack stumbles, head dizzy from his epic exertion.

"S, Sam. M Max?" Jack stammers, stumbling between them.

"Up, we have to go." Jack helping both to their feet, breathing heavily.

"Th, the sound, no . . . no Mrs. Baker, what AP paper?!" Max mutters incoherently.

"Hey, buddy, I know you." Sam shuffles weakly still shaken. Pain shooting through pulsing fingers gripping his companions, Jack pulls the twins to the safety of silence.

"Hff, hff. Thanks, Jack, believe that was the wrong room." Sam gingerly separating to stand on his own, before collapsing again massaging his ears. Jack tapping at his ears signaling his confusion at Sam's words. Unsure of his own words, Sam sinks gingerly into his pack. "What next?" Jack whispers, ears still ringing, the trio burn a few moments to recover as silence settles around them.

CHAPTER SEVENTEEN

PREDATORS AND PREY

Steel and concrete converge enclosing the trio in a network of decisions. Surveying their surroundings Jack wanders back to his new companion's sides. Pausing to think as Max breaks his concentration.

"So all that, we survived the wailing walls! Great, we still in the dark. Now what MacGyver?" Max moans sauntering off to collect his pack. "Damn, screens toast. Great, just great."

"No, guys this isn't the same passage we entered, it's . . . it's different." Jack notes walking ahead pocketing his broken device.

"What? How would you know that? You don't know where we are and back there, at the door! That wasn't exactly MacGyver stuff, Jack!" Max clearly flustered by now.

"I didn't have anything pry it open, just gotta use what you got and hope it works Max." Jack playfully pats Max on the shoulder making his way to the center of the room.

"The floor here is hollower than the perimeter, Sam what do you make of it?" Jack gestures for Sam to come closer.

"Can't be certain, Jack, but I'm certain I don't like this house of horrors." Sam crouching next to his new companion.

"Solid perimeter? Hollow center? SAM, JACK, get away. It's a trap door!" Max lunges and grabs Sam's pack as the floor disappears from beneath his crouched company.

"Whoa, oh shi. . .!!!" Jack jumping towards the top, smashing into an unforgiving steel and falling into the darkness.

"MAXxx!!!" Sam shrieks, sinking simultaneously.

"Sam, gotcha, whoa, NOooo!" Unable to stop his momentum, Max's grip of Sam's pack also pulls him in.

Falling uncontrollably, the trio plunges deep into the baptism below. Silent seconds settle along the surface before a duplicate disturbs it. "PffHUuuu. . . Hhuhuu. Sam? Jack?" Max spits, gasping for air.

"Pff, thpff Mmax, here. I'm here!" Sam splashes desperately.

"No, no good, Sam, there's nothing to grab onto!" Max shouts, slamming his hand forcefully against the solid structure. "It's some sort of reservoir . . . Jack! Where's Jack?" Sam shrieks, feeling blindly as he treads deepening waters.

"He's gone be down there! Huuupppff." Max takes a deep breath, diving below. Short seconds pass before Max resurfaces, gasping for air.

"Pff, pff, Sam, its deep, can't, I can't… you're the, the swimmer. Looks like all those lessons Mother made us take will come in handy." Max coughs miserably.

"Got it. Catch your breath, Max. Fuuupphh." Drawing in deeply, Sam submerges. Kicking hard into the darkness, Sam uses the side to feel for any sense of depth. Being an adept swimmer means little in this abyss below. Seconds sink past a minute; bubbles surfacing, growing further apart, and melting Max's nerves. After several more failed dives, Max smashes water and darkness alike.

"SAM? JACK? Sam?"

"Snff, Sam? Come back, snff" Max sniffs, sending sorrow echoing upward.

"Duh, does he always do that?" A weak voice.

"Hupff, huppf fr, from time to time." A familiar voice echoes in the dark. "Does he always do what, Jack? Ja, JACK? Sam, you son of a. . ." Max turning in surprise, squinting into nothing but hearing all.

"Ahh, ahh, that's your Mother too, Bro!" Sam spits, gasping greedily.

"I thought I lost you guys." Max squeezing the pair, chests heaving heavily.

"Okay, okay. Fine, fine, give us some breathing room. Here, found this, Max." Sam shoving Max back with his own pack.

"Hff, hugs later. Oh, okay, Jack, we need to start making our way up." Sam says, still breathing deeply.

"Hold on, Jack, let the water rise, and then we will escape. Work smarter, not harder. Ole Chap." Max's voice echoing to their salvation above.

Errr. . .click! A heavy grate creaks, clicking into place atop the pit.

"Um, boys, that's not good!" Max splashes frantically.

165

"Calm down, Max. Give me your arms, guys, back to back."
Jack shifting his pack to his front.

Interlocking their arms, pressing their backs against each
other's, the three companions use the strength of a triangle to
walk up the walls. Slowly but surely, barely outpacing the rapids.
At the top of the pit, a solid metal grate blocks their escape. Max
and Jack hold tight to each other as Sam, the lightest of the three,
climbs onto their shoulders. Straining to reach through the grate,
feeling for a release.

"Damn, it's no good that damn thing is bolted down!" Sam
spits exasperatedly.

"What size head?" Max asks, passing up his multi-tool.

"Max, you're a genius!" Sam says, pulling himself up with
one arm, shooting the other, tool in hand, through the grate.

"Yeah, I know, remember lefty loosy, righty tighty, man, I'm
awesmmmm." Max begins before catching a boot from his
brother, forcing his face below the rising rapids.

"Pff, pff. Hey now asshmmmm." Max mumbles as Sam uses
his face to leverage the last bolt free.

"Com'n, you stupid thing… turn, turn!!!" Sam pulls hard
against the last bolt.

"Sam hurrmmyym!" Jack gurgles as his head submerges.

"Hpffff, errr com'n!!!" Sam pulls harder, driving one foot
against the wall, the other pushing down hard into his companions
now below the darkened waters. Straining hard, Sam summons all

166

his limited might until a familiar sound sends him rapidly spinning the loosened bolt with his fingers.

Pressing hard upward forcing the grate open, Sam pulls himself out. Chest heaving heavily, he thrusting his arms into the water frantically feeling for Jack and Max.

"Whoosh. Hoooffff, Hffff!" Jack explodes onto the surface next to Sam, gasping for life.

"Max! Jack, give me a hand, he's too hea, heavy." Sam shrieks, pulling desperately at his brother. Jack jumping to his feet, crouching deep, pulling hard on the lifeless form below. The many years of wrestling serving him well as Jack rips Max from the watery depths. Falling back roughly to the ground, Max's limp form on top of him.

"Max, Max!" Sam's voice stabs sharply through the space, frantically shaking his brother.

"Sam calm down, grab his feet. We have to get him flat." Jack commands, grabbing Max's torso. Jack tilts Max's head back, supporting his neck while laying him flat.

"What are we doing? Hurry!" Sam shrieks. Thinking quickly, Jack breathes deeply, forcing hard, labored breaths into Max. Motioning Sam to take over as he begins deep six-inch chest compressions. Breathing deeply, Sam forces belabored breaths into his brother.

"Sam, Sam. When I stop compressions, then breathe. Calm down. He's gonna make it. One. . .Two. . .Three. . .Four. . ."

Seconds linger as if hours pass while Jack persistently presses deeply.

"Come on, Max. Huuuhhh, pffffff." Sam breathes deeper and deeper.

"Come on. Max!" Sam draws deeply when a rush of warm liquid sprays his face.

"Ugghcufff, cuff. Pfff cuff. Ugh," Max spits weakly.

"Max! Breathe, Max, breathe!" Jack commands, pulling him upright.

"Get it out. Here, hold his arms up. Breathe." Jack continues calmly as Max's breathing slowly recovers.

"Pff. Pff. . .you spit in my mouth Max!" Sam gags, wiping his mouth.

"No. . .nobody t, to, told you to ki, kiss me." Max jests through short, weak breaths.

"Just breathe, Max. Sam, gather our things. We have to get moving." Jack peering over his shoulder at a light growing closer down one of the halls. Shouldering his and Max's pack, Jack pulls Max gingerly to his feet.

"Sam, help your brother. We have to move."

"Move, move where? We almost drown, and then these halls appear! What is all this, Jack?" Sam shouldering his own pack while supporting Max.

"Don't know, but we can't stay here. Com'n this way." Jack commands, sprinting down a random hall. "He's your friend, Sam. I'm still deciding, bruh." Max jests.

168

"Shut up, Max, your breath stinks." Sam pulling Max in Jack's direction.

"Well, technically, it's your breath." Max grins sheepishly.

"Gross, come on." Sam pulls, craning his face away from his brother's.

Adrenaline again courses through the trio's veins, driving them forward.

"This way." Jack shouts behind his shoulder, darting to his right.

"Hold on, I'm dragging an imbecile." Sam shouts.

"Imbecile, you're the imbecile who stepped on my face." Max claps.

"Shhh. Stay here for a sec." Jack abruptly stopping, raising a clutched fist.

"Almost drown, run this way, now stop. Jack, wha wha. . ." Sam begins as a damp finger mashes roughly to his lips.

"The man said stop, shhh." Max motions comically with his other finger for silence.

"Stop that, ew gross, don't touch me." Sam quips slapping Max's finger from his lips.

Jack steps cautiously down the hall before motioning his companions to follow. The room the trio now find themselves in is warm and softly lit.

"Oh great, what now, Jack?" Sam scoffs.

"I don't know; it's like we are being tested or something. My ears have been poppin for a minute, so we aren't that deep underground anymore." Jack begins.

"Didn't notice it before because we've sprinted from place to place so much, but it's like we are supposed to be here." Jack continues, stepping cautiously into the warmed space.

"Let go Sa, let go Sam. Makes sense, Jack, that a super-secret organization just lets people walk through a hidden jungle entrance. Not a chance, but when does it end?" Max pulling away from Sam's support.

"So what now?" Max steps into the warmth, rubbing feeling into his damp chest.

"I don't know, but something about this room creeps me out. There's no doors?" Jack adds, cautiously examining the room.

"The last one didn't have doors until we almost drowned. Maybe this one is really a dead end?" Max adds.

"No, no, it's a game." Sam stepping past his companions.

"Look at the floor, look and the walls. It's like they're made to move or something." Sam continues studying their surroundings. Low lighting above reveal only glimpses of images below.

"What do you mean a game, Sam?" Jack inquires.

"The walls and floor tiles have the same images. The perimeter on our side and the other is one solid piece, but the tiles are different." Sam points at the many different designs on the tiles.

"So if it's a game, what's the objective?" Max asks, brushing past his companions and stepping confidently forward.

"Max NO!!!" Sam lunges forward, grabbing Max roughly by his damp shirtsleeve.

"No, what, Sam? It's just a, whoa, whoa!" Max falters forward, the tile beneath his foot disappearing into a deep darkness.

"Gotcha, buddy." Jack helping Sam pull his brother back.

"What in the Temple of Do Not step there is going on, Sam?" Max screams into the dimly lit space.

"Don't you get it, guys? It's a puzzle. I just don't know how to solve it, yet." Sam continues cautiously tapping his toe, testing each inch of the perimeter.

"A puzzle, yet? Are you sure?" Jack prompts, looking inquisitively at his companions.

"I see it now Sam. It's like that one game we used to play. What's its name?" Max shouldering both packs, tapping his forehead.

"Ice breaker, no. Ice something, umm break, break something break." Max tapping his chin, moving back into the narrow hall they came from.

"Um guys, I found a door. . ." Max spins around, perplexed.

"This wasn't here a minute ago." He continues.

"No, it shut the second you sent that first tile into oblivion." Sam quips, still investigating the patterns on the wall.

"Don't Break the Ice!" Jack blurts out, staring across the tiled room.

"Yeah, that's the game; simple game, Sam, was the best at figuring, which ones not to hit." Max adds still pushing himself against the door away from the tiles.

"Let me guess, you weren't so good?" Jack jests over his shoulder.

"And so? Can't be good at everything. Patterns are Sam's thing, I like building things." Max retorts.

"Jack over here, what do you make of this?" Sam signaling Jack towards his wall.

"It's a pattern of sorts, but it's just random animals." Jack responds. "Right, same ones on the floor. Be a good fella and check the other wall." Sam instructs. "Jack steps carefully so as not to touch another tile while inspecting the opposite wall.

"And, the pattern is?" Sam inquires. "It's, they're all upside down. Read off the animals, front to as far as you can see, Sam." Jack replies.

"Lion, Bear, Falcon, Tiger. . ." Sam's voice trails as further images become more obscure in darkness.

"Your turn, Jack!" Sam calls, squinting hard for any further images.

"A deer, no an Antelope, Fish, Mouse, pig or something can't really make it out. What's it mean, Sam?" Jack replies, perplexed.

"Not sure. One side are hunters, and the other are. ." Sam responds before snapping his fingers.

"Predator and prey! Guys, one pattern is predators; the upside down patterns are typical prey animals, and they're upside down

172

because they're dead." Sam beams with excitement, dashing towards a cowering Max.

"Great, how does that help us? Hey, that's my stuff. Give it back." Sam snatches his brother's pack, tossing it on the nearest tile with an image of a prey animal. The pack lands roughly on the tile, instantaneously disappearing from sight.

"Now look at what you did, jerk!" Max stepping forward before retreating to the safety of the wall.

"Eureka! Jack, the predator tiles must be the safe pattern, and the prey tiles are danger." Sam confidently walks towards the Lion tile, tossing his pack squarely on its center. The echo of the thud fills the room, but nothing else.

"Predators safe, shall we?" Sam motions imitating the mannerisms of a butler inviting his companions onward.

"Predators and Prey, so simple. Good work, Sam, Max come on." Jack stepping past Sam, grabbing up the genius of the game's pack.

"Oh no, you guys first, there's barely enough room for the two of yah as it is. Whoa, what the!" A rumbling behind Max interrupts his whining.

"Max, the wall is moving JUMP!" Jack commands loudly. Reacting to his directive, Max jumps awkwardly towards his companions.

"Gotcha!" Jack grabbing Max roughly, steadying him as the three balance on the crowded tile of the Lion.

173

"I always liked lions, yah know. Fun fact. . ." Max gasps, clutching Jack and Sam.

"Save it, Max, we gotta move!" Jack retorts sharply before jumping to the next predator-adorned tile leading his pack. With each progression, the wall behind the trio moves closer, cutting the space nearer and nearer into the unknown. Tiles of prey outnumber those of predator, tiles of prey dropping at the slightest movement over them.

"Com'n, move, guys, we're doing well, Sam. What's next?!?" Jack shouts through heightened breaths.

"Um, uh, the fox. Damn, that was close." Sam landing roughly, almost knocking his companions onto a bird-adorned tile.

"Whoa, now! Pidgin ain't it, bro!" Max jests as the feathered tile disappears into darkness.

"Shark, cobra, then Mantis, jump, Max!" Sam demands impatiently.

"The room isn't even. There's only prey. What's next, Sam, Jack?" Max screams in terror, landing uneasily on the mantis tile.

"Shh, let me think, fish, bird, deer, orca, human, earth?" Sam pauses, peering at the last only good option. "That's a lot of prey in the rows ahead, Sam." Jack pauses as well, eyes darting between the limiting options.

"Humans, prey or predator?" He responds, turning desperately back at Sam.

"Orca predator, human or earth, I don't know?!?" An exasperated Sam breathes heavily.

"Humans suck . . . prey!" Max, making his decision, leaps forward. "MAX, NOOOOO!!!" Jack exploding into Max, catching his leg, landing roughly on the human tile. The spherical-shaped tile disappearing into nothing as Max falls through.

"SAM!!!" Max screams as he plunges into darkness.

"Gotcha!" Jack straining to keep his grip on Max. Jumping as the wall moves to cover past tiles, Sam leaps onto Jack's legs, pinning him to the tile, resembling their own humanity.

"Hu. .hu. . human. . preda. . .predator." Sam huffs, heaving his cynical sibling upward.

"Ugh, go . . . good, call Sam." Max rolls ridiculously close to the edge.

"Sugarcoated sesamoids. That was close." Max lays, looking up into nothing gratefully.

"Up, Max, Sam, come on." Jack demands as he lands firmly on the other side. Extending his hand and catching Sam's almost ill-attempted athletic feat.

"Gotcha! Max, com'n!" Jack demands firmly. Scrambling to his feet, Max leaps equally pathetic as Sam.

"Gotcha!" Jack and Sam pull Max roughly to a thin edge, now revealed as the final rows of tiles fall haplessly into the darkness.

"Well Gents, we survived the puzzle pit from hell. What next?" Max muses, brushing himself off, as the sound of a door behind the trio jolts ajar.

"That's next, hurry!" Jack sprints through the newly presented path, followed by his companions. Sprinting slows to careful steps as the dimly lit hall spills into a space of unclear dimensions of equally poor lighting.

"Oh great anoth!"

"Shhh" Jack interrupting Max.

"What is it, Jack?" Sam whispers.

"Clapping?"

The clapping grows closer, emanating from above the trio.

"Well done, Gentlemen!" A familiar voice rings above the newly formed faction.

"Wi . . .ley?" Jack begins as lights from above ignite immediately, filling the room with illumination. Shielding their eyes, blinking the image from above into focus.

"Mr. Wiley?" Jack completing his earlier inquiry.

"Yes, Jack Murphy, Samuel, and Maximillian Duval; congratulations and welcome, Gentlemen, to GYAIA." Agent Wiley's voice rings, commanding the room.

"Proceed forward. The real journey begins now." Without another word, Wiley vanishes from his perch.

CHAPTER EIGHTEEN

THE REAL JOURNEY BEGINS

Another door appears as Jack and his companions are ushered forward by sharply dressed cadets into a series of rooms for further processing. Stripped and showered to wash away the grime of earlier events, the trio are ushered hastily to receive new haircuts. Jack's locks sheared into a neat flat top, his sides buzzed into a tight fade. The twins receive looser fades, allowing to retain more hair atop their pristine brains. The boys are fitted with new standard grey uniforms with blue trim.

"Hey now, a little tight around the neck!" Max protests, tugging at his uniform's collar.

"Attention, trainees, this is Cadet Blackshear. He will be your ICC, immediate commanding cadet. He will assist your transition into cadets here at GYAIA." A voice interrupts over a loudspeaker. A smile cracks across Cadet Blackshear's face, observing his new subordinates rubbing the sides of their fresh fades.

"Mighty fine." Making eye contact with Jack, Blackshear volleys before marching sharply to a frontal position before the trio.

The voice overhead continuing the next commands.

"Cadet Blackshear, please proceed with our new trainees to GEPS for physicals and room C-2 for ASVAB skills assessments and further processing."

"Sir, yes, Sir!"

"He saluted the speaker, the speaker? ASVAB, that's for military dudes, what's going on? Hey, let go, Sam!" Max protests, pointing at the speaker as Sam tugs him after a swiftly moving Jack. "Come on, you dope, we're falling behind." Sam urging his symmetrical sibling after Jack, who has already vacated the room.

Sprinting to catch up, Sam and Max struggle to keep pace with Jack.

"Blackshear, more like Swiftfoot!" Max spits sucking in air heavily.

"Shut it, bro, don't be stupid." Sam says, sucking wind equally.

"Keep up guys." Jack shouts over his shoulder, breathing comfortably.

"Keep up; chase the Terminator down the world's longest hallway he says. Did you see that guy? He's jacked." Max continuing his complaints sprinting awkwardly down crisply clean corridors.

"Almost there, ya'll got this." Jack slowing his pace to a halt.

"Ten-hut!" Cadet Blackshear commands standing picturesque outside the desired doorway.

"Hh, hff. Lieutenant Bigfoot, Sir. Reporting for, ooff." Max settles bending at the waist to catch his breath from his brother's blow.

"Sir, don't mind him, Sir. He's the smartest idiot you'll ever meet. Sir." Sam straightens incorrectly saluting the chiseled-jawed cadet.

"Duly noted, smartest idiot. Please proceed to GEPS. I will attend you while you've completed your physicals." Cadet Blackshear salutes and crisply marches away.

"Wha, what was that for Sam?" Max inquires, shoving Sam.

"Max, look at where we are, GYAIA is some sort of military initiation and you're acting like a trailer trash idio . . ." Sam retorts but is cut off by Jack.

"Guys, this is all official. We need to start taking this seriously, because I don't see phone calls home in our future anytime soon. Max, you good?" Jack placing his hand supportively on Max's shoulder.

"Yeah, hffff, hfff yeah, I'm good. Ok, Murph, from here on out, you lead, and we'll follow." Max straightening himself as the trio enter, shutting the door behind them.

A few hours pass as the companions complete various tasks to test their physical conditioning. While Sam and Max tire quickly, Jack excels past other trainees who also perform the initial obstacle courses and array of physical tests their cohort encounters. Max falters early, as Sam shows some resilience before succumbing to his physical limitations. Jack, however, completes many of the various tasks, excelling through sheer will and desire, even dominating some more capable athletes within the age group.

"Dang, how long are we gonna wait here?" Max quips.

"Until Jack is done doing his thing, he's pretty good at this stuff, don't you think?" Sam answers with a question of his own.

"I guess, but what is all this?" Max retorts.

"Bro, I don't even know. I thought we'd be in some lab or workshops developing whatever for the government, dude, I don't know." Sam responds, picking nervously at the floor.

"Sam, what's up?" Max asks, shortly shelving any silly quips.

"It feels . . . feels like we are supposed to be here. I can't rationalize it, but this feels right. I mean, bro, we suck at this running and jumping thing, but Jack, there's something about him. Like we are where we're right where we are supposed to be."

"I don't know about all that, but I can say that this Jack guy wants this, or he wouldn't still be in there climbing over walls and crawling through mud. It's not like us to care about those jock types, but he's. . .he's."

Max pauses to gather his words.

"He's different, I don't know why, and I can't explain why, but he's different, and Max, promise me that you understand that this isn't Georgia Tech anymore. This isn't MIT. This is different, and our best chance of making it has something to do with this Jack Murphy." Sam concludes, resuming his solemn stare at the floor.

"I don't get it either, Sam, but I promise to be better. Until you figure out what it is about him, I'll try." Max, mulling his own emotions, taps impatiently when the door opens.

"Gentlemen, shower and dress in your grays. This way." Cadet Blackshear commands, standing stiffly, peering in one doorway.

"What about Jack?" Sam inquires.

"He's on his way for fitting now, take these, this way." Cadet Blackshear directs with a nod, breaking his initial rigid character.

Following their directive, the twins follow Cadet Blackshear, dress, and proceed to the next phase of processing.

"So how far did you. . ." Sam pressing Jack as they march to another room.

"Don't know, just kept going until there wasn't many of us running around. Shh." Jack presses an index finger against his lips, pointing with the other as other trainees are ushered into a room labeled C-2. Cadet Blackshear directs Jack, the twins, and other trainees to find seating before taking off. A few more trainees are ushered into the testing room, as the Proctor enters promptly. Her hair tightly pulled into a neatly kept knot, clean pressed uniform and skirt. Her mouth drawing sharply as she speaks, instructing the cohort to retrieve neatly organized packets and personal laptops to begin their assessment containing subjects ranging from general science to arithmetic reasoning, word knowledge, mathematics knowledge, and mechanical comprehension. The twins find themselves in their elements, breezing through the computer-based testing. Jack, however, struggles, forcing himself to focus on unfamiliar subjects. Answering every question with his best effort, accompanied by great trepidation and uncertainty. Sam and Max find themselves again waiting in another room, but under much different pretense.

"Sam, Jack seems like a smart dude. What gives?" Max presses impatiently pressing against the cushion of his chair.

"Max, we just took the ASVAB. It's a difficult examination for those not versed in these subjects. We, on the other hand... well, come on, Bro?" Sam hotly stifling his own hubris.

"Yeah, yeah, I get it, cakewalk for us, Bro, but Murph's no dummy."

"Warming up to him, I see?" Sam retorts rhetorically.

"No! Well, like you said, he's got something. It's not like he needs to be us, but he's quick in the moment, which we get stuck. Like he makes quick decisions. Like his decisions aren't just good for him, but what's best for all, who does that?" Max ponders uncharacteristically.

"Exactly, Max, he takes in information quickly and makes decisions that we need time to process in the moment, his decisions so far are instinctual." Sam continues picking at his own chair.

"Well, who cares, Sam? Let him get a crap grade, we can be the brains. You got a 98 on the damn thing, and I know you did that on purpose to beat my 97." Max quips mockingly.

"Oh, shut up, Max. I got a couple wrong on purpose, so they didn't throw me in a think tank or something. You got a 97 because I told you to study in English, but no, you always have to tinker, and I end up writing your papers." Sam snaps back. Minutes melt, quickly evaporating the day before Jack immerges from his testing.

"So how was. . ." Before Max can start up a sharply dressed cadet approaches the three companions. "Trainees Duval, Duval, and Murphy I presume?" His polite voice cutting clearly over Max. "Sir, yes Sir." Jack saluting incorrectly. "Blackshear will fix that later. Follow me gentlemen." Turning swiftly on a dime the older cadet marches several paces ahead of the trio.

"Come on gents!" Jack says collecting his pack before sprinting off with Sam and Max struggling to keep pace.

Marching swiftly the trio are guided through neatly kept halls, walls covered in etched murals echoing eons of mythology. Images of grand battles, rising heroes clashing with failing foes glimmer in the eyes of the three youths as they are escorted to their living quarters. The older escorting cadet nods handing Jack a small neatly folded card containing an access code. "Learn it, flush it, mess call is 1700 sharp, lights out 2100, alarms 0400. . . Welcome to GYAIA Gentlemen." The escorting cadet salutes, turning sharply on a dime marches off.

"Okay?" Jack responses staring at the crisp card when Max snatches it hastily pressing buttons throwing open the door.

"Let's go before the big one comes back." Max mules thrusting his way through the door simultaneously with Sam.

"Oomphh no, me first Bro!" Max squeaks pressing against his duplicate.

The trio settles exhaustedly in their dorm. Finding three neatly prepared bunks, a few basic dressers for clothing, a plain bathroom with a single sink, toilet, and shower. Three small desks; each adorned with small glowing lamps, accompanied by plain chairs nestled in small spaces around the dorm. Jack stares quietly at the ceiling, thinking of Aunt Anna and his friends back home. Sam shifts uncomfortably, failing to find any solace in a stiff mattress, when Max starts up.

"Top bunk, no get down Sam." Max mules pulling his climbing copy down. "Too late, let go Max." Sam kicks playfully.

"No, no I called it first Sam." Max squirms climbing over his copy, claiming his territory. "Whatever Max have it." Sam spits slipping below to his desired spot.

Proudly patting his claim Max sits surveying their small dwelling. "So, is anyone gonna address the craziness of today? I mean, abandoned in the woods, chased through catacombs. Almost deaf, drown us, playin' don't break the ice or fall to death. . ." Max quips.

"Shh, let's get settled Max. 1700 mess is like twenty away." Sam insists, Max only adding to his annoyed state.

"I mean, come on, Bro, this is. . ." Max continues when Jack finishes his thought.

"Nuts, yeah, pretty nuts, and I'd assume it's only gonna get more nuts."

184

"Nuts, maybe, but all those three trials reminded me of that old thing with the monkeys; remember those creepy monkeys at Mom and Dad's?" Sam inquires succumbing to his suffering settling on his bed.

"Yeah, the ones covering their faces and stuff." Max adds settling his pack at the foot of his bed.

"Agreed, those hear no evil, speak no evil, see no evil monkeys. Freaky lil monkeys. Dad had like fifty sets. They were everywhere!" Sam sits up thoughts of their past giving way to their present.

"Freaky monkeys?" Max chimes in.

"Yeah, think about it, Jack, the first room those sirens were so loud we couldn't hear a thing." Sam begins as Max chimes in.

"Yeah, then the drowning pit, can't speak if you're woofin down water." Max jests when Jack begins chuckling to himself, causing the duo to sit up.

"Oh great, Max, look what you did. He's lost it." Sam quips.

"No idiot, he, like most people not named Samuel Antonio Duval, thinks I'm funny." Max claps back.

"har, ha, hee, he said when the evil is loudest, scream louder." Jack fighting to stifle his laughter.

"When evil is the loudest, scream louder. You're right, Sam, he's lost it." Max agreeing with his deliberate duplicate.

"Shh, Max. Jack, go on, he who?" Sam shushing his maniac mirror.

"Wiley, the last thing Wiley said to me when I got dropped off, was some odd riddle. Or at least, I thought it was a riddle, but it all makes sense now." Jack's tone swiftly, shifting from silly to serious.

"What makes sense? Tell us, tell us?" Max insists impatiently.

"Max, shut it, and he could!" Sam snaps, equally eager to know.

"Ok, okay, don't start a fight. The last thing Wiley said was three things. When evil is the loudest, be louder. When the evil speaks wickedly, speak honestly; when the evil sees no path, see the path forward." Jack pauses, surprised at his own accurate recall.

"Whaat???" Max gyrates in his bunk above Sam.

"Hey, stop that. Yeah, that makes sense now. It would have helped when all that craziness was going on, but it makes sense now." Sam smacking the framing above his head.

"Ok, it all makes sense, kinda makes sense, guys, but do tell." Max maliciously moves more maniacally. Jack continues, motioning Max to stop.

"Well, the room with the sirens. When I was pulling at the door, I didn't pull that door open. That thing was heavy. But I heard Wiley's voice saying, scream louder and, without thinking, I did, and the darn thing opened. Weird, right?" Jack directs his question upon his captive copies.

"Yeah, very weird, then the pit with the water, when you and Max were underwater, Max couldn't instruct me any further, so I

186

went on instinct or the maybe the many years watching him tinker away helped me just turn the bolts the right way." Sam adds, leaning forward when Max chimes in.

"Yeah, then the crazy pit with the animals, Sam, you figured out the pattern, as you always do, but it was like Jack said. When evil sees no path, see the path forward. Sam, you totally saw the path forward. Glad you did, or Jack would have totally. . ." Max completing his thought, spinning his finger downward.

"If memory serves, that would've been you, Max, but yeah, Jack, it all makes sense now. Hmm." Sam sinking back into his bunk, satisfied.

"Whatever, Sam, so Jack, which means Wiley knew about those death traps and still. . . " Max begins.

"Yes, Max, he was tipping me off, wish I had remembered those in the moment." Jack settling in his own bunk, reaching into his pocket, and retrieving the trinket Aunt Anna gave him.

"Well, well. Just nuts, but we made it, now what?" Max eager to continue the conversation.

"We'd better unpack mess is soon!" Unhappy with Jack's response, Max kicks his pack to the floor below, jumping off himself. The trio unpack quickly settling into selected spaces when a knock rattles the door sending the trio scattering to attention. Jack pulling the door open revealing the brawny Blackshear engulfing their doorway.

"Trainees, it would seem processing went smoothly, while you may be official cadets in the coming days, remember we do things

187

different than on the outside. We're moving out!" The brawny Blackshear nodding for the trio to fall into formation of awaiting newly minted cadets. Falling in line quickly, the company marches off to the mess hall. The mess hall is a large space with high ceilings adorned with banners of previous cadets and classes. Cadets cheerfully greet each other sharing stories of the day. The trio are ushered through the mess line, seated with other newly minted cadets, eating quickly. Jack rubbing weary eyes, finishes his plate, returning it to its designated spot. Sam and Max unaccustomed to eating swiftly struggle to consume their food before Blackshear ushers his new cadets out the mess hall, returning them back to their dorms.

"Remember Cadets lights out 2100, morning call 0400!" Blackshear boasts, saluting as he ushers his remaining cadets to theirs as well. Jack returning a salute shutting the door behind him. "What a day!" He breathes quietly.

"Well that was new." Max muses picking his teeth with a pen.

"Not my good pen, gross Max!" Sam shooting across the room, wrestling away his property.

"Okay, okay have it." Max mules surrendering the now damp utensil.

"Come on guys lets finish unpacking and get some shut eye." Jack directs turning to a single bed opposite of the twin's bunks. "Good idea. Max want the bigger desk around the corner for your tinkering?" Sam surmises correctly, still wiping saliva from his prized pen.

"How'dya know Sam?" Max muses unpacking a variety of tools irregularly into drawers.

"Figured I'd save ya a fight." Sam says unloading his pack neatly into his selected desk nearest to their bunk.

"Not much to unpack there Jack?" Sam notes surveying the few amenities outside of clothes leaving his companion's pack.

"Yup, except this, I don't think we'll be playing with Legos or listening to many tunes around here." Jack jests modestly placing his few possessions in the dresser.

"Why is that? Don't you have stuff?" Max inquires over his shoulder.

"I have stuff, pack wasn't big enough for the bike and I left my boy Reg in charge of the dekkens, snff." Jack sighs quietly wiping a welling tear.

"Dekkens? As in Dekken Dragon, dekken?" Max presses peeking into Jack's empty pack.

"Dude we love Dekken. Sam and I have like every rare hollow, well except Odin's Wrath, but nobody cold pulls Odin's Wrath." Max muses poking around in Jack's now empty pack.

"We'll be pulling Blackshear's Boot if we don't finish settling in. Leave Jack alone Max, gonna be no Dekken for a while. So Jack, you and your friend any good? What's your go to starting sequence? Densewood over here thinks laying two Whispering Willows and an Earth Spirit is genius." Sam chuckles to himself baiting his brother.

"Listen Mr. Fenrir's Fury, playing Loki's luck is cheating!" Max mules pointing accursedly at Sam.

"Hmm, I'm getting some sleep gents." Jack smiles to himself laying exhaustedly on his surprisingly comfortable mattress.

"Seriously Jack, what's your start? Your deck comp?" Max mules dumping the last of his pack into a random drawer.

"Yeah Jack, tell us about your friend Rhett?" Sam inquires climbing into his own bed after neatly completing his task.

"Oh Reg, he's a good dude, awkward around the ladies, but he's solid. Not as good at Dekken as he thinks, but got a few solid pulls. His deck is fire if you knew how to use it. Betcha ya'll'd like Ari too, Aaahnn!" Jack joins in yawning deeply. The new companion's conversation easily burns past lights out when Sam responsibly turns off their lamps before discovery.

Silence settles over the cramped quarter, as the twins drift off into dreams of Dekken and dragons. Jack soaking in the events of the day, closes his eyes rubbing the trinket still clutched in his hand, whispering to himself.

"What does all this mean, Aunt Anna? Who am . . ." Clutching the mysterious trinket from Aunt Anna, fading into slumber, the young hero finally succumbs to exhaustion.

CHAPTER NINETEEN

"WHO AM I?"

The dawn of a new day is still a few hours away, the companions sleeping heavily unaware of what awaits them. Even Max's snoring is unable to break the trio's shared slumber. Suddenly, their door rockets open, light chasing docile darkness to every corner. Cadet Blackshear marches deliberately to the center of the room, barking orders for the three sleeping beauties to rise and ready themselves. Jack, the lightest sleeper, jolts from his slumber, scrambling for his neatly pressed uniform, followed by Sam.

"Up and at um gentlemen, 0400 is go time! Cadet Duval, get the led out!" Cadet Blackshear bellows, pulling Max's covers off roughly.

"Max, let's go!" Jack shouts, rushing to tighten his boots. Sam and Jack fall in line with other first-year cadets lined neatly outside their dorm as Max rushes about under Cadet Blackshear's watchful eye. Stumbling, still tugging at his own boot, Max fumbles into line.

"First years, A-ten-hut! Forward march." Cadet Blackshear orders, leading his first years to morning mess. Silently, some still sweeping sleep from their eyes, the weary cadets do as ordered. Light sandstone halls adorned by mythical tales, fail to provide any sense of direction, blending seamlessly from one space to another.

"Is this prison?" Max snickers but is quickly reprimanded by Cadet Blackshear, who has somehow found his way to Max's rear flank.

"First year Duval, only speak when spoken to." Blackshear whispers before marching ahead of the line.

The mess hall presents a new set of customs and cadences Jack and his fellow first years must navigate. While older cadets mingle and talk openly, first years are ordered to sit and eat silently once they retrieve their meal, as time is limited before they proceed. Jack struggles to finish his food, as he is accustomed to sitting at Aunt Anna's table having long conversations over suppers prepared with love. His old high school lunch is doing little to prepare him for this pace. Again, first years form a neat single file line, are ushered from room to room for further processing. Gaining schedules, books, and gear specific to their assigned ropes. Ropes come in a variety of colors, and each color is assigned according to the specific duties and responsibilities of the cadets.

First years receive the same color rope as their skills and roles have further defining. Max and Sam receive distinctive purple ropes corresponding to their expertise in technology. Jack is unceremoniously fitted with a green rope, bestowing the responsibility of maintaining their dorm and, more importantly, keeping the twins in check. More or so, to ensure Max is up on time and ready each day. With books in tow, Jack and other first-years take similar courses to ensure consistency in their training.

First-year training is similar to basic training in the military while simultaneously taking courses more specific to each cadet's individual skills as an asset to GYAIA. While the bulk of Jack and the twin's basic training occurs together, Sam and Max's skills in coding and tech fabrication occur within the controlled confines of Professor Brown's lab, affectionately known to cadets as Doc Brown, to his prized pupils Doc Brown's R&D labs are a haven. Jack's aptitude for physical situations, combat, and leadership are tested and schooled, further developing him as a potential asset according to GYAIA's needs.

Courses ranging from geopolitical relationships to wilderness survival test the companions in different ways. Jack struggles to keep up with the density of information, as compared to physical combat training; however, in the scarce quiet moments of their dorm, Sam tutors Jack.

"So you see, Jack, the various tribes that constitute the Feyli tribe of the Diyala Governorate in Iraq or the Chegini tribe of the Fars Province in Iran are all tribes that make up the Kurdish people that still to this day do not have their own sovereignty. Meaning they are not allowed to have their own country, Kurdistan." Sam explains, circling his finger around a map within a rather densely paged book.

"Oh, oh, Sam, tell him about the Reşwan Kurds who mostly populate the Gaziantep, Kahramanmaraş, and Malatya provinces of Turkey and who are also present in the Konya and Ankara provinces of Syria. . .Oh, and don't forget the Qazvin Province in Iran, that milkshake is sure to bring all the girls to the yard! Riveting stuff, let Sam tell yah." Max pipes up from his makeshift workshop hidden in the corner of their dorm.

"Shut it, Max. Jack, listen, Professor Fırat is pretty serious about the suppression of Kurdish people. It's going to be on the final exam. Don't sweat it. I got you."

"Yeah, Jack, just remember Professor Fırat's exam centers around Kurdish independence and the neocolonial efforts of their oppressors whose borders were drawn by the British and French, you know, like, Sykes Picot agreement stuff. Just remember three tribes that you can write about their plights, and you're golden. . ." Max dictates, deflecting sparks from his soldering iron.

Shaking his head, Sam continues tutoring Jack.

"In all functionality, that's true, but Jack the Kurds are a people you should dig deeper than dime store Da Vinci over there. Their independence and sovereignty would signify a paradigm shift away from the thinking of ancient and outdated thought processes, ushering in an era of deeper respect and acceptance for diverging cultures. Kurds are people too, Jack. " Sam quips hotly, settling on a page before continuing Jack's tutoring session.

"I don't understand it all, but I will try." Jack nodding towards Sam.

"You'll get there, Jack. On another note, how's CQC training coming along? Max and I only get the basics, but we noticed you were placed in the advanced CQC course." Sam looks up sheepishly finding his place.

"CQC, it's going okay, I guess. Close quarter combat is rough." Jack tilting his face revealing a fresh cut already encompassed by purple-blue bruising.

"Care to elaborate?" Sam inquires.

"Nothing much to report than Blackshear tossing us around like ragdolls, I mean, I did shoot his legs for a takedown yesterday, but then this is what I got for my troubles." Jack wincing as he sits back on his bed.

"Well, better you than us. They made us go through this obstacle course and Sam almos. . ." Max interjects before Sam cuts him short.

"You mean before I had to pull you over the rope ladder part?" Sam quips, shooting his dubious duplicate with a disapproving look.

"Don't listen to him, Jack. We are improving on the basic obstacles." Sam summarizes.

"Yeah, if finishing last and second ta last over not finishing is considered "improving?" Max gesturing air quotes mockingly.

"Hmm." Jack murmurs to himself, attempting not to escalate the conversation.

"Well, we will have to pick this lecture up tomorrow night, 0400 comes earlier and earlier, guys." Jack motioning his companions towards the miniature bathroom to brush their teeth and get ready for bed.

Days blur into weeks, each day seemingly more intense than the last. Some first years leave or, as Cadet Blackshear refers to, "were recycled". Sam and Max excel in their designated fields, making small gains in their physical training. Jack's training pushes him harder than wrestling ever did. His academic load managed under Sam's watchful eye, finding a few small successes along the way. Days melt away into a multitude of quickly moving minutes. The trio struggle individually to adapt, collectively leaning on each other for support.

"Company halt! Our run resumes in two." Cadet Blackshear jogging briskly to the rear of his company, encouraging Max to pick up his pace.

"He's going harder than usual on Max." Jack quips, removing two fingers from his neck.

"Hff, well heeff, he's the one . . . the one who went into the restricted area of MAD-Sec last night." Sam spits, catching his breath.

"MED-Sec? Do you think Blackshear knows?" Jack inquires, shaking his head.

"Can't confirm, but first years aren't allowed in the lower levels of manufacturing and development, I warned him, but no, he never listens to me. Doesn't help that Doc Brown gave us access, Ur never mind!" Sam straightens his posture as Max jogs by with Blackshear barking orders hovering close behind. "Breaks up firsties, let's move." Cadet Blackshear barks, using Max to push the pace.

"Access to what Sam? Codes to MED-Sec? We definitely gettin latrine duty again." Jack popping Sam on the shoulder, jokingly jogging onward.

"Hey, don't put that into the universe, Jack. I'm serious." Sam sprinting to catch up. The first years complete their morning run, quickly showering and dispersing to their respective classes.

The trio's classes just so happen to head in the same direction, Sam and Jack walking ahead of Max, continuing a conversation on imperial expansion in the late 1800s from the night before. Max simmering in self-pity scribbling sketch device specs in a notebook, resembling a collage of sticky notes and pages of tech ideas.

"Hey, watch where you're walking, you little twerp!" A vicious voice rings out, Max slamming roughly to ground, his notebook spilling its contents. Scrambling to collect its contents, Max grabs desperately at his life's work.

"What do we have here?" A sharp-chinned cadet snatching the notebook, flicking through pages pompously.

"Magnetic fusion properties too unstable for biomorphs? Nanofission unstable? Nerd's too busy to watch where he's going." The sharp-chinned scoundrel scoffs, tossing the tattered notebook to another cadet.

"Hey, give that back, you jerk!" Max lunging past the sharp-chinned scoundrel.

197

"Ooff." Max falls roughly upon unforgiving pavement again, this time tripped by one of the collection of cadets now surrounding him.

"Oops. Did nerd fall down again? Let me help you up!" The sharp-chinned cadet teasing aid, pushing Max down by his face.

"What a dork!" The callous cadet laughing sadistically.

"Just give it back, Jerk." Max whispers faintly, brushing bits of pavement from his hands.

"What was that? Say it again, chump! Get him up." The sharp chinned cadet commands. Many hands, ripping Max from the paved path gripping him tightly.

"You're going to pay for that." Balling his fist tightly driving it deep into Max's midsection, dropping him to his knees.

"Wow, they'll let all kinds of hillbilly trash in these days!" The sharp-chinned scoundrel howls.

"One more that felt gooooo . . . oompf." In a flash, the scoundrel spills roughly onto the paved path.

"Bet that didn't. Piss off or else." Jack now standing between Max and the collection of older cadets. Jack lowering ready to pounce like a panther.

"That stance, where did'ya learn that, gym class?"

The sharped-chinned scoundrel chimes, flicking two fingers for his cronies to cease Jack. Unaware of his skill and experience, the goons rush in foolishly trusting their numerical advantage. Instantly, Jack explodes into the closer crony's leg, kicking the other in the midsection, driving the wind from his frame. Sinking

198

his hips, planting both feet, and thrusting in a twisting motion upward, taking the larger opponent off balance and to the ground with cat-like reflexes. Following the motion with a heavy barrage of elbows, splitting the cadet open. Jack's new training and wrestling background begin merging into one collective calamity.

Rising slowly from his quarry, elbows dripping with fresh fury, Jack stares coldly sending fear into the sharped chinned Cadet. He steps back, snapping his fingers and sending two more cadets cascading from judo flips that are expertly executed.

"No, no! Do you know who I am?" The scoundrel shrieks as Jack fakes a shoot at his near leg, anticipating it to move, catching his firmly planted trail leg. In a flash, Jack feels his torso lift from behind; his armpit hooked flipped roughly to the ground with the force of truck. Limbs tightening around Jack with fury, wrangling consciousness from him.

"Idiot! K got you now! Time for this hick to learn a lesson!" The sharped-chinned cadet rattling off vicious rounds into Jack's midsection, dropping him. Breathing weakly, Jack rises defiantly, quickly a multitude of hands grabbing him roughly from behind. "Lesson time protector of nerds!" The chiseled-chinned cadet spits sinisterly.

"Get off him, you dummies!" Sam running into the fray tugging and kicking at one particularly oversized cadet. Sam's assault lasting only a few strikes. His chubby frame flicked like a flea roughly to the ground.

"Ooff" Sam cries, feeling the searing pain of pavement tearing flesh from forearms.

"What do we have here? Twin nerds? This is too rich, Danzler grab that flabby twerp." The chiseled-chinned scoundrel commanding the oversized cadet. Powerless to aid his companion, Jack watches Sam and Max endure their torment before the group's attention turns back to Jack.

"Enough of these softies. Time for the tough guy here to get his. Hold him tight." Cracking his knuckles, the chiseled-chinned cadet rattling off a flurry of unguarded fists. Smiling sinisterly sighting Jack's solar plexus. Clinching his fist tightly slightly protruding his middle knuckle for maximum menace. An evil grin ripping across his pompous face, throwing his fist back, even with his shoulder.

"Loser!" The chinned scoundrel gloats driving his dastardly destruction hurling at a helpless Jack.

Jack braces, feeling every limb holding him in place squeeze tighter, eliminating any escape. Flexing every muscle possible, Jack winces, willing to accept the beating bestowed on him instead of his friends. Squeezing eyes shut; contorting his face facing his fate, Jack readies himself. Driving hard towards its target, the chiseled-chinned coward thrusts hard and true.

"Wha, ouww! No, don't, ooompf!!!" The chiseled-chinned cadet shrieks, landing roughly a few feet away from where he once stood. With punctual precision, the collection of cronies cascade around Jack. Ferocious blows felling cadets constricting

Jack releasing him hurriedly. Blood that once pumped pompous piety now pumping fear into villainous veins as scoundrels scramble uneasily to their feet, helping their horrendous hero to his feet.

"Ge, get him Childress!" The shrieking chiseled-chinned cadet orders. Standing between Jack, Sam, and Max a familiar frame forms.

"Blackshear???" Sam whispers, catching his breath; a ferocious-looking female steps to the formidable frame of cadet Blackshear.

"Childress? Teach those nerds who I am!" The chiseled cadet commands.

"Your move, Carla." Blackshear beacons, his gaze galvanizing upon the femme fatale before him.

"Hmm. You wouldn't like it, Brian. . ." The villainous vixen scoffs, pressing past her opponent precariously pacing around Blackshear with measured reverence.

"Maybe next time, big boy." Carla purses her bottom lip and biting it suggestively.

"Brush yourself off, get in regulation! Triden, that goes for all ya sniveling wimps. Couldn't finish a bunch of first years. Pff!" The ferocious feline pushing past the chiseled-chinned coward and his disheveled delinquents disapprovingly. Gathering quicker than they assembled, Triden's troop trots off as if nothing ever happened.

Reaching down pulling both biological brothers to their feet with ease, Blackshear turns sharply to assist Jack.

"No, no need, Sir!" Jack waving Blackshear's hand aside.

"I can manage oompff." Jack rises, faltering to one knee, a searing pain shooting through his body.

"My assessment would suggest otherwise, Cadet Murphy." Blackshear's voice low breathing calmly as he pulls Jack to his feet effortlessly.

"Cadets, what were you thinking starting a fight with a group of third years?" Blackshear turns to the twins, assuming their guilt.

"Third years?" Sam begins before Max interjects.

"Sir, Blackshear Sir. We had them right where Jack wanted them. Tell him, Jack." Max projecting confidently, slapping Jack on the back, sending a jolt of pain surging through his body.

"Ahh. Where I what?" Wincing from his wounds Jack steadies himself uneasily.

"Well yeah like you were about to like CQC that crazy bi…" Max interjects before Blackshear cuts him off. "That's enough Cadet Duval. Jack, that group is right there; they are the Untouchables." Blackshear steadying Jack, with an almost brotherly look upon his mature features.

"Untouchables? Sir Blackshear, Sir what do you mean untouchables? You tossed all of them but that ferocious female aside without hesitation." Sam inquires.

"Come, let's take a walk to Sick Bay to get you gentlemen checked out. I'll explain on the way." Blackshear motions, turning sharply, stepping to purpose.

"Hey, wait up, what untouchables? All these unspoken rules. Who are those people, and why is that horrendous hottie so hostile?" Max sprinting off after Blackshear. "Com'n, Jack, got a feeling today's lesson in hierarchy will well worth a listen." Sam strides off, leaving Jack to gather himself.

"Yeah, catch up in a sec. Ugh. . ." Jack wincing weakly at his initial steps.

"Aunt Anna, where did you send me?" He whispers.

Slowing his pace, Blackshear, allowing Max, Sam, and Jack to catch up.

"So these untouchables, are they like royalty or something?" Sam inquires.

"Yeah, like President's kids or something?" Max parroting Sam. "President's no. A Senator, yes!" Blackshear answers, peeking over his shoulder, surveying Jack's status.

"A Senator, which one, the big ugly joker?" Max quips.

"Not exactly, the mouthy one, Triden. As in Senator Triden's son, his pride and joy." Blackshear slowing his pace to a brisk trot.

"The Triden that spoke at the Geneva conference last year Triden?" Sam's face growing faint, losing color rapidly.

"Yes, that Triden, potential President of the free world, Triden."

"So I was right, a President's kid." Max interjects.

"Well, not technically, but cadet Triden's father is one of the most influential and well-connected politicians in the country, possibly the world. You'd do well to steer clear of him. Hear me. That goes for all of you. Especially you, Jack." Blackshear slowing his pace even with a still wincing Jack.

"Stay away from the rich jerkoff, got it." Jack saluting gingerly.

"I mean it. That whole group is connected to some of the top former agents, current agents, or politicians within GAIA and this country. Think of GYAIA as an incubator of future operators and assets." Blackshear's tone solemn.

"Gotcha, Sir. I mean Sir, yes, Sir." Sam attempting to ease the growing tension.

"So, who's that foxy female that almost ripped Jack's head off?" Max asks, murdering Sam's attempt at diplomacy.

"Max, you idiot!" Sam starts as his maniac multiple receives his answer.

"Stand down Sam, no need for formalities; we are only a klick from sick bay. It's ok, C, she's complicated, to say the least." Blackshear breaking character briefly.

"So this C, let me guess she's a former "friend" of yours?" Jack ask implying a romantic relationship.

"Hmm, intuitive aren't you, Jack?" Blackshear shoots Jack a noncommittal nod to stand down.

"So she's not a former girlfriend, but what's with her then?" Jack noticing Blackshear's nonverbal gesture not to alert the twins.

"She's from, how you say, GAIA royalty, both parents' distinguished operatives that sacrificed everything for this country." Blackshear bolting to the lead of the pack.

"So, so you're saying she's like second generation spy?" Max inquires, inhaling heavily.

"No. She's fifth generation. Her family dates back to the Civil War. At least, that's what the records say. Honestly, agent Childress' lineage probably dates back further. Can't be sure. Those records have been sealed for over a hundred years. Point is, Agent Childress is a certified killer, and she's only a second year!" Blackshear says.

"So what you're saying, Sir, is that these older cadets can do as they please and us regulars have to do what? Tough it out?" Sam asks half rhetorically.

"They didn't do as they pleased just a minute ago, cadet Duval." Blackshear retorts respectfully.

"Yeah, well, not all of us are big as hell . . . um, Sir." Max interrupts confidence eroding quickly from a disapproving glare from the gentile giant.

"Back to that, Blackshear, why did cadet Childress back down if she is a trained killer?" Jack adding to the inquiry.

"Childress and I have an understanding of sorts." Blackshear says.

"So Jack was right, former lovers had a falling out, and bound by duty, but secretly longing for each other's affections." Max prods.

"Believe what you want, Gentlemen, that's not it. Our parents have known each other for many years, and so naturally, we knew each other before GYAIA. Regarding romance, that girl does not have a romantic bone in her body. Let her hear you talking like that, and she'd gladly break every bone in yours." An uncharacteristically devilish grin flashes across Blackshear's strong facial features.

"Bre, break all of them. There's over two hundred bones in the human body." Max trembles through his defense, looking nervously over each shoulder.

"Even the little ones." Jack jests, brushing past the terrified twin, having recovered some from his wounds.

"Distinguished, Cadet Blackshear!" A voice from a distance shouts. Making a hard a-bout, Blackshear turns, addressing the voice.

"Yes, cadet Clemons, at ease." Blackshear planting his feet firmly. The young cadet approaching the capacious cadet, whispering something to Blackshear. "Yes, I understand. I'm escorting these first years to sick bay, and I'll be there pronto." With a swift exchange of salutes, the young cadet wheels off to his purpose, leaving Jack and company wildly interested in this new development.

"Ooo, juicy news, let's hear it, Sir, Blackshear, Sir." Max moaning through troubled breathes.

"It's nothing, routine security breach exercise I'm late for." Blackshear turns, bolting back in the direction of the sickbay.

"What's with this guy?" Max meandering forward. The quartet quickly cover the ground in the wake of Blackshear's pace.

"Hy, Hey, now this interrogation isn't over, Blackshear, com'back. Wa, wa, why's he so fast? Com'back." Max spits, sprinting onward pathetically. Jack and Sam sprinting on spiritedly after their enigmatic elder.

"Oh, com'n, guys, not you too!" Max pants panting more pathetically than before. Jack is the first to break stride with Blackshear, who has mercifully slowed his pace. To Jack's surprise, Sam surges ahead of him.

"So Blackshear, as you were saying, the others, are they from some ancient Knights Templar secret lineage as well?" Sam redirects back to the earlier conversation.

"No, their parents are mostly former agents, but they simply ride Triden's coat tale for the most part. A rather useless lot, outside Childress and Danzler. Avoid him, too, Gents. That one's Father is one of the dirtiest active agents in the field." Blackshear resuming the lead ahead of Sam and Jack.

"Yeah, yeah, I remember the name. He was the one Wiley had dumped me off in the middle of nowhere, nice dude." Jack sucking wind to match Blackshear's pace.

"One and the same, steer clear, Danzler is well connected, and his lummox of a son will have those same connections as well. Avoid when possible." Blackshear bolts further ahead of Jack. "Triden, Childress, and Danzler are untouchables, got it!" Jack jolting even with Blackshear, both bolstering each other's energy.

"Hey, hey, now, not so fast!" Max huffs, lagging behind the herd.

"Look alive Gents, sick bay is just around the corner; let me do all the talking." Blackshear orders, slowing his stride.

"Now that's . . . hey now…" Max begins.

"Shh, say nothing, Brother. Blackshear's got us." Sam pressing his hand heartily into Max.

"Blackshear, Sir. . . ." Jack begins.

"Murphy, from here on out, if you address me individually, it's Brian." Blackshear whispers so only Jack can hear.

"But not in front of the Duval's, understand Cadet?" Blackshear bluffing a sense of authority.

Jack nods understanding the directive from his superior. "Yes, Sir. 0400 it is, Sir?" Jack covers, averting any suspicion.

"Sam, Max we check in here." Jack directing the duplicate duo.

"Sick bay eh? More like ooff!" Max begins before receiving a stiff smack from Sam.

"Shut it, Max, thank you, Sir." Sam nods respectfully in Blackshear's direction.

"Com'n, guys." Jack presses. Blackshear enters, speaking to the attendant in hushed tones. Nodding receptively waving the trio for further inspection.

"Jack, Nurse Jess' got you. Anything you need just ask. She's solid." Blackshear nods assuredly, sprinting off swiftly. Jack, absorbing his words, motions for Sam and Max to follow. "Com'n Gentleman, "I'll inform your third-period professors of your tardiness if you get this over with quickly. Check that to 0500 moving forward!" Blackshear, excusing himself, jostling a bewildered Jack forward. Jack and Sam's injuries are quickly diagnosed and treated due to their compliance. Max, on the other hand, requires much more manipulation.

"Wait; don't take that, I . . .!" Max moves manically, avoiding the attending nurse's advances. "Cadet Duval can't help you if you won't sit still!" Nurse Jess jerking Max's arm closer to administer her nurse's needle.

"Whydu need to take blood? I just fell down? Promise all I did was lose my footing, oh this; just a flesh wound. Concussion? No concussion, no, NO, MADAM!"

Sitting silently Sam shifts nervously, waiting for Max.

"How much longer, com'n, Jack." Sam scratching nervously.

"Never mind him, Sam. You know he's just being difficult." Jack jolting Sam back into reality.

"I suppose you're right, Jack. Well, you recovered quickly. You took quite a, a. . ." Sam begins before Jack cuts him off quickly.

209

"No worries, I've had worse. Say, Sam, that cadet approached Br, Blackshear earlier." Jack begins rubbing the worn keychain, which is dangling from his pocket.

"Yeah, that was odd, Jack. What is it?" Sam inquires.

"Well, can't know for sure, but I swear that cadet told Blackshear something about a security breach, but Blackshear played it off like nothing." Jack presses.

"I heard security breach too. Sounded serious. Jack, in a place like this a security breach is highly improbable. Unless. . ." Sam pauses thinking deeply as he often does. "Unless, Sam unless what?" Jack inquires.

"Well, wow, ok, Max, it's ok. Everything's ok!"

"Ok, okay, Max, it's all good. All done. Nurse?" Jack gestures towards Jess.

"He'll be ok, just took a sample to test for any changes in his microbial, he's all yours." Nurse Jess jests.

"Sorry, Mrs. Jessica, but we're late for third period." Sam shuffles, absorbing Max's weight.

"Tee, he. Nurse Jess will do." The nurturing nurse chuckles softly at her new patients.

"Nurse Jess it is. Thank you, Nurse Jess, thank you." Jack covering for Sam and Max's hasty escape.

"Cadet Murphy! I know who you are." Nurse Jessie standing stoically, eyes shifting to the trinket hanging from his pocket.

"I knew agent Anzalone or, as you know her as, Aunt Anna." Stepping back a few paces, a stunned Jack, struggling to absorb her words.

"Y, you, you knew Aunt Anna?" Jack stutters.

"Yes, Jack . . . cadet Murphy, she was a wonderful agent . . . until the acc. . ." Resuming her normal softly stoic self, memories of a long-lived life altering her aura.

"Ma, ma'am, Ma'am, Anzalone? You knew my Aunt Anna, how did . . . how did you know her? What does she have to do with GYAIA? Tell me . . . please?" Jack's shoulders sinking, shaking his head, fighting off emotions of home.

"Please?"

Pausing for the briefest moments, the nurturing nurse knows she has already said too much.

"I'm sorry, Cadet Murphy, but I mustn't. Please understand; your friends are waiting . . . now is not the time to dwell on the past." Stepping swiftly past the young cadet, avoiding eye contact.

His mind racing rapidly, thoughts flooding his immense imagination, searching for answers unknown. Jack opens the door, stepping outside of sickbay, when a weakened whisper breaks the silence hanging heavily in the room behind him.

"Snff Jack, she'd be so proud of you, snff, you've grown so much. Never stop growing. . ." Nurse Jess' voice cracking retreating into the silence.

211

"She? She who?" Jack's inquiry met with continued silence. Sighing silently to himself, Jack exits, leaving her to the solidarity of her singular silence.

"Hey, Jack! If we hurry, we can still make well before third ends!" Max shouts from a distance.

"Com'n, Jack, whatever it is, we'll talk later. Max's right, we got to hurry." Sam resting his hand gently on Jack's shoulder before sauntering off himself.

CHAPTER TWENTY

THE SILENCE OF SHADOWS

The trio makes it to their next class without incident. "Just in time per usual, Cadet Duval." Professor Crane says.

"Oh, both Duvals and Cadet Murphy? A most glorious day this is!" The tall, lanky professor postures ushering the companions inward, pulling the door roughly behind.

"The front, of course, the front." Max kicking the neatly tiled floor, making his way to the front of the class.

"The front it is, Gentlemen, have a seat. We have lots to discuss this lesson."

"Now, class, please retrieve your required reading Tzu's *Art of War,* and your notetaking materials." The course sound of chalk dragging across the milky blackboard sending shivers down the spines of all in attendance. The scrawny Scribe scribbles speedily a collection of scrambled thoughts. Turning swiftly to face his captive audience, wielding the shortened writing utensil as if a sword striking the heart of ignorance.

"Now, class, as mentioned before, first years begin at the end of Sun Tzu's most cherished work. I expect that all have studied and memorized the thirteenth chapter." The lanky professor's eyes darting across the room, seeking his first victim.

213

"Now, who can tell me the essential lesson within the sixth paragraph?" Pointing the calk wildly seeking the inquiry's victim, purposely avoiding the outstretched hands of the twins.

"No, no boys, somebody else, no need for false echoes this time. Aw, Cadet Murphy!"

"Cadet Murphy, recall the sixth paragraph for the benefit of the class if you can?"

"The sixth para . . . paragraph refers to the use of" Jack stutters cut off abruptly by the arrogant academic.

"As I thought, too busy getting into fights to have studied, cadets lacking lineage rarely make it past their first semester!" The angular antagonist scoffs.

Looking up from his dejection, Sam mouthing, "you got this" sending a surge of confidence throughout his being.

"Mr. Duval, I do not believe you were called upon!" Professor Crane glares ghoulishly in Sam's direction.

"The inquiry was directed . . ."

"Knowledge!" The arrogant academic turning swiftly addressing the voice breaking over his own.

"Knowledge of the enemy's dispositions can only be obtained from other men." The voice asserts, reciting the literature perfectly.

"Profe, professor Wiley. What a most distinguished pleasure this is, may, may I?" Studding arrogance evaporating from Crane's now flush face, offering his podium.

214

"Gratitude Professor Crane, but that won't be necessary! Ah, Cadet Murphy, may I speak with you a moment?"

"But, but, of course, Professor Wiley, Sir, Cadet Murphy, you are excused." Crane scrambling to reassure command of his class.

"Bring your effects, Cadet." Wiley waltzing out without another word. Grabbing his pack, Jack nods at Sam, mouthing quietly his gratitude before heading out swiftly.

Shutting the door behind him, Jack's eyes locate Wiley limping spryly down decorated halls, murals of mythical heroes clashing with terrifying beasts rising into high ceilings above. Sprinting when a shooting pain from his earlier encounter slows him to a brisk walk.

"Skirmishes like that always catch up to you, Jack." Wiley's voice echoes wisely.

"Yes, Sir, but Triden and his goons were," Jack begins, stopping sheepishly under Wiley's piercing peek over the shoulder.

"Jack GYAIA is an incredible opportunity for you to be something more than the boy from nowhere, seek its advantages, but learn to know when a strategic retreat serves the cause more than a glorious demise." The still mysterious mentor muses, pausing to admire a terrifying image of a large ferocious wolf standing ahead of his pack defiantly before Zeus himself.

"Yes, Sir, I understand. What's the story here?" Jack inquires standing next to Wiley, shuttering at the sounds of howling wolves calling in Jack's imagination.

"Hmm, another time maybe, I prefer the Norse version. Jack, I have been informed that Cadet Blackshear informed you to avoid Cadet Triden and his group when absolutely possible. Is that understood?"

"Yes, yes, Sir, but they started it. They were targeting Sam and Max, Sir." Jack complies, voicing his concerns.

"Yes, that, which has been addressed. However, the Triden name is well connected, and I feel the forces surrounding that particular individual are greater than your fledgling career here at GYAIA, which is capable of mediating further entanglement." Wiley halting his pace, anticipating Jack's response.

"Yes, Sir, but what do I do when they find the twins again? Stand by as they attack them again. What does that scumbag have against Sam and Max?" Jack protests.

"Simple Jack, young Triden prides himself on being the smartest guy in the room and envies the twin's gifts. When they are ready, they may be GYAIA and GAIA's greatest non-field assets. However, Jack, the Twins have their own journey, and you will not be there to protect them from every bully, like your friends back home. As for your new companions, they must also learn our ways, especially the mouthy one, Max. Now, no more about the Twins. I have a request of you, Jack."

"Yes, Sir, but what do I do if they attack again?" Jack insists.

"Jack, remember the Old Man and Sea?" Wiley replies.

"Mostly, Yes, Sir, I do." The young protégé responds, following his mentor.

"In the end, the old man knew that the sharks would take his catch; he had no choice, but Jack, you have a choice, and you're the catch, Jack. The sharks will strike, tearing away pieces of you until there is nothing of value left. Triden, Crane, and all others are nothing more than such. Treat them as such and nothing more. Your character and perseverance are what you have, traits the Triden's of this world do not. They have never needed those traits to be where they are. As for the twins, I will speak with Madam Director this afternoon about the matter. You disapprove?" Wiley pauses, rubbing his leg and kicking sensation back into the long wounded limb.

"No, Sir, I understand. That limp is pretty noticeable. Why not get a cane?" Jack inquires.

"An ancient injury, I assure you, Jack, but I am not that old. I can move when the moment calls for it." Wiley jumps suddenly stumbling under his weight.

"Whoa, easy there Sir!" Jack, jumping into action, catching his mentor, securing his balance.

"Maybe you are right. These old legs don't move like they once did."

"Har, har, enough jokes, Jack, the request." Wiley wincing as he does.

"Yes, Sir, the request?" Jack adjusting his pack taking a step from the cavalier coach.

"Yes, the request, Jack this must strictly be between you and me. There is to be an attack on GYAIA, but not in the traditional sense, a cyber-attack of sorts. I feel that Max will be blamed." Wiley steadying himself.

"Max?" an astonished Jack takes another step back.

"Yes, he's the perfect scapegoat, are you familiar with this term?" Wiley whispers catching his breath weakly.

"Yes. Max, but why Max?" Jack presses.

"Shh, yes, Max, he's the perfect scapegoat. There has been a series of security breaches in research and development. Max has been sneaking off and tinkering in R&D. Professor Brown has undoubtedly aided in these excursions. I am afraid he is well-intentioned with the twins. Now, Jack I have seen the footage. Max has taken an interest in the Seteria prototype, an anti-gravity aircraft, which has only wasted GAIA's resources to this point. However, while he has the intellect to make that waste of space useful, someone else has accessed R&D's mainframe searching through said mainframe for encrypted files." Wiley pauses, rubbing his leg.

"Max, encrypted files? Sam?" Jack's eyes rivet from wall to wall.

"Yes, Sam is the encryption genius of the pair; I fear that they both will be implicated. . ." Now standing strongly under his own power, Wiley ridged in his intent.

"But, Sam and I are rarely. . ." Jack begins as Wiley continues.

"Yes, Agent Duval, Sam. While he has the skill, he does not yet possess the tact to execute such an operation." Wiley stepping gingerly forward.

218

"Tact? Wiley, what are you asking me to do?" Jack steps closer concernedly.

"Nothing, I am asking you to do nothing. Whoever is behind this breach will present themselves if you don't get involved." Wiley stepping a few paces ahead.

"Do nothing? I can't, I won't, and I don't understand Mr. Wiley?" A perplexed Jack inquires.

"Jack, there are forces at work far beyond your understanding. I need you not to get involved." Wiley insists, shuffling forward.

"But why? I'm a first year. Why does my involvement matter so much?" Jack presses.

"Jack, your particular skill is not tuned to being, as we say covert. To reveal this threat prematurely will reveal only the symptom, not the cause. Jack, I need . . . we need you to stay in the shadows on this one."

"Stay in the shadows, Sir? I don't understand." A curious look caressing the his face.

"Yes, Jack; allow the *divine manipulation of the threads* do their work." Wiley pivots, securing his surroundings. "Jack, you still have that copy of *Art of War,* correct?"

"Yes, Sir. I do." Jack answers.

"Good, study it, especially the thirteenth chapter. Crane will not let up on you until you have committed it to memory and action. Understand?" Wiley leans close affirming his point.

"Yes, Sir. It will be done." Jack leans to peek over Wiley's shoulder as the sound of footsteps grows in the distance.

"Good, Jack, we haven't much time in the shadows. One last thought: outside of myself, the twins, and Cadet Blackshear, trust no one. No one, Jack. No further questions, study, train, and keep to the shadows. You have five minutes till your next class; do not be late." Wiley stepping past his young protégé, placing a reassuring hand on Jack's shoulder before whisking himself out of sight.

Like few times in his life, Jack stands alone, unsure of his next step. The events of the day weighing heavier than each step, like many times before, his mind filling with unconcluded thoughts.

"Yes, Sir. I don't understand, but I will try. I will try." Jack whispers to himself, heading off to his combat skills course.

CHAPTER TWENTY ONE

THE SOUNDS OF SILENCE

Peering cautiously around every corner, Jack makes his way to the locker room to change for combat skills. Stepping softly upon cool tile, slipping past undetected to his locker changing quickly storing his pack as the bell blares, sending many pupils hectically hurrying through halls. Cadets from the previous period populating the locker room, showering and changing frantically making their way to individual destinations. Avoiding detection, Jack opens his locker, feigning exploration until the numbers reduce. His eyes cutting back and forth nervously, attempting to conceal his premature presence.

The Dojo's floor contains a large raised central platform for sparing, surrounded by various training weapons lining the walls. Hanging high above the space, semi-dim lights focusing upon the platform below. The smell of wood and wax settling the senses as a few straggling cadets sprint into formation. Taking his place in line, Jack and fellow cadets stand at attention awaiting orders.

"Cadet Murvhy!" A booming voice breaking over the commotion, sending a shiver down Jack's spine.

"Cadet Murvhy, early bird doesn't always get vorm!" A thick Russian accent booms.

"Cadet Murvhy, we have vords." Motioning Jack closer to the hulking figure.

"Ye, Yes Professor Volkov?" Jack strides forward sheepishly.

"Vhy cadet Murvhy early bird today?" The immense instructor inquires, eyes darting around his dojo of destruction.

"I, Sir, I was speaking to . . . speaking to my dorm mates about yesterday's lesson, and I apologize for my lack of execution in counterstriking. Won't happen again, Sir." Jack mutters, searching the hardwood floor foolishly.

"Counter striking not problem vor cadet, Cadet Murvhy has too many minds in moment." The burly brute bellows deeply.

"Cadet Murvhy must learn to valk before learn to run. Cadet Murvhy, running from past. No good, no run from past, embrace present, fight in present. Har har!" The burly brute raps Jack roughly on the back affirming his point before stomping off. Catching his breath, a bewildered Jack returning to his position in line, perplexed at the exchange.

The training session proves surprisingly fruitful for Jack. Under Professor Volkov's tutelage, Jack bests many of his contemporaries, some with equally surprising ease.

"Yes, Cadet Vurphy, vinish him, vinish No Mercy! Enemy deserves no mercy! Vithout torture, no science. Good! Blood good!" The burly brute instructing his pupil to pummel further.

"Good, blood dries. Victory not vhipped away so easily! Good, is all for today, tomorrow we vearn to take weapon vrom opponent!" As directed, a disarray of clobbered cadets scramble to their feet, escaping quickly to their lockers, showering and changing swiftly, making their way to their next destination.

Pressing against the unforgiving wooden floor Jack rises gingerly. Panting roughly, Jack hustles off when a forceful hand grips his shoulder halting any further progress.

"Cadet Murvhy, we have vords." The gargantuan grip releasing, revealing a softer tone foreign to the burly brute. Turning to face his immense instructor, Jack settles his feet.

"Yes Professor Volkov?" The diminutive dynamo responses.

"Cadet Murvhy learn fast. Cadet go far as cadet vant. Volkov knows secrets when secrets silent. Vothing as vurdensome as secret. Volkov keep cadet's secret safe." The burly brute placing a heavy hand on Jack's shoulder, saying nothing further. A smirk sears across the Russian rhino's stern features as he walks away.

Perplexed, Jack stands, wiping sweat from his brow.

"Secret silent? Keep secret safe? Divine manipulation of threads? Can't remember a paragraph, but can toss around second years in combat skills, no problem? What's going on, Jack?"

"Maybe Sam can make sense of all this." Jack shaking feeling into his sore shoulder before heading off.

"Think Jack, next class is PT, damn. Professor Bray gonna kill us if we're late. Combat skills then physical training, who the frick made this schedule?" Jack murmurs.

Navigating the bustling halls, Jack makes his way to his destination.

"Jack! Wait up, Jack, com'n, bro! Outta the way, red stripe!" Max' voice ringing over the crowd.

"Jack, what the heck, dude?"

"Crane starts in on you, and then Wiley appears, and you disappear?" Max inquires.

"Shut it, Max. What this idiot means is we will talk later. Professor Bray was very clear that today's PT would be ridiculous, gotta hurry." Sam surmises, pressing past them both.

"Jack, what's going on?" Max maneuvering himself between a cache of cadets, making his way to Jack and Sam.

"Max, PT now, Jack's situation later. Don't you have R&D anyways?" Sam says, pointing in the opposite direction.

"Oh yeah, they switched my schedule. I'm in Bray's with you guys now!" Max shifting into position, pushing a path toward their collective purpose. "Com'n, we can make it!" Max bellows, continuing to push a path for his companions through the crowded space.

"Com'n Sam!" Jack pushing past passing pupils, propelling Sam forward.

"Hey, not so rough, Jack. I need that arm!" Sam squeals. The trio trudge through the teaming masses. "Almost there, Sam, where? Oh, there you are, Jack, is it always, Ooofff!" Max maneuvers himself into the dense Danzler.

"Watch it, nerd, if Father was here, I'd, I'd!" The dimwitted dunce begins cut off sharply by the chiseled-chinned cadet himself.

224

"Well, well, well if isn't! Hey watch it!" Triden begins before Jack brushes past him swiftly down the hall.

"Sorry, didn't see you there Triden, not good to see yah, gotta go!" Jack jests, jolting Sam past the frenzy of fiends.

"Jack, that's the . . .!" Max pausing his progress, allowing Sam and Jack to catch up.

"Jerk, yes, let's go. No, Max, let's keep moving. Can't be late to Professor Brays." Jack grabbing both, tugging them forward.

"Jack, why, we could!" Max protests.

"Nope, can't do anything to them now, yup, yes and we're moving!" Jack willing his companions through a side door into a surprisingly empty narrow hallway.

Pausing for a second, Jack's eyes dart around the narrow hallway, noting the change in style of tile and greyish stone walls. Gaining his bearings, Jack steps tapping tile with his boot, listening carefully for a hollowing sound. "Ah there you are." He sighs silently, pressing a loose cool stone that rockets out of sight sending a clicking sound reverberating behind hollow walls. "Com'n?" Jack nods entering the dark slender passage. Max unimpressed by this secret passage, continues his earlier argument.

"Just sayin' Jack, ole she-beast wasn't with Trundlehead. You could've taken Danzilurch out by yourself, and it would have been three-on-one?" Max protests, ripping himself free of Jack's grip.

"Yeah, and then what, Max? Have a US Senator wondering why GYAIA allowed his only son to get beat up in the hallway by some common stick hicks?" Jack says, slapping Max's hand effortlessly.

"I'm no common stick hick Jack?" Max replies, swiping air.

"Don't be dull Max. What Jack is trying to say is Triden isn't it, and besides, what would we do? Slap him into submission?" Sam surmises, mocking Max's awkward fighting stance.

"Hey now, slinking scarab is a legitimate stance. Ask anyone!" Max scoffing as he stomps off. "Let's go, we're gonna be late." Jack flicking his finger under Max's still-present abdominal girth.

"Hey, stop that, Jack, not the piggly wiggly!" Max stepping back before following his companions.

"Com'n, last class of the day, gentleman." Jack motioning his companions forward into a small hall closet.

"Snff, snff! Where are we, Jack?" Sam inquires as the trio squeeze into the limited space, dust wafting gently underfoot.

"Short-cut, was doing some reading in the library when I came across the original blueprints of this place. You guys wouldn't imagine how many secret passages that go to practically wherever you'd like." Jack lowers his voice, pressing firmly against a hard aged wooden panel, revealing a small opening. Smiling, he steps into the dim light, fresh air mixing with the passage's stale musk.

"Jack, when do you have time to spelunk?" Sam perplexed by Jack's boldness.

226

"Sam, don't get mad, but I may have accidentally told Ma . . . x" Jack begins, before Max cuts him off.

"Hey now, Jack, you said it was our little!" Max interrupts, looking sheepishly at his brother exiting the passage.

"Little what? Secret? Jack, spill it!" Sam protests.

"It's quite simple, really. Max has been sneaking out after lights out." Jack begins with Max shaking his head behind the pair.

"I followed Max one night sneaking into R&D, and we barely got back to the dorm before Blackshear caught us." Jack explains, checking his notes intermittently.

"And that's it; the both of you are now keeping secrets from me?" Sam protesting the notion stops to lean against clean sandstone walls.

"Yes, Sam, look, Max can't help himself. He's a troublemaker." Jack doubling back to shut the passage door, addressing his hurt companion along the way.

"So what let him get in trouble? We are supposed to be!" Sam turning to break eye contact with Jack.

"Sam, you're such a hard sleeper, and this joker just disappears. Come on, we're gonna make it." Jack pats Sam's shoulder softly.

"Oh poo, let him sulk, Jack. He's always following the rules; look this place is stuffy and boring outside of Doc Brown's and getting beat up by that turd Triden. What is it, Bro? D'ya feel left out?" Max jokingly jostling Jack's shoulder, seeking approval.

"And if I did?" Sam replies.

"Well, then, just come with us silly; be like old times when we'd break into Pop's toolshed." Max smiles nervously.

"Yeah, just like old times. Always getting me into trouble. Max, did ya ever think that maybe some people actually want to be here? That some of us kinda like all this?" Sam's tone trailing off, anticipating Max's ridicule.

"Look, Sam, I didn't know. I mean, you have been doing much better in PT than me and all." Max mirroring his multiple's tone.

"Hey, Sam, we have like a minute to get to class. We will talk about this again at the dorm, tell ya everything, promise! Right Max? Besides, neither of you said anything about Professor Brown's access codes, now, did ya?" Jack gesturing for Max to respond appropriately.

"Yeah, oww, sure, everything. Stop that, Jack. How'didya know bout that?" Max slapping Jack's hand away from his midsection.

"It's settled then. Follow me, out this door, take a slight right and a quick left." Jack jolting off, waving his companions onward.

"Darn, Max, ya blabbermouth, you I expect, but dragging Jack into your shenanigans." Sam sniffs, pressing past his brother disapprovingly.

"Oh yeah, Max sneaks off to a restricted area and I'm the bad guy, sheesh, Sam. Sam, wait up, you wouldn't believe all the cool stuff down there!" Max muses, sprinting off to catch up.

228

The trio place distance between themselves and the secret passage, entering a small passage into an office space connecting two classrooms and slip into the regimentally arranged class, taking seats apart from each, careful not to draw attention to themselves. Professor Bray's physical training class passes without incident. Sam continues to show strides, Jack finishing in his usual effortless manner, as Max continues to struggle through the various physical elements of the class.

"Well, that was uneventful!" Max huffs.

"Sure, whatever, Max. Jack, we got R&D now, yeah they added PT for us. We still got to go to Doc's now. Busy busy. Catch up to you at mess. Why don't you go to the library and look into MEC specs if you can? Here, take this." Sam pushing a device into Jack's pocket.

"What's this?" Jack digging it deep into his pocket feeling Aunt Anna's trinket as he does.

"It's, well for the most part. It's a phone, Jack. Use the camera to, you know, "study" something." Sam nodding suggestively, pressing Max in the direction of Doc Brown's lab.

Jack returning a suggestive nod the trio exchanging a quick salute quickly making their way to their respective places. Jack making his way to the library wandering the robust array of resources. The immense library of literacies line each wall, packed with bookcases reaching towards the ceiling with knowledge carefully collected from every corner of the world. Jack wanders trying to gain a sense of direction.

"Ok, if I was MEC specs, where would I be?" Jack whispering to himself tapping his forehead.

"They must have a Dewey, oh, here we go." Finding a rolodex reminding him of all the hours after school, Jack would help Aunt Anna categorize books back into their proper places.

"Hmm, natural sciences . . . no, that's not it, think Jack. Oh, here we go, gotta be applied sciences right?" Jack hums quietly to himself finding his groove.

"M, mechanical, gettin close, oh here we go MEC specs. Wow Sam, not exactly specific about what to look for. There's a zillion things here." Jack thumbing through the thick throng mechanical specifications in GYAIA's sphere of interests.

"Ok, think, Jack, think."

"Think like Sam, what would someone find high priority?" Jack jammed up with information, flicking through the robust rolodex.

"Wish you were here, Sam. You'd know what to look for." Squinting closely at the various references of resources Jack's mind spins.

"I don't know what a MRSs or MEC HAs are, come on think, think." Thumbing nervously.

"Looking for something in particular cadet Murphy?" A velvety voice rings out from behind the young cadet, stunning him in place.

"Stop that, Max, we're almost there. Quit it, will yah?" For once, act like the genius that you are . . ." Sam protests, slapping Max's wandering hands.

"Ah, gentlemen, you've finally arrived! Always shuffling schedules, shuffling schedules around here. Come quick got something to show, something to show. Now, where did my spectacles run off to?" A manic man patting his white lab coat pocket ushering Sam and Max through a pair of heavy doors left ajar.

"G'afternoon Doc." Sam smiling, fending off one last attempt from Max.

"Yes, yes, good afternoon, gentlemen, good afternoon. Hurry, hurry, so little to learn, so much time."

"Well, scramble my grits, no, no, that's not right! Doesn't matter who doesn't like eggs? Come, come." The maestro of maniacs musing his multiples to join the others, starting class promptly.

Surrounded by a ridiculous amount of technology, Sam and Max are in heaven. While Doc Brown typically starts a lesson sanctioned by GYAIA, most classes quickly evolve into him manically meandering between stations of students tinkering with various tech.

"Good, Max, good now, reverse the polarity. Be careful now, careful now. Remember to keep our charges balanced. Mustn't recreate our happy little accident from last week. Good, good!"

231

Doc Brown clasping Max around his shoulders, eager to observe the results.

"Excellent, now carefully increase charge ratios. *Rather elementary if you know what you are looking at.* Excellent, you've successfully executed vertical thrust, now, can you figure out forward locomotion?" Doc Brown claps Max gently, congratulating him on his progress before meandering off.

"No, it's not a functionality error. Come on, Sam, check for control flow errors. Nah, looks correct. Syntactics look good. Where did I go wrong?" Sam wearing out a worn keyboard, pecking purposefully.

"Tinkering with your A.I. master program, I see cadet Duval. Tricky for even fourth years, very tricky those race conditions are." The manic maestro muses, tapping the screen, averting Sam's attention to his solution.

"Hold on a sec, wait, what? That's not . . . how did you know Doc?" Sam inquires suspiciously.

"Well, you know, when I was developing B.E.S.T.Y, she kept having race condition errors. Just plum forgot to let the old girl rewrite new data over the old. Simple fix here, Sam, let's check your calculations while we're at it."

"Aw, here we go, here we go, see there, Sam. Your calculations were telling us to only receive information but not synthesize the present with previous inputs. Simple fix, simple fix. Hold tight, I know it's here somewhere!" The manic maestro stepping away momentarily, riffling through papers in an antique desk. A bewildered Sam, observing his professor's panic-stricken self.

"What is it, Doc?" Sam inquires.

"Not here, not here! Well, cook my goose, must've left it in my office. Be right back, right back. Sam, check for data mismatches. I'll return, yes I'll return." Shuffling off swiftly, Doc Brown leaving Sam thoroughly perplexed.

"Data mismatches? I thought they were condition errors?" Sam sits patiently perplexed, picking up where he left off. Minutes melt away in Doc Brown's absence, leaving Sam to his work. Combing his codes, Sam forgetting his panic-stricken patron.

"Oh no, cadet Gosling its JavaScript, YES JS baby, JS the object-oriented pro lang! You're not creating an Einstein-Rosen bridge! Yes, like that. It's good to keep at it. Be back in a sec, in a sec." The manic maestro strides purposely back to Sam's side.

"Apologies, cadet Murphy, nepo-babies. Nepos everywhere." Doc shakes his head disapprovingly, producing an old tattered notebook. He looks over his shoulder and observes the opulence of obscurity beyond Max and himself.

"Doc, Doc Brown!" Sam snapping his finger, regaining the nutty professor's attention.

"Oh, Duval, are you still here? Third session was over hours ago." The peculiar professor pacing purposelessly.

"Um, Max and I got switched to, never mind. Doc, you left to retrieve something. What was it?" Sam presses, knowing the period is about over.

233

"Um, yes, yes, my notes. Yes, notes. Here, Sam, take these. Missing something, missing something, but they're all here." The manic maestro, pressing the tattered notebook into Sam's lap.

"Take care of them, care of them. Yes, in your pack, in your pack." Doc Brown signaling Sam nervously, eyes darting anxiously.

"Ok, okay. Got it. What are these, Doc?" Sam presses.

"No time, time is not. Sam, my secrets. Secrets not safe." Doc assisting Sam, cramming the notebook deep into his already opened pack.

"Alright, Doc, it's in there. Sheesh! Max, we gotta go!" Sam shouting as he does.

"Shhh. Other cadet Duval mustn't know, mustn't know. Here, take this too."

"Duval, secrets. They deal in secrets. Study them, know them, and trust them."

"I don't understand, Doc. Why can't Max know?" Sam inquires, pulling both straps, shouldering the pack's weight.

"Know, Max, no. No, that's not right, Max . . ." The panicking professor starts silencing himself as Max nears.

"Know what, Doc?" Max interrupts, eyes evaluating the precarious pair. "Nothing, Max, Doc Brown was just encouraging me not to give up on my A.I. program. Have lots to go before I can get the bugs worked out. Isn't that right, Doc?" Covering for his panicked professor.

234

"Um, yes lots to go, must go now, yes, lots to go before E.V.E. is ready. Yes, E.V.E. good name, cadet Duval. Good name, yes." Doc, breaking eye contact, nervously looks over the pair's shoulders.

"Ahh, I know what's going on here!" Max exclaims, raising his voice.

"No, no, he mustn't, he . . ." Doc Brown begins before Max cuts him short.

"Clear as day, Sam, you finally named that A.I. you've been tinkering with forever." Max concludes confidently.

"Uh, yes, sure have. How'dya know, Max?" Sam presses, noting Doc Brown's bewildering bugging eyes, eagerly nodding his head in Sam's deception.

"Com'n, Max, Jack must've found something by now. Com'n, tell you about E.V.E. on the way." Sam says, pulling Max towards a side exit.

"Yes, have good talk, gentlemen, yes, good talk." Doc Brown awkwardly waving before slinking off to his office.

"Yeah, that's really cool, Sam! So happy for you!" Max exclaims loud enough for Doc Brown to hear before lowering his tone as the pair sprint off.

"Com'n, Sam, what's with Doc? He was acting weird the second he left his office before talking to you. Spill the tea. What gives?" Max presses as the pair make their way down the hall.

"It's nothing really." Sam proclaims, pulling ahead of Max.

"Uh, no. It's not nothing, Sam. Talk!" Max commands, pushing his pace to catch up.

"Really, he thinks E.V.E. is a solid name for an A.I., I just have to work out some control flaws, and she should be up and running in no time. Where do you think Jack will be? The library or the dorm?" Sam stepping up his pace, attempting to escape Max's inquiry.

"Ok, okay, have it your way, Sam, keep secrets. I have a few of my own." Max closing on Sam.

"I'm sure, really think Max. Where do you think Jack is?" Preoccupied with avoiding Max's forgetting his own logic.

"Well, wouldn't hurt to try the library first, and if he's not there, then we head to the dorm. Nothing to it." Max says, making a not-so-subtle attempt to feel Sam's weighty pack.

"Stop that, Max. We aren't far from the library. Com'n, there's a shortcut through these rooms. I'll tell you when we find Jack." Sam says assured they are far enough away from Doc Brown's lab before rocketing into an unmarked door.

"I knew it. Sam's got a secret. Sam's got a secr . . . whoa not so rough!" Max exclaims, Sam pulling him roughly into the room.

"Ahem. Cadet Murphy, is there something in particular I can assist you in finding this afternoon?" The velvety voice repeats.

Scrambling to pocket the device, Jack stands at attention, his pockets spilling onto the floor. Panicked Jack, pushes back his chair flooring it abruptly. Jack sheepishly apologizing, attempting to conceal the devious device.

"He he, no apologies necessary, cadet Murphy. Here, let me help." The velvety-voiced librarian setting the chair upright before kneeling beside the caught cadet.

"Here that's everything. Happens to me all the time. Apologies, I've given you quite the scare." Her velvety voice barely breaching a whisper. Her young and soft smile reassuring Jack, calming his nerves.

"Thanks, ahem, thank you." Jack, clearing the lump in his throat, returns a shaky smile.

"There you go, all there." She smiles again, sending a warm sensation through the young hero's cheeks.

"So what's a combat cadet doing at this hour combing through this old thing?" She inquires, pointing toward computers that serve the same purpose. Sheepishly running fingers through locks that are no longer there, Jack responds quickly. "Um, I'm writing a paper for Professor Crane's on armament capabilities of enemies and allies of GYAIA. Thought I'd start with MEC specs, yeah, that's what I was doing. Tryin to get ahead start before semester's end." Jack biting his lip, kicking himself for the stupidity.

"Oh, I see MEC specs, odd thing for a first-year to be required to know. Well, there's a lot of them archived here at GYAIA. Are you looking for any in particular?" Her velvety voice trailing off into deeper thought.

"Yeah, I'm in the advanced placement program. Honestly, not sure where to start. Just trying to get an early start and all. So you like the head librarian around here?" Jack recycling the lie, burning it into his brain, wiping a faint taste of blood from his lip attempting to redirect her intrigue.

"Advanced placement, Jack. Really this isn't College Board, you idiot." Thinks to himself, his thoughts broken by the soft cue of a dove. "Well, I suppose you must narrow your field. And no, more like an assistant to the assistant's assistant librarian." The velvety voice vaulting off to a computer almost buried amongst piles of papers and books. The soft lighting and glow of the screen line the soft features of her feminine features.

Unsure of his next move, Jack follows, stepping over piles of books littering the floor.

"What's all this, ma'am? Reduce my field?" Jack inquires, feeling secure in his deceit.

"Oh, this? Apologies, I get carried away with reading that it all just kinda accumulates here and there." Giggling to herself, her voice soft like a dove veiled in velvet.

"Come sit. I think this may help. You have to reduce your field of inquiry. Like countries and organizations of interest. It's pretty rudimentary, really."

Removing a stack of books revealing a stool seated beside her chair. Running her fingers across the antique's grains, she reminisced about a myriad of memories from its texture, patting the seat invitingly. Smiling sheepishly, feeling his cheeks again warming, Jack sits leaning away from the young woman's frame as she leans into his space. Sitting quietly, observing her click

238

feverously through the library's master MEC spec inventory, Jack waits patiently.

"Ah ha, the ultimate starter pack of specs to get you started." She raps Jack's thigh with excitement.

"Oh, um, that was easy." Jack spits nervously, pulling his legs tightly together.

"Here, I'll print you off the list so you can research them yourself. The printer is . . . it's around here somewhere." Her velvety voice trailing off, shuffling through piles of papers and resources bound for greater academic purpose.

"Here it is, I think?" Jack delicately removing a stack of dusty books and scrolls, revealing a state-of-the-art printer entombed in the tech of a bygone era.

"Oh, there you are. Haven't seen you in ages. How embarrassing. You must think me a . . ." The young woman turning to conceal her own cheeks. Cutting her off, pulling the stack of warm pages from the machine, Jack chuckles.

"No, not at all. This . . . I understand."

Circling his finger, alluding to her overwhelming workspace, pausing in his own memories of Aunt Anna's often-similar workspace. Nodding approvingly, Jack reaches for an empty folder, when a small number of papers pour upon the floor below, revealing a picture enclosed in a worn wooden frame. Stepping back, Jack's eyes rivet from memory to present like pistons of an engine. Eyes flaring frantically seeking answers unknown.

"Oh, sorry bout the mess, been meaning to get things in order. You know, work, work around here." The velvety voice echoes hollowly like white noise upon the young hero's senses.

"Murphy? You alright? That should be all you need to get you . . ." The velvety voice silencing upon his discovery.

"Oh, well, look at the hour. It's almost chow time, right?" Stepping between Jack and the sight before him.

"Cadet Murphy? Will that be all?" Her velvety voice calls calmly.

"Oh yes, thank you. I feel rude. You know my name, but don't know yours." Jack contests containing thoughts racing through his mind.

"Anza . . . Arella . . . It's Anita Arella. Cadet Arella, the Ls make a slight "y" sound, though." The velvety vixen stepping hard into Jack's personal space, sending him backward stepping carefully over piles of resources.

"Anna, Anita. I mean cadet Arella. Glad to meet you. I gotta . . ." Jack stepping awkwardly, turning respectfully coming face to face with a searing sensation of similarity.

"Good to finally meet you as well, cadet Murphy." Cadet Arella agreeing with an appealing smile.

"I, I gotta go. My dorm mates are waiting."

Clutching his quarry, Jack salutes awkwardly, jolting off from Arella's sight. Sighing heavily, cadet Arella saluting the young hero, sinking dejectedly into her seat. The sounds of silence surrounding her in halls that speak volumes.

CHAPTER TWENTY TWO

"WHAT'S GOIN' ON?"

Footsteps pounding one after the other, Jack races thoughts running through his mind, outpacing every step taken. Clutching the prints tighter with every step pounding underneath.

"That picture can't be."

"Whoa! Jack, slow down! Jack, slow down, Jack!" Max's voice.

"Jack, what's the hurry? We were coming to see if . . . Jack is hiff, I, hiff, is every . . hiff. . thing okahhhhmpff?" Sam stops sucking wind as if stolen from Aeolus himself.

"Not here, mess now talk later, come on." Jack stammers gathering his senses, stuffing papers into his pack, while ushering the trio to an uneventful meal before heading back to their dorm hastily.

Unlocking their dorm door, Jack rushes in.

"Max, only a few lights. What did you find, Sam?"

"How was the library? Find any specs?" Max mastering maturity in the moment, prying Sam's pack lessening his burden.

"Um yeah, specs, in the library. Yeah, where to start." Jack pulling a third and final chair close to his companions, throwing down the file folder filled with specs.

241

"Wait, what? This looks like maybe 20 max. Like how many more are we talkin Jack?" Max inquires, flipping through specs under lamplight.

"Dunno, could've been thousands, maybe more." Jack leaning in tilting Sam's shoulders back again.

"GYAIA's got a crap ton of them on file. MEC specs isn't exactly specific, you know." Throwing his palms up slightly exasperated.

"Fair enough, these are just briefings of specs, but it's definitely a start." Max combing through each entry, riffling through the pages pulling a highlighter out of Sam's pack.

"What's that for Max?" Jack inquires, leaning over his shoulder.

"I'm highlighting military-grade weapons designed for combat or agricultural production graded specs." Max chewing deep impressions into the bright yellow cap.

"Agricultural grade, like food pro? Why?" Jack leaning even closer now.

"Simple, agri-pro feed the masses and . . ." Max begins as Sam, now recovered from his run, completing his brother's exact thoughts. "and weapons to protect food supply chains that control the masses. Keep em fed, keep em happy." Sam stands on shaky legs, walking to the bathroom sink, drinking deeply from cupped hands.

242

"Wait, what's goin on? Supply chains, controlling masses? Not sure where you're goin with this guys?" The twins perplexed partner sitting down, rubbing his racing mind.

"It's just a hypothesis, Jack. As of right now, we don't have any hard evidence, yet . . .O, oh Sam come here." Max snapping motioning for his tired twin.

"Jack, there's got to be a connection. Speaking of connections, Jack, what did Wiley need to say to you in the middle of Crane's class earlier today?" Sam inquiring before Max who is preoccupied with his potential discovery.

"Um, Crane's class? Oh yeah, he informed me that someone has been breaking into R&D and looking for something. Odd really, not sure why he'd tell me that." Scratching his forehead Jack attempting to reflect from any deeper inquiries.

"He was almost warning me, quoting Art of War, something about divine threads and sticking to the shadows. Then her picture, why would Aunt Anna be?" Jack mulling a multitude of events blurring his memory.

"Hm, not much to go on. Picture, what picture? Do you suspect he knows about Max's late-night excursions?" Sam presses, mostly revived from his run.

"Can't be sure. He was rather cryptic; this person of interest defiantly was searching for something important in Doc Brown's workspaces. What that is, he didn't say." Jack continuing to redirect.

243

"Hm, indeed, this mystery person Wiley was referring to might have something to do with Doc Brown acting very off-kilter today in class. Wouldn't you say, Sam?" Max looking up from the list of specs briefly.

"No doubt there's a connection. He's a kooky cat for sure, cautious, but not paranoid like he was. What picture Jack?" Sam answering Max, before Jack speaks up.

"The librarian had an old picture of my Aunt Anna and a few others . . . could've swore that was . . . never mind. Paranoid? Like how?" Jack interjects.

"Like buggin out after he spoke to Sam about something. Care to inform us what spooked the good doctor?" Max says without taking his eyes off his analysis.

"Sure, he was helping me make corrections to E.V.E.'s programming, and then he went off to his office looking for something. That's when he noticed something missing and started acting frantic." Sam answers.

"Frantic is a nice way to put it, Sam, the man was manic. Even gave Sam something before we left." Max tapping Sam's dense pack with the highlighter.

"Oh yeah, he did. Before we left, he stuffed something in my pack. Give me a sec." Sam unzipping the bulging baggage digging deep into its contents.

"Ah, here it is!" Sam pulls a worn notebook from his pack and sets it in the light on the small desk.

"So this is what all the fuss was about? Better than some old picture." Max muses stacking spec lists neatly into to organized piles of checked and unchecked.

"Maybe? So what do we have here, guys?" Jack lifting the warped cover, the crackle of pages contained creaking painfully within.

"Well, let's take a look, Sam suggests snapping on a pair of latex gloves before investigating.

"Gloves?" Jack furrowing his brow intrigued by his process.

"Yeah, he does that. Something about oil from your fingertips is ruining the dexterity of the pages. Give us a few." Max waves nonchalantly, snapping on his own pair.

Quiet moments pass, an exhausted Jack embattled by a multitude of memory, settles comfortably on his bed, nodding off momentarily. Thoughts of the day's events giving way to exhaustion, drifting deeper into restful R.E.M. . . .

A full moon hangs brightly above slowly cooling shadows below. Tall wooden sentries tower high above a densely packed forest floor. Nightfall descending quietly broken by footsteps frantically fleeing in all directions. The crunch of gravel underfoot dissipates as Jack slows to a halt. Stepping cautiously, he stands alone on a loosely packed gravel path, surrounded by forestry in all directions.

"Reg! Ari! Hey guys its late we should be heading back!" Jack shouts with cupped hands. "HEY REG, ARI! I'M TIRED! WHERE ARE YOU GUYS?" He shouts louder peering into the darkness of the woods surrounding him. Horrendous howls rising in the distance, sending a shiver down Jack's spine. "Wolves?" Jack strains to hear faint, but familiar cries in the distance. "Reg! Ari! Max, Sam . . . Sam . . . Max? Hold on, I'm coming!" Jack shouts sprinting down the darkened gravel road, the crunch of unevenly packed bedrock below dispersing into darkness under each frantic footstep.

Desperate screams of youths rise with every step, trembling with terror, stealing serenity from the once silent night sky. "JACK! HELP, GE. . . GET AWAY FROM ME! OOOWWW!! NO NeeeOOOOO!!!" Ari's voice shrilly slicing through shadows.

"ARI! I'M COMING! WHERE ARE YOU?!?!" Jack shouts dashing desperately in her voice's direction before falling to his knees. "Oww! Sssffff . . . phfff!" Searing pain shooting through his knees, feeling every painful pebble dig deeply. "MURPH HELP! THEY'RE GETTING Clos . .e. r! NOOoooo murph!" Max's voice moans outward into the nothing surrounding Jack, as he rises for another attempt. A cruel breeze whips across Jack's face rustling densely packed palmetto bushes along the gravel path. Canine howling pierces the cruel commotion colliding from all directions.

"Owww! Damn that smfff!" Jack winces burying his face into his forearms, peeking through the slimmest of creases. Darkened green hues of palmetto leaves lashing as the wind whips wildly.

"JACK, no! Let me go . . . no, no, mmmmm. . ." Sam's voice falling silent only a few helpless feet away from Jack. "SAM!

246

SAM!" Jack lunging desperately, knees collapsing; crashing roughly onto unforgiving gravel. "Ahhh, mmmm hffff!" Jack spits, settling upon harmed knees, helplessly unable to stand, brushing small bits of gravel from scrapes burrowed into his palms.

"Get up Jack . . . get UPPPP!!!" Jack spits willing himself, stumbling to his feet. "JACK! WHERE? I'M HERE! NOOOooo. I'm here, he's here, help m . . . me, Gurg, uhhhel, pfftt. . . ." Reggie's voice calls out weakly in another direction sending a surge of energy through Jack's bones. "Ugh. I'm . . I'm coming Reg. . . I'm coming. Oomphh!" Jack falters back to his knees sending searing pain deep within. "JACK!" "JACK! NOOOOO!" "WHERE ARE YOU JACK?!?!" HELP US JACK . . . help us. . ." Voices shriek from the darkness deafened by howling of Hell's hounds tearing and thrashing hidden within fearful foliage, howls echoing hatred into the night sky. Jack rises painfully once more, stumbling in all directions and none simultaneously. "I . . . I can't. Get up Jack, get . . . up . . . oomph! Nooo!" Jack sobs sinking exhaustedly into pain searing his body. Heinous howling tearing innocence from bone haunting every sensation, Jack sinks lower into his despair as bits of gravel and dirt digging deeply into his face, neck, and forearms.

"Get up Jack . . . get up!" Jack thrusting raw hands roughly upon unforgiving gravel, commanding lifeless limbs onward. Wiping soil and sorrow from his face, Jack rises slowly his eyes meeting the burning eyes of a scarred hound's stepping cautiously

247

from concealment. Its growls rumble dangerously from deep within as the hell hound steps confidently forward. Fangs dripping with blood and bane; the hound circles its prey cautiously, readying its final attack. Bearing teeth and brutality, the worn wolf stepping slowly into the light of a full moon above. For a moment Jack senses a moment of familiarity fading fast into a night sky above filling quickly with howls heckling from all directions. "J, j, ja, ck . . ." The sweet sound of Aunt Anna's voice incoherently gurgles from a distance. "No, no please no . . ." Jack sniffs faltering to a knee as more hounds materialize from sorrowful shadows, licking blood soaked fangs wickedly.

From one knee, clasping a fistful of rock and soil Jack readies his final stand. Trembling greatly the young teen rises facing his fate. "Devils . . . snfff, they were my friends snfff. . . my family!" Rage rising in his voice, the young teen stands. Growls surrounding him hiss as if laughing. "Shut it DEVILS!" Jack shouts fists clutched tightly, lunging losing his footing on loose gravel. Falling roughly upon unforgiving floor the pack swarms, biting and tearing viciously. "NOOOoooo . . . noooo!" Jack kicks flailing wildly.

"Jack! Jack wake up! What devils?" Sam shaking Jack to his senses. "Murph its ok, here drink this." Max pressing a cold glass of water against Jack's cheek while dodging a disoriented fist flailing wildly.

"Wait, what? You're a . . . alive?" Jack stammers, drinking gratefully.

248

"Alive? Why wouldn't we be Murph?" Max muses seeing his companion's heaving chest begin to slow. "Jack, you just experienced a very intense night terror, care to share?" Sam offers, attempting to make sense of the recent chaos.

"Um, um. I uh, I don't know where to start." Jack sighs hanging his head rubbing dried tears from his eyes.

"It will be difficult, but please try Jack." Sam's soothing calming voice settling his companion. "Yeah Murph you were only out for like an hour. What's up?" Max patting his companion's back awkwardly hoping to soothe.

"I . . . I, an hour?" Jack inquires confusedly. "Yes Jack. Max and I were looking over specs and you started thrashing, going on about devils and hounds. When you started screaming no repeatedly we woke you. What happened?" Sam asks leaning in attentively.

"I was in the woods, back home I think and . . . you were there with Max and. . ." Jack pauses staring blankly between his companions. "And what Murph?" Max popping Jack back into reality. "Oh and my friends back home Ari and Reg. Think I heard Aunt Anna's voice too, but it all happened so fast. So fast." Jack sighs finishing his water, returning the empty cup to Max.

"Odd Jack that we'd all be there, given we've never met your friends back home. Jack try your best to describe what you remember." Sam settling into his chair like a therapist. "Yeah Murph take your time, what happened?" Max leaning in eagerly awaiting his companion's tale. Minutes melt by as Jack describes his nightmare. As details of darkness illuminate his companion's

249

imagination Jack concludes his tale. "Then your voices went quiet, the wolves swarmed. From there, I just remember kicking and swinging as they attacked. Snff . . . what's goin' on guys?" Jack lowers his head fighting not to relive the memory again.

"Murph that's rough dude." Max concludes astonished at Jack's retelling. "Jack, while I'm not sure what this dream means, it's clear these wolves represent some danger and people you care about will be in danger if these "wolves" aren't dealt with. Did any of these wolves have distinguishing features? Features resembling people or events, these wolves may be avatars for?" Sam inquires leaning forward. "Yeah Murph, were they Canis lupus or Canis lycaon? Dimensions maybe?" Max presses eagerly adjusting the width between his hands.

"Canis what? They were big wolves, not comic book big, like this big." Jack throwing his hands apart attempting to answer Max's question. "Ah Lupus, definitely greys." Max muses pleased with his assessment. "Yeah sure they were mostly grey." Jack sighs rubbing his face still shaken from his experience. "Lupus or not, what do you mean mostly grey Jack? Any other features?" Sam pressing past a convinced Max.

"Um, yeah the leader or alpha I guess had a scar and kinda limped a little as it circled me. It was pretty dark and everything happened so fast I couldn't . . . that's really all I remember." Jack concludes rubbing his legs gingerly.

"Maybe the subspecies doesn't matter, what matters is what these wolves represent. I'll do some research on dreams,

Max are you gonna?" Sam nods in his duplicate's direction. "Oh yeah Sam give Sleepyhead the update." Max muses bounding off to the bathroom.

"Doc's notes?" Jack asks easing himself from bed, sauntering over to Sam's side, blinking fatigue from weary eyes.

"Think so." Doc's handwriting is closer to cuneiform than English, but we may have something here." Sam pulling Jack near.

"Okay . . . Whoa, what am I looking at? . . ." Jack stumbling slightly sitting roughly next to Sam at the small desk.

"So there's so much here to sift through, gonna need at least a week to really do these notes justice. Doc has notes of renewable energy, advances in A.I., alternating current modulators small enough to fit inside your pocket but powerful enough to power an entire street. Real Tesla stuff here. It's all theoretical of course, but these notes are extremely detailed. Just too much to digest in fifty minutes." Sam's eyes darting from Doc's notes to his own, ensuring correctness. Pages are missing towards the back, some sort of history of something, I need more time to research and correctly translate some of these languages in Doc's notes." Sam's voice trailing off into his task.

"Ok, so how can we help Sam?" Jack rubbing moisture from his exhausted eyes.

"Well, funny, you should ask, Jack!" Max stepping into the dim light of the desk, dressed and ready.

"Oh no. No, guys, it's past 2200. Get some sleep 0400 comes fast or was is 0500?" Jack protests, knowing his objection falls on duplicated deaf ears.

"Jack, you have to, but these missing pages could still be somewhere in Doc's lab. All I need is a few pages. Can't translate blank spaces." Sam waves the notebook in the air.

"Ok, okay. I'll get ready." Jack patting himself, stretching, when a sudden realization freezes him in place.

"Um, Sam, I think Jack's broken again?" Max muses.

"Jack, what is it?" Sam striding over, investigating Jack's catatonic state.

"Yeah, he's broken alright. I blame the food, could be the dream. I mean, it's not bad, but come on yeaooww!!! What gives Sam?" Max pacing backwards rubbing his arm.

"Jack, what's the matter? Jack, Jack?" Sam waving his hand at his cemented companion.

"It's gon . . . gone." Jack's voice trailing frantically searching disheveled covers of his bed.

"Oh no! Doc Brown must've bit him. He's gone cuckoo, too!" Max exclaims excitedly.

"Not helping Max. Communicate, please. What's gone, Jack?" Sam setting his notes aside to assist his companion.

"Aunt Anna's, I must've lost it when!" Jack's eyes widen without finishing his thought.

"Ok, when? Where?" Sam presses.

"When that young librarian startled me earlier, I accidentally pulled everything out of my pocket and tried to hide this." Jack beginning to calm down as reason sets in, waving Sam's device in his direction.

"Oh good, I was looking for that. Get any good pics?" Sam adds, snatching the device from Jack.

"No. She printed them for me." Jack pointing at Max's neatly stacked piles, dressing quickly.

"Young librarian you say? The hot one with the velvety voice?" Max starts smacking his lips.

"Eww, stop that Max, gross. What's wrong with you?"

"Ok, okay let's go." Jack jolting for the door signaling for Max to join.

"Alright, late field trip." Max clapping quietly mimicking one last biting gesture at Sam.

"Ewh, get off. Hey, don't be out past 0100. I'll translate Doc's notes. Good luck with your trinket, Jack. Be safe and Max . . ." Sam's pause grabbing his brother's now limited attention.

"Don't get Jack caught, will yah?"

CHAPTER TWENTY THREE

SECRETS IN THE SHADOWS

Jack and Max move swiftly through the halls, accessing passages to the library. The young cadets go undetected, beginning their search, communicating with a simple system of hand gestures. At night, lamps turned low emit a soft glow upon desks and computers alike. Large ancient decorative wooden bookshelves looming large like redwoods containing more books than forests have leaves.

Worn metal buckles and golden lettering glimmer as the pair sneak stealthily to the old rolodex Jack occupied hours earlier. Turning to the desk and its surrounding area, circling his finger down and around shrugging silently, unsure of its whereabouts. Nodding equally silent, Max draws a question mark in the air, dotting the end.

Rolling his eyes in return, the two play charades as Jack attempts to describe the trinket. Twisting his hand, mimicking starting a car while tugging at an imaginary chain around his neck. To Max's amusement, clapping silently, understanding clearly, beckoning another clue. Tapping his forehead, Jack crouches lower, arms spread apart, and rocking back and forth in a wavelike motion. Throwing Jack two thumbs up, Max begins the task. Having rushed out so quickly neither properly pocketing a flashlight to assist with the search. The dimly lit lamplight offering little assistance save for the desk tops, the pair patting the floor under and around the desk for the keychain.

Minutes seem to pass like hours for Jack, and a sinking sensation surges at every failed pass of his hands. Turning to check Max's progress, crawling to Max, who is lying straight on his back, eyes closed and hands folded neatly across his chest. Rocking his calm companion gently, a rising fear befalls Jack. Checking his surrounding head swiveling in all directions for signs of other intruders when the sound of a snicker squeaks silently from the form below. Staring down through furrowed brows, scowling at his companion's ill-timed act, mouthing Max's name simultaneously.

Suddenly, Max sits up slowly; still shut, with hands affixed to his chest. "Psst quit playing around, dude." Jack breathes, staring face to face with Max. Suddenly, Max's eyes shoot open, staring past Jack blankly. Before Jack can poke his comedic companion's ribs, Max's arms extend forward parallel with the floor below. Peeved and perplexed by this act, Jack pulls back swiftly to deliver the painful poke, sending it to Max's exposed ribs. In an instant, Jack pauses inches from his intent as something glimmering in the glow of lamplight dangles from Max's now outstretched fingers.

Snatching the surfboard-shaped keychain swiftly, running fingers across worn words reading, *sunshine summers*. Clutching it tight to his chest, Jack mouthing thank you at Max.

Still in his seated position, Max mouthing quietly, "Your welcome. So where's hot girl's coffin? Gotta be round here somewhere, right?"

Jack's sternly staring down at his companion, pressing a finger to his lips, pointing towards a disturbance in the distance. Without a word, Jack slinks around the desk, pointing toward the nearest exit. Clutching his cherished charm, the two young cadets creep from shadow to shadow exiting without detection. Cautiously crossing through corridors, concealing themselves inside a cramped corridor camouflaged as a small custodial closet.

"Wff, finally, mmm." Max begins before Jack muffles his mouth.

"Shh, I think we're being followed. Com'n, two rights and a left." Jack whispers, tugging Max in the dark corridor and stuffing Anna's keychain into his pocket.

"Jack, two rights and a left. Where we going? Doc's lab has two lefts and a right; we're goin in the opposite direction." Max whispers, hugging close not to lose his guide in the shadows.

"If I'm wrong, then we're not being followed, and we'll be doing the following. Let's move next, right at the crossroad." Jack tugging Max to follow, both stepping cautiously. Taking a few paces down the darkened corridor, Jack sinks low against rough sandstone, feeling rough granules grabbing his shirt. Motioning for Max to mimic him, the pair pauses in place, allowing shadowy seconds to turn into profitable pauses. Distance footsteps faintly pass, turning left opposite to Jack's right decision.

Patiently, the pair wait, assuring no other persons pass.

"All clear, on to Doc's." whispering, tugging Max near.

"Wait, what? Jack, that could be Wiley's mystery dude. Ah na, it's late we can go back." Even in shadows, Max's uneasiness is clear as day.

"Maybe, maybe it's a vampire." Jack jests, jolting off in the direction of Doc's labs.

"Har har, maybe it's a shadow person, maybe it's a vampire, not funny, Murph." Alone, Max hurries, fearing falling behind. Carefully, the pair navigate a narrowing corridor crawling through a crevice barely big enough for either to fit.

"Glad I've slimmed down. Don't prefer the shortcut." Max wiggling himself free of the crevice. Motioning for silence, Jack places a metal panel aside carefully pushing open a tall locker door disguising the passage behind it.

Stepping into the dimly lit room, Jack checks for signs of activity before motioning for Max.

"Hold up." Max whispers throwing his arm across Jack's chest, causing him to look down.

"Been workin out, buddy? You feel, strong. Ok. Okay, jeeze." Max chuckling softly, holding up his pointer finger, motioning for a momentary pause.

"No, for real, for real. Hold up."

"My bad, forgot about security resets." Jack whispers, bending his knees while they wait. Audible clicks faintly reverberate around the expansive space filled with the faint buzzing of various sleeping tech.

"Ok, first stop, Baby girl." Max saunters off silently, making his way down a dark but familiar path.

"Good grief, Max. Let's make this quick." Jack sighs, rolling his eyes, following close behind his smitten companion.

"Com'n almost there." Max claps excitedly, pressing through a short corridor into a vacant elevator. Jack hustling in just in time, doors shutting behind him.

"Excited are we?" Jack asks rhetorically, but Max's mind singularly focused on his baby tapping impatiently. Descending levels below her hanger, the elevator settles quietly. Max bolts through the slightest of cracks, sprinting to her underbelly, running his hand along its length, speaking sweet nothings to her.

"So this is Soteria?" Jack inquiring skeptically.

"Yup, one and only. The Temptress of turbulence herself."

"Looks small." Jack jests.

"She's the only large-scale Magnetospheric-Propulsion System in the world. She can do Mach 5 in her sleep bro, polycarbonate cockpit enclosure, vertical take-off and landing capabilities, onboard anti-UAV system, 360-degree cloaking, when Sam and I get the bugs out of course. Radio and laser altimeters. Can't beat RF and LF am I right?"

"Plus, plus she produces zero SAFs, unlike those LM fuel guzzlers out of Fort Worth. Murph, you hear what I'm sayin?

Zero atmospheric emissions, Zero, zip. She's quiet, like real quiet." Max gloats, grabbing Jack by the shoulders.

"Wow, all that huh? When's the wedding?" Jack sniffs sarcastically.

"Oh poo, Murph, I wouldn't expect a small-town tumbleweed like yourself to understand what true love is." Max kicking imaginary rocks, crash-landing as he does.

"Max, she's an amazing piece of machinery. She just doesn't . . . you know, fly!"

"Well, she flies in the simulator Sam developed. I've almost mastered every maneuver she's got. Just can't get her off the ground." Max admits boyishly.

"Every source code checks out fine, I just can't figure out why she won't just fly." Thrusting his hands upward dejectedly. "Murph, its hard loving something that doesn't love you back." Kicking at nothing stuffing hands in his pockets.

"Hey, Max, I know a little something about that." Jack says, walking towards some sort of control panel.

"Yeah, what would you know about that Murph? You're mister all-American back home, I'd bet. Probably dated the prom queen and everything. Signing babies at homecoming type stuff."

"What, signing babies at homecoming? Max, have you ever been to homecoming? Prom? Besides, I was only a freshman. Freshman aren't "Prom Kings"." Jack throwing air quotes mockingly.

"Honestly Max, my best friends Ari and Reg back home are nerds like you and Sam. Well not your level of nerd, but they're nerdy, you'd like Reg I bet. No, I wrestled in middle and was on track to be all-county as a freshman, but then I just . . ." Jack's voice trailing off into the soft glow of the screen below, illuminating suddenly solemn features.

"Wait, so, Murph, no prom queen?"

"Well, she would've been Prom Queen during our senior year, but that's beside the point. Point is I grew up just wanting to make friends, wrestle my way to college if I was lucky, and come back to be a small-town nobody. Look at me now . . . got in trouble, sent here to be in some super spy school, with a history nobody tells me jack about, and now I'm sneaking around a dark hanger with one of two boy geniuses looking at a jet that doesn't fly."

"Whoa, that's deep, Jack, real deep Murphy. Guess you do understand. Whoa, whoa, I know you're fired up, but that doesn't mean we fire her up too!" Exclaims Max, peeling Jack's fingers from Soteria's control module, snapping Jack back into reality.

"Why not fire her up? Give her a good old kick in the ole jet engines and fly off away from it all at Mach 30." Jack conceding Max's efforts, pushing the control panel, pacing away, collecting his emotions.

"Jet engines? What part of Magnetospheric-propulsion do you not understand? She's calibrated for Mach 5, Mach 30 would kill us; never mind, you ok, Murph? Been under a lot of duress, we've

260

all seen it, hell we've felt it too." Max clicking off controls before turning hastily catching up with his conflicted companion.

"Murph, wait up, where you going?"

"Com'n, Max, let's look around Professor Brown's workspace, find something useful for Sam, and get out of here." Jack pressing a button, sending the pair ascending upward.

"Soteria, huh? What's that mean, anyways?"

"Oh, yeah, I forgot, Soteria is the Greek Goddess of safety and deliverance. Ancient Greeks believed she protected them on their travels. So, Soteria is a vehicle that, when functioning, will *deliver* her passengers *safely* from place to place." Max elbowing Jack, amused by his own clever wordplay.

"Makes sense, cool name, let's go." Jack sending a stiffer elbow deep into Max's ribs, jolting out of the elevator and down the hall.

Doc's lab, while extensive in resources, is rather simple in its layout. Research and development seamlessly integrated without separating from the textual academics required by GYAIA. Students use their textual resources to identify and solve real-time problems. Given this structure and chaotic randomness of Doc Brown's instructional style, Jack and Max must wade through workspaces of unfinished projects. A task in itself under a bright canopy of lights during class, however, shadows now saturate the space.

"It's like an obstacle course in here, Max." Jack whispers, stepping over and through the projects that are laid about.

261

"Yeah, you get used to it. OH, here's Tully's miniature particle accelerator, which is totally lit when she figures out that her electromagnetic field is the issue. She'll figure it out. She's brilliant. " Max giddily skips by.

"Have you told her that, Max?" Jack quips quietly.

"No, would totally kill her learning process. Failure is essential to every success." Max muses, sauntering in admiration between various projects.

Jack smirks stunned by Max's maturity when in his element.

"Always a surprise with you, Max." Jack breathes to himself, the pair inching closer to their purpose.

"So this notebook was pretty old. Where do we start, Murph?" Max making his way into Doc's personal office.

"Dunno, needle in a haystack if you ask me." Jack whispers, shifting papers around.

"Can't see a darn thing, I'm gonna." Max begins clicking the office light on when Jack stops him. "No, Max, no lights, we work in the shadows on this one."

"In the shadows? We'll never find it at this rate." Max, seating himself in Doc's chair, spinning in place.

"Stop that, Max, focus. Think Professor Brown gave Sam his life's work for some reason. Those missing pages are either here or already gone." Jack quips, halting his circling companion.

"Stop playing around, or I'll." Jack jamming fingers deep into Max's ribs pinching playfully.

"No, not the piggly . . ." Max squeals silently. Falling to the floor, wrestling about as friends do when a clatter of metal upon the floor reverberating roughly throughout the laboratory.

"What was that?" Max whispers through weighted breaths.

"We're not alone." Jack muffling Max's mouth, returning to a crouched position.

"On my go, move." Jack whispers, inching his way around Doc's oversized desk.

Peering through a window Jack detecting a form motoring in their direction. Thinking quickly, Jack grabs the first thing his hand lands upon, hurling it out the office doorway into the dark distance. Jack's desperate heave is hammering some poor cadet's creation, sending their mysterious guest to investigate the collision. Pulling Max roughly, the pair sneak swiftly using shadows to their advantage. Stowing away under desks, careful to avoid detection. Calming themselves Jack and Max listening patiently for their unintended guest. Steps shuffling strenuously into Doc's office. A flash of light strobing inside, seeking something. Files flutter frantically, forfeiting scenic silence.

Gymnastically maneuvering through workspaces, Jack and Max seeking sanctuary of shadows swallowing their presence. Distance and discretion directing the cadets concealing themselves inside the crevice, counterfeiting as a locker. The young cadets careen down covert corridors, hearts pounding faster than footsteps below.

Papers settle upon the floor back in Doc Brown's office. Labored panting, pacing the space. "Brown, you sneak." Whispering wickedly to themselves, pausing in place.

"Time's up tonight." The mysterious figure spits, stepping dejectedly over piles of paper strode across the floor, resting awkwardly on something in the shadows.

A flash of light revealing the novelty nestled underfoot. Snatching the trinket tersely throwing light upon its worn features.

"Hmm. *Sunshine Summers*? Murphy . . . always a Murphy." Pocketing the twice-lost trinket the Phantasm evaporates escaping into the shadows. Clicks of security cameras are coming online, and silent sentries are safeguarding Doc Brown's lab once more.

Stealing shadows from silence, the young companions navigate hidden corridors. Stepping silently, carefully avoiding sentries above and bipedal. *click* "Murph, that was close." Max leaning heavily against the door securely locked behind.

"Max, whoever that was, knew they weren't alone." Signing heavily, Jack kicking off his shoes, pulling impatiently at his socks.

"No way, we totally disappeared back there. Dude, we were awesome."

"No, they knew. They knew."

"Murph, how'd they know? Gets pretty dark in Doc's lab."

"Dmm, pff, Don't know, but whoever they were, they didn't expect company tonight."

"B, pfff believe what you want, pff pff they know nothing."

"Then why did they panic and toss Brown's office as we left?" Jack inquires, sinking under his sheet still wearing clothes.

"Maybe they were in a hurry like we were? Only a couple of minutes before the cameras came back online." Max flexing foolishly in a small mirror before retiring to his own quarter.

"Yeah, that's what gets me. Who else knows about the security shutdown, Sam? Brown?" Jack rubbing fatigue in his eyes.

"Doesn't matter? It's 0132, ya both late." a third voice breaking the pair's ponderings. "Sam? Oww damn." Max es and jams his toe on their bunk.

"Get some sleep. We'll figure it out later." Sam protests, punching Max in the head thwarting an attempt to touch him.

"Ow bro, ow my toe. Not the face, not the. . ." Max mules.

"Didn't touch your face. Go to bed." Sam states, shifting himself back to sleep.

"Sam's right, Max, see you gents in a few." Jack settling comfortably in his bunk.

"Oh, so now, you both want to be cl mummumm." Max catching two pillows on the face.

"Mmmaa, I see how it is, keepin' these." Max stuffing two new arrivals between his legs and head. Silence swiftly stealing into the shadows, exhaustion exacting its heavy toll upon the trio.

265

CHAPTER TWENTY FOUR

HARD LESSONS LEARNED

Shortened slumber slipping by as 0500 arrives swiftly met Cadet Blackshear blasting the companion's door and rousing the rogues from their rest. "0500 Gentlemen, let's go, let's go, let's GO!" Blackshear bellows. The trio scramble changing into appropriate attire. Blackshear marshalling his company to morning meal with little time to digest their food, the trio eat quickly, releasing cadets to their respective classes.

"Dunno bout you guys, but I feel oddly refreshed. Kinda don't mind PT so early. So about last night, last night was crazy, right?" Max jogging ahead of his companions.

"Glad so . . . someone is. Let's get PT out the way, got combat skills after." Jack stretching, fighting off another yawn.

"Speak for yourself, Max. Keep it down, Max. We'll talk later." Sam stretching alertness into his limbs, shaking his head at Max's boldness. Physical training flies by, Max posting his most productive day, Sam and Jack dragging themselves through. The twins change out of their physical training gear for Professor Brown's lab.

"Convenient for you, Murph, don't even have to change your PTGs." Max tugging at Jack's attire.

"Don't listen to him, Jack, tough run. Bray then Volkov. We got time, we'll walk with." Sam pushing Max away.

"Thanks, Sam, won't be necessary. Saved some for Volkov's, just other first years anyways." Jack grinning wolfishly.

"Woooo! Whatever you want, bro, feeling invincib . . . oompff!" Max says, spilling roughly to the floor. Sam plodding pitifully into a wall of muscle, spilling simultaneously.

"Watch it, nerd!" The mound of muscle, known as Maddox mocks, mashing Sam roughly.

"Hey, je . . rk ugh!" Max motioning towards Sam, finding himself underfoot of the vicious vixen herself. "Pathetic!" Carla attempting to step over Max disrespectfully when a jolt, sending her hurling off.

"Murphy!" She howls as the densely defined Danzler steps to her defense. The large lurch lunging at Jack who swiftly dodges his attempt. Shooting Danzler's near leg, lifting with all his might, sweeping the other, sending his hulkish adversary crashing heavily. Stepping forward, ducking a massive fist from Maddox, Jack jolting past the sloth to Max's side. Stepping protectively past Max, standing eye to eye with the vicious vixen.

Tense moments merging each foe's ferocity.

"Hmm. Figures." The vixen sneers sadistically. Adrenaline and contempt race recklessly between burgeoning rivals. Not giving an inch, Jack losing track of Danzler and Maddox, who have slipped behind him. "Murph, look out!" Max shouts, wincing under heel. A sinister sneer shredding across her vicious face. Hands shooting solidly lifting the two brawny brutes by their belts. Maddox and Danzler dangle disillusioned from their doings.

"Wat we ave ere? New play tings, Volkov like new play tings."

Tossing muscular miscreants aside staring disapprovingly into the dangerous Delilah's eyes.

"New recruits elp virst years. Come, class start now. Same siblings come too. Childress, Danzler, Maddox elp wiv virst years today no!" Volkov commands, marching the bitter brigade to his dojo. Slowing his pace, Volkov settling behind Jack, whispering. "Vhy cadet Murvhy look rouvgh?"

"We uh, I didn't sleep well last night, toss'd n turned all night, Sir." Jack marching slowly, allowing distance between everyone else. "Sleep good. Vhy no sleep? Mind need sleep, no?"

"Just got a lot on my mind, I guess . . . Sir."

"Haarrr. Har har har. Murvhy has secret. Vothing as vurdensome as secret. Volkov keep secret. Volkov vas secret too." The immense mentor mocks slapping Jack stiffly on his back, striding ahead as he does.

With all in attendance, plus the unexpected addition of Sam and Max, Professor Volkov pairs his pupils. Other first-year cadets stand unready across a line composed of more advanced aggressors. A muscular Maddox sneers from across the mat in Jack's direction. Uneasy about his approach, Sam shys away from the violent vixen. Cracking his neck confidently, Max extending his hand, motioning for the densely defined Danzler who stands

268

dormant, ready to dominate. All cadets ready themselves for Volkov's command.

"Last sessions, ve focused on veapon removal, but vhat if opponent is veapon?" Volkov vexing his young victims.

"Not all opponent need veapon to be veapon!"

Volkov spouts, clapping as he sends the line of accomplished cadets to their task. "Wait hold UUUPPPP ooff!" Max screams under Danzler's crushing strength, slamming him deeply into the mat. Sam dodging the violent vixen's first attempt catching a lightning leg sweep spilling to the mat below. Maddox, while muscular, is gradual because of his girth. Jack even exhausted sidestepping his immense enemy tripping him for his efforts. Allowing Maddox up, Jack dodges another attempt patiently picking his spot. Maddox, frustrated from earlier lunging over his toes when Jack strikes, throwing him off balance, both crashing to the floor. Jack seizing the opportunity, taking the muscular menaces' back, cinching a chokehold deeply. Rolling his opponent belly down, thrusting hips upward, kicking into a bridge Jack jerking life from the foolish follower. Failure foreboding his muscular frame, eyes bulging; Maddox's massive hands pounding pathetically before passing out before his peers.

Silence stunning students, the heated hero releasing his grip, kicking a motionless Maddox aside, rising slowly, eyes fixated upon the vicious vixen, inciting her innermost aggressive appetites.

269

"Good! Good Murvhy, aggression good!" Volkov, clapping thunderously. "Cadets be like cadet Murvhy, attack vith no mercy. All bones break, all bodies breathe . . . vell not all bodies." Volkov, smirking to himself, motioning for Maddox's removal from the mat.

"Next!" The immense instructor, initiating the next matchups.

First years continue enduring similar punishments as Volkov's guest cadets easily crush their untested counterparts round after round. Sam sustaining an injury sending him to Nurse Jessie. Max clumsily capturing victories over less skilled older cadets. Jack surviving multiple skilled strategies, dispelling each with renewed vigor and unequaled viciousness.

Multiple rounds pass in the waning moments of class, Volkov checking his time commands thunderously.

"Vone more. Murvhy, Duval and Danzler, Childress again!" Volkov motioning the four forward.

"True test in combat comes at a cost."

The immense instructor elicited enigmatically. Jack standing slightly ahead of Max, shielding his companion from the cruel combination. Danzler steps forward cracking his knuckles, searing vengeance in his eyes. Cadet Childress stepping forward scoffing at Max's static stance.

Eying her sadistic stare, Max mouthing mutely through his mouthpiece. "H-E-L-P!" Unaware, Jack's eyes fixated on his feminine foe waiting for his command.

270

"Cadets . . . Combat!" Volkov booms. Danzler dashes, driving densely at Jack, who dodges him easily evading. Cadet Childress paces patiently closer to her prey. Max panics, lunging awkwardly to avoid his fate.

"MURPH! LET'S TALK BOUT THISS PRETTY gir OOFFF!!!" Max shrieks Childress, catching him easily and tossing him roughly to the tiled floor beyond the mat.

"Hu, hu, HUUUuuuu." Max lands, driving wind from his lungs.

"Har hrrr" Volkov chuckles.

Finding himself outnumbered, Jack calms his breathing patiently waiting for a mistake made by the dangerous duo. Hiding from sight, cadet Childress crouches behind Danzler's dense frame. Danzler again attempting a similar assault lunging, shooting toward the singular savior. Accounting for the danger ducked behind the dense Danzler, Jack grabbing a gargantuan wrist, driving it hard into the mat below. Swinging hard driving two daggers into the surprised vixen's midsection. Writhing in pain, Danzler clutching his wrist, wails weakly, rolling himself from combat.

Rolling to her feet, heels digging deep anger seething within the vicious vixen, slinging arrows into her adversary. Jack's feet dig deeply, readying himself.

"Childress, not staring contest ATAKA! ATAKA!" Volkov commands.

271

Nodding, the dangerous Delilah dashes forward, eyes burning deep into her target. Jack takes one last breath, calming his heart, and leaps, evading her leg sweep, landing low grappling. Suddenly hushed by a quickness never experienced, the vicious vixen explodes, throwing punches and kicks, sending him shielding his face, catching blows deep to his ribs. Deflecting a few blows, Jack jolted backwards, attempting a leg sweep of his own, finding the vixen's vapors.

Landing crisply, the vicious vixen vaulting high overhead. Seeking his shot, Jack flips his hips, sending his heels driving into her lead leg. Driving the devious Delilah downward. Grappling gruffly iris' sharing searing sensations close enough to sense each other's labored breaths. The fire in Jack's eyes setting the beauty's brutality ablaze. Enjoying the struggle serenading him, the immense instructor allows his prized pupils to continue their combat unobstructed. Skillfully blocking her rapid but painful blows, Jack shoots her trail leg, attempting a takedown. Sensing such a move, the vicious vixen sending an elbow deep to the back of his neck, followed by a swift uppercut driving devilishly into his cheek, driving Jack to the mat below. Rising slowly, spitting blood, Jack clasps weakly for his mouthpiece. Stumbling to his feet, a feat on its own versus such a vicious victor, the humble hero beckoning her forward.

Barely breaking a sweat, the violent vixen vectors forward, tantalized by a terminal blow jolting forward, blocking

272

his defense away, grabbing her prey roughly when the bell blares, releasing cadets to their next class.

"Good vork. Good vork today. Tomorrow, we learn counters!" Volkov claps.

"Childress, take Danzler to medicals. Vall dismissed!" The immense instructor orders, stepping to Jack's position waving the vicious vixen away. Shoving Jack to the mat roughly, Childress spits searing her insult internally.

"Stick hick. . ."

"Cadet Murvhy . . . good vork today. Don't . . . !" Volkov begins boisterously, Jack stepping silently past his immense instructor. Limping into the locker room showers struggling to wash away his deluge of defeat. Water racing down his body, draining faster than his racing mind.

"What are you doing this for Jack?" The young cadet spits, wiping foam from their face.

"Murph, you in here?" Max's voice rings out from around the corner.

"Yeah, bout done. Give me a sec." Jack responds, rinsing shame away as best he can.

"Max, throw me that towel, please!" The crushed cadet commands.

"Oh yeah, here!" Max tossing a dry towel out of sight. Barely a minute passes before Jack steps past Max, changing into his fatigues.

"Ready?" Jack inquires, staring past Max.

273

"Yeah, yeah, Sam's with Nurse Jessie now, let's go." Max responds, looking his companion head to toe.

"Dude, you alright?" Max murmurs, catching a look from Jack, he has never seen before.

"Good, all good. Let's go check on Sam." He commands, setting off for sickbay.

Without another word, Max following the humbled hero. Dashing between cadets cascading into classrooms, Jack and Max maneuver expertly to sickbay. "Doors closed, Murph?" Max investigates ignorantly.

"And?" Jack jerking the door ajar, ushering his companion in.

"Cadet Duval and Cadet Murphy, what a wonderful surprise! I was just telling Sam, err, cadet Duval, that other than general soreness, he should be ship-shape in no time. Jack, err, cadet Murphy, what happened to your face?" The nurturing nurse leaving Sam's side checking Jack completely.

"I'm alright, just a scratch, really, I'm fine."

"How ya holdin up, buddy?" Jack jolting past her attempts at aide.

"Overall, I'm good. Just a few bruised ribs, and achy back, but I'm fine. What happened to you, Jack? It looks like you went through hell." Sam inspecting his friend closer, searching Max for answers.

"It's nothin; you should see the other guy, well gal." Jack jests.

"Oh, I see! Volkov made you spar with that witch, didn't he?" Sam presses.

274

"Well, doesn't matter now." Jack brushed the concerned cadet's hand away.

"VOLKOV! Should've known, that bully!" Jess interjects. Her tone transforming from a nurturing nurse to a maddened mother. Grabbing her coat, attempting to storm off.

. "I'm gonna give him a piece of my mind!"

"No! Nurs . . . don't." Jack jolting between her and the doorway.

"Out of my way, cadet! He's no right to subject first years to this!" She commands.

"Ma'am, please! Max, say something. Ooff!" Sam adds, jumping gingerly off the table.

"Say, what, Sam? She's right! We missed Doc's for what an epic as . . .?" Max begins as the maddened madam cuts him off.

"At ease, cadet!"

"Gentlemen, this isn't how we do things here at GYAIA. Let me handle this! Out of my way Ja, cadet Murphy!" She stomps impatiently when a familiar voice booms from beyond the doorway.

"Ah, here you gentlemen are." Cadet Blackshear steps forward. "Oh, don't here you gentlemen are, me cadet Blackshear! I know what is going on here. This isn't boys will be boys, now out of my way!" She fidgets futilely.

"Nurse Jessica, good to see you again. I've taken the liberty of reporting the incident once I heard. Gentlemen out, let Nurse

Jessica see to cadet Murphy. I'll debrief him later. Ten-hut!" Blackshear barks direction the twins out shutting the door behind.

"Now gentlemen, let's discuss why you missed Professor Brown's!" Clasping both cadets, corralling them down the corridor.

Shaking her head and hands trembling, Nurse Jessie washes her hands, drying them before fitting a fresh set of gloves.

"Ma'am, it's nothing really. Nurse Jess . . ." Jack spouts sheepishly.

"It's not nothing, Jack! First years are not permitted direct combat with advanced assets!" She scoffs, prepping her instruments. The twins, you, could've been . . ." She begins biting her lip.

"You all could have been seriously injured. That Childress has always been a menace, and Triden makes her worse. Now sit!" She commands. Checking the young cadet thoroughly before divulging her diagnosis.

"Well, you look like hell, but you check out. That's a nasty contusion below your eye. The general soreness in your neck should subside with rest. While you're cleared for combat, I'm not clearing you from checking in two days about those rib contusions. Jack, this cadet, she's expertly trained to be a . . ." Jess' voice trailing off, removing her gloves.

"She's what? Jess, please?" Jack pleads, pulling his shirt over his head.

276

"She's an assassin asset! Her sole purpose is to disarm, dismember, or destroy any target that impedes her mission." Her voice trailing, struggling to contain herself.

"Assassin asset? Oh, I thought you were going to tell me . . ." Jack jests gingerly tucking his shirt.

"Jack, I'm serious. Steer clear; you have nothing to prove." Turning to conceal emotion welling in her eyes.

"What is it, ma'am? Oh, okay, okay I will, but. . ." Jack says, noting her tender tone.

"Nurse Jess got a question. Before I left, Aunt Anna gave me an old keychain. A surfboard with the words *sunshine summers* on it. I feel like now is the time to dwell on the past." Patting his pockets, realizing the keychain is missing again.

"What the hell, where is it? Wore these last night?" His eyes rivet from pocket to pocket, patting pathetically.

"She kept it . . .," whispering to herself, concealing a comforting chuckle and turning wicking wetness from her eyes.

"Jack, Jack, what's the matter?"

"It's not here. It was in my pocket when . . ." Stunned silence sets in when a heavy rap on the door wreaking any reckoning from the room.

"Nurse Jessica? Cadet Murphy, all done?" Blackshear's voice melting all memories away.

Turning to the nurturing nurse, speechlessly searching for words, Jack steps silently. Nurse Jessie jolting to her office, leaving the door slightly ajar, sniffing softly to herself.

"Ok, come in!"

"Cadet, you ship shape?" Blackshear belts boorishly.

"Snff. Yeah, all's well, Sir." Jack turns his gaze, tugging tersely from the silhouette of serenity sobbing singularly within her office.

"Swell. Debriefed the twins, they are safely in Professor Brown's laboratory. Now, just a few last things to tie up. Come Murphy; let Nurse Jessica do her work. I'm sure she's catching up on past patients." Blackshear ushering Jack hastily.

CHAPTER TWENTY FIVE

DESCENT INTO MADNESS

Pushing past Blackshear, Jack strides off silently, struggling to understand the quickly changing world around him. The pair navigate to an empty corridor adorned with stories from bygone eras etched in all directions. Quiet moments fade between Jack and Blackshear before the burly cadet addresses his distressed companion.

"What's the hurry cadet?" Blackshear easily catching his quiet quarry.

"Hurry? You're in a hurry, Sir." Jack retorts, jolting ahead.

"Fair point, but for good reason, Murphy, Murphy! . . . About-face cadet!" Blackshear booms, departing his usually even tone.

"As I thought. I'll be speaking with Nurse Jessica about her diagnosis. At ease cadet." Blackshear nearing his young cadet.

"Jack, I have no idea what's going through that mind of yours, but I . . ." Blackshear begins dropping all decorum before Jack cuts him off abruptly.

"What's going through it . . . is that I'm not built for this. I'm just a nobody from nowhere, which I felt for fifteen years. Fifteen years! I'm no secret agent or asset or whatever. I'm just a kid, a troublemaker. Sam and Max are genius anomalies, and almost everyone else is some kinda spy royalty. Me, I'm just Jack, the nobody from nowhere." Sighing heavily, kicking at his presumptive self.

"I'm not special . . . not special." Still kicking at nothing, his tone lowers, showing respect for his superior.

"You're definitely not nobody, Jack." Blackshear's tone regaining its benign self.

"Could have fooled me. For a minute there, I thought I was good, but today. I've wrestled older wrestlers before, but today will continue, won't it, Sir?" Jack's head hanging low at the prospect.

"Not sure, Jack, Volkov was out of line, and it's being investigated, especially given noncombatant assets were involved." Blackshear placing a reassuring hand gently upon Jack's shoulder.

"So, I've heard, but it will for me. Soon, I'll just be a joke to those people. Just a stick hick that . . ." Jack sulks, hanging his head lower.

"NO! They'd be wrong. You're so much more!" Blackshear bolstering his position, looking over each shoulder before speaking again.

"Jack, I don't know why you're here, but it was clear from the beginning that you're different."

Pondering his peer's persistence, Jack presses.

"Different . . . I've felt that way for the longest. Nothing new, but why me, Brian, why me?"

"Hmm, that I do not know, Jack. I do know that different isn't necessarily a negative. I would've advised against taking on Carla." Blackshear produces, searching to console his cadet and catching his own personal connection.

"Carla? You mean cadet Childress?" Jack turning away, rubbing his cheek carefully.

"I'm sorry, Jack, our history is complicated, as you know, and it's not important here. You are." Blackshear pivoting the topic away from her.

"Yeah, maybe. Don't care what the history is, I want to trust you, but I don't know who to trust now. Volkov trying to get my head torn off, Crane humiliating me in front of everyone, some mystery person in Doc's lab, Nurse Jess knowing Aunt Anna . . . nobody is telling me anything that makes sense." Jack's voice trailing off into his own thoughts.

"Ooofff. You have a lot going on, Jack; I can see that . . . I'm here for you, but the real reason I'm here is more concerning." Blackshear pausing in place.

"More concerning?" His superior's words piquing Jack's interest.

"In all that happened today, Triden was absent. There was a reason for this. He . . ." Blackshear begins.

"Triden? He what?" Jack interjects.

"Triden is why I'm here, Jack." Blackshear begins.

"Triden has been on the warpath all day. Not to worry, I have it on good authority Wiley is giving him and his crew a proper chewing as we speak."

"I know you need no reminding, but I'd be remised if I didn't remind you to steer clear of Triden and his crew. I'm serious, Jack, I've solid intel that Triden will look to gain some credibility back and in a big way from today's setback." Blackshear pauses, knowing Jack is chomping to respond. Allowing Jack to speak freely, Blackshear nods for him to do so.

"Set back, what set back? In a big way?" The inexperienced first-year inquires.

"While you don't see it this way, you've embarrassed him more than you know. You stood up to him and his troop. Triden types only have power over those that fear them." Blackshear continues cautiously surveying the corridor. Murals of mythical moments line the silent corridor's rising walls. Still new to GYAIA's traditions and history Jack presses ignorantly.

"Ok, I follow, but what big way?"

"The . . . The Trials of Titans, of course."

"Trials of Titans? Some cadets mentioned it at mess once. What's the big deal?" Jack inquires ignorantly.

"The Trials of Titans is a multi-stage gauntlet, an obstacle course, but not any run-of-the-mill type. Designed to test more than physical endurance; it's a test of one's will, Jack."

"Hold on, this Trials of Titans, what's it got to do with me?" Jack presses.

"My intel has informed me that . . . Triden has filed to enter The Trials of Titans as a singles challenger." Blackshear continues, confident of the confidentiality of their conversation.

"So what, that wuss can enter all he wants. Without his goon squad, he'll never. . ." Jack interjects, but Blackshear cuts in coldly.

"That is why I am here, Jack!" Blackshear, raising his voice, grabbing Jack's undivided attention.

"First years are typically barred from competition . . . however, a single challenger is not allowed to test the Trials of Titans alone . . . they have, by rite of rule, to choose a fellow competitor." Blackshear continues shaking his head at Jack's naiveté.

"So he what chooses an opponent to compete against, right?" Jack speaking out of turn.

"Yes, Jack, and he has." Blackshear hanging his head.

"So what, his big way to get back at me is to choose you? Then what? Defeat you, an accomplished cadet, and embarrass your entire unit, too?" Jack, pressing his superior.

"No, the original challenger can select any active combatant cadet. That cadet is . . . is you, Jack." Blackshear's voice cracks, signaling the severity of his revelation.

"Me? Wait what? I'm a first year; you said first years are barred from these trials." Jack stepping into Blackshear's view.

"That's not entirely true; the precedence was set years ago and to a most disastrous result. If my Intel is solid, Triden will challenge The Trials of Titans and select you, not me, as his rite of rule opponent." Blackshear turning away, pacing nervously, reassuring the hall's secrecy.

"Me? Why a first year? Jack inquires.

"Retaliation Jack. You disrespected him by not fearing him. That's why." Blackshear responds, checking his watch.

"Too bad for him, he's the jerk. I'll accept his challenge. These trials are toast." Jack defiantly responding to this revelation.

"I was afraid you'd say that, Murphy." Blackshear's voice somber in tone.

"So you fear I'll fail?" Jack retorts.

"No, no, I don't. Failure isn't the fear. Descending into madness willingly is when we fall the furthest, Murphy, please . . ." Blackshear's voice trailing off at a break in the silence of a nearby hallway.

"Well I appreciate your vote of confidence Sir, but I'm lost. You're acting like I'll die or something. So what is it, Sir?" Jack responds, reading deeper into his superior's enigmatic expression.

"Murphy, the Trials of Titans has never been completed by a first year; even seasoned cadets never complete the Trials." Blackshear rubbing his shoulder, looking distantly down the hall.

"Wait, you've tested these trials before, haven't you?" Jack presses.

"Yes, yes, I did once, and it nearly cost me." Blackshear marveling at his young cadet's conclusion.

"Cost you? Who was you're challenger then?" Jack speaking silently, allowing random groups of cadets to careen by.

Blackshear pauses, exchanging customary salutes acknowledging his station as they pass.

"The short version, cadet Childress and I both challenged each other. We were close back then; she's always been driven . . . not to best me, but driven to prove herself, I suppose. Not important, she won. We were equal til the Escape from Tartarus. I lost my grip, she didn't. Childress won, and the rest is history." Blackshear rotating his shoulder, rubbing it in remembrance.

"So what happened? What did it cost you not being friends anymore?" Jack now intrigued by their history.

"Something like that. Success has a way of attracting the wrong type of people. As for me, I was awarded the dubious duty of looking after knucklehead first years when I recovered from my injuries." Breaking a smile Blackshear jests.

"Success . . . wrong types, yeah, I know something about that. So Triden took interest . . . wait, what injuries?" Jack presses.

"All healed now. I warned her, but their parents go way back, and so, you know." Breaking character, once more, Blackshear briefly allowing Jack to peer into his personal perspective.

"I get it. You became the champion of chumps and she became Triden's champion attack dog." Jack halfhearted attempt at humor, failing on his superior.

"Yeah, sure, something like that. Cadet, these trials take everything you got. Most don't even make it halfway. Murphy, these trials aren't just treacherous. They're downright dangerous. Accepting Triden's rite of rule will do only one of three things . . .

you fail, risking irreparable injury in the process, or you best Triden in these trials and embarrass him permanently, placing a target on your back for your entire career here at GYAIA. The third option, of course, is to reject his rite of rule, thus giving him the satisfaction of your fear." Blackshear pauses, gathering his final thoughts on the matter.

"Murphy, there is no recourse if you fail, excel, or deny his challenge." Blackshear prudentially paces, anticipating his young cadet's response.

"So it's a lose, lose, lose scenario either way?" Jack responding rhetorically.

"Correct, the professor's council will not intercede, Professor Wiley cannot intercede without accusations of bias, only Madam Director can resend the rite of rule, and no acting director has ever done so. Triden doesn't deserve this right of rule, but his connections are above our pay grades. He's gunnin' for you." Jack's stout superior solemnly states.

"Sir, I'm not ready. I know this, but I am not afraid. If I've learned anything so far, is that there will always be bullies, size doesn't really matter . . . and so what if the bullies of my past weren't some Senator's son. They're still bullies, ya know, the best way to stop a bully?" Jack pausing, gathering his words, staring daringly into Blackshear's eyes.

"Yeah, Jack, what is that?" Blackshear beckons, dropping decorum, bewildered by his cadet's courage.

"Simple, punch em in the mouth. Bullies never like to bleed and I like makin' bullies bleed." Jack confides coldly. Absorbing his cadet's confidence, Blackshear digs deep into his pocket, producing a device driving it deep into his young cadet's chest.

"True, very true. Well, if you're gonna make the bully bleed, then bloody em good, eh!" Blackshear stuffing something in Jack's hand, salutes before turning to soldier off.

"What's this, Sir? Sir?" Jack forwards, fumbling the contents of his hand.

"Trial specs. Give them to the twins for analysis! Oh yeah, cadet Murphy tell the twins lights out at 2100, not 0200, not 0300." Blackshear nods, pressing his uniform back into regulation, regaining his superior status before bolting down the hall.

"Yes Sir 2100, Sir. Bloody em good?" Jack salutes, digging the device deep into his pocket before checking the time.

"The twins should still be in Doc's. Wait till they hear bout this!" Peddling towards Doc's laboratories, fears fleeting faster than footsteps fading underfoot.

CHAPTER TWENTY SIX

STORMS STRIKE SILENTLY

"Yes, yes, Sir. Yes, disproportional balance between magno-receptors. Got it, Doc!" Max muses to his maniac mentor.

"Now, Samuel, I sent you manuals on basic pro langs Python, Java, Julia, and a few others. Read them, I mean it. Don't just skim. Read them. I'll quiz you later." Doc Brown persists.

"And when I ace said quiz, when do I get to see BESTY's langs?" Sam jests in return.

"No, no, not my BESTY, not my girl. Well, butter my biscuits! You've decoded my notebook. Very impressive, Samuel. Yes, very impressive!" The thought turning the eccentric egghead's tone to proud papa.

"Well, not all of it, only eight percent, give or take a page." Sam states sheepishly.

"Eight percent, you say. Well, slurp my Slurpee, what parts?! I prefer cherry, by the way. Outside of the BESTY bits, do tell?" Doc Brown's eyes, illuminating eagerly.

"Well, BESTY used blowfish, but you only referred to her script specs but left out a lot of lang. I'm familiar with some blocks and algorithms." Sam staring at the ceiling searching his catalog of knowledge.

288

"Oh goodie, block, algorithm, caesar, hill, transposition. I used them all or most of them, even the ones I developed myself. Say how you figured I used blowfish for BESTY?" Brown brandishing a big grin.

"Easy, you've mentioned your pet blowfish, Besty, only a million times during lectures. Kinda obvious, don't you think?" Sam jokes.

"Well, bait my blowfish! Incredible Samuel, Truly!" The peculiar professor proudly preens.

"Rather elementary if you know what you're looking at." Sam slyly surmises.

"Ahh, another Brownism, I see. Is this the part where we L . . O . . L out loud?" Brown boasts.

"No, no, Sir, there will definitely be no LOLing." Max slapping Sam softly on the shoulder.

"Yah, no LOLing, Sir." Sam shaking his head at their put-down professor.

"I will read up on those scripts, Doc." Sam nods supportively, stepping into Jack.

"Oompff, gotach Sam! Professor Brown, Sir." Jack says steading Sam, saluting Doc.

"No need for such pleasantries, Cadet Murphy." Professor Brown bunglingly, saluting the young cadet. "Gents, mess time. Sorry for the . . ." Jack begins.

"No, no nourishment necessary, very necessary." Brown boasts, pushing the trio towards a well-deserved dinner.

"Thank you, Sir. Thank you . . ." Jack nods respectfully.

"Cadet Murphy, don't pull . . . just swing with it." The peculiar professor perplexingly proposes pulsating back and forth.

"Yes, Sir, swing with it. Got it. Gents?" Jack saluting, simultaneously steering the twins towards suppertime.

"Dude, I've almost got it, Murph." Max meandering ahead.

"Soteria?" Jack inquires.

"Yeah, Doc says I'm close, but can't help but feel like I'm looking at it all wrong Murph." Max motioning for Sam to catch up.

"I'm catching up, Jack how did combat go?" Sam presses.

"Yeah, bout that . . . defeated Danzler and Maddox easily. Big oafs just can't figure out how not to get over their toes." Jack answers.

"And the she-beast?" Sam inquires. "Don't call her that!" Max blurts out, eying the wall for support.

"Yeah, ok, so Childress?" Sam correcting his previous inquiry. Pausing searching for words, rubbing his elbow, Jack responds.

"Childress she's . . . she's different. Fast, aggressive, technically flawless. She's just different, my dude, and got one heck of an arm bar." Jack presses forward.

"You good, though, right?" Sam catching up, pressing his luck.

"Yeah, hey what did Doc mean back there?" Turning to Sam, eyes teeming with tremendous trepidation. "Whoa, you're not good. What's going on, Jack?" Sam sensing a shift in his friend's spirit.

"Tell you when we get back to the dorm. Doc said, *"don't pull, just swing with it"* Why would he say that?" Jack questions.

"Not sure why he'd say it, but what he said must be referring to something an object of sorts. You must already know what this IT he is referring?" Sam suggests centering his glasses.

"I know you're right, Sam, but what is it?" Jack scanning the floor for answers.

"Well, whatever it is, not gonna taste like them herb taters, hurry up my dudes." Max hustling ahead hungrily.

"Whatever it is, we'll figure it out, Jack." Sam states supportively, speeding off himself, lifted by heavenly aromas aerating the hallway.

"It's a clue, Cadet Murphy!" A familiar voice, rousing Jack to attention.

"Professor Bray, Ma'am." Pausing in place Jack stiffens, saluting at attention.

"At ease, cadet. A word, please?" Bray saluting, accepting an agreeable nod from the young cadet.

"I'm aware Blackshear has spoken to you about cadet Triden's right of rule challenge. Cadet Murphy, I professionally object to first years participating in the Trials of Titans; however the decision is above my paygrade." Bray begins briskly checking over each shoulder.

"But I digress; do you still have the specs?" She inquires.

291

"Yes . . . yes, ma'am." Jack feeling his pocket remembering what he's gained and lost.

"Good, keep it safe and make sure those boy wonders don't get a hold of it." She states stepping aside returning salutes to a group of cadets passing by. Pausing until the path is clear, she nods and continues.

"Professor Bray, please tell me what's going on? Why me? Why am I?" Jack stammers through an ocean of questions surging.

"Storms strike silently. Cadet, you're the storm they didn't see coming. Find me tomorrow after your classes conclude." Bray offers.

"Yes, ma'am, may I ask why?" Jack fidgets, feeling foolish for asking.

"Before Volkov took over close-quarters combat, I instructed the course. I'm sure there's a particular pupil of mine you're having trouble with. We'll speak after class. Get some sleep tonight, cadet." The mysterious ma'am nods, saluting before swiftly stepping away. Stunned in place, pondering the meaning of her wisdom.

"Storms, Volkov, pupil? What's going on, Jack?" Questions flooding his mind, stomach rumbling; rescuing the young cadet.

"Man, what a day." Whispering to himself and making his way to the mess hall.

Grabbing a tray passing through quickly Jack makes his way to the twins sitting alone to themselves.

292

"Sup, gents. How's them taters?" Jack says, stealing a bit from Max's plate.

"Hey, get your own Murph." Max protests, pulling piled potatoes from reach. "So Jack . . . eat, eat. I've been thinking . . ." Sam starts wiping his mouth.

". . . about what Doc said. Swing, not pull. Where were you just now? You . . ." Sam begins cut off by Max spitting potatoes particles in their direction.

"Who were you talking to? Whatcha not telling us, Murph?"

"Cover your mouth, Max." Shaking his head in disgust, Sam interjects. "What this idiot means is Doc knows something we don't at this time. Max, Max, wipe your whole mouth, not just there you go." Sam, shaking his head again, regaining his composure.

"So what is it, Jack?" Sam presses. Peering over each shoulder skeptically, leaning close disclosing one word.

"Trials of Titans . . ." Sending Sam sinking into his seat, Max leaning in. "The trials, that's for experienced cadets. Whatcha mean trials, like the Trials of Titans Murph?" Max mimics his downtrodden duplicate.

"Yes. Blackshear said the older Triden's influence giving the younger a right of rule challenge in the Trials of Titans. He's gonna challenge me." Jack pauses, soaking in his own words. "He can't do that! When?" Max standing slightly in his seat looking around the mess hall.

"Max, sit, sit. If Blackshear said so, then it must be true. What will you do, Jack?" Sam pulling his manic multiple downward.

"Beat him, of course. Not sure how, but I have this, and I have you guys." Jack stabs at his plate, producing the device Blackshear gave him.

"Oooo, me likey!" Max's eyes light up at the device, waving before his eyes.

"What's on it, Jack?" Sam inquires side, eying his crazed copy.

"Blackshear said Trail specs are for you guys to analyze." Jack answers, waving his hand past Max's eager digits, placing the device in Sam's guaranteed grip.

"Oh, no fair, ur a trickster, Murph." Max mules pawing pathetically at his brother.

"Get off me, you idiot." Sam pushing Max away.

"We'll look into this tonight. When is this challenge occurring, Jack?" Sam questions.

"Funny enough, don't know. Blackshear only told me Triden would challenge soon." Jack shrugs, collecting their purged plates.

"Challenge accepted then, we'll be ready." Max muses manically, contemplating his catalog of creations.

"Hold on, he doesn't have to accept." Sam states, slapping Max's hand away.

"No, but if I don't, then we'll be worse off." Jack jumping up, throwing their trash away. "Come on, gents, we got some homework."

"Yes, yes, homework me, likey homework!" Max tapping fingers together, eagerly awaiting the device's contents. The trio trot off undeterred to their dorm.

"What a crazy few days." Max kicking off his boots jumping onto Sam's bed.

"Gentlemen gonna catch a shower first. Sam, would you do the honors?"

"Way ahead of ya, boss. Got a guess at the encryption, Bro?" Sam inquires, slapping Max's sweaty feet off his bed as his computer screen glows to life.

"Ooo, gotta be AES. I mean, GYAIA is a gov outfit, right?" Max responds, posting a chair next to Sam's.

"Maybe, let's see. Could be twofish. Ok, here we go, not two fish. You guessed it, Bro, AES. Hello there. Are we a 192 or 256? They wouldn't go 126 would they?" Sam talking to himself, both completely in their element.

"Well, let's find an access point." Sam and Max go about their task as Jack attempts to wash away the events of the day. Muted minutes melt away until Jack returns from his shower-soaked psyche.

"Any luck Gents?" Jack asks, jumping on to his bed and stretching out.

"Well, we'll have to back door this encryption, could take a while, but we'll get there." Sam responds, pecking away.

"What's the hold-up? Doesn't it just use a password?" Jack jests, chucking the towel at Max.

"Har, har. If we knew the password, we'd just type it in now wouldn't we?" Max retorts, ripping the damp towel off his head.

"Passwords are nice, but these encryptions can be tricky. Open to suggestions." Sam states, staring deep into his work.

"Who gave you this again, Blackshear?" Max questions, contemplating a shower of his own.

"Yeah, but I don't think it was his originally." Jack responds, reading through his worn copy of Art of War.

"What do you mean not his originally? Then who's?" Sam presses, pausing his task.

"Before mess, Professor Bray stopped me in the hall and spoke to me about a few things." Jack grows quiet as his mind wanders.

"A few things, like what?" Sam scooting his chair back.

"She wants me to see her after class tomorrow. It has something to do with Childress; she's really working me in Volkov's." Jack pausing his half-hearted studies.

"Volkov, that dirty rat. Ohh, what I'd give to rumble with that Russian reject!" Max muses, waving clinched fists foolishly.

"Yeah, he'd pretzel you in a heartbeat." Jack jokes, catching his towel effortlessly.

"That's beside the point; he still deserves a good . . ." Max mules, Sam interrupting Max's emerging ill-mannered comment.

"So the password did Blackshear or Bray give you such a thing? A clue or riddle, maybe?" Sam snorting, silencing a sneeze.

"No, he focused mainly on Triden's challenge, tell you later, but nothing useful outside saying they were Trial specs." Jack jostling his head, hoping to jog his memory.

"Well what's that big lug Blackshear up to; maybe we can guess his password? Protein powder good, or maybe muscles for days!" Max mocks swiveling in place.

"Hold on now, Max, Jack, you spoke to Professor Bray about somethings, did she say anything odd or out of the ordinary?" Sam taps his mouse.

"Well, she did mention something about me being the storm or something, but Doc made that weird comment earlier, too. I dunno man." Jack turning away from his companions. The twins pause, gathering each other's thoughts with a glance.

"Come on, Murph, what's up?" Max making his way to the edge of Jack's bunk, poking him comically.

"I don't understand it, guys, why me? Why all the secrets? Why are some professors helping and some hurting me?" Jack sharing thoughts mounting in his mind.

"Not sure on the whys, but there's plenty of alphabets before Y. We should start there. So what did Bray say exactly?" Sam inquires, distracting his conflicted companion.

"Oh, shoot... give me a sec . . . storms silently strike. No, um, oh! Storms strike silently and then told me I was that storm. Dunno what if that's helpful." Jack sinking deeper into his bunk.

"Storms strike silently? Storms have thunder. They're not silent at all." Max says mockingly.

"Eureka! It worked!" Sam shouts.

"You're telling me every day feels like a surprise. What worked, Sam?" Jack jumping from his bed. Max and Jack leaning over Sam's shoulders.

"The silent striking storm or whatever, that was the password. Let's see, hmm, small files to unzip, less than a Gig on this thing, wow GYAIA just WOW!" Sam exclaims, wrinkling his face at the basic device.

"Is that bad? Broke?" Jack inquires, fearing the worst.

"No, no, Murph, the USB is just standard hardware. Don't mind Sam, he's being a tech snob. When secretly transferring data always go basic devices. Think small easy to hide in something, cheap to replicate backups. Only idiots go super fancy with disposables. Good encryption what's important. There are only about six hundred megabytes here. We're not talking bout Frontier or Lumi computations here, Murph!" Max muses.

"Shoot fire look at this!" Sam exclaims, shifting his glasses.

"Oh, baby there she is. Let me see . . ." Max pawing oddly at Sam's mouse.

"Stop that weirdo." Sam slapping his hand away.

"So this is it? The Trials of Titans?" Jack's voice stiffening upon inquiry.

"Yes, Jack, I'm sure of it. According to this, this file is only days old, but there are files with much older creation dates.

Hmm." Sam states, rubbing his chin, clicking intensely through files of photos.

"Hmm, what, Sam?" Jack jolting him back to reality.

"Oh, I think this must be a recent configuration, not the one you will face." Sam shares silently, continuing to click.

"I think you're right, Bro. There must be versions of past trials, and these pics are oddly specific given few share the same timestamps; likely not from the same set of trials. Question is, what does it all mean? Hmm. . . ." Max mimicking his multiple mannerisms subconsciously.

"So basically Murph . . ." Max begins cut off by his quicker companion.

"Basically, someone is trying to tell me what to prepare for." Jack interjects, staring stoically, reflections rifling by his eyes.

"Exactly! The real question is the sequence of these elements. Can't just build you any old thing." Max says, clicking on his desk lamp, sketching hastily.

"Build what?" Jack asks, peeking past Sam. "Your own personal training simulation, of course." Max chuckles to himself, scratching ideas hastily.

"Wait, what? Triden hasn't challenged me yet, and who says I'll accept. Maybe I'll back down. Public humiliation isn't so bad after a while, did'ya think of that?" Jack jumping back making a scene.

"Yeah, ok! Don't think you even know what those words mean, Murph!" Max jests, pointing at photos on the screen and sharing a silent conversation with Sam. "What words?" Jack craning his neck, catching a glimpse of genius at work.

"Back down, Jack . . . yes, I see it... write that down . . . it's kinda your thing Jack, you don't back down, and neither are we." Sam states, pointing at various details for Max to scribble down.

"Wait, hold on, what are you guys talking about?" Jack sitting down confused. "Look, Jack, get some rest. Max and I will finish breaking these specs down. Lots to do, lots to do. You think Doc will let us use his ExoLifts?" Sam waving Jack away continuing his conversation with Max.

"For sure, let's me use them for Soteria mods all the time. We can clear out section C tomorrow and begin to build preps. Nobody even knows bout that dump. Gonna need a lot of 550 paracord for this one." Max responds, eyes bulging with anticipation.

"That looks like 550 but this one's less than 1.2 milly. What's micro holding up?" Sam wiping sleep from his eyes, pointing at a peculiar picture.

"Well, at least someone is enjoying all this." Jack sighs to himself. Brushing his teeth, settling in bed, rocked gently to sleep by twin companions tossing ideas back and forth nearby.

CHAPTER TWENTY SEVEN

"I JUST BELIEVE!"

0500 arrives quicker and quicker, alarms blaring, rousing the small dorm's inhabitants. Jack's sore but surprisingly rested, wrestling his fatigues, pressing them into place.

"Come on, gents get in reg. We gotta go." Jack jostling Max from a well-deserved slumber.

"No, Mom, Sam did it." Max murmurs.

"Get dressed, you idiot! We got work to do." Sam kicking his sleepy sibling.

The trio fall into the routine of rank and file waiting in the hallway.

"Good morning cadet Singh, De Mendes, Ruiz! Good morning cadets, who's ready for a brisk morning run? Where are those three?" Blackshear booms, marshalling his cadets looking for his missing trio.

"There you are! Cadets Duval and Duval, you're exempt from morning run the next few days for injuries accrued in class. Report to Professor Brown, morning meal should be waiting on you. Busy days ahead, boys." Blackshear lowering his voice, nodding in Doc's direction.

"Murphy fall in!" Blackshear booms resuming his commanding tone.

"Thank you, Sir. I did have this pain in my . . . Oww, we're going, and we're going!" Max saluting foolishly fumbling as Sam shoves him to their directive.

"Yes, Sir, on the double, Sir." Sam says, saluting respectfully. Blackshear and Sam, exchanging understanding nods.

"Let go, Bro. Wow you've gotten strong, wait what's going on?" Max mules.

"Shh, tell ya on the way. Hurry up." Sam stepping swiftly down the hall.

"Get the lead out, cadets, MOVE, MOVE, MOVE!!!" Blackshear bellows, bolting ahead leading his cadets. Morning runs finish quickly, finding Jack eating morning mess alone in the twin's absence.

"Well, well, well, what do we have here? A cadet with no company." Maddox meanders into Jack's plate, spilling its contents on the floor.

"Oops. Didn't see you there, tiny!" Maddox mocks fist-bumping Danzler, who settles roughly next to Jack.

"Got something for you in Volkov's little man." The dense dummy divulges, displacing his hated host hastily.

"Loser seating not so bad. What you think, Maddie?" The dimwitted dunce dissing on his own.

"Don't call me that in public, Daniel!" Maddox mashing Jack's head down settling stiffly next to the young cadet.

"Double D? Ur Mom name ya?" Jack jests, clapping Danzler's dorsal densely.

"Hey bro, you can't uoompff!" Maddox grabs Jack roughly before ripped to his feet roughly.

"Not starting trouble, are we, gentlemen?" Blackshear pushing Maddox easily away, staring sternly into Danzler's eyes.

"No, no, Sir." Maddox mumbles moronically.

"Just talkin with Murphy bout Volkov's, weren't we?" Danzler responds rising eye to eye with Blackshear beckoning for battle.

"Best move on." Blackshear barks backing down the two behemoths.

"Sir, yes, Sir." The pair salute sadistically in Jack's direction. Staring steadily till the two step away, Blackshear holds his ground.

"Got a lot to learn about dealing with size and numbers, Murphy." Blackshear eying the dangerous duo.

"Those two twits? Haven't beaten me yet in Volkov's." Jack interjects ignorantly. "Alone, maybe, a wolf is weak. Wolves attack in a pack. You know this, Jack." Blackshear keeps an eye of the dubious duo.

"I know why you're here, Brian." Jack responds, picking up his breakfast from the floor, brushing its contents, contemplating its consumption. "Here have mine, Jack, already ate." Blackshear's stare searing seriousness into his cadet's eyes.

"Triden will challenge today . . . say nothing but what's been decided, Jack." Blackshear whispers pushing a tray towards his cadet.

"Sir, what if . . ." Jack begins accepting the meal gratefully.

303

"Know you're not alone, cadet." Blackshear nodding, saluting passing cadets.

"Sir, yes, Sir." Jack eating eagerly, a feeling of security flooding from each bite. "Got rounds. See to the twins' cadet, lights out at 2100." Blackshear nods brushing past his prized cadet, saluting cadets as he passes.

Jack finishes his meal hastily making his way to his first class. The day, absent of Sam and Max continues without incident.

"Late again, Murvhy. Vines cadets take position!" Volkov voices vehemently. Taking position against Maddox, Jack readies himself.

"Атака!" Volkov shouts. Maddox rushes as usual, Jack side-stepping the muscled menace, tossing him easily. Stepping back into position, daring the deviant director defiantly.

"Good, good, vight vid vigor, vight . . . Murvhy?" Volkov veers vexed by the visual of Jack's victory. "Murvhy, Childress." The villain vents.

Stepping close, the vicious vixen vexing vision upon her victim.

"Let's get this over with." Jack whispers, stepping forward. Childress acknowledging her adversary, adjusting wrist-wraps willingly. "Stop givin me you're back, won't ya." The vicious vixen voices readying herself.

"Come get it." Jack jolting forward, shooting sideways, attempting to surprise his foe. Faking a shoot on her forward leg, sliding sideways taking her trail leg driving the dangerous Delilah

304

to the ground. At lightning's length, the vicious vixen spins grappling Jack's shoulder cinching deeply, forcing him to tap.

"Hmpff. . .hmpff nice, got me there. You're instep is insane." Jack wrangling his arm free, offering an olive branch.

"You're smart but slow." Slapping his humbled hand away spitting as she does.

"For now, for now." Jack whispers, holding his index finger and thumb together. "You're not close, first year." The victorious vixen storms off clearly bored with her hasty victory.

"Murvhy, Maddox next. Dis time no tap little man." Volkov venting frustration.

"First year too cocky we fix dat. . . Maddox Раздавить!" Whispering his directives to the muscular Maddox. Sighing deeply, Jack settling to his feet, readying himself for another round.

The hardwood feels firm underfoot, Jack catches a glimpse of his reflection. His face serious and stern. The boy in the mirror staring back at him over the years fading within each bead of sweat. Whipping his forehead, Jack steadies his breathe surrounded by adversaries incased by walls rising into cold lifeless steel framing. Banners randomly dot the steel ceiling frame, swaying calmly, quietly cheering him on when a smile creases Jack's face.

"Come on, yes, step left, then overhand right as always. What a predictable oaf." Jack smirks to himself, dodging the dense dummy's attack with ease.

305

"Oh I'll get yah, promise. Oh, a shoot really? This was your master plan?" Jack thinks silently cinching in a headlock, choking the muscular menace out. Flipping into a bridge, maximizing his mayhem upon the muscular moron. The heavy thud of Maddox's mold laying limp leaving Jack staring at the vile Volkov.

"Not bad, Danzler Go! Vipe smile off face!" The insidious instructor instructs. "Hmmpff, whatever you like, jerk." Jack whispers, dodging his dense opponent.

The twins work quickly, removing crates of randomly forgotten hardware examined and removed swiftly, as a massive hangar revealing ancient bones opens up. Beams rise and fall, quickly stacked for use or removal.

"No, no, Max! Those go to section B, subfloor 3 good, good! Yes, Sam, you got it now! Getting good using the Exolift! Place those there!" Doc directs.

"Yes, Sir. Doc, where did'ya get all this?" Sam starts, cut off by Doc's directives. "Government good at spending taxpayer' taxes. Yes! Gently now, gently, Max! Good! Sam, take those last crates away! Good! Now we build!" Doc delightedly dictates, surveying the empty space.

"Remember, boys, stick to the script. Everything must go in its proper place!" Doc directs, stepping away, attending his other cadets.

"Bro, that was easy with these Exolifts!" Max manipulating his metallic members.

306

"Yeah, yeah. You were right, we got work to do. According to the specs vaults go here, and runs go here." Sam starting to piece together their version of violence.

"Yup, yup. Specs say drops should go right about here!" Max shouts, moving mayhem into place as he shifts large beams into place.

"Say, Sam, why d'ya think Doc made so many adjustments to our original configuration?"

"Elementary, my dear duo, Doc designed this year's Trials of Titans! He's just not sayin it! No, Max. Specs say this run goes after this balance, followed by the vault. Yeah, like that!" Sam stabilizing his side of a daunting drop. "Point taken, this is much better than MIT!" Max muses manipulating framework, erecting another sadistic structure.

"Say, Sam, why doesn't Jack just train on the real deal? I mean, it's got to be somewhere on campus?" Max questions fitting his work to purpose.

"Good question. Security would be tight, I'd assume, nothing we couldn't hack, but Blackshear gave us these specs, and given nobody knows about section C, Jack can train without anyone ever knowing." Sam suggests settling steel into place.

"What bout Doc's mystery visitor?" Max inquires, inserting beam after beam to construct their colossus.

"Ya know, he hasn't been as jumpy since he gave us his notebook for safekeeping. Max, I figured whatever else was in that notebook was what our mystery person wanted. Doc has been his usual uncanny self hasn't he?" Sam surmises, setting the sizable structure seamlessly and with ease.

"You're probably right, no, not there, Sam. Specs say jump to ring thingies go here!" Max corrects connecting corresponding pieces together. "Got it. Say, Sam, do you think Jack can actually beat this thing?" Max ponders, patching away.

"I believe he's capable, not sure he believes he's capable." Sam surmises, sifting through sizable steel beams.

"Bro, Murph, Murph doesn't even know what he's capable of. That dude has so much going on right now. Once he figures it all out, Bro, he's gonna be something special." Max manifests manipulating manifolds according to specs.

"No cap on that!" Sam says, setting sizable pieces into place.

"Max, why do you think he does it though?" Sam inquires, inserting piece after piece. "Dunno; he's not wrong, though." Max continues.

"About what?" Sam inquires, setting another piece into place.

"He's being targeted. He's just an orphan from some nowhere town and, suddenly, he's here being called out by some powerful senator's jerk offspring. For what . . . being better? Bro, you know pieces are missing." Max replies, rigging parts together tightly.

"More than we know, I'm sure. Could also be a trap? Triden may also have access to these specs. Hopefully, this contraption will help shed some light when Jack beats that jerk." Sam admits breaking from his usually reserved opinions.

"How do you figure?" Max shrugging inquisitively. "Domino effect, something will fall soon, revealing what's really going on. Max, no, not there, that obstacle's out of sequence." Sam corrects, sliding another piece into place.

"Hopefully, I really don't know how he takes those beatings in Volkov's and gets up wanting another like he does. Dude's certified insane!" Max mechanically muscling mesh into place.

"Ain't wrong there. Dude's a warrior for sure." Sam setting another piece of the sadistic structure into place.

"Sam gotta ask, why you so sure bout Murph?" Max presses the piping into place.

"Max, sounds weird to say out loud, but for the first time, I think we're actually going somewhere. I mean, MIT was somewhere for sure, but Jack makes me feel invincible like him. For the first time, we're not just nerds to be used for our brilliance. Like we're part of something much bigger than ourselves this time. Come on, he doesn't even know about all this, and I believe in him. . . I just believe." Sam swiveling his Exolift's hand heftily.

"Well, if you believe, Bro . . ., then so do I!" Max motioning to his duplicate continuing their work.

"What'dya mean by trap?" Max inquires, massaging his shoulder.

The groans of soar cadets fill Volkov's dojo as the Russian rhino roars with excitement at the scene unfolding before his elated eyes.

"Har, Har, Har! Murvhy can't take defeat. Typical Americans! Boy is tired, Danzler, finish him." Volkov vents mockingly. Jack dodging another devastating deluge from Danzler.

"What are you afraid of, little man?" The dense Danzler demands.

"Hmm, huff, huff. His shots are almost hitting home. Think, Jack, think." Jack jumps, rolling from another narrow escape.

"Ok, big guy, this gonna hurt one of us more than the other." Jack thinking quickly on his feet. Attempting to surprise his opponent, the young cadet carelessly falls into Danzler's dense physique. Sinking into a spin quickly, hooking a heavy leg, hoisting it off the ground, running his feet rapidly driving deep into the mat below.

"Whoa, no ugh!" Danzler shrieks, crashing densely downward. Spinning on his back, flipping his hips and faking an arm bar, Jack jolts into place. Danzler's definite strength advantage setting the trap as the dense dummy defending his exposed appendage. Swiftly sliding to position his prey, flipping the immense enemy onto his belly, taking Danzler's back.

"Not this time, little man!" Danzler rocketing to his feet, exploding high into the air and landing on Jack, driving wind from his chest.

"Ooff." Jack spits, kicking wildly, avoiding heavy blows beaming down upon him. Waiting patiently through the punishment, Jack lunges, locking in a headlock, arms becoming anacondas.

310

"Pff, ug . . .fff." Danzler gasps for air.

"Enough. Murvhy, hit the showers!" Volkov vaulting into place, pulling Jack roughly from the heavy heap of humanity.

"Virst years no use advance holds, point goes to cadet Danzler!" Volkov shouts vehemently, tossing Jack aside. "Class dismissed!" Volkov commands, checking the downed Danzler's vitals and shoving Jack aside.

Wiping blood draining deeply from above his eye, Jack limps away angrily.

"Hmm . . . this one's different." Cadet Childress notes surveying the scene, slipping off silently.

CHAPTER TWENTY EIGHT
CHALLENGE ACCEPTED!

"Good, good, Gentlemen! Well, settle my score! You boys did almost three-day's work in one. Should be operational in no time." Doc doting on his prized duo, inspecting their work.

"Fantastic, Sam, sequencing is superb! Almost time for supper, clean up, Gentleman. I'll check the specs. Can't be too sure when toppling a tyrant." Doc directs, fitting himself into an Exolift.

"Thank you, Doc, for letting us . . ." Sam begins.

"No, no need, Sam. Take care of those injuries. No time like the present! Don't be late for supper!" Doc winks, whirling away to his work. Saluting, Sam and Max make their way to wash up.

Slamming his locker shut, Jack pressing a towel tensely above his eye.

"Freakin Volkov, giving the point to that putz." Jack stammers to himself, checking the time.

"Oh, shoot, gotta hit up Bray! I can make it." Jack jolts off. Dodging clustered cadets thrashing through throngs of threatening thoughts. "That's him, the first year. Yes, I'm sure."

"Him? He's too small. He'll lose for sure."

"Heard he cheats in Volkov's." Cadet's comments cut deeper than the gash above his eye. Pushing on, pausing to pack cloth deeper into his wound. Jack jetting past pupils, positioning for passage making his way to Professor Bray's classroom.

"Ahh, cadet Murphy! Starting fights again, I see!" Professor Crane comments condescendingly.

"Yup, gotta catch em all, Sir!" Jack salutes, sprinting past the pompous professor. "Arrogant little . . . Triden will deal with you soon." The scrawny scholar grins gauntly.

Dodging through a hall of hurtful hisses, slowing his pace, he approaches Professor Bray's door, noticing it is slightly ajar. Bray's voice emanating from her office speaking to someone on the phone. Jack creeps close enough to hear.

"I know J, I know you're worried, but the . . . of course I am, but the time's not right. He already has so much going on, and now that tyrant Triden is . . . I can't, J. The professor council has already convened on the matter and voted to uphold Triden's right to rule. Of course, I voted against it, but Crane, Volkov, and a few others are all on the Senator's payroll. Well, what was I supposed to do?" The perturbed professor punctuates.

"J, talk to you soon. I have to go. I will, I will. Calm down, please. We'll talk soon, promise." Ending her call, the powerless professor leans solemnly on her desk. "You can come in now, cadet!" Her voice cutting clearly through his concealment.

"Wait, how'dya? I didn't hear much. You said to . . . to." Jack stammers stumbling through desks, making his way to her office.

313

"Doesn't matter what you heard, cadet. CADET?!?" Bray bolting to her bloodied beginner.

"Murphy, what happened? Let me see that!" She orders.

"Oh, this, I'm alright, just a little souvenir from Volkov's." Jack stumbles, shaking his head, blinking blindness away.

"Yeah, sure, sit down and don't move." Bray directs, digging into her desk and producing a bleed kit.

"No, really, I'm good, stopped bleeding back in . . . back there. Oww, that stings." Jack wobbles as Bray attends to his wound.

"Shh, keep your head still. Jess would be pissed if she saw this." Bray breathes, sending the suture straight and closing the canvas above her cadet's eye.

"Hold still, almost done. Ja, Murphy, this isn't ok. Hold this." She commands placing the damp towel in his hands. Gauze is placed over the wound, and its perimeter is taped precisely.

"Ok, all good here. Now, Murphy, I'm gonna have to check you for a concussion. Look straight ahead . . . not into the light, straight ahead." Bray instructs, studying her pupil's pupils.

"Hm. . . Hard to tell could be from blood loss, definitely a slight increase in intracranial pressure. Got your bell rung. It's good for sure; here, drink this." Bray handing Jack a bottle of orange juice from a mini fridge nearby.

"Why would Nurse Jess be mad Professor?" Jack asks between grateful sips gently scratching her patchwork.

"Leave it be. Murphy, go straight to your dorm. I will have supper sent there. We will resume training tomorrow, you need rest." Deliberately dodging his question.

"The twins should still be in Doc's, standby cadet." Breaking eye contact, Bray returning to her office to forward a call, cracking the door.

"Professor Bray, may I speak with Professor Brown . . ." Bray speaking in hushed tones too low for Jack to hear the conversation, returns moments later.

"Ok, Murphy, straight to your dorm, talk to no-one. You hear me, no-one?" She commands, settling a cap on his head, and pulling it low over her patchwork.

"What's this for?" Jack adjusting the cap, itching his incision.

"Triden's got eyes all over campus. They can't see your injury. Wish you were more discreet." Tossing his bloodstained towel in the trash.

"Why would that matter?" Jack inquires, finishing his drink.

"See, all good!" The young rogue wincing as he does.

"Negative cadet, you're excused from PT and Volkov's tomorrow. I still expect you here after classes conclude, say 1600. Keep the lights low, and no screen time. You can finish Crane's paper on armament capabilities later." Bray's eyes piercing sharply.

"You're dismissed, cadet!" Saluting seriously, returning to her office and fielding another call and leaving the door ajar.

315

"Professor Bray, requesting a ration sent to cadet Murphy's dorm . . . make it 1700. On the double with that order . . ."

Standing to attention saluting, Jack stumbles, shaking sense back into his leg. Exiting Bray's pulling the cap low, Jack checking the time. "1700? That's like in fifteen. Pff, screw that jerk, Triden. I'm not eating mess alone in the dark." Jack murmurs to himself. Suspecting Bray may be spying on him, Jack meanders towards the barracks before turning down halls leading to Doc's labs. Casual cadence transforming into a ginger gallop nearing his destination, careening the last corner carelessly.

"Ooompff!" Jack crashes hard to the floor.

"Cadet Murphy, barracks are back that way. On the double cadet!" Blackshear booms.

"Yes, Sir . . ." Sulking through his salute.

"Cap stays on cadet. I'll check on you at lights out." Blackshear commands standing stoically staring down his young cadet's correct corridor.

"I'm going, sheesh everyone is acting weird all of a sudden." Jack says silently, sauntering off. Sensing a sizable silhouette shadowing his steps, Jack gallops gingerly to his dorm, slamming the door behind.

Showering quickly, carefully covering his wound, he dresses and jumps on his bed. Any attempt at rest wrestled away by thoughts of the day searing his mind when a knock upon the door raps. Jumping from bed, he answers the door to a cadet, who presents Jack his meal. Thanking the young cadet and saluting as she sets off, Jack shuts the door behind him, shadows seizing the room. Silently, Jack eats angrily alone in the dark. Gripping an empty tray, checking the time.

"Mess will be over in five. I can make it." Jamming a foot into his boot. Checking the hall for superiors, Jack jogs briskly towards the mess hall.

"Murphy, why can't you listen? We're just trying to protect you." A voice whispers.

"Nice, minutes to spare." Congratulating himself, Jack returning his tray, eying the twins eating alone.

"Whats'up, gentlemen?" Jack clapping the bewildered brother's shoulders.

"Murph, hey, you're not . . . Oww, that hurt, bro!" Max begins before catching an elbow to his ribs.

"Jack, you're supposed to be resting in the dorm!" Sam shooting enigmatic eyes at Max.

"Supposed to be, had to return my . . . Oompff!" Jack spreading his hands, stepping back into a muscular menace.

"Watch it, shrimp!" Maddox shoving Jack forward hard into the table.

"Oh, lil man finally showing his face? Did I do that?" Danzler daring Jack to retaliate.

"Pff, finally woke up, I see. Volkov must've used all his smelling salts to wake you, or maybe he just. . ." Jack steps, craning his neck, staring down both behemoths.

"Cute when he's mad, isn't he Maddi . . . Maddox?" Danzler dismissing their expected guest.

"Walk away before . . ." Jack spits when a cheer rises from cadets' ranks as Triden enters the mess hall. Raising hands randomly and pointing out cadets, a triumphant Triden trots confidently. Waving his hands, soaking in cheers of cadets before stepping on a table and clambering for decorum. Standing above his peers, echoing ideas in his head, Triden hushing the horde.

"Fellow cadets!" Pausing pretentiously soaking in ill-gotten adulation. Raising a single finger for silence.

"Fellow cadets, I bring good news!" Pandering further patronage permeating his peers.

"I . . . Teivel Anwir Triden, have secured my Right of Rule!" A sinister smile searing his chiseled chin at the roar of cadets cheering his conquest.

Raising his hands for silence once more, Triden triumphantly touts.

"With this Right, I will challenge The Trials of Titans!" Triden turns, bathing in his boldness.

"I will not challenge by right of the collective! I, Teivel Triden, will test my skill against a single challenger!" He announces to excited audience.

"GYAIA has always been a haven for honor, in defense of diligence, a commitment to craft, and to this challenge. I dedicate my victory to our past, our present, and OUR FUTURE! . . . We are GYAIA and we must protect from provocateurs; foreign and domestic!" Triden touting to tremendous applause.

"WHO? WHO? WHO? WHO?!?!" Cadets commanding his challenger.

Closing his eyes, soaking in energy not of his own, Triden striking a powerful pose. Peering into the distance, gallantly tapping just above his eyes, cutting mockingly in Jack's direction.

"GYAIA must be protected, must be rid of all weakness undermining our illustrious legacy, GYAIA must be strong FOREVER! As my Right of Rule . . . I challenge the first year, Jack Murphy!" Triden points triumphantly to cheers filling the mess hall. Cadets pound tables in thirst for competition, excited by the calamity contained within the Trials of Titans.

"They hate you now, Jack!" Sam says, sinking his head.

"Don't listen to him, Murph. We got that crooked-chinned creep . . . We got him!" Max motioning for Jack to stand on their table. Staring sternly through crowding cadets, Jack rises to hushed tones snickering around the hall.

"I . . . I, Jack Joseph Murphy, accept!" Jack barks, barraged with a roar of boos.

Silencing sinisterly, Triden raises a single finger once more.

"Two weeks cadet, two weeks till we remove weeds weakening GYAIA!" Triden boasts boisterously. Cadets roar raucously ranting Triden's name.

"Time for us to go, Jack!" Sam pulling Jack's pant leg purposely.

319

"He's the weed, let's go Murph!" Max mimicking his multiple, fighting every impulse to cause a scene. Traveling tensely through throngs of cadets cheering their counterfeit champion, Jack and his companions attempt an escape before any altercations can escalate.

"Oh, leaving already, nerds?" Maddox muses, shoving Max and grabbing him roughly.

"Yeah, what's the hurry?" Danzler demands snatching Sam.

"That's enough, boys . . . losers need their sleep!" Childress chucking Max from Maddox's muscular meat hooks.

"Whoa, what . . . what womanhood?" Max mocking the massive mauler's moxy.

"You've accepted Triden's challenge, now go!" Childress cutting her eyes between the trio.

"We'll see who the losers are in a couple of weeks." Jack spits, dashing dangerously, daring her to action. "Not today, Murphy, go." Childress whispers leaning close.

"Cadets about face." Blackshear booms from behind, returning swift salutes from Childress and company.

"Lucky your buddy's here, little man!" Danzler says, shoulder-checking Jack disrespectfully.

"See you in Volkov's har har!" Maddox muses maniacally, striding off to Triden's side.

"Let's go, cadets. . . Murphy, we will have words. March!" Blackshear marshaling his herd to their dorms.

320

"Morning run will commence at 0300. Some lessons need learning, it would seem." Blackshear addressing his whole company, drawing daggers digging deep in Jack's direction. Dismissing his company, Blackshear turns his attention to Jack and the twins.

"Duvals dorm on the double! 2100 Duvals 2100, no exceptions!" Blackshear barks, dismissing Sam and Max.

"Not you, Murphy. You were given strict orders to stay in barracks. Were you not?" Blackshear beacons his young cadet. Looking down, searching for wiser words, Jack responds. "Sir, yes, Sir, but you were the one who told me Triden would challenge, were you not?"

Pausing, gathering the last of his patience, Blackshear clinching his jaw, sending muscles shooting across.

"Professor Bray and myself both gave strict instructions, and you breaking rank back there . . . Jack forces are at work here to destroy your opportunity here at GYAIA. You must . . ." Blackshear begins broken by his conflicted cadet.

"Opportunity to what, get beat up by Triden's dogs? Be hated on by all these nepos who cheer that giant jerk? I never wanted this stupid opportunity. I don't belong . . ." Jack continues, cut off by his superior.

"Nobody ever said this is fair, and I know you didn't ask for this, but standing up to Triden put a target on your back. You accepting his challenge only fed his obsession. 2100 cadet, lights out at 2100. 0500 comes fast. Your body requires recovery."

321

Blackshear salutes tapping just above his eyebrow, dismissing his conflicted cadet.

"Sir, yes, Sir." Saluting solemnly, retiring to his dorm. "And you thought keeping peace between Ari and Reg was hard, what are you doing Jack?" Whispering to himself, closing the door behind.

CHAPTER TWENTY NINE

"OPERATION TITAN-FALL!"

Kicking his boots off and blasting them into a corner, Jack slumps onto his bed, itching his injury.

"I Triden the turd challenge this weed. What a clown?" Jack jabs.

"It was a stupid speech, for sure. How you holding up?" Sam says, sitting at his desk still drying his hair.

"Yeah, stupid speech, Murph, give me that!" Max echoing Sam's statement, snatching his brother's towel.

"Hey, I wasn't done with that!"

Shaking his head, Sam opens his computer, clicking keys copiously.

"Doesn't matter, Sam. Win, lose, or draw, I can't . . ." Jack says, sitting upright.

"Can't what? Win? You sure as heck can win, Murph?" Max hollering from his shower.

"Hmm, how ya figure, Max?" Jack quips, searching the floor for answers.

"Well, with this, come take a look." Sam states confidently. Peeling away from self-pity, Jack steps, looking over Sam's shoulder.

"Is that it?" Inquiring ignorantly.

"No, this is our replica according to specs provided. Couple days, and this bad boy will be operational. Whatcha think?" Sam shoving Jack playfully.

"It's bigger than I thought it'd be." Jack responds.

"That's what she sa . . ." Max adds before Sam cuts him off.

"Yes, it's quite the construction; we bout two-thirds complete. Sequencing is correct, and to scale, we should have the necessary space to complete the remaining elements tomorrow. Give or take a day for mishaps." Sam concludes.

"Mishaps?" Jack inquires, searching the screen intently.

"What he means if we don't run out of scraps. Doc's supply accounts were frozen today. Can't order proper building materials. Odd dontcha think?" Max meanders over, settling next to Sam.

"Stop that, you'll get my keyboard wet." Sam slapping his damp duplicate's hand.

"Oww, show Murph that last element sim. Dude, this thing is ridiculous!" Max prods preening his hair, wicking water purposely.

"Quit it, you idiot, I'm going . . . I'm going. Here, happy?" Sam wiping water drops from his glasses. "It's just a rope?" Jack inquires, investigating its sadistic simplicity.

"It's not any "rope" it's a sub 2mm micro 90 paraco . . . oompff! What the heck, Sam?"

"According to specs, this paracord or rope, Jack, is rated for a hundred-pound load." Sam eying Max slapping away his retaliatory attempt.

"Yeah, what's the problem, guys?" Jack inquires ignorantly.

"Well, Murph, unless you're only 99 pounds, that para won't hold you. Triden is at least 190, by my best estimate. I can't see how this part can be completed unless the real trial uses another extremely thin cord that holds way more than that!"

"Look, Jack, we got plenty of heavier paracord, but a simulation is only as good as its details, which is concerning. Whatever this cord is; it's super thin, like cut straight to bone thin. Maybe these specs are wrong, and it's not a para?" Sam contemplates, concerned for his companion.

"Hmm, what about suspension bridges? Don't they use super strong steel or something?" Jack interjects.

"Well, yes, Murph, but the mili's are way thicker than these specs say." Max motioning their roundness with his hands.

"We thought of wire and, yes, it's possible, but using steel wire for a climbing element isn't just difficult, it's dangerous." Sam completing his and Max's thoughts.

"Dangerous? I'll just wear gloves, those tactical types with Kevlar pads." Jack proudly produces.

"Negative ghost rider, rule specs say no gloves or padding of any type. Singles challenges are serious!" Max retorts roughly, eying an opportunity.

"Dang, really? Can hide them in my pockets." Jack jests, adjusting uncomfortably.

"Jack, these Trials of Titans are a beast, and this end element vexes me!" Sam says, pointing out various elements to his companion, slapping away an attempt from Max.

"Oww, hey, Murph, want to see it?" Max motioning over his shoulder.

"Oh no, Max. Blackshear was pretty peeved. Best not tonight." Sam says sliding his keyboard away from Max.

"He was pretty pissed at me out there. Too early for an expedition wouldn't you say?" Jack, gesturing Max behind Sam's back.

"You two better not, but given you're gonna have to train after hours anyways, who am I to stop ya?" Sam slyly states.

"Best bro ever!" Max muses, kissing Sam's cheek. "Ew, gross, stop that!" Sam protesting another from Jack. "Max, you got Soteria mechs to work on. Jack if you're goin out, best get some rest. Blackshear is serious bout that 0300 run. Unfortunately, 0100 being optimal time to travel, want me to loop camera feeds again?" Sam suggests when he notices an unread email.

"Hmm don't know no Banshee . . . sunshine summertime for a call, what kinda title is that?" Sam whispers, wrinkling his face thinking hard.

"What's up Bro?" Max mushing his face into Sam's so he can read. "It's a video, for Murph, odd! Who's Angel's Kiss Sam? Sounds hot!" Max muses puckering his lips mockingly.

"I don't know, stop that. Hey Jack come here, someone sent me a link for you. Max hand me that laptop you swiped from Doc's." Sam commands snapping his fingers in the direction of Max's workspace.

"Huh, huh, what laptop? Okay! Okay! I'll get it Jeeze Bro!" Max muses dodging a screw driver, now dug deeply into a corner wall.

"I'm here, settle down Samurai Sam. What's up?" Jack jumps from his bed settling next to Sam. "Not sure, hold on a sec." Sam pausing his companion typing quickly on the laptop Max retrieved.

"Ok almost, here ya' may want these Jack." Sam handing him a pair of earbuds along with the laptop.

"What is it Murph?" Max mashing his face beside Jack's as the glowing image of familiar faces populate the screen. "Sam, you broke my laptop! Some goofy lookin' nerds popped up!" Max exclaims as Jack shoves him away playfully.

"Hey now who that hottie, Aunt Anna?" Max wiggling his eyebrows suggestively.

"Alright Max had your fun, leave him be." Sam says tilting his head for Max to tinker.

"Snff. Thanks Sam." Jack sniffs quietly to himself settling in the earbuds, as a pre-recorded video plays.

327

A smile emerging across Jack's face, tears welling in his eyes at the sound of Anna, Ari, and Reggie's voices dance in his ears. Ari and Reggie's typical banter reminding him of the twins, Jack breathes deeply when Aunt Anna speaks. The sound of her sweet voice filling him with confidence and calm. Rejuvenated, Jack closes the laptop as the video, sitting quietly on his bed for a few minutes.

"You good Murph?" Max askes shaking his previous silliness.

"Yeah, thanks guys I needed that." Jack says handing Max back his laptop.

"We didn't do anything, still not sure who this Banshee is." Sam pipes up from his desk.

"Nap time then Murph, we'll head out after lights out." Max suggests, making his way back to his workshop.

"Yeah, probably be best. Thanks, man." Jack responds, sinking between sheets and snoring softly seconds later.

"Really, Murph's out! . . . Shh, let em rest . . . remember what Bray said." Sam silencing his sibling into secrecy.

"My bad, er um E.V.E. scripts?" Max whispers from around the corner.

"Yeah, Doc thinks I'll get her script right soon." Sam responds, peering purposely at his screen. "Gotcha, gonna tinker for a bit, then catch some shut-eye." Max whispers willingly.

2100 ticks to a knock on the trio's door. Answering hastily, Sam steps into the hall.

"Sir, yes, Sir. Max is wrapping up Soteria mods now. Jack? Studied some for Crane's, few asleep before 2000 Sir." Sam divulges deceitfully.

"Sir, yes, Sir. We did. Operation Ninja Warrior is a go. Tonight? Replica isn't complete . . . Yes, Sir, thank you, Sir." Sam salutes, closing the door.

"Set your alarm Max, be back before 0200 please." Sam staving off sleep.

"Just dropping off, I'm not training on that . . . ahhhh-hhaaaaaa, thing." Max mouths through a yawn.

"I'll set my . . . no, got it, all good." Max cutting off his scheduled sibling. "Get some sleep, Sam, got a lot of wor . . ." Max snorting himself to sleep.

Quiet halls sit empty, soon filled with excitedly chattering cadets in the coming days. Murals of mythical epics rage throughout silent halls. As GYAIA sleeps, silent hours slip by before Max's alarm rings, rousing him from slumber. "I'm up, Murph, get up, Murph?" Max falling out of bed motioning in the dark. "Get dressed, Max." A voice resonating silently from shadows.

"Oh, there you are. Where are my . . . there they are." Max meanders, pulling on his boots.

"Shh, come on." Jack producing a note from Sam.

"Loop's only running an hour tonight, let's go." Jack gesturing towards their door. Sneaking between barrack halls, checking their six occasionally as they move silently.

329

"All clear, move." Jack motions, moving silently, unaware of their silent shadow.

"Going somewhere Murphy." Their shadow whispers. Making their way through passages placed in shadows, Jack and Max advance.

"Shh, toes up, Max." Jack whispers, stepping carefully over obstructions.

"Got it, replica is in section C. We'll be there in a jiffy." Max motoring behind his companion.

"Shh, let's move." Jack gesturing jolting around another corner. Sticking to shadows and secret corridors, making their way into Doc's lab through the secret locker like before.

"Shh, you hear that?" Jack pauses, the hairs on his neck standing at attention.

"Yeah, security cameras are still on. They loopin for another forty-eight or so. Gotta go Murph." Max mashing his companion forward.

"I guess, lead on Max." Jack placing the faux locker aside, stepping silently.

"Section C is just down these steps. There's no elevator where we're goin', come on." Max motions sprinting off. Making their way down towards the dusty old storage garage.

"Whoa, Max, this thing's big enough for a football field easy." Jack jolting ahead, surveying their work.

"Yeah, not sure what that means, Murph ov'r here. Got something for ya." Max motioning Jack towards a rusty locker.

"What's this?" Jack inquires, digging through dingy garb.

"Can't have you ripping fatigues when training. These may be a little big, but you know, "budget cuts" Max mimicking air quotes, handing Jack a well-used uniform.

"Wait what? I'm not training tonight. Am I?" Jack questions.

"Murph, we'll have this thing done by tomorrow, maybe. Right now, Triden is probably talking bout his victory, and that clown doesn't even know what he's up against." Max motioning for Jack to change.

"I don't even know what I'm up against." Jack jests.

"Sure you do. He's not up against some high school gym bro. He's up against Jack Freakin Murphy!" Max muses, motioning for Jack to hurry.

"Murph, you only got like forty-two minutes before loop is up." Max turns monitoring the space.

"I'm movin, I'm movin. Triden probably has specs, too. Dontcha think?" Jack jousting a leg into pants.

"Most likely, but he doesn't have this." Max clicking on lights illuminating the destruction awaiting his ally. Lights above harmoniously hum to life, lending illumination below.

"Whoa!" Jack stands, adjusting his attire. "Yeah, impressive, we know. Commencing Operation Titanfall, have at it, Murph. Be back before 0300 would'ya?" Max motoring off.

"Wait, where do I start?" Jack jerking Max back.

"Specs in the locker. Hey, Murph, don't fall. There are not many foam pads sitting around down here. Oh yeah, there are

331

some earbuds and an old mp3 with those eighties tunes you like, uploaded courtesy of Sam." Max motions at the dusty before making his way up the stairs.

"Max, where ya goin?" Jack whispers confusedly.

"Sorry, Murph!" Max salutes dashing off.

Jack breathes to himself, checking his watch, rifling for specs.

"Even the twins keepin secrets now. Ok, Jack, thirty to get dirty let's go." Stretching gingerly, rubbing his ribs.

"Danny Boy got me good today. Here we go, start here!" Sizing up the sinister structure, plugging in headphones, pressing play. Nostalgic sounds surge, sending Jack back in time. With Whitesnake willing him on, Ratt rushing him from ring to ring and rope to rope, Foreigner forcing every exhausted effort forward, Jack journeys through few elements effortlessly.

"Oommpff! Only a few, Max, try none." Landing solidly, sending searing pain piercing his hurting husk.

"Get . . . get up. Missed timed that one." Jack willing himself upward, standing defiantly he continues his task. Metallica motivated the day's hero, jumping and thrusting himself through obstacles missing another bar hurling heavily below.

"Ow!" Jack groans, gearing himself for another run.

Stirring silently, a shadow surveying his harmonious harm.

"Hmm. So this is what you're up to Murphy." Peering perched out of sight cadet Childress observing the young rogue reset for another reckless run.

"Not like that, twist and swing . . ." She spits silently.

"Oommppff! Yeah that's it for the night." Wincing trekking gingerly returning the contents of the rusty locker. Checking his watch, Jack cutting the lights out unaware of his hostile audience. Legs heavy from each step up the stairwell, bracing himself against the wall.

"Only two weeks, Jack. You got this . . . whoa ain't got these steps though." Jack sucking wind stumbling to the top. Slipping through secret passages and making his way back in time. Opening the door slowly, silence settled in hours ago. Sam and Max sleep peacefully. Falling flat on his bed, head pressing heavily into the cool pillow. Tossing tensely each agonizing his autonomy. Finally exhaustion ferrying his form to sleep. His shadow speeding by breaking the light beneath their door.

Childress slinks silently back to her dorm, pausing before entering.

"Seems I'm not the only shadow this morning . . . Brian." She whispers coldly.

"Not here for a fight, Carla." Blackshear, stepping around the corner, confronting his old comrade.

"You and Wiley sent that boy on a suicide mission. He's got heart, but he's not ready."

"Wasn't my call to make, just following orders on this one." Blackshear begins, met with the coldest of shoulders.

"Same . . . take care of that shoulder." The vicious vixen ventures off, leaving Blackshear behind.

"Hmm. Never change Carla, never change." He sniffs stiffly.

333

CHAPTER THIRTY

"ALL ANY OF US CAN DO!"

Waking to rousing raps on their door, the twins dress, shaking Jack awake.

"Get up, Murph. No that one with the holes are mine, giv'me Sam." Max stretching, shredding the sole survivor.

"Now, look what you did!" Sam shouts, shoving his sibling. "Oh man, now we gotta steal Murph's again." Max storms off.

"Jack, hey, Jack, wake up. Mornin' run in five." Sam shakes his companion sneaking socks hidden from Max.

"Can't believe that brute Blackshear is making us run at 0300 freakin . . . freakin love that guy!" Max muses, saluting stupidly.

"Rise and shine, Gentlemen! Six quick ones gone now!" Blackshear bellows, saluting Sam before storming off.

"Bigmouth, probably get another mile, thanks jerk!" Sam shoving Max away soldiering off.

"Hey Murph, get up. Murph, you gotta change outta that old uni! Here, use Sam's, he hides a clean one under his mattress!" Max hovering over his companion.

"Yeah, ugh, I'm up. Max stall a bit, would'ya?" Jack groans rolling roughly out of bed.

"Gotcha back, Murph!" Max, slapping Jack on his back before jolting off.

"Oww . . . thanks, ahhh." Jack changes, racing off into formation.

"MOVE IT, CADETS, MOVE IT, last ones on the double!" Blackshear barks ahead of the pack, marching in place, giving Jack a chance to catch up.

"Somebody stayed up too late. Get that lead out, Murphy and Duval!" Blackshear barking berating the back of his pack.

"He huuu, he's huuu gonna keeelll hhhUS!" Max sucking air pathetically.

"Shh, breathe, just breathe." Jack jogging just ahead of Max, who finally completes the run patting his penultimate partner.

"No mo . . . no more. Can't do . . . ." Max falls to a knee, whimpers weakly.

"Shut it. Complaining will get everyone else another. I deserve this, they don't." Jack spits, lifting elbows over shoulders drawing deeply.

"Nice sentiment, Jack, but they hate our guts right now." Sam whispers, striding through a throng of thorny stares.

"Good pace today, cadets, only 0318, hit the showers, then the library for a thirty-minute read period! Be there by 0330 on the double. Hupp! Hupp!" Blackshear bellows before bolting off himself.

"Oooo la biblioteca!" Max tapping his fingers together.

"Hurry up, Max!" Sam shouts already several paces ahead.

"Com'n, Murph?" Max popping Jack again on his back.

"Ye, yeah. Mmpff." Jack says sorely following for the first time.

Cadets' shower darting damply down halls devoid of classmates. Blackshear's troop making their way quickly to the quiet cavernous library. Shelves of knowledge rising high towards the ceiling. Rows of shelves of neatly organized texts tempt cadets as they pass in search of their selection. Of course Sam and Max, already familiar with the place of literary worship, break away seeking texts containing tech. Jack still sore from the past few days, saunters gingerly as fellow cadets careening to favorite nooks nestling in for a good read.

"Have at it, gents, got some script reading to do." Sam says, sauntering off.

"So Murph, what you goin for?" Max mulling his options.

"Not sure, man . . . how's Professor Crane's paper coming along Murphy?" Jack spinning sorely addressing their new companion.

"Armament capabilities, was it? No MEC specs?" Anita's velvety voice, alleviating her visitors.

"Good'mornin, Anita. Have you met my? Max Du, dude?" Jack swirling in place.

"Morning Murphy, tehe." Chuckling to herself pointing at a nearby bookshelf. "Don't be rude, Max, come here."

"Oh no, go ahead Murph can't get enough Kafka ya know. Murph, you and this guy have a lot in common, gotta go." Max says sheepishly, melting behind a bookcase.

"Was good to meet you, Max, can't go wrong with The Trial; it's a classic." Anita nods knowingly.

"Come, Murphy, I have something for you."

What's this?" Jack brushing fingers over its worn reddish brown cover.

"*Mythology* Edith Hamilton? This a history of Pegasus'?" Running his fingers over the golden-winged stallion, smells old." Jack jerking back, sniffing pages between fatigued fingers.

"Tehe, it's a book, silly. Specifically an original 1942 first edition of Edith Hamilton's *Mythology*. Here's your copy. Already checked out and everything. Hope it helps."

"Wait, what's going on? Anita, please tell me something . . . anything. Please." Jack jolts, cutting off her escape.

"Cadet, I can't . . ." The lovely librarian looking nervously over each shoulder.

"Please. I've been in the dark for months now, please!" Jack begs boyishly.

"Murphy the Trials of Titans represent the twelve titans that Zeus and the Olympians battled for a decade, banishing them into the underworld, Tartarus. Jack, you must best the twelve Titans and climb from the pit of Tartarus. No more Jack, I must go, just read." Anita's velvety voice vexing her visitor, pointing to tabbed pages.

337

"Twelve Titans? Pit of Tartar sauce?" Jack rubbing exhausted eyes settling in a nearby seat.

"Whoa, how'd ya do that, Murph? She's totally into you!" Max muses, settling near Jack. "Do what?" Jack inquires, sinking comfortably into his seat.

"Talk to Ms. Naughty Hottie!" Max gyrating suggestively. "Not now, Max. What do you make of this?" Handing the immature multiple his copy.

"Oh Hamilton's *Mythology: Timeless Tales Of Gods and Heroes* is a good read. Is that?!?!" Max jumps, eyeing the reddish-brown book in Jack's hands.

"Shhh!" Hushes from fellow cadets careening from across the room.

"Oh, shush yourself, nepo know-nothings." Max stands surveying his surroundings.

"Sit down, Max. What do you make of this?" Jack repeats, rubbing exhaustion from his eyes.

"Well, this is an original print of Edith Hamilton's *Mythology*." Max brushing his figures over the cloth cover, sniffing it sensually. "Yeah, I know smells old." Jack jests.

"No smells like expertise and education." Max's eyes glowing from the golden Pegasus prancing about its cover.

"So whatcha think?" Jack jabbing Max's ribs. "Ow, stop that. Oh, this piece here is a wonderful collection of Greek and Roman myths with some Norse mythology thrown in somewhere. Murph

338

the gilt is still in great condition given its age. Can we keep it?" Max massaging the text reverently.

"No, that's the library's copy. Anita gave me this copy. Whatcha think?" Pointing at the newer edition in Max's lap.

"Hmm, let me see . . . well, someone did their homework. Check this out." Max leans closer, counting neon tabs protruding from its pages.

"Ok, someone did their homework. Is that for me, ya think?" Jack leaning gingerly.

"Bingo." Max pointing out posted pages.

"Murph, these pages detail how Cronus, leader of the Titans seized power from his daddy Uranus to rule the cosmos. Most Greek mythology are succession myths, very complicated stuff. The real intrigue here are these notes about each Titan. Hey, Murph, got an idea. Let's find Sam, have to confirm something." Max handing Jack the older copy.

"Go see your girl Murph, meet me in Computer Sciences." Max hustles off, still clutching Jack's copy.

"She's not my gf, whatever, man." Jack tripping Max as he leaves. "Oomppf! Hey what the he . . .!" Max squeals mulling about on the floor. "Shhh!" A chorus of hisses, hurling their way.

"Oh, shush yourselves . . . nepos." Max mules before hustling off with Jack's copy.

Jack jogs gingerly to Anita's cluttered desk.

"Oh, thank you. Learn something, cadet Murphy?" Her velvety voice, soothing soreness away.

339

"Yeah, you could say that." Jack handing her the heralded hardcover.

"Happy to help. Have a great day Cadet Murphy." Brushing hair from her face smiling with satisfaction.

"Thanks again." Jack smiles, attempting to hide a grimace.

"Cadet Murphy . . . good luck. You got this." Her velvety voice invigorating his hurting husk.

Smiling to himself, Jack jolts away, finding the brainiac brothers bickering.

"Shh, keep it down. What's going on Sam?"

"Jack, I solved your riddle . . . hey, give it back." Sam swiping at the text.

"Hold on, solved what? Here, I'll take that." Jack jerking the book free from Max's grip.

"Ok, one at a time. Sam first, solved what?"

"Elementary, really, these notes are clues to solving each obstacle. Even the thirteenth obstacle is all so clear now." Sam summarizes, staring stupidly, mimicking Max's expression.

"Ok, sounds good, now, Max?" Jack motioning Max on.

"What he said . . . he stole my part about the last obstacle, but yeah, that." Max mean mugging his multiple.

"Good work, Gents. Talk more before I head out tonight, should head to mornin' mess soon." Jack checking his watch, catching Max's hand before landing on his back.

"Could use a break for a bit, c'mon." Jack says falling into formation, forming around the door. Following Jack's lead, Sam and Max fall in as well. Blackshear appearing only seconds later, pleased with his unit.

"Morning mess it is, Ten-hut." Blackshear mouths motioning his cadets' onward, saluting Anita. The lovely librarian winks, returning her own salutation.

Blackshear's cadets are the first to arrive for the morning meal, eat, and move on before most cadets make their way through. Giving short instructions, Blackshear releases his troop to class without further conversation.

"Well, that was weird!" Max moving ahead. "What's so weird?" Sam pushing past his dense duplicate.

"Gotta admit, Sam, was kinda odd. Whatcha thinkin?" Jack jogs ahead of the melancholy multiple.

"He's hiding something, they're all hiding something." Sam shaking free from his companions.

"Who, Blackshear? Bray? Doc? Triden?" Jack jests, jolting to face his friend.

"Yeah, I know, but it doesn't matter because I got you guys. My secret weapons."

Jack jiggling their midsections, sprinting off gingerly. "Hate when he does that! Get back here. Gonna get ya good!" Max motoring after his courageous comrade.

341

"If you only knew Jack. If you only knew." Sam sinks, sauntering after.

Professor Crane's class concludes like most. Sam and Max easily schooling their pompous professor, guarding Jack from further academic atrocities. Parting ways, Sam and Max make their way to Doc's, continuing to construct the colossus of section C as Max has deemed it.

Outside in the fresh air, the sun rises ushering dawn to another day. Jack executes Bray's physical training exercises slower than usual. Cadets careen by shooting stabbing wounds with their eyes.

"See how tough you are when them Trials get you." One cadet checking Jack to the ground on their way up a wall climb.

"Murphy! Thought I told you to sit the next few out!" Bray bellows.

"Yes, Ma'am, you did, but I needed the exercise." Jack spitting soil, saluting softly.

"Not here, you don't." Bray's piercing eyes, eyeing a pull-up bar nestled quietly away from other circuits. "Wides, Scaps, L-sits, Commandos till failure, cadet!" Bray tossing the weakened warrior two towels.

"Don't need these. I won't quit, Ma'am." Jack retorts respectfully. Stepping close enough to breathe his air.

"I know . . . . Towels till failure." Nodding her orders, sending him off, barking commands till other cadets fall about like weeds wilting from summer's sun.

Doing as commanded, Jack completes each pull-up till failure. Hands tremble between each set, finishing each later than before. "Gotta keep, goin. Keep go . . . Oompf!" Jack groans, gripping the frame, pulling himself up for another searing set after searing set.

"Good work today cadets. That should be enough to keep those gossiping gobs gagged till tomorrow!" Bray bellows, her piercing pearls darting about studying exhausted cadets.

"Hit the showers, loose lips! Move! Move! Move!" Cadets dejectedly dragging themselves under her piercing eyes.

"Not you, Murphy . . . drop and give me till failure!" Bray commands loud enough for straggling cadets to hear. Standing over him, posing purposely. Checking her six, calling him up.

"Good for today, Murphy. Here, take this." Bray pushing a small device into inflamed hands.

"Take this to Nurse Jess, she's expecting you." The piecing professor salutes, marching off turning her attention to other matters.

Returning her salute, Jack shaking soil and sweat from his uniform.

"Why not, why not." He whispers to himself, jogging off gingerly. Pacing himself through throngs of threats, cutting corners, and passing Volkov's dojo, Jack does as commanded.

"Hey, what's the hurry, little man?" Triden teases, tossing Jack roughly into a wall.

"Out of my way, Triden. I'll deal with you later." Jack dodging Triden's grasp, ramming roughly into dual densities.

343

"Sup gentlemen, wouldn't know where the ladies' room is would ya?" Jack jests, jolting from reach.

"Little man got jokes!" Triden spits stupidly. "Oohh did Bray put lil Jack in the corner? Look around. Nobody's laughing with ya." Triden snickers, checking Jack, as he passes.

"Come out an play, little jerk, got somtin for ya!" Danzler driving his elbow into his hand repeatedly. "Nah, wittle jerky werky got a booboo and can't come out to pway!" Maddox tapping just above his eye. The trio laughing tyrannically.

"That's enough, boys!" A vicious voice surges sternly through the society of scumbags.

"Ah, Childress, would you care to teach Murphy another lesson?" Triden sneers, shoving Jack roughly.

"Another day, I'm sure, off with you, boy." Childress stepping near sending a shiver down their spineless backsides.

"Volkov said don't be late. He's pretty pissed his favorite punching bag won't be attending for a few. C'mon, move out." The lethal lioness prowling past her pompous pride. Sensing his opportunity, Jack slips away, jolting down the hall.

Jack does as Bray commanded, nearing Nurse Jessie's office. Her door slightly ajar, attending to another cadet Jack takes a seat outside. Waiting patiently, picking at stitching above his eye.

"Your arm is set, and I've recommended that you not attend Professor Volkov's for at least a couple weeks. Keep it in the sling for now; I'll check on you in a few days. You'll be ok, cadet Singh, was very brave of you to take on Danzler. Ok, off you go."

Her nurturing voice resonating as the young cadet exits. Jack looking up at the skinny cadet exiting Jess' office.

"Hey, Singh, was it?" Jack inquires, stepping close.

"Um, oh cadet Murphy, yes, Singh, my name is Yuvraj Singh. I . . . I, I tried my best . . ." The skinny Sikh sniffs adjusting his purple patka.

"I'm sure you did. Don't let that big doofus Danzler stop you from being the best cadet you can be. Pretty brave takin him on."

"Thank, thank you Jack Murphy. Cadet Murphy fight like the Akali. Once I am healed, I will show Jack Murphy that I am strong like him."

"Hmm, sounds good." Jack smiling, returning the slim Sikh's salute.

"Cadet Murphy, is that you?" Nurse Jess' nurturing voice rings from her office.

"Yes, Ma'am, Professor Bray told me to report." Jack stepping sideways concealing his cut.

"No need for that, Murphy. Shut the door and let me see Bray's dressing." Nurse Jessie motioning for Jack to sit. "Hmm, not bad for a field dressing. Her ends were always a little loose. Hold still, and let me redress that cut." Nurse Jessie controlling Jack's chin, gently inspecting his wound.

"Good news it's not that infected, gotta keep these types of lacerations clean. Oh, don't be a baby, Jack." Jess gently, jerking his head close.

"Oww that stings!" Jack jiggling in his seat.

345

"There, all closed up! Now, shirt off. Let me see those ribs."
Jessie tugging simultaneously, slapping her patient's hand away.

"Ok, okay, jeeze. Just a little sore." Jack gingerly, plucking his
arm out.

"What I thought, multiple contusions running anteroposterior
to posteroanterior. These clusters here are newer. Started training,
I see." Nurse Jessie side-eyed her patient's exposed elbows.

"Darn you, Doc." Nurse Jessie disapprovingly tossing gloves
away.

"Eh, um, yeah, something like that. Sorry. . ." Jack says
sheepishly, slipping his shirt on.

"Leave it off, this way." She motions, leading Jack into a
large, dimly lit room.

"What are these?" Jack inquires, pacing prudently.

"Advanced Cryotherapy pods. Cadets call them Poke'pods.
Not sure why, though." Jessie clicking on a single Cryo-pod.

"Jack, you'll spend a few minutes in sub 140C temps. Blood
will flush from extremities into your core. After a while blood
rushes back to your extremities, enriching the body with oxygen,
enzymes, and nutrients necessary for recovery. This process
targets damaged muscle groups and tissue. Total process doesn't
take long at all. Ok almost ready." She says, checking the
machine's readiness.

"I'll need to check vitals Jack. Put these here and here . . .
almost set." Jessie sticking small sensors over his heart.

346

"Wait, what, so it's like an auto ice bath?" Jack peeking into his pod, pulling his socks and pants off.

"Same premise yes, Here put these on." Jessie handing him gloves and a mask big enough to cover his nose and mouth, before turning away.

"Get in. Bray, give you a drive, correct?" Jessie, reaching out toward the almost bare boy.

Fumbling foolishly in his pockets protecting himself, Jack handing her the device.

"Thank you. Undergarments will suffice for future reference cadet." Jessie turns uploading contents of Bray's device.

"Blast you, Bray, why?" She spits, shaking her head.

"Oh, sorry, standard issue you kn . . . what is it, Ma'am?" Jack jests stepping in.

"Nothing, here put these on. It's gonna get cold. Just breathe and focus on the training modules Bray's prepared." Jessie settling VR goggles on Jack's head, plugging earbuds gently into each ear.

"All good?" Her nurturing nature returns, ratcheting down the temperature.

"All gooOOOOD GOD THATS COLD!!!" Jack jitters, jerking about.

"Give it a few minutes. Focus on the modules! Just breath, good just . . . there you go!" Speaking over her patient's frigid fidgeting.

347

Minutes melt away as Nurse Jessie checks his vitals for any abnormalities.

"Ok all done. I'll take those, vitals check out cadet. Not concerned about yesterday's concussion symptoms. . ."

"Arella, Blackshear, Bray, Brown, Wiley, you . . . what's really going on?" Jack placing gloves, VR, and mask in her hands squeezing, feeling strength return to his hands.

"Jack, I can't, not now . . . please understand. Doesn't matter what I think about you entering the Trials of Titans . . . all any of us can do is our part. This is mine. Oh sweet Jack, promise me that whatever happens, the sweet boy Anna raised . . . promise that you'll never . . ." Sniffing away memories.

Jack pauses, words forming from his frostbit brain.

"I promise, whatever the weakness, regardless of reward, I'll topple any trial . . . I promise I'll never change . . . promise." Breathing deeply, daring weakness away.

"Snff, snff. I know you won't snff . . . snff Bray believes these Cryo-pods will, will . . . see you tomorrow. I have another snff." Stepping away, the nurturing nurse nods, wiping memories menacing her mind. Setting her attention on cadets cowering from casualties caused in Volkov's.

"So they all know something." Jack dresses, rocketing off rejuvenated for tonight's second round.

348

CHAPTER THIRTY ONE

THUNDER IN HIS HEART!

Pacing himself, jogging through empty halls, making his way to Professor Bray's classroom. Opening her door cautiously, concealing himself from sight. Minutes pass when a bell blares, dismissing cadets cascading into halls hastily. Bray consoles a cadet complaining about their ankle, asking for exemption from class tomorrow.

"I'm sorry, cadet, that just won't be possible. You may go see Nurse Jessica, but I assure you the ankle isn't broken. Put some ice on it. See you tomorrow."

"Hpff . . . nepos!" Bray stepping towards her office, turning swiftly.

"Been waiting long?"

"No, ma'am, thought I'd nap for a sec." Jack materializing from behind mats mashed in a corner, eying them longingly.

"Hmm, I'll tell the twins. You ready then?"

"Yes, ma'am, those Cryo-pods are something else." Jack jests stretches, readying himself.

"Sure are, you're still recovering. Watch the film carefully when you recover in Cryo. We'll start with the basics today. First lesson, guard and framing to maintain head and arm control. Tomorrow side-control, bridging, and creating angles. Murphy, this will take time. Childress is the youngest black belt in GYAIA history. She dreams of Ju-Jitsu. I'm only teaching you this for survival, can't keep you out of Volkov's for long. Don't get cute with her. Childress was my very best pupil. Let's begin." Bray stuffing stray strands into a tightly pulled ponytail.

"Yes, ma'am." Jack responds, rejuvenated. Silencing questions queuing, courage coursing through cardio, soaking studiously like a sponge. . . .

As Jack trains to defend himself from his skilled adversary, the twins work expertly under the watchful eye of Doc Brown to complete their own task.

"So let me get this straight! You really think each Titan contains a clue to each Trial? Come on, Sam, even for me, that's nuts!" Max manipulating another mount.

"I do. Some are straightforward, but a few of these will take Jack time and practice to master, so we must follow specs best we can. Max you sure these are all the pads?" Sam settling the slimmest of soft landings.

"Yeah, unless we start stealing professor's and cadet's mattresses, that's it!" Max motioning empty hands.

"It's not enough. Outside of Prometheus' Pendulum we're almost done." Sam whispers, wiping sweat from his brow.

"No worries, bro, Murph's got this. Just gotta put padding where it counts." Max pointing purposely at perils nearly touching the ceiling.

"Gonna have to. Max gather the rest of the 550. It's out of specs for Prometheus's Pendulum, but it's all we have." Sam instructs.

"Only have about twenty feet or so. You sure?" Max mimicking his multiple's melancholy demeanor.

"No, but it's what we have." Sam shrugs.

"Could this help?" Doc stepping forward mechanically, maneuvering his own Exolift, brandishing thinly braided wire.

"Hey, let me see that!" Sam inspects the braid. "Sure is thin enough. What its tensile strength Doc?" Sam stretching the cord with his Exolift.

"Oh, that old thing, it's plenty strong, yes, plenty strong." Doc chuckles to himself.

"Gonna have to, let's see, measures just under specs. We'll make it work." Sam surmises. "Doc do we have time to construct Prometheus's Pendulum?" Max asks, checking his watch. "No, but we can start framing today and finish tomorrow. Cadet Murphy isn't ready to make the climb yet. No, not ready. We have time, Boys! . . . he will be, he will be . . ." Doc sizing remaining materials whispering to himself.

"Agreed Doc, where do you want these resistance torches?" Sam carrying three large welding torches.

351

"Oh, that's what I forgot. Good call, Sam. Here, attach mine if you would." Doc setting beams aside.

"One sec, there you go, all set, Doc." Sam securing Doc's torch to his Exolift.

"Well melt my MIG, let's get started, boys. We'll have this heinous high-rise up in no time. Remember, boys, gotta have a wide base and tapered top." Doc settles goggles on his eyes. Sparks spitting in all directions, the sadistic structure surges, pushing painfully to its peak.

While the twins work diligently, Jack continues his secret session with Bray.

"Oompf" Jack groans, struggling to flip his hips, braking Bray's hold.

"Don't fight me, roll, roll with me create space. Good, Jack, good, and that's how you break guard." Bray, breathing calmly, stands.

"Now we bow, even if you don't respect your opponent, always bow out of respect for the art." Jack's piercing professor beacons with a bow.

"Ohufff, oh, yes, sorry." Jack mimicking her mannerisms.

"Remember, use your forearms and elbows when framing; your hips are for escaping and setting guards. Ju-Jitsu isn't about power; it's about technique and multilateral movements. You'll get there, promise." Bray turning to check the time.

"Yes, ma'am. I will." Jack pants collecting his pack.

"Same time tomorrow, oh cadet . . . don't stay out to late tonight." Eyes piercing her point home.

"No, ma'am, I won't" Jack nods leaving Bray's makeshift dojo.

"Almost supper. Let's go see what the guys are up to." Jack, checking his watch, dashes off, avoiding any unwanted conflict.

"Good work, gentlemen. Welds looking straight, yes very uniform, no holes good Samuel." Doc piling praise on his prized pupil.

"Hey now Doc, how's mine? Less splatter this time, dontcha think?" Max motioning Doc near.

"Oh, yes, your welds don't look like microwaved Swiss cheese anymore. That's very good, Maximillian!" Doc patting his protégée proudly. Max smiling stupidly at Sam.

"Whatever, bro, your welds aren't trash anymore. Thanks, Doc, for letting us. . . ." Sam begins, cut off by their manic mentor.

"Oh, no need for gratitude Samuel. The thought of a first year besting the beast, conquering Cronus, traversing Tartarus is enough for this old relic." Doc eyes dazzling in a deluge of daydreams.

"Doc to earth, come in, Doc!" Max motioning their manic mentor.

"Oh yes . . . Maximillian, you're dismissed. Samuel, a word, please." Doc waving Max away.

"Yes, Doc?" Sam shoving Max towards the stairwell.

"Oh, ok, I know when I'm not wanted." Max making his way up.

"Yes, Professor?" Sam leaning near.

"Samuel, Max mustn't know . . ." Doc whispering wisdom to his prized pupil.

"Yes, Sir, understood. I'll let him know, yes, Sir." Sam responds, listening intently.

"Aw, right on time." Jack slowing his pace, allowing cadets to career by.

"Green light, thank you." Jack slipping past preoccupied pupils into Doc's lab.

"Ok, let's see, section C is oh right over here. Looks so different with the lights on." Jack jests to himself.

"Murph?" Max motioning Jack to his workstation.

"Whats'up Max, where's Sam?" Jack questions, looking around at empty workstations.

"Oh, Doc needed him for something; I don't know what. Dinner time?"

"Yeah, we going out tonight?" Jack jabbing his companion jokingly.

"You can. I got Soteria sims to run. Sorry, Murph." Max securing supplies.

"Speaking of the Soteria, have you ever thought about bees or hummingbirds? They fly so effortlessly." Jack handing Max supplies.

354

"Hmm . . . hummingbirds. What's your angle, Murph?" Max amusing his companion's offerings.

"Maybe you're too focused on linear speed when multilateral mobility is where it's at." Jack offers, impressed with himself. Pausing, allowing his mind to race, Max musing his companion.

"You may be on to something, yes, multi. Pack those, too." Max motioning Jack on.

"Ah, cadet Murphy! Looking quite fit. To what do we owe the pleasure?" The peculiar professor ponders.

"Good to see ya, Doc. You know, escort duty." Jack jests, jabbing Doc jovially. "Har, har, none of that, you kidder. Remember, Murphy, just swing with it . . ." Doc dodging behind Sam.

"Oh, Sam, don't forget our deal, solve them cyphers, and BESTY's yours." Doc says, using Sam as a human shield.

"Got it, Doc. Come on, gents, or we'll miss mess. Quit it, I'm hungry." Sam saluting his manic mentor. Jack and Max mimicking Sam's salute, the trio traversing tense halls consuming calories, returning promptly to their dorm without incident.

"Pffff, what a day!" Max kicking off his boots.

"Yeah, crazy day. Hey Sam, ever heard of Cryotherapy?" Jack inquires, returning Sam's uniform.

"Sure, athletes and celebs use them to recover. Went to see Nurse Jessica, did we?" Sam shedding his own uniform.
"How'dya know?" The rejuvenated rogue rocketing wore socks away.

"Elementary really, Jack. You were pretty beat up this morning and now you're a new man. Can only be Poke'pods." Sam surmises shoving Jack's sweaty offerings into their laundry bin.

"Didn't see you in Bray's today. What gives, Murph?" Max mashing his fatigues deep into the bin.

"Oh yeah, Bray made me work in a corner. Hey, good job, Sam, you're really getting over them walls well." Jack jolting into the bathroom before Max.

"Check this dude out, spends one day in a Poke'pod, he's back to normal!" Max mules, conceding his spot.

The trio refresh, readying for their task ahead.

"Jack, check this out." Sam motioning his companion near.

"So we've almost completed Prometheus's Pendulum, but we still have work to do. Take it easy tonight. Focus on these three tonight; time yourself. Remember, our replica is roughly half the real trails, and it is designed for at least two participants." Sam explains pointing at various elements.

"Gotcha, so whatcha make of these?" Jack handing Sam his copy of Mythology.

"So all these obstacles are related to a corresponding titan. Some trials aren't descript, consisting of multiple segments stealing your stamina, but these here are strictly based on their specific titan." Sam pointing out each obstacle's obscurities.

"Ooo, tell him about Hyperion. I built his obstacle." Max motioning his multiple.

356

"Hyperion's obstacle includes a timing element. Jack, find your footing and be patient. Wait for each rotation, then jump to the next orb. Be careful. Kinda rushed footholds on the orbs, probably harder than the real deal. So Hyperion is represented by his three children, Helios the sun, Selene the moon, and Eos the dawn. See these notches." Sam points.

"Look, Jack, just practice prior titans, adding Hyperion tonight. Specs for Oceanus and Tethys could be a problem. No worries for now. I'll figure it out tonight. Stick to these, please. You have time . . . stick to the script." Sam staring sternly at his audacious ally.

"What Sam's sayin, Murph, is that you should pace yourself, no rush." Max adds.

"Ok, I will. We have what ten days till trials. I'll master what two a day, and that leaves me with a few for full test runs?" Jack asking anxiously.

"Something like that, Jack. Max is right, should pace yourself. Any fall could cause a major setback. Poke'pods don't heal broken bones." Sam surmises.

"Gotcha, no setbacks. Well, got some studying, gonna take a nap time. . . Sam, Max, thanks. That means a lot." Jack states stoically. "Don't mention it Jack. This is bigger than any of us." Sam nods, turning to his work.

"Good luck, Murph, just like those eighties movie training montages." Max making his way to a much-needed shower. Hours pass for settled siblings soaking in sleep. A light glows, rousing Jack from rest.

"I'm up. Keep it simple." Dressing silently, stowing off through shadows Jack trains as instructed.

"Ooff almost lost it there. Wrong tunes, yeah, that's it." Jack settles, searching through a cathartic catalog.

"Thanks, Sam!" Placing a speaker on the ground, pressing repeat. Sound surging to the heavens heralding a new age of hero. *Thunder in your Heart* thundering throughout the house of horrors. Jack jolting from obstacle to obstacle, hushing hatred heaped upon him. Every move, like lightning harboring his heart thunderously. Heart heaving like a lion, moving moments truthfully and triumphantly traversing tyranny. Landing roughly, rousing himself for another round. Jack pushing past points of no return, readying himself to rectifying his wrongdoers.

"Oompph! Ugh, Oww." Jack winces, willing himself on. Jack peeling himself purposely off the floor, unaware of the shadow surveying silently above.

"One more, maybe two. Gotta get this right. Man, wish I had some chalk." Rubbing reddened palms, preparing for another run his voice venturing upward to uninvited ears. Farnham hammering him onward, Jack jumps, swinging skillfully, timing each movement of truth, completing his task for the night.

"Hmm . . . really likes that thunder song." Childress whispers, watching her prey push through his remaining runs. Slipping off into the shadows before Jack finishes, contradictions collide challenging conclusions, no longer concluded within the young vixen.

Exhaustive minutes pass before the you rogue finally surrenders to soreness.

"Ok, that's it." Stuffing gear randomly in the rusty locker, thunder thriving in his heart, disappearing into shadows, making his way back undetected.

"Made good ti. . . time." Tugging off boots and socks silently showering quickly, careful not to disturb the duo of synchronized sleeping siblings. Resting wearily, rocking himself to sleep.

CHAPTER THIRTY TWO

STONING A SIBLING TAKES STONES

Rising rejuvenated for another day, going about their usual routine. Morning run, mess, and off to classes. Crane's class becoming nothing more than propaganda promoting Triden's touted triumph. Jack settles quietly, keeping to himself, counting seconds away. Bray's class is more the same.

"Add some mixed-grips, Murphy, till failure." She salutes, sending Jack again to the pullup bar away from other cadets.

"Rest of you warm up. Today, we break out the sticks!" Piercing eyes surveying her cadet's excitement.

"Aw, man, not pugil sticks." Sam sulks, pocketing his glasses.

"AwwYeahh!!!" Max manically, marching off to his warm-up line.

"Alright, cadets, strap up! De Mendes, Singh, pair up! Ruiz, Wagner! Duval . . . Duval pair up!"

"What the hell? Thought she was on our side?" Sam sighs, slipping on his gear.

"OH, BABY, let the battle for bathroom supremacy begin!" Max motioning his readiness.

"Two lines, cadets! On the hop!"

"Warm up with the basics, cadets! Gonna have ourselves a tourney!" Bray belts to a thunderous ovation. Cadets excitedly hack and stab, connecting with their opponents. Anticipation ascending enthusiastic cadets clamoring for competition.

"ATTENTION! Second loss elimination! Here's the brackets!" Bray holding up a whiteboard, cadets crowding around.

"Singh? Doesn't seem fair, but ok." Max mouths to himself.

"Wagner first, really. Whatever, let's get this over with." Sam stepping to face his opponent. Cadets circle, cheering their champion.

"Cadets ready? . . . FIGHT!" Bray barks back, stepping away. Setting his feet, Sam readies for Wagner's first assault. *Jab, left swipe, he'll sweep . . . Wagner always sweeps.* Sam sliding side to side, expertly jumping into a joust, jostling Wagner's headgear roughly.

"Point Duval. Singh, Duval, center!" Bray barks, marking her whiteboard.

"Ready . . . FIGHT!" Bray backing out, sending Singh and Max to their task.

"Alright, let's go, Singh, hey where's your sling? WhoaOoampfff!" Max shrieks, tripping on Singh's stick.

"Point Singh!" Bray bellows, bringing forward her next pairing.

"Hey, no fair, he was wearing a sling at mess yesterday!" Max protests, peering into piercing eyes.

"Never mind, point Singh, got you next time, Singh." Max grumbles to himself.

"Sam 1-0, Max 0-1 sounds bout right." Sam whispering in his stunned sibling's ear.

"Lucky shot." Max mumbles, smacking Sam's stick from his nose.

"Boop!" Sam teasing his humbled half.

Cadets cheer raucously round after round, lessening the pool. Max recovering from his earlier defeat, scoring five victories earning a final four spot. Sam continues his streak of victories, pacing himself as well.

"Point Singh! Final four are set! Ruiz, Duval! Duval, Singh!" Bray points pairing Sam and Singh. "Ruiz, Duval, you're up first!" Bray barks, matching Max versus an also undefeated Ruiz.

"Ok, let's do this." Max mouths, steadying his breath. "Cadets ready . . . FIGHT!" Bray barks. Max dodging Ruiz's early aggressive assault, blocking stray strikes.

"Nope, nada, nice try!" Max muses, dodging her taxing attack, leaving Ruiz panting.

"Whew, my turn!" Max lunging lethargically, faking a slow weep, sending his stick swiftly into Ruiz's chin, knocking her into the other cadets crowded about. "Point Duval!" Bray barks, marking Ruiz's last strike.

"UrrggRAHH! You slow-played me, Duval!" Ruiz whines, rubbing her chin.

"Yeah, I did." Max smirking confidently, hyping fellow cadets.

"Duval, Singh set! . . . Ready? . . .FIGHT!" Bray beacons both. *Sling right? No sling left dude can barely lift his left. Sorry, Singh.* Sam surmises, mapping his attack mentally. Jousting gingerly, the skinny Sikh stabbing weakly. Sam blocking, bolting from side to side picking his target. Like a surgeon, Sam changing his stance, seeking advantage, stabbing swiftly, pinning the skinny Sikh's shoulder to his side, tossing him roughly out of the circle and colliding into crazed cadets.

"Point Duval! Quick break, hydrate finals in five!" Bray bellows checking on Singh.

"Yes, Ma'am, all good." Singh sighs, devastated by his defeat.

"Com'n, Sam, you knew he was injured." Max addressing his sibling's savage sendoff.

"No, you idiot, didn't want him landing on it." Sam spits, walking away.

"Ohhh, makes sense now. Won't work on me, jus so ya know!" Max muses, drinking greedily.

"I'm sure it won't . . . Good effort, Singh. Made it to finals on one wing." Sam congratulating his comrade.

"Oh, thank you, thank you. I'll train harder, be ready next time." Singh smiles, rubbing his sore shoulder.

"Yeah, dude . . . that was nuts . . . why risk it?" Max presses between gulps.

363

"I want to be strong like him." The skinny Sikh says, staring over his shoulder.

"Met the Murph, did ya? I get it. He's pretty tough, I guess . . . WHAT FINALS? NO, I'M NOT SURPRISED, SINGH!" Max flexing foolishly as a couple of female cadets stride by.

"Good luck, Duval!" One of them winking wishfully.

"Don't need lu . . . phff, uck, ack. What the hell, Sam?" Max whines, wiping his chin.

"Those girls totally respect my Rizz! Did'ya see them wink at me?" Max muses overestimating his moxy.

"Yeah, ok, watch your . . . boop!" Sam poking Max's nose comically.

"Hey, stop that. You'll ruin the rizz!" Max swiping at his sibling.

"Max, may I?" Singh tapping the maniac multiple's hand.

"What now Singh? Want my rizz too?" Max pulling himself away foolishly.

"No, your water, please." Singh bowing respectfully.

"Yeah, sure, you can my rizzwater." Max handing the skinny Sikh his mostly empty bottle.

"Thank you." Singh bows respectfully, running off.

"Odd, dude. Sam, aqua pov favor." Max reaching ridiculously.

"Knock it off. Finals start in a minute." Sam shoving his maniac multiple away.

"Ooff. . . pff, pff . . . bit my cheek again." Jack groans, spitting blood and wiping sand from his mouth. *Till failure, how bout till fu* . . . Jack spits sand and blood when a bottle shakes before his face, breaking salty thoughts.

"What's this? Oh, Singh, thanks, man." Jack sips, swishing the contents of his mouth.

"Noticed you were without my friend." The skinny Sikh smiles, rewarding the simplest kindness with another.

"Gulp, ulp. Tha, ulp, thanks again, brother." Jack draining the bottle gratefully.

"Brother? . . . Maybe in another life. Best of luck, my friend." Singh bows respectfully, returning to the crowd of cadets circling.

"Hmm, maybe." Jack pausing, puzzled by Singh's statement, scratching sand from his hair.

"Winner, S. Duval!" Bray barks cadets crowding about, cheering their hero of the day. "Darn you, Sam, you boop't me! Boop't me right on my nose in front of girls. All gone, all my rizz gone!" Max whines, watching Sam carried off on the shoulders of congratulatory cadets.

"Win some and lose some, Max. Com'n, get up." Jack extending drained digits.

"Not now, Murph."

Jogging off to shower and change, Jack meets up with Sam, still surrounded by congratulating cadets.

"Sup Sam, got time for us plebs?" Jack jokes, shaking Sam's hand, nodding in approval.

"I suppose, say, Jack, how long is Bray gonna banish you? You would've totally toasted everyone at sticks today." Sam states.

"Dunno, concussion protocol, I'd guess." Jack itching the cut above his eye.

"Stop, got training tonight." Sam slaps sternly.

"Ow, hey, where's Max, ya'll gotta get to Doc's?" Jack surveying the scene.

"Oh, he's convinced he can talk Bray into takin her training pads." Sam surmises. Sam and Jack join Max, bargaining with Bray in her classroom.

"Yes, Ma'am, I understand we got tuck and rolls tomorrow, but can't we do those in sand? Same effect, right?" Max motioning to padding stuffed in a corner.

"Yes, yes, just take them. I'll message Professor Brown concerning their return. Cadets all showered up?" Bray breaking from Max's manic motion.

"Yes, Ma'am, all good. See you tomorrow." Sam answers, pulling Max from padding.

"Hey, she said I could!" Max hugging pads humorously.

"We'll be back with transportation. Come on, Max, we'll be late." Sam salutes, shoving his manic multiple out the door.

"So, I'll. . ." Jack begins, broken short by his professor's piercing persona.

"Go walk your friends to class, Murphy. Jess is expecting you." Bray commands, shooing him away.

"Max, it's not a big deal. People get boop't all the time." Sam striding ahead.

"True, but on my nose? A leg, an arm, heck, you boop't Singh's shoulder. His shoulder, bro!" Max mules.

"A tenth grader told me once he got boop't by a senior in the bathroom." Jack interjects, catching his quarry with ease.

"Ew, gross, Jack. That was something else." Sam shivers.

"Probably right, don't think noses were involved." Jack jests, searching his memory.

"Of course, noses weren't involved. Nobody should be runnin round boopin noses. It's blasphemous to the bro code!" Max exclaims, working himself into a frenzy.

"Ha, ha, Bro code?" Jack jests playfully poking his companion.

"Don't laugh, Murph, it's a thing, and he broke it!" The deranged duplicate dances about.

"Thanks for guard detail, Jack. See ya at mess." Sam salutes, absorbing another earful from his manic multiple. Shaking his head, stifling a laugh jolting off in Nurse Jessie's direction.

"Yes, it looks bad, but really it's just a mild bulla, a blister. I can either drain it here, or you can?" Nurse Jessie jostling a jittery juvenile when Jack arrives.

"Cadet Murphy, good to see you. Cryo's ready go prep, be there in a sec . . . no, you can't just walk it off!" Nurse Jessie jerking the fidgety cadet back on her table.

Jack readies himself, slipping on gloves and mask, slipping past Jessie and the painful pollex. Booting up Bray's VR module, stretching soreness from his frame. Moments later the nurturing nurse, freeing herself from a line of cadets.

"Sorry bout that, blood and blisters all day, every day." Jessie jokes, brushing hair from her eyes.

"Already booted up, well aren't you a smart cookie." Jessie jests, adjusting the VR comfortably over his eyes.

"Thanks, Jess, so blood 'n' blisters, huh?"

"All day, that Volkov keeps me busy. Vitals much improved today. Ready?" Clicking away, checking on her cherished cadet.

"Yup, I mean, yes, ma'AMMMUTHER OF FREEZERS!" Jack fidgets frigidly to focus.

"Just breathe, there ya go, you're a regular ole Jack Frost now." Nurse Jessie jests, exits, attending another cadet.

Permafrost prickling beneath pores rejuvenating the young rogue. Jack shivers through another session, purging his pain. Moments melting by before Nurse Jessie returns.

"Ok, checking vitals . . . hmm, no sign of cranial contusions." Mouths under her breath, stepping away attending another ailing cadet. "Burrr." Teeth chatter chewing his gloves shivers as warmth returning. Setting gear aside, dressing quickly before the nurturing nurse discovers his escape.

"Them poke'pods really do the trick." Jack jogs clinching healed hands, hustling to his piercing professor's classroom.

Slipping silently into his corner, catching a quick nap. Cadets clearing the room, rousing Jack from rest.

"Suit up, Murphy, hope you studied." Bray beckoning him on. Testing his studies, Bray breaks his bridge by bestowing knowledge between each failure and sowing another successful seed.

"Good! Now bring your hips, drive, drive! Very good, Jack! Now frame, grip 'n' flip my hips, don't pull guard so quick. Good, good!" Bray sucking wind recovering from her surprisingly spry sparring partner.

"Yuhhu, yohhu . . . you learn quick Murphy. Cheater, watched ahead, did we?" Bray presses rhetorically.

"Yeahhu, yes, ma'am. Jess was busy, so I . . ." Jack wiping sweat itching above his eye.

"Shower up and get out of here cheater." Bray smirks proudly pulling her Gi into place.

"Yes, ma'am." Jack bowing respectfully races off. Bray bows.

"He's just . . . just like you Phoenix . . . just like you." Breathing silently, searching her soul for strength within silence.

CHAPTER THIRTY THREE
SLEEP WELL, MURPHY, SLEEP WELL

Jack, jolting past pious peers, pressing onward he sprints.

"Just missed em. Mess hall it is." Checking his time juking juxtaposed juveniles.

"What's the hurry, Murphy? Still gonna lose, loser!" Danzler densely decries as Jack dashes by. Meeting up with the dynamic duo, devouring dinner hastily hustling his comrades. "What's goin on . . . someone tryin to beat us up . . . let go, Murph?" Max tugs.

"For once, I concur, Jack, what gives?" Sam protests, tearing himself away.

"Nothing, no time to waste." The rejuvenated rogue, ripping past his companions.

"Must be them Poke'pods?" Max muses, motoring to catch up. "Must be. Slow down. What's the hurry?" Sam spits sprinting after them.

Jack ushering in his companions, slamming their dorm door. "Hff, hff, Murph, you're acting crazy. What's up?" Max crouches, catching his breath.

"Glad you asked, so Theia and Rhea. . . ." Jack clicking Sam's desk light on, rifling through notes.

"Whoa, slow down, Murph, those are classified!" Max making his way to their hysterical hero.

"Classified my ass. Theia's challenge uses lights and lots of em. Where are they?" Jack jamming specs into Sam's chest.

"Ok, okay, Jack, them Poke'pods got you . . ." Sam protests, pressing his caged companion.

"It ain't the pods, something Max said." Jack rifling through notes, searching suspiciously.

"Ok, you're officially freakin us out, Murph!" Max plucking papers, perplexed.

"Sorry, sorry like you said, Sam . . . different Titan, different trial, right?" Jack fumbles frantically.

"Yeah, so you're running Theia and Rhea tonight. What's goin on? . . ." Sam stacking notes meticulously.

"Sorry, sorry. Here it is!" Jack slamming his copy of Mythology on their desk.

"Ok, Murph, what's going on?" Max presses.

"Never mind, look . . . Theia's challenge isn't bout brilliance. If I just look at her shadow, I should be good, right?" Jack shifting aside.

"Theoretically, yes, but how'd you? " Sam searching for flaws in his summary.

"Elementary, really! Right, Sam? I may have tested her last night, could only see the floor. Mad LEDs, Max! Were those stadium lights?" Jack shifting frantically.

"Yeah, all we have, thought you were gonna stick to the script, Murph?" Max asks.

"I did. Ran through Coeus and Crius at least ten times. Just gotta know where my feet go for Coeus. Crius is all upper body with them rings." Jack taking a sec to catch his breath.

"Having Hyperion after Crius is rough on my hands. Got any chalk?" Rubbing his hands.

"Chalk?" Sam searching his memory.

"Sorry, Jack, Max chalk?" Sam shrugs.

"Sorry, Murph, fresh out." Max motioning empty-handed.

"Darn." Jack kicking himself for not asking Professor Bray when a knock raps roughly on their door. "I got it!" Sam shooting swiftly.

"Who is it?" Jack pushes past Max.

"Looked like Blackshear, hey now, Murph!" Max pushing Jack back. Fighting for position.

"Yes, Sir, won't happen again. Yes, Sir!" Sam says, saluting his superior when the door swings open.

"Murphy, Duval . . . Duval… good, all cadets accounted for. Duval, get that bunk back in regulation. Have a good night, gentlemen." Blackshear salutes, stepping off, completing dorm checks.

"What did Blackshear need?" Jack inquires, inspecting his bunk.

"Nothin, we didn't check in after mess. Told him Max wasn't feeling well, we're good." Sam shutting the door, settling down and studying his notes.

"Oh good, no biggie. Why do I need to make my bed if I'm just gonna mess it up in a few hours?" Max muses, tugging the top sheet tight. "You know how it goes round here, Max." Jack settling next to Sam, continuing their earlier conversation.

"So we have a few design flaws due to logistical issues. We're not able to simulate Oceanus, the great river titan. Specs suggest he's a perimeter swim, and Tethys involves diving elements. Sealing section C and pumping that much water would be a logistical nightmare, sorry, Jack." Sam scratching his chin, searching for a solution.

"Aren't there Olympic-sized pools in recreation?" Jack pressing for a solution.

"Yes, but first year's need clearance during the day Jack." Max adds as a plan forms in his head.

"Hmm, don't recall any hidden corridors leading to rec." Jack itching above his eye.

"Stop, Jack, it's finally healing." Sam slapping his hand.

"Okay, okay, oww!" Jack playing up his pain.

"You'll live, here. Study these notes for Crane's quiz tomorrow. Know and be able to apply each of the nine situations, chapter eleven." Sam returning to his own studies, scribbling new notes.

Finishing his studies, Jack fades into a dream about a pretty girl with golden auburn hair. Max and Sam work to fatigue on their own projects. Bouncing ideas off each other when necessary. Hours later, Sam and Max making their way to bed as Jack rises from a restful embrace, readying himself. "Ptss, Murph, Murph." Max motioning Jack near.

"Yeah, what's up?" He whispers.

"Pretty sure Doc swims after class. Could duplicate his credentials and get you access. Interested?" Max whispers over his snoring sibling.

"Sure you won't get into trouble?" Jack inquires, leaning near.

"No prob, got you tomorrow after class. Oh, Murph, don't fall so much. Ya almost tripped security sensors last night, oh yeah here. Wish it was chalk." Max placing a pair of earbuds with earhooks in his hand.

"Full charge. Good luck, Murph." Max whispers, cozying himself.

"Thanks, man." Jack slips off into shadows and resuming where he left off.

Flicking the switch sending a buzz around the room. Lights illuminating his rusty locker. Switching uniforms, Jack turns, kicking an object rolling into shadows.

"Chalk? Sam and Max said they didn't . . ." Pouring powder, pondering its existence.

"Thanks, Doc." He shrugs, powdering pleased paws.

374

"Pff, what would Brown know?" A shadow spits silently, surveying her quarry.

Readying himself turning up eighties tunes, Kansas carrying the wayward son onward. Toughing out test trials, jolting through the first three Titans transitioning to Theia's blinding brilliance. Shimmering gems designed to disorient. Falling from floating steps, doubt poisoning his person penetrating painfully. "Can't see steps." Jack shields his eyes from Theia's brilliance noticing the slightest of shadows outlining each step. Keeping his eyes low, jumping from shadow to shadow, avoiding Theia's blinding brilliance. Lights twinkle, tempting false steps.

Searching for shadows, Jack jumps, missing the first of five dangling disks crashing hard.

"Ooampf!" Groaning gearing up for another run. Averting eyes shadows sway sinisterly overhead. Testing depth and distance, Jack jumps, jerking the first disk and swinging himself towards another shadow, dancing dangerously. Multiple runs ending in failure fatiguing forearms.

Imagining Triden falling repeatedly, petty thoughts pushing him past the hanging heartbreakers. Rubbing feeling back into his hands, transitioning to the next Titan. Rhea, GAIA's great-mother generating more fails, forcing him to test multiple methods. Gripping tightly rolling with the log lacking padding, spinning to safety. Shaking life back into his forearms, handling the handlebars descending into a swing, squeezing abs, carrying momentum from bar to bar. Swinging through another transition,

375

focusing attention on detail. Muscles memorizing every step, taking another step closer to completion. Savoring small victories, vaulting himself on.

Zigzagging tilting temple tops. Jack jumps, landing roughly, readying himself for another round of rings. Lamenting Lapetus's litany of loosely levitating levels. Entering an expanse of sinisterly swinging spikes. Testing a plethora of paths, Jack dangles desperately. Bon Jovi is beckoning Jack to live on a prayer, propelling himself to now or never.

"Hff, hffff, damn cramps." Jack sits rubbing a knot forming in his forearm. Glancing down at his watch, he wills himself through another few runs. Trading the taste of defeat for blood, bolting through his last run of the night.

"Hhff, hhff. Good for now." Jack spits, stretching as soreness sets in. "Good ole Doc." Tossing the can of chalk into the rusty locker, dashing off into shadows.

Silence settles around the sinister structure, as a shadow saunters forward.

"Pff, what would Brown know?" The dangerous Delilah rocketing something small at the rusty locker.

"Sleep well, Murphy . . . sleep well."

Jack returns without incident, running this routine for days, carefully avoiding Triden and his goons. Days into Operation Titanfall seeing Jack and the twins returning from evening mess once again to their dorm. Continuing collectively with Sam and

Max, Jack puts Themis in her proper place, committing Mnemosyne to memory-sourcing knowledge from literature.

"As you can see, Jack, the titan Phoebe was a prophet of sorts, shining to light the way." Sam suggests pointing to the text.

"Ok, but you said the problem was with Tethys and Oceanus' challenges." Jack interjects.

"True Murph, Tethys, and Oceanus are connected as are all rivers are to the great river, Oceanus." Max answering before Sam.

"Correct, we couldn't simulate the water components of those challenges. As Tethys is connected to Oceanus, Phoebe shines her light, showing the way through Tethys' many children, aka Earth's many rivers. Once you ignite Phoebe's light, she will show you the way. Don't lose her light, Jack." Sam suggests running his finger across the map of many routes representing Tethys' many children.

"Gotcha, so I swim through these seven levers, allowing me to follow Phoebe's light through Tethys?" Jack inquires, running his finger along the path.

"Correct, fall behind, and you lose her light. Max, did you?" Sam turning to Max.

"Of course I did. Here you go, Murph." Max completes Sam's thought, handing Jack an access card with Doc's credentials.

"Nice, so why couldn't you guys just get me an access card to the Trials? I could just train on the real deal?" Jack, taking the card, inquires smartly.

"Simple, once Doc completed its designs, he was restricted too. The completed trials are under constant camera surveillance. Had trouble looping them, we tried Jack, we tried." Sam says, concluding the question.

"Dang, oh well. So what do specs say about each lever?"

"You will need to hold your breath long enough to dive and activate the lever without losing her light. Once you've navigated Tethys' children, Oceanus' half-kilometer swim circles around the Trials leading to Cronus' compass." Sam signing heavily.

Noticing his companion's waning confidence.

"What's up, Sam? I'm a strong swimmer, saved my buddy Reg from a riptide once." Jack includes confidently.

"A riptide, really? Quit playin' Murph. Those will kill ya." Max questions, unconvinced.

"Sure did. Just swim parallel with the shoreline until ya feel the current calm. From there just swim ashore and count your blessings." Jack answers confidently.

"Dude, that's nuts. Murph, tell us another crazy 'I survived Florida' story!" Max musing him on.

"Ever escaped an angry moccasin?" Jack indulging the maniac multiple.

"Why you runnin from footwear?" Max asks moronically.

"Snakes stupid! He's talkin bout snakes, Agkistrodon piscivorus to be precise." Sam interjects, shaking his head.

"OOooo, pay him no mind, Murph. Sam's a serpent simp!" Max mocking his multiple moronically.

"Whatever wolf whisper, no, Jack we've never escaped a common cottonmouth." Sam slapping Max's finger from smudging his glasses.

"Yeah, well, it's no picnic. So Sam about Cronus, says here he was the youngest and leader of Titans. Why is the youngest their leader?" Jack inquires, refocusing the conversation.

"Unfortunately, I hadn't time to read all of Hamilton's work, but he ushered in the Golden Age of peace until his children took him down. Jack I'd need more time to answer your why, but he's the final titan before Prometheus's Pendulum." Sam says searching through notes.

"So can I?" Jack jabbing Sam for a response.

"Tonight, run through each trial under twelve? You can try, Cronus should be ready for an attempt." Sam submitting to the courageous cadet.

"Yes! So Cronus looks to be a simple cane lane type." Jack starts, cut off by Sam.

"Well, no, remember you will have swam Tethys and Oceanus. Your uniform will weigh you down." Sam surmises.

"Oh, good point, so without swimming them first, how do I . . . what the hell Max?" Jack jostling in his seat, catching a weighted vest.

"This, this is how Murph!" Max chuckles, returning to his seat.

"Could'a warned a brother, thanks man." Jack jests, sizing the worn vest.

379

"Don't mention it, Murph. I stole it from Bray." Max motions amusingly.

"Stole? Bray?!" Jack rising at the ready.

"Calm down, Jack. Bray gave it to us the other day. We didn't steal anything." Sam states, defending his dubious duplicate.

"Wait, why didn't she just give it to me herself?" Jack inquires confusedly.

"Dunno, maybe she was busy makin you do pull-ups till ya puke." Max muses.

"Maybe, so who left this?" Jack questions, producing a small container with a mouth guard.

"Dunno, left where?" Sam inquires.

"Found it by the locker the other night. Max?" Jack returning the inquiry.

"Not me, Murph. Why do you need a mouth guard?" Max motioning lost at his inquiry.

"Not me, I don't think Doc would either." Sam surmises. "Left one night, and the next, it was there. Thought it was you guys or Doc." Jack scratching his head sheepishly.

"Not us, Murph honest. What's it for?" Max inquires.

"Been bitin my cheeks and lips when I fall, haven't since, though. Sure it wasn't Doc?" Jack presses.

"Not a detail he or we were aware of Jack . . . Weird." Sam surmises.

"Yeah weird. Glad to have it." Jack rubbing his cheek. "Lots of strange happenings lately. Mysterious Marauder milled through professor's offices. Triden challenged without earning the right of rule, random chalk appears and now a mysterious mouthpiece. Bray punished you in a corner all period without causation. Lots of . . ." Sam stopping his list searching his companion.

"Doesn't matter who gave you the mouthpiece. We have an operation to see through." He concludes.

"Yes, Operation Titanfall, down with the man!" Max muses.

"Ha, ha, we'll see. So Cronus? Just a cane lane type to me." Jack jests, focusing his friends.

"Yes, Cronus' cane, well, scythe, really. Jack, the difficulty is you'll be drenched and depleted from Tethys and Oceanus. Take a minute to breathe." Sam suggests.

"Yeah, Triden probably won't be around at this point. Sam's right. Take a sec, oh, here for the swim." Max tossing Jack a sleek swimsuit.

"Whoa, these are small! This is smaller than my first singlet. I can't fit into it." Jack stretches, searching for space.

"Feet first, Murph, its design reduces drag. Should save some extra exertion navigating Tethys and Oceanus." Max nods.

"Gotcha, thanks, man." Jack says, stretching the stiff wetsuit.

"It'll fit, Jack. Now Cronus' Compass has five components . . ." Sam produces, pivoting back to his point. "Using Cronus' scythe, you must hit all four cardinal points. Starting south, etch east, work west, and navigate north. Bringing Ouranos' Eye into focus. Without the cardinal directions you'll never make that jump without lowering his eye. It's too high." Sam states stoically.

"Once his eye's in focus, I swing to center, slaying the sky." Jack completing Sam's instructions.

"Hmm, someone's been studying. Correct . . . Slay the Sky, Ouranos." Sam surmises, satisfied.

"Ok, so, tonight, I'll train with the vest, but why don't I just complete Cronus' compass and Prometheus' Pendulum in my wetsuit?" Jack inquires, gathering his growing gang of gear.

"You could. I'm sure that lynx of a librarian wouldn't mind Murph!" Max mocks.

"Don't listen to him, Jack. The vest simulates resistance during your swim before Cronus' Compass. Couple of laps should do." Sam suggests.

"Run, run as fast as you can, won't catch Murph he's the . . . Oww!" Max motioning a running movement with his fingers across Sam's keyboard.

"Quit that! About the best we can do, given spec limitations. Good luck tonight, Jack." Sam says, smacking Max's hustling hand away.

"Makes sense. Thanks, gents, gonna need a nap for this one." Jack jokes, setting gear aside and settling comfortably.

Leaving them to their work, Jack rests before another painful practice.

CHAPTER THIRTY FOUR

BE GOOD TO YOURSELF

Another routine day passes as Jack and the Twins hustle from class to class and task to task, purposely avoiding unnecessary conflict. Excitement grows in every hall as the Trials near. Competing cadets converse about their chances to enthusiastic younger cadets, dreaming of their own opportunity in their future. Jack finishing his academics steals off to Nurse Jessie's to recover from last night's abuse.

Mist hissing harmlessly, Jack jolting for another rejuvenating round.

"You're a regular ole polar bear now, cadet." Nurse Jessie jokes, collecting his gear.

"Yeah, these Poke'pods been a real lifesaver, Nurse Joy!" Jack jests, patting her warmly on the shoulder.

"Get out of here, you rogue . . . still don't understand the reference!" Shoving him playfully, smiling to herself.

Jogging past pious pupils, Jack makes his way to Volkov's, readying himself for another round.

"Murvhy late!" Volkov's villainous voice venturing from behind.

"Today's lesson . . . group assault." Volkov hisses with delight.

"Oh boy, this is gonna . . ." Jack sighs, slipping in his mouthpiece.

"No, let's see what the boy's learned since his return." Childress interrupts, stepping between Jack and Volkov. The lethal lioness tugging her Gi tight, settling her stance.

"Har, har vhy vight two vhen boy vight army!" Volkov howls, delighted with the dangerous Delilah's proposal. Waving Danzler and Maddox away, Volkov sanctioning their sparring session.

"Cadets ready! VIGHT!!!" Volkov howls, eagerly anticipating another annihilation. Jack settles heavily on his back foot, careful not to rush her like before.

"Hmm, seen that before." Childress spits sarcastically, stepping forward. Cautiously avoiding a mistake, dodging her first attempt sliding to safety.

"Get in there, little mouse!" Danzler demands hyping fellow cadets to do the same.

"Get in there, tough guy! Get em good, Childress!" Cadets chastise chomping for carnage.

Setting her trap, Childress fakes a sweep, tucking into a roll, taking Jack's loaded leg. Twisting him to ground roughly. Cadets cheer excitedly, expecting his end. Tugging himself into guard, pinning her arm expertly. Shock surging through the vicious vixen, Childress sinks, pressing her weight on his chest. Torqueing torsos tussle for top position. Both begin breathing heavily, confusing cadets and Volkov alike.

"How boy know?" Volkov spits silently.

Careful to conserve energy, Jack frames himself to test her. Gripping each other's Gi, tugging and dodging for dominance. Taking a trip down memory lane, slipping her hips, taking her back, driving his forearm deep beneath her chin. Gripping his wrist tight, Childress, sensing his skill, tearing it taut. Unable to complete the hold, Jack releases, reaching for her hips. The momentary mistake affording her opportunity. Tugging hard, spinning her hips, Childress thrusting his thorax to the ground, flattening his hips. Pulling guard again, the rebellious rogue receives a quick crack to his gut driving wind from frame.

"Huffooampff!" Jack gasps weakly, tugging her Gi.

"Save it for later." Breathing belabored into his ear, cinching in her stranglchold, releasing quickly, kicking his heaving husk away. Cadets cheer, applauding her performance.

"Good show, Childress. He almost got you there. Ooomph!" A random emboldened cadet shrieks upon clasping her back. Ripping him roughly to the ground, Childress bows respectfully, addressing both her still prone opponent and professor before storming off.

The sinister Soviet staring skeptically, returning her bow.

"Hmm, secrets." Volkov motioning for his remaining cadets to pair up, proceeding as normal.

Scraping himself from the ground, sucking air angrily.

"Boy did vell . . . Murvhy dismissed!" Volkov spits, stepping between Jack and an approaching Maddox.

385

"Boy's done for day!" Volkov waving the muscular menace away.

"hfff, hfff . . . never done . . . hff." Jack gasps gingerly, dragging himself off.

Leaning against a wall, catching his breath, Jack changes gingerly before trudging towards Bray's. Sneaking into his usual shadow, settling uncomfortably. Moments pass, blaring another bell, sending cadets careening about. "Murphy?" Bray's piercing eyes scanning her room.

"Yeah, I'm hff . . . here. Let's get this . . ." Jack spits, stepping forward.

"No, not today. Childress got you good today, I see." Bray jokes, brandishing an odd-looking device.

"No training today?" Jack questions, rubbing his stomach.

"We can resume combat training after the Trials. Today, you swim. Go change; Twins left a wetsuit in your locker. Meet me in rec in five. Hustle up, cadet!"

Jolting off to his locker, struggling to fit into his wetsuit Jack tugs hastily. Dressing in his uniform, tugging on tightened spaces Jack heads off to the rec pools.

"You're eight seconds late." Bray presses, checking her watch.

"Yes Ma'am, this thing does zip itself." Jack tugging the taut fabric beneath his uniform.

"Eight seconds is enough to lose the light. Let's go." Bray swiping her card.

Doors open revealing large pools used for all types of aquatic exercises.

"Whoa, these are big!" Jack exclaims, investigating their length.

"Yeah, they're too short, but they'll have to do." Bray tossing the last device in, sinking swiftly.

"So today's exercise replicates Tethys' trial. You will have to dive and operate each device. Once done, you may surface for air. Without triggering each device, you cannot progress. I will be at the topside shining this light into the water. Follow the light. It only pauses temporarily on each lever before moving on. Murphy, you must stay on schedule. We only have the pool for twenty-two minutes. Let's begin." Bray bolts off, settling high above.

"Follow the light cadet! Begin!" Bray barks, dimming the overhead lights, shining hers.

Forgetting to disrobe his uniform Jack jumps into the pool, pulling hard to keep pace. Lighting pausing, peering into depths below, sending Jack deep. Jack breathes deep, diving deeper, solving the first device, triggering a green light. Lungs burn as he kicks, breaching the surface. Sucking wind greedily, kicking hard to keep up before diving again.

Light barely penetrating the depths, Jack fumbles, frustrated with the second device barely triggered its light, sending him to the surface. Sucking air, heart pounding like a train down its tracks. Swimming slower, digging deep not to lose the light.

Drawing breath, he dives deep tripping the third device with ease. Driving his legs hard along the bottom, propelling himself up. Breaching the surface, sucking oxygen obstreperously. Losing the light, Jack wades weakly after. Light settling for only seconds, the young rogue resists the urge to dive, calming his heartrate. Wicking water from his nostrils, sucking life into his chest, diving once more. Kicking deep, Jack driving downward, drowning fear and insecurities. Fidgeting frantically with the final device when the light disappears. Bubbles bursting from his mouth, Jack kicks weakly underwater in frustration before he surfaces.

"Three out of four on your first run, not bad, cadet. Not bad at all!" Bray strides over, pulling her exhausted cadet from the pool of peril. "Hff, hffff, I hff, was, hfff!" Jack spits.

"Shh, just breathe, just breathe."

"Next run, lose the uni quicker, shall we?" Bray patting his sopping shirt.

"So heavy, so hfff, hfff." Jack, leaning back, body begging for mercy.

"Back in a sec. Breathe, cadet." Bray pulling hair tight, slipping off her uniform, kicking heavy boots aside, revealing a sleek athletic physique. Jack turning to hide the warmth returning to his cheeks.

Diving deep without a sound, resetting each device two at a time, before resurfacing. Water drips delicately from Bray's firm frame; toweling off, checking her time.

"Little slow, Hff." Whispering to herself.

388

"Ok, cadet, let's try this again. Got time for one more run, take position." Bray orders, returning topside, readying her light.

Hands still shaking, Jack tugging his soaked uniform, kicking heavy boots aside.

"Keep your socks on!" Bray instructs from her bird's eye view. Looking down, Jack feeling their weight, sighs readying for another run.

"Position . . . BEGIN!" Blaring her light piercing a path. Calming himself, Jack jumps in swimming swiftly. He cuts through wayward waters with ease, diving deep, disarming each device before resurfacing completely spent.

"Got em all, good job, cadet! Last one's tricky, but you pulled through!" Bray tossing Jack a towel.

"Hff, hfff." Jack sits weakly, catching his breathe.

"Meet here tomorrow, same time. With only a few days left, must time your transitions." Bray peering over the pool, eyes piercing its dangerous depths.

"Hff, transitions, hff?" Breaths belaboring his question.

"Time to disrobe, Tethys' trial, and swim Oceanus himself. Triden's been training too. Time is everything." She states coldly, staring over troubling tides.

"Triden, I'll kick his . . ." Beginning his thought broken by Bray's piercing pearls.

"No doubt you will . . . Jack preparation is critical. Tonight, take three laps, pushing each faster than the last. Your lungs will be screaming when you rise from Oceanus' waters before taking on Cronus' compass. Pace yourself. Got a few days till the Trials, Jack." Pointing to a dry uniform in the corner, Bray nods, tossing her towel aside, dives, retrieving each device in one go.

Jack, wringing his soaked uniform, changes, checking his time before hustling off. Jack showers, enjoying silence before Sam and Max bust through the door. "Hey now, no, I was first!" Max maneuvering past Sam, thrusting his arm into the air.

"Whatever, tripper!" Sam settling at his computer, ignoring Max's idiotic celebration.

"I'm the winner, speak the devil; the usual Murph?" Max inquires strutting about foolishly.

"Usual what?" Jack asks perplexed, when his stomach rumbles.

"You know, mess, study up, little nappy nappypoo, then get some swinging in?" Max muses.

"Probably best skip studies, we'll make notes. Get some extra rest Jack." Sam adds noting his companion's fatigue.

"Sounds good Sam, Tethys' swim is no joke. C'mon let's get mess." Jack acknowledging Sam's concern, patting his depleted stomach.

The trio step into the hall closing their door behind them when a familiar voice halts their progress.

"At attention cadets!" Blackshear's voice booms, causing the three to stiffen in place.

"You three take evening meal the next few days in your quarters. Ma'am Director's orders." Blackshear booms when Jack protests.

390

"But Sir . . ." Jack blurts, before Blackshear nears.
"Tensions critical, since Max's little scene earlier today. That's
extra laps Cadet!" Blackshear's eyes cutting away from Jacks
momentarily.

"Sir, what scene?" Jack presses fearing the worst for Max.
"Duval can speak for himself. Back to your dorms, mess is on its
way. Dismissed!" Blackshear barks still eyeing Max
disapprovingly. Waiting a moment until the trio have followed
orders, Blackshear gathers his remaining troop, heading off for a
well-deserved meal.
Slamming their door behind them, Jack grabs Max roughly by his
shirt.

"What the hell Max, you said you'd be good!" Jack
shouts, loosening his grip when Sam intervenes.

"Settle down Jack, we're just following orders." Sam slips
revealing an unfortunate truth.
Turning to address his collected comrade, Jack throwing his hands
up slapping his thighs roughly. "Following orders? Whose?" Jack
presses hotly.

"Can't say Jack, trust us it's for the best." Sam surmises
ashamed of his role.
"Trust, I can't trust anyone around here!" Jack turning away
avoiding eye contact with his companions.

"Murph, things are getting crazy right now. Triden's
support is ridiculous. Blackshear can't be everywhere at once. Just
gotta be this way for a bit." Max states somberly for once.

"So what! What did you do then?" Jack presses, still not looking at his companion.

"Well, I may have tripped Maddox in the hall. Don't be mad Murph, he had it coming, right?" Max muses attempting to break the tension.

"You tripped him and now we're in timeout for the next few evenings?" Jack shaking his head, looking around their humble dorm for answers.

"Well, it may have started a small scuffle in the hall. Professors had to break up the two factions, but nobody got hurt. Ok so Crane may have taken an elbow to the beak." Max chuckles to himself unable to hide his satisfaction.

"Crane got it?" Jack's voice softens stifling his own satisfaction.

"Yeah Jack, it was a right bloody mess, but that wasn't part of the plan Jack, honestly. We were just told to give a reason to separate that's all." Sam adds wishing he'd said less.

"Ok whatever guys, I'm hungry and tired. This all just doesn't make sense." Jack concludes sitting on his bed when a knock on the door cut their conversation short.

"Ah smells good, thank you, thank you." Sam greets the young delivery cadet before shutting the door behind him. The trio eat quietly, speaking only about trial specs before Sam and Max go about their business, leaving Jack to slip off into slumber.

Hours pass as a buzzing alarm rouses Jack to his task. Sneaking carefully as before Jack prepares himself for another night of successes and failures. As instructed Jack runs each trial, checking the time, pacing himself and stopping only to catch his breath. Running as instructed, Jack sheds the heavy vest, readying for the great Titan himself. Hands tremble, tightening his grip. Cronus' compass proves more challenging than expected.

"Oooamphh!" Jack groans, gripping his chest as he rises for another run.

"Eye of Ouranos, damn things a pinhole." Jack spits, brushing off his mouthpiece. Rising from rough run after rough run. "Thppt, tunes all wrong. Need ya, John!" Farnham whispering Jack on.

"HELLYEAHH!!!" As the selected symphony surges the young hero hangs before swinging to safety.

"We got this, John." Jack whispers to an imaginary Farnham.

Stepping to the final trial, craning his neck upward, sending a shadow deeper into darkness.

"Prometheus' Pendulum, dang things an upside-down ice cream cone. How the heck?" Jack tugging the thin wire.

"Oww, damn!" Kissing his cut.

"Sharp lil devil?" Stepping back, investigating its rise.

"Can't straight climb this razor." Jack ponders applying pressure. Checking the time, leaning on a stack of forgotten mats, Max failed to disperse. Closing his eyes, catching a breath.

"Preparation critical, think, Jack, think!" Jack sighs, snapping his finger.

"Doc said swing with it; hmm I wonder?" Removing heavy boots soaked with sweat, wrapping sopping socks around his hands tight, salt searing his cut.

"Ahh, Alright John, let's see what we got." Pressing play throttling thunder through his heart. Cinching cord deep into wraps, running in a circle, building momentum, ripping off each wall, kicking hard. Risking it all, every move like lightning lifting him upward.

Slinging slack, Jack gripping tight, thrusting hand over hand, kicking walls wickedly. Heaving himself heavily halfway, swinging swiftly, and setting sights on the summit when damp feet slip beneath him. Releasing the razor, reaching desperately. Slapping smooth surfaces, aiding his frictionless fall. In an instant, hues of blue flash faintly from the floor. Contorting his body, bracing himself, he screams.

"AHhhhhhhOamph!" Jack's body bouncing bluntly off the stack of mats rag dolling him roughly to the floor.

"Ugh." He groans lying motionless for a moment.

Rolling slowly, checking for broken bones, Jack settling uneasily on one knee.

Stay down, stupid boy, Childress mouths from her perch.

Gathering all he can spare spreading pads in a square pattern. Tightening his wraps, the titular teen flings himself into another attempt. Faltering once more, falling short of his first run.

"Damn! Get up, Loser, GET UP!" Slapping himself, adjusting his mouthpiece, tugging tautly. Racing across mats, losing speed atop sinking steps, crashing hard into the wall.

"RRRAAAHHHHHH!" Exploding with a resentful roar whipping the wicked wire away.

"This is you, Jack, this is you . . . loser!" Pounding ground, sobbing into shaking hands. Pulling knees close, wishing it were all a dream, weeping weakly. Silence settling around the sinister structure, a faint echo etching hope into his despair. Patting empty ears, Jack crawls towards the melodious music. Feeling about in the dark, beat growing louder, begging him to be good to himself. Closing his eyes, soaking in soulful sounds. Rubbing stiffness settling in his shoulders, hanging up his sweat soaked socks for now. Returning gear to the rusty locker, leaving everything else in place, Jack retreats for the night. Stepping from shadows, Childress pacing memories pugnaciously, peering at the painful pendulum's pinnacle.

"Stupid boy won't quit." She whispers, staring at a fate once hers.

CHAPTER THIRTY FIVE

ALL JOURNEYS END

Rising for their morning run, Jack and the twins eat morning mess under Blackshear's watchful eye as cadets career excitedly about.

"Triden gonna weed the garden! Heard he's been blowing through trials training! First's years got no chance!" Chattering cadets' converse carelessly between classes.

"Don't listen to them, Murph, you'll figure out Prometheus." Max moving cadets from their path.

"Hey shrimp, what's the . . . oh cadet Murphy, my apologies right this way." A cadet motions, moving classmates aside.

"Thank ya, thank ya, Murphman's best friend here, thank ya, not ya, thank ya!" Max maneuvering ignorantly.

"All titans fall, Murphy!" The cordial cadet winks motioning Jack on.

"What's going on, Sam?" Jack whispers into his confidant's ear.

"Trials were moved up a day. They're tomorrow. Dunno why, Jack, they just were." Sam anticipating his comrade's next question.

"Nurse Jessica best look at that shoulder today, Jack." Sam sliding past chattering cadets.

"Double da Poke'pod Murph!" Max muses, mushing cadets aside who are making their way through throngs of stoked students.

Excited cadets chatter, converting curriculum to conversations of the coming calamity.

"Dude, this is insane. We're celebs, Murph!" Max motors mimicking a red carpet walk.

"They don't, never mind . . . off to Doc's. Stop by if you have a sec, Jack!" Sam shouts over-enthusiastic cadets.

"Sure, sure, Sam, I'll try." Jack jostles away, pulling himself from cheerful cadets.

"Cadet Murphy!" Blackshear's voice booms over eager cadets.

"A word, move aside, move aside!" Blackshear bellows, clearing a path for his cadet. Slipping past cadets, the pair proceed to a calmer corridor.

"Yes, sir?" Jack asks.

"Trials aren't usually this crazy; Triden's turned them into a spectacle. Sorry, how you holding up, Murphy?" Blackshear inquires.

"All good, headed to Volkov's. What's up, Sir?" Jack pressing his superior.

"Take this; it's an excusal note from Bray. You have orders to skip Volkov's and report to recreation. Bray will meet you at 1400 sharp at rec. Seen Nurse Jessica about that shoulder yet?" Blackshear comments.

"No, Sir, not yet. I'll stop by after rec, promise." Jack answers.

"That'll work. To avoid any issues, we'll take mess early. After mess, I'll inform you and your fellow cadets of tomorrow's schedule." Blackshear attempting a dismissal salute when his young cadet interrupts.

"Yes, Sir, there's something else, isn't there?" Jack presses.

"Yes, Jack, there is . . . No training tonight. You have too much at stake to get hurt or be too exhausted to perform. Please don't make me put you on lockdown. Be smart, Murphy." Blackshear instructs, saluting Jack before jogging off.

"Sorry, sir, can't do that, got unfinished business tonight." Jack whispers, returning his superior's salute. Jack, checking his time, jogs off towards the rec center. Using Doc's card, Jack slips in, changing quickly, stripping down to his wetsuit.

"Remember, socks on!" Bray beacons from behind.

"Yes, ma'am." Jack salutes respectfully.

"At ease, cadet. Here for the shoulder." She salutes, tossing him a small roll.

"K-tape, nice!" Jack snatching swiftly, wincing as he does.

"Hmm, supra, come here I'll tape you up." The piercing professor positioning his arm, anchoring two strips supporting Jack's shoulder front to back.

"Supra?" Jack asks as she completes her task.

"Thank you, I'll get that." Jack reaches for empty strips.

"Warm-up cadet, let's get started." She commands, sniping a nearby waste bin.

"All good." She smirks, stepping to the edge of the pool. Her sleek physique shimmers with sensuality as she stretches.

"Wait, what about the light?" Jack stretches, straining not to stare.

"Hmm . . . no light today, cadet. You'll be racing against Triden, an accomplished swimmer. Phoebe's light only shows Tethys' way. Falling behind in Oceanus' swim affords your competition time to rest. Would be a mistake. Only one Cronus' compass, can't afford any advantage to Triden." She states, shaking life into her lean limbs.

"Aren't there two canes?" Jack asks, adjusting goggles and taking position beside his picturesque professor, limbering his own limbs.

"Correct, but there's only one pendulum." She says, inhaling deep before diving deeper.

"Heeey!" Jack breathes, bolting after her.

"Keep up, cadet!" Bray spits, submerging again.

Drawing deeply, blowing fire from his nostrils, lungs burning like a furnace, forcing himself under again. Diving deep, suffocated muscles aching for salvation. Willing himself harmfully, hands ripping calmly, controlling each device. Green light's glow dotting the water's surface as the amphibious assault battles below. Surfacing, Jack draws life, desperately plunging once again after Bray. Pulling effortlessly, lithe limbs slice, shooting to solve another device. Calming his mind, Jack swims along the surface, swiftly sucking air before diving after the

Madonna mariner. Sleek sinew rippling rhythmically, the majestic mermaid manipulates her final device, drifting to check Jack's pace before surfacing. Driving deep, grabbing hold of the weighty device, steadying his aching body, and activating his last device. Breath bubbles surge from burning lungs as Jack kicks, driving defeat downward.

"HUuHuUu!" Breaching the surface, gasping deeply. He weakly swims to the edge.

"Hff . . . hfff!" Composing himself, wicking water from his face.

Clap! Clap! Clap! "Very good, Murphy, great job adjustment. Catch your breath; eight hundred meters doesn't swim itself." She congratulates stretching lean legs.

"Fff, for a second there, thought those turned to fins." Jack jests, calming his chest.

"Hmm . . . Murphy, Oceanus is a marathon. Find your pace and maintain it. Six laps around should about do it. Let's go!" The piercing professor, fitting her goggles snuggly, dives in like a droplet.

"Hffff, six laps. Gonna have to triple Poke'pod time." Complaining as he adjusts his goggles. Finding his pace proves to be tougher than he'd expected. Bray's lead tempting him to surge forward.

Find your pace, Jack. She's testing you. Just breath, four more, just breath. Swimming some distance behind, beckoning him to speed up. *Smooth is fast Jack, smooth is fast.* He reminds

400

himself attempting to stay calm in the moment. Staying true to his training Jack digs deep to complete all six laps. Lungs burning as he pulls himself from the pool.

"Good swim cadet!" Bray tossing him a towel, tying her hair knot tight. "You could have smoked me easy. Why didn'tya?" Jack dabbing himself dry. "The lesson wasn't to win. It was to train pace." Her eyes piercing truth to principle.

"Hmm, I did, but on that last lap, you sped up. Why?" Jack inquires, removing his soaked socks.

"Simple, wanted to see if you could keep up." She smirks, motioning him near. "Bring those socks, want to show you something." She saunters over towards a thin wire dangling from the rafters.

"Hey, this is like . . ." Jack begins careful not to grab the wicked wire.

"Yes, same tensile strength. Same millimeters." Bray informs, grabbing one sock and pulling and twisting it as thin as possible.

"Do you know any Boy Scouts back home, Murphy?" She asks, motioning for him to do the same.

"Yes, ma'am, planned on being an Eagle Scout one day." He replies, pulling and twisting as instructed.

"Good then, you know knots. Have you heard of the Prusik?" She pauses, securing both ends together.

"No, ma'am, but I know a fisherman's bend when I see one." Jack mimicking her movements.

"Wrap it around the wire, making a Lark's head. Make sure to clear your fisherman's bend, and now feed it through like such. Yes, like that, Murphy, well done. Practice the Prusik tonight; you will need two to make the climb."

"I get it now." Jack sliding both independently, pulling one securing taut to the wire.

"Good, grip the fishermen, then climb. You have twenty have at it!" The piercing professor stepping to a control panel, sending the wicked wire dangling over the pool below.

"What the?" Jack stepping to the edge in amazement.

"Now, make the climb." She commands.

"What if I fall?" He asks sheepishly, rubbing his shoulder.

"Hmm, then fall." She smirks, waving her over the water's surface.

Tossing his goggles aside, diving in, and swimming towards salvation. Gripping the taunt knot, sliding the other with ease, repeating the pattern, pulling himself upward. Droplets drip, freeing him from the deluge below. Tensing his muscles, Jack slides one, pulling the other downward. Heroes rarely ascend on their own. Jack ascends, water wicking, weighing him down no more. Pulling hard, pausing to shake fatigue from weary wrists. Biceps burn, fried forearms forcing Jack to focus on one hand at a time, inching his way to the punishing pendulum's pinnacle.

Fingers tremble, tugging tautly, thrusting his legs upward, taking tension from aching arms. Inch by inch, the apex appears, tempting him upward. Sliding his last slide, tugging his last tug, grabbing the beam, pulling himself onto scaffolding hidden in the canopy's construction. His chest heaves heavily, arms aching, lying limp at his sides. Wincing to himself a smile etches weakly across his face.

This is who you are. Jack ponders saving his breathe.

"Excellent cadet! Care for another run?" Bray barks.

"No, no more madam mermaid!" Jack jests, massaging his limp limbs.

"Madam Mermaid? Get down there before you earn pullups till failure!" Shouting through a smile. Pulling himself painfully descending to his proud professor.

"Well done, cadet. I believe Jess' got a Cryo with your name on it." His piercing professor postulates.

"Thank you, ma'am." His legs failing him into an irregular embrace. Catching her collapsing cadet, a feeling absent for some time, allowing the embrace for only a second.

"Okay, okay, get dressed, to sickbay with ya!" She exclaims, pushing him away.

"I'll clean up, wear these tomorrow. You're dismissed, cadet." Bray tossing Jack a pressed pair of socks. "Umpf. Thanks, thank you."

"Murphy, all journeys end." Bray saluting stoically, sending him off.

Exiting recreation, checking his time, Jack jogs gingerly through vacant halls. Dragging himself around a corner, spilling roughly to the floor.

"Har, har. Look, Maddox, the little mouse came out to play!" Danzler stepping on Jack's ankle, pinning him painfully.

"I think little mouse man wants some cheese! Say cheese, little mouse!" Maddox raising a fist, driving it dangerously.

"Oomph!" Maddox spilling swiftly to the floor.

"Childress, what the hell? We were just, Ahh! AHhhh, oomph!" Danzler shrieks, sailing next to his brash brethren. "Did you dunces forget what Triden said? The runt is his and his alone!" She spits. "Outta here, runt!" Childress hisses, stepping between Jack and Triden's bruised brutes.

Eying the lethal lioness, Jack rises cautiously before dashing away. Hustling through hollow halls, Jack strolls stiffly. Entering sickbay, settling on a bench, and waiting his turn.

"Murphy, is that you?" Nurse Jessie pokes her head out of her office.

"Yeah, yes, ma'am, just nappin." Waking weakly, Jack answers. "Come on, you poor thing. Got you a pod ready' n' waiting."

Following there previous processes, the pair work in concert allowing Jack to recover. The frigid sensation extracting inflammation and pain from his harmed frame.

"Almost over . . . there all done." The nurturing nurse coos completing her task.

"Burrr! Thanks, Jess." Shaking feeling into limbs, Jack dresses quickly.

404

"What's the hurry?" Nurse Jessie jests, placing the sensors away.

"Oh, nothing big day tomorrow . . . I'm sorry shouldn't have said that." Jack nearing the nurturing nurse.

"Been under a lot of Ooooff!" Jack freezes, feeling her warmth wrapping around him.

"Hey, hey, won't get hurt, I promise."

"How can you . . . when hurt is all you've known?" She weeps softly, squeezing his healing husk.

"Ow, okay, I get it. I'll be fine." Jack patting his pitiful patron.

"Snff, snff, not with that terrible tape job, you won't." Sniffing though sensitivity, picking peeling tape from his shoulder.

"Yeah, another Bray special." Jack jests.

"Snff, she was always terrible at field dressings, snff." She sniffs peeling tape from his shoulder.

"Hmm, suppose you could do better?" Jack jabs her playfully.

"Sit, cadet!" Jessie jolts to her office returning with fresh wrap.

"Bray said something bout my supra?" Jack offers.

"Shh!" She instructs, feeling his shoulder.

"Bursa seems fine, Subscapularis' a little loose, Gleno-humeral's concerning, Teres minor's solid. Odd." She states sinking fingers massaging lax ligaments.

"Well, doc, do we have to amputate?" Jack jokes.

"No, hush now. I'm concerned, but overall, the shoulder checks out. Jack, please be careful tomorrow." She suggests taping his shoulder expertly.

405

"There, that's as tight as it's gonna get." Storming off, sulking in her office. Sensing her hurt, Jack dresses and enters her office. Searching for words unfound, eyes darting around her office.

"For what it's worth, I know Aunt Anna sleeps better knowing I've got you. Thanks Miss Jess." Jack states confidently before slipping away.

"Snff, snff. You did well Anna, now it's our turn. Snff." Sobbing silently to herself, memories of better days surfacing under her eyes.

Feelings of apprehension and angst rise, riddling Jack's psyche as he runs.

Run faster Jack, faster. No, smooth is fast, smooth is fast. Prutskin, Pulaski? What did Bray call that knot again? Think Jack, think. Hope the guys are ready to go, I'm starving.

Checking his time, Jack jolts towards Doc's lab. Making good time, swiping Doc's crooked credentials, Jack slips through security, stowing past pupils pining away at projects.

"Yes! Well, bake my bacon! Yes! Max, you've perfected her polarities!" Doc shrieks in surprise.

"That's enough for now! Set her down! Set her down!" Doc congratulating his prized pupil. Max does as instructed, monitoring his baby's delicate descent. "Careful! Yes, there you have it!" Doc congratulating Max with a clap on his back.

"Sweet . . . AHHhhh, Murph, you bum!" Max jumps, rubbing his ribs.

"Congrats, Max. Sam at his station?" Jack jests dodging a swipe from Max.

"Cadet Murphy lookin fit. Did'ya get the swing of it?" Doc nods knowingly.

"Sure did, not much swinging, but I'm "knot" giving up!" Jack jests retuning a knowing nod.

"Do ya'll need a room?" Max mocking with his own unknowing nod.

"Yeah, Sam's pecking away as usual, Murph. Hey, I've got to run diagnostics reports real quick, and I'll oh yeah, Sam's over there." Max motioning him in Sam's direction.

"Gotcha, see ya in a sec." Jack jolts off, dodging another attempt.

"Eureka, I got it! Gotta show Max. Oh, good afternoon, Jack. Thought you'd still be swimming?" Sam surmises.

"Done for the day, got what?" Jack inquires, investigating lengthy lines of code.

"Oh, well, I finally got E.V.E.'s base command codes working. Just sent them to Max. What's up with you?" Sam smiles, pumping his fist, celebrating silently.

"I'll tell you when Max gets here, so who's E.V.E.?" Jack asks, patting Sam on the back.

"Oh, E.V.E.'s my first operational A.I. Right now, she's a basic conversational command. Eventually, I'll expand her capabilities to learning, cognitive computing, etc." A twinkle dancing in Sam's eye as he gears up.

"Nice, maybe she'll take over the world and hunt humanity."
Jack jokes, quickly realizing he'd insulted his companion.

"Kidding, of course, you'd never do that. So, what's E.V.E.
stand for?" Jack dodging his own ignorance.

"Got a few contenders. My way to early concept is Electronic,
Virtual, Essence. It's stupid, I know." Sam sinks into his chair,
hearing his idea out loud.

"Virtual Essence, E.V.E. It's good Sam, simple. Easy to
remember ya know!" Jack jabbing his humble partner playfully.

"It's stupid, I know." Sam sulks, shutting off his computer.

"Nah, man, it's a good start. Better than falling fifty million
times the last few days. As you said, she's only gonna get
beEEETTERR! OWw!" Jack jumps, absorbing Max's malice.

"Gotcha, Murph, you jerk!" Max muses, mimicking Jack's
gesture.

"You did. Com'n, gents, I'm starving." Jack jolting away from
Max, checking his watch.

"Sounds good to me, Jack. Max, I sent you E.V.E.'s files for
mobile integration. We'll work on it tonight." Sam says, slapping
away an attempt from Max.

"Ow, gotcha. Figured out E.V.E.'s commands did'ya?" Max
retorts rhetorically.

"Yup, let's report in with Blackshear before heading to the
dorm." Sam ushers his companions on.

The trio trot jovially, joking about the day.

"So wait, socks, Murph? Used your socks, whole climb and everything? Get outta here!" Max muses in disbelief.

"Yes, socks, learned this knot, a Prius I think. Show ya'll tonight." Jack waves the pressed pair Bray gave him.

"All this hinges on socks, ridiculous Jack. We believe ya, but socks?" Sam states skeptically.

"Yup, simple problems require simple solutions, I guess." Jack jokes, jabbing both in their ribs.

"Omph, Murph, you get back here!" Max dashing after the charismatic cadet.

"Hmm, simple solutions. Hey guys we're eating in our dorm! Guys! Err, that's gonna be laps." Sam ponders, sprinting after his misbehaving companions.

Racing through lines netting nutrition, the trio taking their seat, eating hastily. "Mmm, mmm. Here, Jack, you need the protein." Sam scoops half his salmon onto Jack's tray.

"Nom, nom. Nom these too. Can't get enough carbs, Murph!" Max mashing potatoes onto his trey.

"Whoa, whoa. Can't eat all this, got practice tonight." Jack jerking his trey from the tandem.

"Betta eat fast, Murph." Max motioning foolishly with his fork, surveying the growing congregation of cadets.

"Best to pace yourself, Jack, gonna need every calorie. If my estimates are correct, your nightly excursions burn at least a thousand calories alone. The trials alone will burn, hmm." Sam lowering his head, scribbling calculations on a napkin.

409

"Okay, ok, I'll eat, I'll eat. Max, you gonna?" Jack gestures to his fruit cup.

"No, not the fruit cup." Max mules placing produce on Jack's plate.

"Oh, antioxidants are great!" Sam states scooping away fruit.

"Okay, ok, I get it, guys. Thanks for carefully, I'll be fine tomorrow . . . Promise." Jack eats gratefully, nourishing his body.

"Eat quick, Murph. Blackshear hasn't seen us yet and Sergeant stupid's here." Max leans hiding his friend's feast.

"Best we all finish up." Sam mimicking his multiple creating a canopy of concealment.

"FRIENDS! CADETS! COMRADES!" Triden taking a tabletop shouts spewing sewage.

"We stand at the precipice of purification!" Triden touting his tyranny. "Yes! Yes! Tomorrow, competitors will rise . . . and competitors will fall!" Sinisterly staring over subjects, Triden continues his reign of rubbish.

"Tomorrow, TITANS FALL AND A HERO RISES!" Triden touting tentacles of tyranny.

"I, Teivel Anwir Triden, Tamer of Titans, Guardian of Greatness' gates . . . tomorrow Titans stand tall and pretenders perish!" Triden touts to a chorus of cheering cadets.

"TRIDEN! TRIDEN! TRIDEN!" Cadets chant.

"You're dismissed, cadets. Gonna cost ya Gentlemen!" Blackshear bellows barely breaking boisterous bullies.

"Yes, Sir!" Sam tugging Jack from mouthfuls.

410

"Mmm, mnot done yet!" Jack chocking down calories.

"Gotcha, Murph." Max migrating morsels into a napkin.

"Go now!" Blackshear barks barring bodies forming. The trio dash to their dorm.

"Well that was interesting." Max making his way to the shower.

"Stupid sheep." Sam spits, wiping sweat from his brow. "Doesn't matter what they think." Jack sits, storing calories gratefully.

"Mmm, thanks, gents." Jack gobbles gratefully when a knock raps on their door.

"Got it!" Sam shouts, sliding the door ajar. "Yes sir, yes, Sir. Will do." Sam says, before shutting the door.

"Blackshear?" Max motioning at the door.

"Yeah, trials start at 0800."

"Oh good, we get to sleep in!"

"Not for us, we still got morning run at 0500. Jack report to Bray at 0700." Sam nods.

"Wait, what, we got?" Max mules, preparing to shower.

"Max, we got plenty of time to . . ." Sam pointing to his computer.

"Yeah, shut it, Murph." Max mules, making his way off.

"Don't mind him, Jack. I know you want to train tonight, but don't . . . Just don't." Sam confiding his confidant.

"Probably right, Sam, but I must . . . just must." Jack massaging his swaddled shoulder.

411

"Hmm, we know, Jack, we know. I'll run interference tonight. Good luck, Jack." Sam sighs, tossing him a loose shoelace, spinning around, pecking purposely.

"Thanks Sam." Jack sinks comfortably on his bed, practicing the Prusik, pulling each loop into place, sliding off to sleep.

Hushed hours pass before Jack slips off into the shadows. Readying himself, running through trials, memorizing mistakes, and picking himself up from every failure. Testing each trial, Jack jumps, twists, and swings, slinging himself onto the next intimidating titan. Sending Cronus' cane through the eye in the sky, Jack jaunts onward.

Wicking sweat from his brow, readying himself for harm. Twisting and tying soaked socks around the wicked wire. Shaking feeling into his shoulder, Jack presses play, sending thunder surging through his heart. Jumping into a series of slides and pulls, inching his way up. Pulling his weight close, carefully avoiding its evil entanglement. Breaking to breathe, Jack continues. Biceps burn, begging fingers for failure.

"Alm . . . most there!" Eying the punishing pendulum's pinnacle, continuing his rigorous rise. Feet away from its cruel crest, Jack pulls powerfully slicing a sock from the wicked wire. Feeling himself freefall, tugging his only tether taut, Jack dangles dangerously over the darkness below. "Ohhh, ahhh, just breathe, breathe. Pffff, pfffff!" Calming himself, strain surging through his shaking shoulder.

"Not that far, damn, that's far. Here goes nothing!" Jack kicking his feet back and forth, building momentum. Swinging swiftly, careful not to slice his lonely tether, Jack jolts, driving hard off each smooth surface, rocketing his reach towards the sinister summit. Fingers exhaustedly exerting upward, Jack stretches with every inch. Silence befalls the benevolent behemoth in a single shot, garnering a gasp from the shadows. As one journey ends, another one begins.

CHAPTER THIRTY SIX
TRIALS OF TITANS

Eager cadets excitedly enter and exit morning mess. GYAYA's halls are electric with energetic cadets quickly completing various tasks in order to attend the Trials. Murals of myth surround first years and advanced cadets alike hustling excitedly through their hallowed halls, optimistically awaiting another champion to rise from their ranks. Conversing cadets profess potential winners loudly proclaiming Triden's assured victory, as hushed tones whisper another. A pair of such hushed tones converse nervously to themselves as they eat.

"I don't know, bro. Maybe he left for an early jog." Max pushing his trey away.

"Max, this isn't like him not reporting in." Sam tossing toast aside.

"Gentlemen, good effort today at morning run. Hope Murphy enjoyed the extra winks this morning!" Blackshear's voice booms over crazed, chattering cadets. The troubled twins searching the floor for an answer.

"Gentlemen, he's still sleeping like you said, correct?" Blackshear nearing his serious features to the twin's guilt-ridden faces.

"He snuck out to that crazy contraption last night, didn't he? Didn't HE?" Blackshear barks.

"Yes, sir." The timid twins answer anxiously.

Pausing to gain his composure, pacing anxiously, Blackshear presses. "Gentlemen, at any point, did cadet Murphy return last night?"

"Not, not sure, Sir." Responding simultaneously, the siblings sit, dreading disaster.

"Sam, this is on you. You should've reported this immediately." Blackshear stares sternly, shaking his head.

"All fun until assets get hurt!" Blackshear spits, stroking his shoulder.

"Hey, that's not fair. Sam only looped the cameras. I showed Jack them secret corridors, well some of them." Max divulges densely.

"Dorm, now, I'll escort you both to the arena myself. You're both dismissed!"

Enthused cadets career about, hurrying through meals. Cadets excitedly chatter past halls pointing out Titans clashing within mythical murals along the walls. A thrill for skill daring danger hangs heavy as Blackshear breaks his stride entering Doc Brown's lab.

"Cadet Blackshear? What do I owe the?" Doc begins confused by the big cadet's presence.

"Section C Doc, I'm requesting access to section C, please Sir." Blackshear saluting his confused host.

"Of course, of course. Well grill my cheese, where'd that tablet go? May I inquire about your purpose?" Doc saluting, oddly accessing his lab, inviting Blackshear in.

"Lost cadet, sorry, Sir, this is most abnormal." Blackshear's eyes dart about, surveying his surroundings.

"Hmm, har har. You're here for cadet Murphy?" The perceptive professor, hushing his humor suddenly no longer confused.

"Yes, Sir, is cadet Murphy here?" Blackshear paces like a prowling panther.

"Oh no, cadet Murphy left a while ago. Sam's loops are good, but I'm the teacher still cadet Blackshear. Cameras show cadet Murphy entering around his usual time and then leaving later than usual. Here he's entering sickbay around 0300." Doc stifling a twinkle tepidly.

"Why would he do that, Doc?" Blackshear ponders tapping his forehead.

"Confusing creatures' you teenagers are. Would you like to see the footage? It's quite impressive for a first year." Doc offering his tablet to Blackshear.

"Impressive? Doc, he hasn't reported in." Blackshear watches in disbelief, Brown pausing the painful footage.

"Understand now?" Doc smiles pressing the screen closer.

"He couldn't have, that's impossible!" Blackshear stumbling back, settling against a desk. "They mustn't know, but I recorded every success and every failure your cadet endured. Science,

416

digital or physical; can be measured. Data collected, patterns plotted, but spirit tricky. Spirit, yes, a very tricky entanglement. The human spirit cadet Blackshear . . . the human spirit is both incalculable and incredible, rife with outliers." Doc nods assuredly in his assessment.

"He's an outlier!" Blackshear peering into the pragmatic professor's eyes.

"Hmm, we'll see, we'll see." Doc's chuckles, sending Blackshear sprinting off.

The twins banter down a hall leading to their dorm, a normal scene completely unnoticed by cheerful cadets cascading to complete various task, ensuring their attendance to the Trials.

"Bro, I'm gonna . . . doesn't matter, he can't speak to subordinates like that." Max thrusting their dorm door ajar.

"Blackshear's right we shouldn't have . . . Jack?" Sam slamming the door behind them.

"I'm up, I'm up." Jack jumping from his bed. "Murph, we're gonna kill ya! Get em' Sam!" Max misses moronically, spilling onto the floor.

"Everyone SHHHHhhh! Jack, Blackshear's been up our butts like a bike with no seat. Where've you been?" Sam states sternly.

"Sorry guys, I was tired after that final run, so I decided to rest a bit." Jack dodging a pillow from Max.

"A nap? We gonna get laps over a nap? Murph, in a few hours, you compete in the Trials of Titans, and your only defense is "I took a nap"?" Max readying another rocket.

"Okay, okay I messed up. I admit it, but the weirdest thing happened last night." Jack pauses, pressing memory to return.

"Ok? Care to elaborate, Jack?" Sam inquires.

"Completed a few runs, was kinda tired, but no issues. So decided to run some more, so I was swinging, and my sock snapped. From there, I must've fell asleep . . . and woke up in sick bay on a couch. Did you guys know Jess has a couch?" Jack attempting to conclude when Max interrupts.

"A couch, was is comfy? No, no all exhaustion aside, whatcha mean I fell asleep?" Max mules working himself into a frenzy as Jack concludes.

". . . yeah woke up in sickbay? Dunno know how I got there, but I did, and Jess was like "Your tapes coming off," and I was like, "yeah my shoulder hurts". She shined a light in my eyes and put me in a Poke'pod, patched me up and let me take a nap. Must've dreamt it because Childress was *YAAAWN* Whoa, I'm tired! So I missed mess, but I was. . ." Jack yawns, sinking sound asleep in bed.

"Murph? MurMmm!" Max mumbles, slapping Sam's finger.

"Let him rest. He's so tired he's delirious. The trials start in a few hours anyways, and luckily, Triden's the final challenge." Sam states, settling a blanket over the snoring savant.

"Max, let's go to Doc's and review those Soteria specs again. E.V.E. isn't synching for some reason. We'll be back before Jack wakes, come on." Sam suggests grabbing his laptop. The pair leave their companion in peace, returning hours later to check on their companion. Hours pass before a knock pecks peacefully at their door. Max taking command of their computer, sending Sam to the door.

"He is . . . didn't say . . . yes, still sleeping." Sam nods, taking a trey of food prepared for three, shutting the door behind him.

"Mmm, lunch is served!" Max picking away at all three treys.

"Get outta here." Sam whispers, slapping Max's hand away.

"Oww, hey, who was Mmmm." Max munches.

"Good morn . . . afternoon gents." Jack checking the time, rubbing sleep from his eyes.

"Good, you're up. Here, eat something. Older cadet's heats still going, you're about an hour out." Eating light, Jack drinks water greedily.

"Hey now, not so much, Murph, you'll get . . ." Max attempting to stop Jack.

"Leave him be. Here, Jack, eat a few of these. Specialty blend for energy." Sam shoving Max aside, handing Jack three small gummies.

"Thanks, man, what are they?" Jack popping in all three simultaneously.

"Cadet Arella makes them herself." Sam answers, stabbing at his meal.

"Mmm, not bad. Tastes like skittles." Jack washes them down with a swig of water.

"An hour, you said?" Jack stands, stretching from head to toe.

"Something like that, Blackshear should be . . ." Sam begins interrupted by a banging on their door.

"Got it, Murph." Max rocketing across the room in his chair.

"Cadet Duval, get dressed and get that bed in regulation!" Blackshear bellows, barging into the room.

"Blackshear Sir, I'm . . ." Jack begins.

"Cadet Murphy, we'll talk later, finish mess, and get dressed. Wetsuit under your fatigues cadet. Sam, a word." Blackshear states, motioning for Sam to step out of the dorm.

"What's with him?" Jack inquires, dressing as commanded.

"Oh, he's just mad bout earlier, should've check in Murph." Max finishing his meal, picking through Sam's before making his bunk.

"Understood, yes, Sir." Sam salutes, shutting the door behind him.

"So?" Jack leans urging him to share.

"You don't want this tea, trust me, Jack. Get ready. We head out in five. Tight, Max, pull the sheet tight." Sam says, standing over his messy multiple. "It's tight, it's tight." Max tugs, leaving to ready himself.

"Jack, those socks Bray gave you, wear them." Sam instructs.

"Okay, okay, I'm going. A little tight, what are these made of?"

"Besides, how'dya?" Jack begins before Sam waves him off.

"Feels like woven Kevlar fibers. Other tea later Jack, let's go!" Sam steps out, wiping his glasses.

420

"Everyone bein suspish!" Jack shakes his head and follows after.

"Ok, all present?" Blackshear surveying his cadets waiting as Max mossies' out.

"Good, all accounted for. Duvals' you sit with the unit. Murphy, you're with me. Move out!" Blackshear barks marshalling his talented troops.

Making their way through throngs of excited cadets Blackshear steers his cadets through an awe-inspiring arena.

"Whoa, this thing is huge! Definitely missed some specs Sam." Max mouths gawking at the gargantuan gauntlet waiting below.

"Shh, stupid." Sam shaking his head at his moronic multiple. Pausing to peer over a rail surveying the anger that awaits. Jack stares, studying the sinister structure.

"How's the shoulder?" Blackshear asks, leaning into evil's imposing inevitability. Good, more or less." Jack jabbing the big cadet's shoulder playfully.

"Hmm, mine was after." Blackshear whispers under his breath.

"Come, cadets, waiting room's this way." Blackshear bolts off.

"Thought we weren't invited?" Max says, the trio shrugging collectively.

Pushing to keep pace following Blackshear's furious footsteps.

"What's with this guy?" Max moans.

"We did get out of morning run!" Sam spits.

421

"Stairs, of course, he takes the stairs." Max mules, making his way after his companions.

"In here, cadets!" Blackshear motioning his cadets in.

"Whoa! VIP, me likey!" Max moving towards a comfortable couch.

"Don't get comfortable cadet. When Ja . . . cadet Murphy competes, I'm sending ya south." Blackshear settles, overlooking the sinister structure.

"So you know?" Blackshear inquires, massaging his shoulder.

"Not everything. I know enough. So you and Childress?" Jack inquires.

"Yeah, we were close. We once earned individual rights of rule. We were young and foolish then." Blackshear pauses, peering upon punishment and piercing his memory.

"So what happened? We were strangers just months ago, and all of a sudden, you're super pissed at me for training last night?" Jack presses, peering into his insurrection.

"For some, it's anger, others's envy, but my motivation Jack, is neither . . . I know the dangers these trials present. I empathize with your struggle, Jack." Blackshear stops searching for words of wisdom.

"So, that's it. You're scared, ain't ya?" Jack turns, facing his muscular mentor.

"Yes, Jack, I'm afraid. How are you not?" Blackshear, rubbing his shoulder.

"Simple, fear never helped anyone. Courage and experience sure, but fear only chains us to who we are, not to who we can become . . . for years I wanted to become, more than my home town could offer. Maybe this is . . . No this my chance to . . ." Jack pauses, allowing words to waft over the wickedness below.

"Hmm, to what?" Blackshear shoulders, sinking, assuming his cadet's response.

"To break those chains." His young cadet concludes, staring daggers deep into the demonic destruction below.

"And so you will, so you will." Blackshear states settling his hand upon his cadet's shoulder, sending security into his cadet's soul.

Trumpets tearing serenity from silence, sending cadets cascading to seats. The arena filling instantaneously, cadets' crowd cheering for chaos. "Cadets, learned professor, and esteemed guests, WHAT ARE WE HERE FOR?" A voice booms over the loudspeaker, sending the crown into a frenzy.

"TRIALS! TRIALS! TRIALS!" Cadets chant chaotically.

"BY RIGHT OF RULE, CONTENDERS PRESENT!" The voice commands. Older cadets file in forming two lines. Cadets cheer, lights illuminating hopeful heroes below.

"Why isn't Jack down there?" Max presses Blackshear.

"Only cadets with the right of rule are introduced!" Blackshear concludes to chaotic cheers as Triden steps into the spotlight.

"So cadet chinface gets a, Ooamph!" Max mouths, stumbling from a sharp elbow from Sam.

"CONGRADULATIONS ON YOUR ACHIEVEMENTS! MAY MOTHER GAIA GUIDE YOU ALL!" The voice confirms. Cadets of all ages cheer on their champion. A chorus of chants cascades, covering cadet Triden, raising his hands, sending cadets into hysteria.

"That jerk didn't even!" Sam protests.

"Sam, SAM! It's all good man! Crowds cheer. It's what they do!" Jack settling an incensed Sam.

"He didn't even!"

"Doesn't matter, man. He'll get his!" Jack jerks his companion, closing in on an edge evanescence.

"First years don't present!" Blackshear bellows.

"What's he so happy bout?" Max shoves swayed by a chorus of cheers.

"Sit, sit cadets, seasoned vets aren't the main course!" Blackshear barks, sending Sam and Max to their sets.

Senior cadets compete, taming few trials. Introductions rousing raucous cadets, frenzying at every failure. Failing flights of Crius, crushed by Coeus' chaos, laid low in Lapetus' lethal labyrinth cadets' collapse to choruses of cheering cadets. Trial after trial consuming pairs of proudly prepared participants.

"Bout that time, cadets!" Blackshear states, standing by an open door, signaling his companions.

"LET'S GOOOO! Operation Titanfall is a go!" Max jabs, shadowboxing an imaginary Maddox.

424

"All suited up?" Blackshear searching for something in his pocket.

"Think so, wetsuit, goggles, all taped up, socks on my feet . . . shoot, forgot my chalk!"

"Hmm, here, powder up, cadet." Blackshear smirks, tossing Jack a small container.

"Nice, how'dya?"

"It's time, down the steps, take a right, then a left. Good luck, cadet!" Blackshear ushers his offering. Motioning for the twins to follow, Sam stepping to his companion.

"You got this, Jack . . ." Sam pauses patting his ally anxiously.

"Thanks for everything, gents." Jack salutes, jogging down the steps as instructed. High above the crowd, a curious conversation commences. "Good afternoon, cadet Childress!" Wiley waltzes past the lethal lioness.

"Sir, been a while!" She nods, staring at the sinister structure.

"Hmm, been busy . . . it would seem that I'm not the only one." Wiley nods knowingly.

"He's exactly as you described him, Sir." The lioness leaning against the rail.

"We'll see . . . noticed Triden was given priority trial training clearance last week. Report?" Wiley winces, relieving weight from ancient injury.

"If you count posing every five seconds as training, then sure." Childress comments coldly.

"Ha, ha! Well, we can't all be a champion. And Murphy?" Wiley inquires, massaging malice.

"Hmm, resourceful and relentless." The lethal lioness staring over the sadistic structure.

"We'll see . . . we'll see." Wiley nods, leaning heavily, awaiting the coming commencement.

"IN A RARE TREAT! WE HAVE BY RIGHT OF RULE, THE ESTEEMED CADET TRIDEN CHALLENGING . . . FIRST YEAR CADET MURPHY!" The voice blasts, beckoning the boy. Triden thrusting hands triumphantly coercing cheers from comatose cadets. Blackshear and the twins, seating themselves in the stands, surveying the sinister structure below.

Stepping to the starting position, Jack accepts jeers from peers hissing for his demise.

"I'll make this quick little weed." Triden smirks.

"COMPETITORS ON THE READY . . . BEGIN!" The voice bellows, sending both bolting forward.

"Ooamph!" Jack crashes hard, absorbing a solid shoulder from Triden.

"CHEATER! He can't do that!" Max's protest concealed by a chorus of laughter.

"Game on, jerk!" Jack swiping a thumb roughly past his nose, sniffing soundly, refusing to relent. Powdering his hands, Jack rises, rocketing through Coeus with ease. Finding his footing, Jack jumps, dodging disaster. Catching Triden careening through

426

Crius soaring through the sky rocketing from ring to ring, cadets roaring excitedly.

"WOW BOTH COMPETITORS DISPLAYING INCREDIBLE SPEED! BUT CAN THEY SLIP PAST HYPERION'S HORIZON?" The voice bellows to an ever roaring crowd.

Pausing to catch his breath, shaking life into hurting hands.

"Keep up, little weed!" Triden taunts, timing his jump, hugging swinging orbs, carefully setting his grip.

"Damn, he took the little one." Jack spits, timing his jump, landing roughly on a large moon orbiting the outermost route.

"Take your time, Jack . . . no, no, now!" Sam squints, shielding his eyes as Jack jumps, gripping another orb orbiting into focus.

Managing moons, dodging the dawn, Jack hurls himself around the sun shielding his eyes. Tapping his timing, Jack jumps expertly from orb to orb, digging deep. Moments melt, managing Hyperion's children, Jack jumps, landing with a roll. Cadets cheer.

Catching his breath, looking ahead, noticing he's alone, a rush of confidence collects within. Unsure of his next step, Triden lunges, clawing his way to safety. "What an oaf!" Max mocks, receiving a barrage of boos. Steadying himself, the chiseled-chinned cadet claps, rousing his contingency. "TRIDEN! TRIDEN! TRIDEN!" Cadets' chant, cheering their champion.

427

"WOW WHAT A CLOSE ONE! WHAT WICKNESS LIES WITHIN LAPETUS' LABRYRINTH?" The loudspeaker laments.

Baiting Jack, Triden dashes towards his entrance, allowing Jack to enter his own entrance. "Yes, little weed, trigger all them traps, and I'll just waltz through." Triden snickers.

Lapetus' labyrinth walls reach higher than the twin's replica. However, training in shadows prepared the young pupil's pupils. Feeling first with his toes, keeping one hand against a wall, Jack feels for danger. Darting from wall to wall, panels' plunge, splashing below. Jumping over fractions of walls firing from nowhere, tripping trap after trap, Jack carries on cautiously. Dodging devils darting from darkness, tucking tightly hugging walls, Jack pushes past points of no return. Feeling for firmness beneath his feet, Jack flings himself, flying over the final panel, propelling upward, swinging closer to safety.

Building momentum, he leaps, gripping cold steel, swinging from steel to steel, sweat cooling his face as he flies from bar to bar. Dismounting, tucking into a roll, he rockets rhythmically, wasting little time twisting through a narrow nook, kicking the wall, ensuring a safe dismount. Cheering cadets settle silently as Jack steps into the light, leaving the labyrinth behind. Saluting the mob mockingly, claps from a few friends fill the settling silence.

"Next one's for the real ones," Jack whispers when an explosion of encouragement drowning his thoughts as Triden emerges from Lapetus' lair.

428

"TRIDEN! TRIDEN! TRIDEN!"

"BOTH COMPETETORS HAVE LEVELED LAPETUS' LABRYRINTH!" The announcer heralds, hyping the crowd.

"Thanks for the assist, little weed." Triden taunts, taking position, producing a pair of shades as Theia's brilliance beams. Blazing brilliantly blindness befalling below. Gems gleam and glitter, sending light in every direction, disorienting crowd and competitor. Fashioning his shirt into a shemagh, shielding squinting eyes. Jack powders his hands, throwing excess billowing into the air, a shadow forming below, outlining his first ring.

"THE CLOCK IS SET! COMPETITORS MAY THEIA LIGHT YOUR PATH!" The speaker informs.

Jack, catching a final glimpse, gallops, snagging his first ring. The crowd cheers, peering through hands, shielding their eyes. Jack swings, searching for shadows, swaying softly. Swinging from ring to ring, feeling rough runs ripping fingers raw. Making use of muscle memory, Jack motors on. Triden blindly fumbles using length, looking down, searching for salvation, he swings. Shrieks shrouded in cheers, he screams in frustration at every miss.

Building momentum, Triden swings, grasping desperately, dragging himself over the final obstacle. Squinting through shades, eyeing his dismount. Swinging hard wind wicking sweat and tears from fear as he jumps, landing roughly near the cursed cadet. Jack sits, calming chaos combating his chest, rubbing faith

429

into fatiguing fingers. Blinding light dims, concealing the trial's truth.

"AMAZING WHAT A SHOWING BY CADET TRIDEN! SHOWING REAL DETERMINATION ON THAT LAST ELEMENT! GIVE IT UP FOR BOTH COMPETITORS!" Cadets cheer wildly at the remark.

Controlling himself, Jack rises, readying himself. Stretching life into hollow hips, Jack pulls his shirt into place, tucking it neatly. "Give up, weed! I've surpassed my own expectations! Clear sailing from here!"

"I haven't . . ." Jack whispers.

"MOTHER GAIA, GIVER OF LIFE! GIVE LIFE TO DEAREST DAUGHTER! RISE RHEA RISE!" The voice rumbles, stirring a chorus of cadets' chants.

"RISE, RHEA, RISE! RISE, RHEA, RISE! RISE, RHEA, RISE!" Jack's feet rock, readying for Rhea's revenge, sending Triden to a knee.

"Keep up, Triden!" Jack turning the tyrant's taunts against him, pillars rumble as they rise. Closing his eyes and imagining each foothold and every entry point, tightening laces deliberately. Wiping sweat streaming down his face, Jack jaunts forward, facing his fate.

Jaunting on, Jack steps, sliding like in practice; perceiving each obstacle without issue. Triden stepping back, allowing Jack to provide the blueprint mimicking hated rival's movement.

"INCREDIBLE BOTH COMPETITORS CRUSHED RHEA'S REVENGE!" Cheers cascading cadet's corrupt champion.

"AS ALL THINGS! WE MUST ALL FIND OUR PROPER ORDER! COMPETITORS THEMIS AWAITS . . . BEGIN!" The announcer sends Jack and Triden onward.

Searching memory, righting Themis' order, Jack mentally maneuvers and slides solutions into place.

"Yes, that one, no, no! Yes, then . . . yes . . . he's got it, he's got it!" Sam slapping Max's shoulder excitedly.

"Quit it, that hurts, Bro!" Max mules slipping swipes from his sibling.

Triden tailing his rival, stealing solutions; the chiseled-chinned cadet carries on covertly. Swiping summarizing pieces in place, Jack jolts into place, rising before his rival. Sliding stolen solutions into place, Triden teems with confidence.

"AMAZING! TRIDEN THOUGHT THROUGH THEMIS EFFORTLESSLY!" Announcing another anecdote.

"Sure he did." Jack's calming, corrosive comments circulating in his head.

"MNEMOSYNE MEMORISIZES ALL! COMPETITORS BEGIN!" The speaker states, sending Jack jolting jubilantly. Solving each problem piously, Jack jaunts ahead of his hated rival, rocketing resentfully.

"Slow down, don't forget, he got it, dang finished that fast!" Sam settles, swiping fog from spectacles.

431

"Murph's crushin!" Max muses, slapping cadets and sibling alike.

Making Mnemosyne a memory, Jack jolts, jamming jargon into place. Triden trudges timidly, copycatting his competition's configuration, sprinting off after Jack, who's already stripping down to wetsuit and socks.

"Socks, gettin cold feet, little weed?" Triden taunts, tossing boots and socks aside.

"Hmm!" Jack turns from the taller tyrant, focusing his thoughts, pocketing chalk, and adjusting his goggles.

"WHAT AN EPIC RUN! GIVE IT UP FOR BOTH COMPETITORS! READY YOURSELF GENTLEMEN!" Lights dim drawing attention to punishment pooling below.

"This is where you sink!" Triden taunts, taking position. "Just breathe, just breathe," Jack whispers, crouching low.

"FOLLOW PHOEBE'S PROPHESY! TETHYS AND OCEANUS AWAIT! BEGIN!" Dual lights diving deep calling competitors in her depths, Triden and Jack dive deep. The chiseled-chinned cadet cuts the water and plunges perfectly, leaving Jack in his wake. Swimming swiftly disabling his first obstacle, Jack surfaces, drawing breaths before diving again, searching for guidance. Triden completes his second obstacle, diving deep. *Don't panic, just breathe!* Jack's thoughts focus, forcing fatigue further into his frame. Kicking smoothly, sending his second and third obstacles aside, surfacing gulping greedily.

Losing light, he dives, pulling powerfully, entering a submerged structure and searching blindly. Lungs burn, bubbling hope away, hands feeling foolishly. Suffocating fear, Jack driving hands deep, settling upon salvation. Clicking the final obstacle into place, he twists, hamming his head into a hard surface above.

"Something's not right!" Blackshear bellows.

"What's not right?" Sam asks, squeezing the rail rigidly.

"He's been down there too long! Divers! Divers!" Blackshear descending stairs swiftly, motioning for the safety team's attention.

"What's with him? OWWwww!" Max shrieks, rubbing his ribs. "He should've been up by now!" Sam screams. Safety divers dive into dim depths, resurfacing, throwing up empty hands.

"Where is he?" Sam panics, pushing past pacified pupils.

"Look! Murph's tailin Triden!" Max shouts.

"I'm gonna kill him!" Sam sinking to steps below, tightening trembling hands.

"He's good, Bro! Murph wasn't lyin bout them riptides!" Max muses, patting his drained duplicate.

"Incredible, he must've been under for four, five plus." A bewildered Blackshear boasts, counting fingers.

Breathing as he swims, Jack pulls, punishing his body. *Find your pace, breathe, Jack, just breathe,* willing himself, trailing Triden.

"THIS IS INCREDIBLE, LADIES AND GENTLEMEN, BOTH COMPETITORS HAVE ENTERED THE GREAT

RIVER GOD, OCEANUS! TRIDEN'S PULLING AHEAD! HE'S CRUISING TO CRONUS' COMPASS!" The announcer emits, erupting cadets cheering chaotically.

"Waves? Waves weren't in specs?" Sam scratching his head.

"Whoa, look at Murph go!" Max jumps, knocking neighboring cadets to their seats. Jack draws burning breaths, diving deep. Kicking smoothly, skimming safely beneath the surface.

"Interesting." Blackshear stares, settling on a rail.

Oceanus' fury flings Triden into a frenzy. Waves whip him around, ruining his ridiculous pace. Frustration infuriates the tyrant, tugging himself along. Failing to prepare, prepares all to fail. Surfacing, Jack lifts his chin, inhaling over every crest, toughing each trough. Sighting strokes, exhaling exhaustion, Jack controlling calmly. He kicks hard, rides rough waves, and dives when necessary, and, his pace propels him through wicked waves. Surpassing the sly serpent's struggling strokes, toughing the titular titan's trial.

"INCREDIBLE CADET MURPHY'S INCOMPACITATED OCEANUS! TRIDEN'S LOSING STEAM! BOTH LOOK ABSOLUTELY EXHAUSTED!"

"Speak for yourself, dude." Jack spits, inhaling gratefully, gripping the rope ladder leading to Cronus' Compass. Lifting himself over the edge, Jack lays for a moment. Unzipping his wetsuit, allowing lungs to breathe. Triden complains, ascending the rope ladder careful not to lay like his rival. Rising to his feet, sending fans frenzying.

"Hfff, hff, hf! That's right, hff, hf . . . Stay down . . . where you belong!" The corrupt cadet taunts, tossing his goggles aside.

"Gonna need those, jerk." Jack whispers, rubbing a cramping calf. Twisting his socks, tying them around aching ankles, wicking water from his hands.

"CADETS PREPARE YOURSELVES! THE FINAL TITAN IS AT HAND! CRONUS CONSUMER OF CADETS RISE . . . PREPARE YOUR COMPASS!" The announcer agitates the chaotic crowd again. Chains clink, raising the cruel contraption high above a pool of darkness swirling sadistically. Striding over, Jack powders his hands, taking position. Triden still breathing heavy, copying the young cadet.

"CADETS, AS CRONUS ROSE, MAY HIS COMPASS GUIDE THE TRUEST OF TITANS! CADETS TAKE YOUR SICKLE AND BLIND THE EYE OF OURANOS! . . . BEGIN!" The announcer commands.

Sibling sickles rise from hidden pedestals beside each competitor. Triden taking the sickle thrusting it high. Crazed cadets cheer, crowning their champion. Jack spinning the width of the handle in hand, powders it quickly, testing his grip. Waving his sickle like a sword, Triden runs, jumping, connecting with the first rail sliding east.

"Hmm, start south, east, west, then north. Hff, here we go." Drawing his last unlabored breath, Jack jolts, exploding into his first rail, sliding southbound, swinging swiftly, keeping his momentum. Ripping his scythe from rail to ring, ring to rail, sliding south, pulling the first point into place inching Ouranos' eye suspended high above Cronus' compass.

"So that's what you're up to!" Triden hisses, heaving himself after Jack. Building momentum, Jack jumps, sending sickle clanging another rail sliding into a swing soaring through the air. Cadets gasp at every fearful flight. Jack jerks, dodging a kick from Triden.

"Hff, not today!" Jack whizzes by, willing himself east, clanging calmly, pulling another point into place. As Ouranus' Eye inching closer to center.

"Yes, little weed, do my dirty work!" Triden taunts wickedly, whirling after Jack.

"Hmm!" Focusing on his next connection, clanging solidly, swinging north.

"Not if I get there first, flea!"

"COME ON STUPID RING RELEASE!" Triden whines, the worm wiggles.

"Sorry, dummy!" Jack waves whirling west. Sending sickle true, chains clink carrying Ouranus' eye just out of focus.

"No little weed, I'm a Triden!" Triden howls, heaving his sickle up, driving down, pulling north into place. Chains clink, centering Ouranos' Eye between the jousting juveniles. Cadets stand cheering chaotically, clambering for the coming collision.

Both building momentum, moving into position. "Hhhhffff! Screw it!" Jack jolts, swinging swiftly, eying the prize.

"Yes, little weed." Triden whips wickedly. Riding rails, rocketing off rings, the dueling duo dart dangerously.

Careening on a collision course, the cadets collide. Anticipating another kick, Jack swings, soaring high, evading Triden's evil attempt. Clanging canes on the same rail sliding to the center, the serpent sends long legs to constrict Jack's waist, squeezing wickedly.

"Time to go weed!" Triden hisses twisting Jack side-to-side, pain shooting through his shoulder. Jack's grip peeling from pommel, the young cadet centers his focus. Sighting his target, releasing lighting into Triden's torso.

"PFFFfff!" The tyrant gasps, spitting from his spine. Loosening his stranglehold enough for Jack to escape. Ceasing momentum, the moment Jack driving feet deep into Triden's thorax, reaching reassuring his grip.

"NOOOOOooooo!" Triden shrieks, splashing into the darkness below. Sinking out of sight, gasps gather around the arena.

"Drink up, jerk!" Jack adjusting his grip, pulls balancing his weight over the rail. Collecting his breath, rubbing rising pain from his shoulder.

"Not done yet."

"UNBELIEVABLE! INCREDIBLE! TRIDEN HAS FALLEN! TRIDEN HAS FALLEN! WE CANNOT CROWN A CHAMPION AS THIS UNKNOWN CADET. . . CADET MURPHY HASN'T COMPLETED . . . OH MY GAIA!" Silencing from shock, Jack dangles, diverting attention from the addlebrained announcer.

Crowd clapping cautiously. "Holy hell, he did it! He threaded the needle!" Sam stammers.

"Hell yeah! Told ya Murph got this!" Max jumps.

"It's not over yet!" Blackshear barks, pointing towards grinding gears, revealing the final trial.

"Oh shoot, forgot bout that!" Max fidgets fearfully.

"Prometheus' Pendulum! Definitely didn't meet specs, Max." Sam stares, fearing for their friend.

"AS THIS INCONCEIVABLE RUN CONCLUDES! CAN CADET MURPHY TAME TARTARUS, ASCENDING TO GAIA'S GREATEST GLORY?" The announcer agitates concerned cadets. "PROMETHEUS' PENDULUM PROVIDE THIS PUPIL PATRONAGE OR PUNISHMENT!" The voice vexes, silence searing cheering lips shut.

Surveying the sinister structure, stepping into shadows, Jack twisting socks securing salvation.

"Kevlar socks, Bray?" Jack jests to himself, prepping his pair of Prusiks.

"All . . . all him now." Sam stammers, sinking into his seat.

438

"Stupid things taller than specs!" Max mules, Blackshear motioning for silence.

"Don't fall, cadet . . . don't fall," Blackshear whispers, clutching his shoulder. Cadets' crowd, peering impatiently.

"Nice and dry, sweet, let's do this, John!" Jack speaking to shadows, producing a pair of earbuds, pressing play preceding past pain. Thunder in his heart, wrenching wire, heaving himself ascending into insanity. Shoulder searing, Jack pulls, pressing the pendulum's pinnacle. Biceps burn, digging deep, Jack climbs the wicked wire cautiously. Pausing to shake sensation into his shoulder, Jack refusing to submit before setting eyes on the sadistic summit. Gasps grow at every slip, plunging progress.

Breathe, Jack, just breathe. Igniting emotions embodying every defeat, painfully pressing Prometheus' pinnacle. Body aches condemning continuation, sighting the summit. Pulling painfully, Jack reaches relentlessly. Fingers rising roughly, clasping evil's edge. Swinging with all his heart, hurling himself heavenly. Landing limp, chest heaving heroically.

"UNBELIEVABLE! HE'S DONE IT! HE'S DONE IT! NO FIRST HAS EVER . . . OH MY GAIA!" The announcer anointing GYAIA's newest champion. Fickle fans explode with excitement, bolting over barriers, rushing to their collapsed champion. Crowding cadets settle their exhausted champion upon shocked shoulders. Throngs of jubilant juveniles jockey for position to touch their champion. Burying behind Blackshear bulldozing bodies, Max and Sam jump joyously through the crowd of cadets.

"Murph! Murph! Out of the way, normie!" Max mashes milling minions.

Attending Professors clap, cheering along with cadets pushing past Crane. Rolling his eyes, the pompous professor claps mockingly, slipping his slim frame through crowding cadets and escaping the cheering crowd. Blackshear muscles through thickets of thrilled cadets circling Jack.

"Congrats . . . make way! Make way, just put you there!" Blackshear displacing pupils.

"There you go! Congrats, Murphy, first ever first year. Well done, well done!" Blackshear extending his hand, shaking Jack's.

"Let's hear it for the Titan King!" Max shouts.

"TITAN KING! TITAN KING! TITAN KING!" Jubilant juveniles joining in joyously. Maximizing the moment, cadets carrying their triumphant champion around ridiculously chanting their new battle cry.

"Okay, okay! Thank you, Thank you! Love you too, man!" Jack sits uneasily, fist-bumping and high-fiving fellow cadets.

"Alright, enough of that, put him down!" Blackshear grabs Jack, placing him on his own two feet.

"Back down to earth. EVERYONE, YOUR ATTENTION PLEASE!" Blackshear booms.

"Thank you, thank you. Listen up, cadets! Chow in ten! In light of recent events, double dessert rations are available for everyone courtesy of Cadet Murphy!" Blackshear announces to an explosion of excited cadets clapping in celebration. Clapping ridiculously himself, Max elbows Sam, yelling over the cheers.

"He can do that?" Sam says, adjusting his glasses.

"Well, if he can't, gonna be a different type of riot, its ice cream night." Max retorts.

"It's what? Can't riot in ice tonight?" Sam looking perplexed unable to hear over the roar of the crowd. Shaking his head, Sam pushes ahead not to lose sight of Jack.

Childress peering from her perch above the slowly dissipating assembly below.

"He did it; he really did it, just like practice." She whispers, nodding in approval.

"Professor Wiley?" Stepping perplexed, realizing she's alone.

Jubilation harmonizing the halls, and professors corral the chorusing crowd to the mess hall. Jack and his companions walk with a renewed sense of accomplishment. Max waltzing ahead, waving his arms as if conducting an imaginary orchestra.

"Can't believe we actually did it!" Max says. Sam always quick to correct his blabbering brother.

"We? . . . We did nothing. All we did was watch Jack go to work." Sam motioning between himself and Max.

"Hold up now! Who built that monstrosity in section C? Huh? Huh?" Max points, mimicking his brother. Sam slapping Max's hand smudging his glasses. "Stop that weirdo! Now look what you did!" Sam stumbles into Doc's backside.

"Apologies!" Sam squints.

"No worries, Sam. Jack, my boy, congratulations!" Doc shaking his sore shoulder.

"Ahh, than, thanks, Doc. Max's got a point. Couldn't have done it without any of you guys." Jack smiling ear to ear, darting between the two, throwing his arms around both their shoulders.

"Hate it but, have to admit he's right." Sam begins before Blackshear's boom breaks the surprising silence of the corridor.

"Good to see you, Doc. If these two digital Da Vinci's get credit, then I suppose all the times I caught these three out of the area after lights out without reporting it counts too." Blackshear jokingly clapping all three on their collective backs. Stunned to silence, Max's mouth moves mutely.

"Told ya we'd get caught." Sam professing his correctness. Pulling away from the pack, Jack jokingly jabbing at Max.

"Well we know who Max's ghost was now. Woooo Wooo wooo!" Jack jabs Max playfully, causing the trio to laugh at Max's expense.

"Not funny guys!" Max mules.

"Oh speaking of fun, I do believe you boys left a mess in section C. The Exolifts are all charged up and waiting for you tomorrow." Doc salutes leaving Sam and Max's mouths agape.

"No, no Doc come back! It's Murph's mess. It's his mess!" Max mules.

"Quit complaining, Max, it's ice cream night. Hey, guys, I'm stopping by the dorm, can't get my glasses clean." Sam states, sprinting off.

"Suit yourself, Sam. Hey, Blackshear wanna race?" Jack jabbing the muscular militant.

"Please, you outta gas! Here, get in reg first." Blackshear tossing Jack dry fatigues before bolting down the hall.

"Who cares about ice cream? Guys, wait up, gotta run everywhere. Ugh running." Max moans, making his way to mess.

CHAPTER THIRTY SEVEN
SON OF A SAM

Blackshear bests Jack easily to the mess hall entrance. "Not bad, Murphy, not every day I get to beat the Titan King!" Blackshear jokes, steadying his cadet. "Hmm, could'a let me get dressed first." Jack jests, tucking his shirt.

"Hff, hff, ugh. I can't . . . Dying, I'm actually dying." Max collapses comically upon the perfectly waxed floor, sucking wind weakly.

"Get up, cadet." Blackshear kicking his cadet's boot.

"I'm up, hfff, I'm up." Max crows crawling to his feet.

"Where's Sam?" Jack presses, peering down the hall.

"Hff, hff. He, hff said he was stopping by the dorm, something bout his glasses." Max states, straining to breathe.

"I'll go get him." Jack jolts jerked back by Blackshear.

"He'll be fine. We gotta get in there before all the sprinkles are gone." Blackshear responds, rubbing his stomach.

"Sprinkles?" Jack jests, pointing at Max.

"Call me Sprinkles and morning run starts 0200, Titan King or not." Blackshear barks, buffaloing towards tasty toppings prepared neatly.

"Sprinkles." Jack jokes, fist-bumping Max, making their way into a melee of starved students. Chants careen around the room's high ceiling when Jack enters. "TITAN KING! TITAN KING!" Cadets cheer.

"Titan King, sit here! No, sit here, Titan, King!" Cadets coax, clambering for the champion's attention.

"Champs busy, come on Murph." Max tugs seating away from the mayhem.

"Hmm, Mmmm." Jack eats gratefully, filling his gut.

"Good move, Blackshear, er, Sir. The ice cream, Sir." Max motioning to his malted dessert as cadets swarm Jack and treats alike.

"Was Wiley's idea, actually!" Blackshear says, scooping spoonful's of sprinkles.

"Wiley? Really, he's missing quite the feast." Max licks his spoon clean.

"Hmm, missing!" Jack jabbing the remains of a well-deserved dinner.

"What's up, Murphy?" Blackshear inquires, stealing sprinkles from Max's melting meal.

"Where's Wiley been all this time? I know he's off recruiting cadets, but we haven't spoken for over a month?" Jack jousting julienne potatoes. "That's not odd; Wiley is GAIA's top special asset acquisitions." Blackshear informs, destroying surviving sprinkles.

445

"Guess you're right; he spent months undercover as a high school teacher." Jack says, tapping his trey.

"There you go, Murphy; maybe he was recruiting the next Titan King!" Blackshear jokes, walking off to return his empty trey upon a quickly amassing pile.

"Haa, har, har, he likes that one, Murph. Speaking of missing, let's go find Sam." Max motioning to return his trey. Pausing Max takes a moment to absorb the many framed pictures of former cadets adorning crisp uniforms. "One day, one day!"

"Wait up, Max, I'll come with!" Jack rises, rushed by flocking fans.

"I got it, Murph. You're gonna be busy, Champ." Max muses, tossing Jack a marker.

"Wait, Max . . . what? Of course, I'll sign your forehead." Jack says, surrounded by star-struck students, packing themselves tightly around their newly crowned king.

Tossing his tray, Max waltzes around the mess hall, chuckling to himself. "Ha ha Titan King! Can't believe that hit." Making his way down empty halls leading to their dorm Max noticing their door ajar.

"Sam wouldn't leave the . . . what the heck?" Clicking on the light revealing a littered mess, Max motors cautiously among their belongings scattered about.

"Sam? Bro, you in here? Oh no, not the notes!"

"Hey Sam, this isn't funny, bro. Where are yah?"

Dashing from disaster into the hall, hurtling himself hastily, Max motors.

"Hope he's still in . . . in a . . ." Max stutters stiffening to attention, shaking as he salutes. Laughter fading into the distance, sweat beading upon his brow, fingers fidget pressing nervously into his forehead. Standing stiffly at attention, uttering not a single syllable.

"At ease, cadet." A commanding yet reassuring voice acknowledges the young cadet's efforts. Sounds of sprinting echoes down pristine halls. Standing shoulder to shoulder with Max, Jack, and Blackshear saluting their senior officer.

"At ease, cadets. Remember your training, breathe." Madam Director commands, nodding for Blackshear to step forward. "Came right away, Madam Director. I take full . . ." Blackshear begins.

"No time, cadet, we have a situation. Central command, this is Director Stingley, Bray report!" Turning on a dime, motioning for the trio to follow.

"This is Bray, code 001 confirmed!" Bray's voice breaking over swiftly sprinting feet. "10-4, Central Command lockdown the premises. This way, gentlemen." The determined director directs dashing down halls. Boots stomp steadily, echoing along perfectly manicured pathways.

"What's a code 001?" Max whispers, struggling to keep up.

"Missing asset, shhh." Blackshear motion for silence as Director Stingley slows her pace. Placing her hand over a dimly glowing touchscreen, peering into the retinal scanner, heavy doors dart open revealing an elaborate array of screens anchored above desks filled with monitors displaying various readings from around the campus.

"This way, cadets." She commands.

"Agent Bray, report?" Madam Director commands.

"Madam Director, asset Duval was abducted roughly after 1700. Records show cameras looped from 1705 to 1710. Simple five-minute loop, cameras were backdoored by someone using credentials "Max_Wlfhund@Ibiz_Laik@Estre_Ylkshr"." Bray completing her analysis, eyes piercing the copied cadet.

"That doesn't make sense! Max was with me and Blackshear majority of mess!" Jack divulges, defending his companion. "Blackshear, keep cadet Murphy in line!" Bray barks.

"Time's ticking. Speak freely, cadet Duval, are these your credentials?" Madam Director commands.

"No, no, Madam Director, it's a cypher." Max trembles, trying hard not to mumble.

"A cypher? This is clearly a joke!" Bray baulks. "Continue, cadet." Director Stingley shoots Bray a stinging stare.

"Ye, yes, Ma'am. It's a simple message, really, may I?" Max grabs a pen, scribbling quickly.

"Sam addressed it to me, Max. The rest are dogs breeds, abbreviated, but their names aren't important. The acronym is." Max scribbling symbols.

"W-I-L-E-Y . . . Oh, my GAIA!" Max gasps, dropping his pen upon the spotless floor.

"Wiley? Bray, locate Agent Wiley's access history." Director Stingley commands.

"One sec . . . library, arena, Doc's lab, Volkov's, VOLKOV!" Bray pauses, petrified by a premonition.

"Bray search Volkov's access history." Director Stingley snaps Bray back to reality.

"Yes, Ma'am . . . professor's quarters, arena, transport subsurface, dormitories . . . transport floor level. Volkov accessed transport five minutes ago!" Bray belts, banging the desk.

"They're fleeing, but why? Bray, pull up transport cameras!" Director Stingley commands. Bray clicking quickly, sending footage to a large screen overhead.

"There's Wiley and Volkov. Who are they stuffing in the SUV . . . Duval identify, is that cadet Duval?" Stingley commands.

"Yes, ma'am, that's Sam. What's going on?" Max the mystified multiple melting to his knees. Slumping upon spotless tiles, Max catches his own reflection staring fear back into welling eyes.

"He's the one; Wiley must be who wrecked Doc's lab!" Blackshear begins, cut off by Bray.

"We don't have time for this Director. I'll take a bike and pursue targets!" Bray beacons sprinting to the door.

"You'll never make it." Jack speaking softly drawing the room's attention.

"Cadet this is no time for riddles, never make it?" Bray barks.

"He's headed to the airlift. The one we were landed at when we got here." Jack concludes confidently, lifting Max to his feet.

"Director, permission to take a Hawk and intercept targets?" Bray beacons fidgeting frantically with the keys under her fingertips.

"Waste of time. Volkov probably disabled air supports." Max stands solemnly whipping a tear from his eyes, steadying on Jack's shoulder.

"Cadet Duval's instincts are valid. Doc Brown, do you copy? Your services are required in R&D restricted. Do you copy?" Director Stingley pauses, waiting in a room filled with glowing screens offering no solutions.

"Was bout to take a swim, restricted Ma'am; are, are you sure?" Doc Brown's voice cracks on speakers anchored overhead.

"Fire up Project Safe Salvation!" She commands. "10-4 Madam Director." Doc responds.

"Whoa, not my baby!" Max moans.

"Zip it, cadet! Director, that thing has zero flight hours. I've never flown her class?" Bray debates.

"No, but Max does." Jack offers, pushing forward his solution.

"Wait, Murph, No, thousand flight sim hours don't count! Soteria's not, she's not ready!" Max protests.

"Soteria? Doc status?" Director Stingley commands.

"Soteria, I mean Project Safe Salvation will be online in five minutes. Well, find my fiddle. That's where I put ya!" Doc's voice echoes.

"It's settled then. Bray, you will escort cadets Duval, Murphy, and Blackshear to restricted and retrieve cadet Duval."

"Yes, Madam Director but, what about Wiley and Volkov?" Bray presses.

"Retrieving GYAIA's asset takes priority. Bray, go to Doc now!" She commands sternly, sending Bray away with a dismissive wave.

"Madam Director Stingley. I want to for Sam, but I . . . I'm . . ." Max mumbles. "Cadet, do you believe you two were recruited to be babysat by Blackshear?" Director Stingley's statement stunning the young man. "Just because you're unsure of the path beneath your feet, doesn't dismiss its purpose." She states, nodding knowingly in Blackshear's direction.

"On the hop cadets!" Blackshear orders, returning her nod with a salute. "Max, you got this." Jack comforts his companion.

"No, Murph . . . we got this." Max states maturity matriculating throughout.

"On the double cadets!" Blackshear barks bursting down the hall well ahead of his cadets. Jack and Max follow suit, striding

451

swiftly. Careening close corners, hurling halls hastily Jack and Max race recklessly.

"I finally get to fly her Murph, isn't this Oomph!" Max crashes, spilling roughly to the floor.

"Oww." Max moans rising slowly upon hard spotless floors.

"Grab him, Maddox!" Triden hisses.

"Hey! Hands off!" Jack struggles to free himself.

"Thought Triden's just disappear, do we?" Triden taunts, slapping Jack sinisterly.

"Stop that loser! Oww!" Max shouts as Maddox squeezes him roughly.

"LOSER! I'm a Triden, we don't lose!" Triden readying a sinister shot.

"Whoa, ah, Oomph!" Triden shrieks, sliding roughly across hardened tile. "Childress, you snake!" Triden spits, slithering to his feet.

"Let 'em go, boys." Cracking her knuckles, the lethal lioness readies herself for harm.

"Turncoat, how dare you? Wait till Father here's about this!" Triden hisses.

"Run ta Daddy, hit the showers, losers!" The lethal lioness threatening his thugs. Releasing Jack and Max, Danzler and Maddox retreat cautiously. "LOSER! Get her! Wha'ya wimps doing? Get her!" Triden whelps. "Piss off, Triden." Childress cuts.

"CADETS, come on! Carla, what are you . . . Triden!" Blackshear barks.

"Cadet Blackshear, we . . . we were just congratulating your cadet. Weren't we . . ." Triden hisses before Blackshear cuts him off.

"Com'n, cadets, these boys need a shower." Blackshear steps, sending the sniveling serpents slithering.

"Com'n, don't have time for this!" Blackshear bolts backed by the boys. Carla kicking easily ahead of Blackshear.

"Brian, lockdown, whatcha know?" She inquires. "Classified! Sorry, Carla!" Brian breathes, blowing through hallowed halls.

"Wiley's got Sam, Volkov's with him. Want in?" Jack offers, jolting into the conversation.

"Stand down, cadet; ya don't have the authority!" Brian boasts, bolting ahead of Carla.

"Com'n, Brian, you can't win, you gonna need the help." Carla pointing to their rear at Max, who has fallen behind.

"Argh. Come on, we ain't got time for this." Brian lifts Max onto his back like a pack.

"Whoa, whoa! Just needed a breather not beast of burden!" Max bounces, mimicking a jockey.

"Hi-Yo, Silver, Away!"

"Is your friend always this dramatic?" Carla shaking her head.

"More or so, yeah. I'm Jack, by the way." Jack nods, extending an olive branch.

"Hmm, don't get friendly, Champ!" Carla careening ahead of the pack.

"Wait, you don't know where we're goin?"

"After the trials, I followed Volkov. He was disabling aircraft in the subsurface hanger, and then he headed down to floor level." She spits, sprinting harder.

"Ok, wouldn't an aerial escape have been faster?"

"Yes, but all the aircraft have trackers. Their SUV is out of circulation; harder to track would be my guess." She speculates as the group enters Doc's lab.

"Childress, you're not authorized for this outfit!" Bray begins when Jack speaks freely.

"No, ma'am, but we could use her skills."

"Hmm, Director Stingley, do you copy?" Bray contesting his conclusion.

"Bray, brief Childress on the way. Doc, Soteria status report?" Director Stingley directs.

"She's ready, just waiting on her pilot." Doc confirms.

"We're here, Madam Director." Blackshear bucking Max off his back.

"That'll do sprink . . . Sorry." Max grinning moronically, abandoning his comment. "Suit up, team!"

"Nice, just like the movies, Murph!" Max muses.

"Hurry, Max, Wiley's gonna hit that airfield in ten." Jack tossing fatigues to the floor. The group dresses, docking quickly.

"Will this thing get there in time?" Carla comments, clicking her harness.

"We're gonna find out! Doc launch bay door, please!" Bray communicates, checking navigation.

"Good evening, this is your Captain speaking . . ." Max begins, berated by a chorus of commands.

"LET'S GO! PUNCH IT!" The group shouts as the craft rises to life, lifting effortlessly.

"Stabilizers set. Hit the jets cadet!" Bray barks.

"Sorry, co-pilot, she ain't got those!" Max laughs, thrusting the throttle. Sucked into their seats, Soteria rockets down the runway, darting dangerously out the hanger.

"Too fast, cadet, too fast!" Brian bellows, gripping his seat.

"Oh no, big buddy, she's just wakin' up!" Max laughs maniacally, mashing the throttle. Humming hastily, Soteria soars, leaving landscape in her wake.

"No banking, Duval, keep her even . . . KEEP HER EVEN!!!" Bray shrieks.

"Good evening, cadet Duval. May I be of assistance?" A synthetic voice speaks.

"E.V.E.!?!" Max exclaims, evening out Soteria.

"Who? What's going on Duval?" Bray pants for breath.

"Oh, E.V.E.'s Sam's A.I., didn't know he integrated her already. E.V.E., locate Sam, please." Max commands, clapping childishly at her response.

"Searching, stand by . . . cadet Duval's tracking beacon indicates a north by northwest course of convergence. Is this course correct?" E.V.E. sending calculations to Bray's screen.

"Negative E.V.E. set coordinates to this location." Max setting their course to the airfield.

"Wait, Max, maybe I was wrong." Jack offers.

"No, Murphy, that idiot Volkov didn't take off his watch, tracking now." Bray, collecting her nerves, taps impatiently.

"Gotcha, Volkov's beacon places them en route to the airstrip. Good call, cadet." Bray states, reaching for the throttle.

"Sorry co-pilot, Soteria's built for supersonic speeds. E.V.E., please provide the current rate of speed and ETA." Max asks, slapping Bray's hand away playfully.

"Ooo, you'll run for that cadet." Bray baulks gripping her seat tighter.

"Current rate of speed seven hundred and fifteen miles per hour . . . estimated time of arrival three minutes, eighteen seconds." E.V.E.'s analysis sending shocks through the cabin.

"Slow down, Max, we'll make it." Jack pulls forward, patting his companion.

"E.V.E. commence vertical descent in one minute, thirteen seconds. Set elevation to one hundred feet." Max commands, checking his math.

"One hundred feet! Cadet we'll crash at that rate of entry!" Bray bellows. A tense minute flashes by in a second, as Soteria sinks like a lightning bolt.

"Max, buddy, this isn't funny!" Jack squeezing his seat, Devil's Drop feeling like the teacup ride.

"WHOOOAAAAA!!!!" Blackshear belts throwing his hands in the air.

"E.V.E. execute "SILENT STOP!" Max shouts suddenly. Cleanly clearing treetops, Soteria stops suddenly.

"E.V.E. descend to five feet and standby." Max orders. Like a feather floating softly, Soteria descends silently.

"You're nuts Duval, there in the hanger. They know we're here!" Carla concludes.

"Doesn't matter, we're ready!" Max settling Soteria safely in the shadows.

"Did my part, now go get Sam." Max settling her safely to a chorus of unclicked buckles.

"You got itm Max." Jack patting the maniac multiple approvingly.

"Team, I'll make first contact; you three secure the perimeter." Bray barks.

"Whatever happens cadets, don't engage unless ordered. Keep coms open. Let's move." Bray, Carla, Brian, and Jack exit. The trio of cadets surround the hanger. Bray sneaking into the shadows surveying the scene silently. The musk of rarely used hardware rising all about.

"Jet's ready Wildwolf, time to go! Vhat of?" Volkov tosses a tied and gagged Sam roughly on the cold floor, causing dust to rise from the aged unkempt flooring.

457

"Leave him; he had what we came for . . . Of course she'd send you!" Wiley whipping around, facing his piercing peer. Stepping from shadows of the aged hanger, Bray readying herself.

"Why?" She spits, stepping over a short stack of flight logs of out of service aircraft.

"Simple, the other guy pays better." Wiley wickedly tapping the case in hand.

"Not talking about that guy!" Bray steps, baring access to his escape.

"Hmm, of all people, you'd surely understand Bray or should I say . . . Banshee!" Howling at his own humor.

"I'm not her anymore!" Bray barks, digging her feet, searching for advantage.

"Well, unless you got that spineless spitfire Stingley hidden in your pocket. I suggest you move. Volkov knows his orders har, har, har move Banshee!" Wiley angling to agitate.

"Shut up, Wiley, you'll answer for your crimes. He's just a babe, and you brought him here! Why?" Bray barks, turning his toes towards a nearing Volkov.

"Why? Well, that's a different reason all together . . ." Wiley limps, rubbing life into ancient injury.

"Acquiring the twin twerps to GYAIA was easy but, forced to acquire that ordinary little orphan. . . . That one really sizzled my steak for a bit. It's all clear now; you ladies thought he'd be like them! But he's not, he's no killer! Anna softened him up real

458

good! Made him read and care about feckless loser's feelings!" Wiley whips wickedly.

"Take that back, they weren't killers!" Bray bellows, seething with anger.

"Hmm, course they were. You all were Banshee. Hmm, a forbidden bond bound by blood. Makes me sick!" Wiley winces, feigning a fall averting her attention. Volkov vaults into action, striking hard, sweeping her feet, and sending Bray crashing hard to the old concrete floor below. Volkov pinning lithe limbs, squeezing breath from her frame.

"Get her up!" Wiley nearing her flimsy form.

"So beautiful, your body's so . . . so fragile. I like fragile . . ." Wiley whispering warmly into her ear.

"LET HER GO WILEY! WHERE'S SAM?" Jack demands, stepping into the light.

"HAHAha! Well, if it isn't the parentless pupil himself?" Wiley wrenches wickedly.

"I said let her go or I'll . . ."

"Or you'll what Jack?" Wiley warns, slinking closer to the young cadet.

"Step off, gimpy! You fell, I didn't ya gimp!" Jack sneers, staring insecurity into Wiley.

"Volkov, snap her neck! We don't have time for this!" Wiley's wail reverberating wildly off the tin roof above.

"Enough, loser! Funny thing about your buddy Triden . . ." Jack dragging his leg, kicking up dust, mocking the Wildwolf.

459

"When that turd Triden challenged me, I took a trip to the library . . . and you know what I found in Trial records? . . . You losing, again, and again! You lose so much; they should induct you into the hall of failures!" Jack spits spitefully.

"YOU KNOW NOTHING BOY!" Wiley howls.

"The old man knew how his story would end . . . Or were all those talks just an act?" Jack responds, lowering his tone, drawing the villains into a false sense of security.

"Yes, but you misunderstand the narrative! Unlike the old man . . . I'm refusing the sharks their feast!" Wiley wheeling himself from harm, clutching his case.

"So that's what this is all about, you greedy loser!" Jack baring Wiley's escape.

"Hmm, greed, how juvenile! Final lesson, Jack . . . espionage is about knowledge acquisition. Knowledge of your enemy is power over your enemy. Spies are replaceable, you and I are replaceable . . . hell, GAIA herself is replaceable. But this . . . this knowledge is irreplaceable." Wiley waving the case in his hand, taunting Jack to act.

"So what's that got to do with Sam?" Jack presses, inching closer.

"Ah, Jack, always so inquisitive . . . well, that little piggy was just too smart. Samuel figured it all out weeks ago; however, he was so busy helping you prepare for the trials. Young Sam even figured out your wolf dream. Didn't take him long, once he discovered my call name. But, who was he to tell?" Wiley pauses pointing to himself, chuckling to himself.

"Hmm, not proud to admit, but it took me a little longer to figure out what Brown did with his precious notebook . . . luckily you left me a clue!" Wiley producing Jack's keychain.

"That's mine!" Jack lunges, missing the wily wolf.

"HAHAHAHAhahaha! My hand trembles with terror just thinking about all Doc's projects powerful enough to evaporate empires. Knowledge capable of shredding capitalist chains shackling generations to the disease of debt, damning them to a life of cyclical servitude! All my years of painful patience finally paying off in perpetuity! And all that concerns you is some stupid memento!" Wiley wrenches wickedly, tossing the trinket onto the dilapidated tarmac.

"I'LL END YOU!" Jack jolts shooting Wiley's legs, but misses wildly.

"Hahaha! Enough of this snap her . . . Snff!" Wiley says, sniffing his surroundings.

"Hmm, Blackshear . . . snff... Childress, turned did ya?" Wiley willing them into the light.

"Wiley, you rat!" Brian barks, stepping from the shadows.

"Shut it, snake . . . Volkov, no more words!" The lethal lioness laments.

"Vildvolf Go!" Volkov voices venturing between, tossing Bray's breathless body crashing carelessly into a pile of old wooden crates.

461

"You'll pay for that gimp!" Jack jumping Wiley, Brian barreling towards the roided rhino. Carla checking Bray before joining Brian. Wildly, they wail on Volkov.

"Com'n, cadet, let's see what you've learned!" Wiley dodging a furious flurry.

"Weak! Gotta, Ooamph!" Wiley reeling from Jack's relentless rockets.

"Sh!" Jack dodges, sending shots searing Wiley's sides.

"Oomph! Titan King, Oomph!" Wiley spits sustaining searing shots, the wily wolf reaching into his bag of tricks.

"AHHhhh ugh!" Jack falters, swinging stupidly to the unforgiving concrete floor.

"Jack!" Brian, blocking a brick formed from Volkov's fist, opening for a ferocious shot. "urgh . . ." Brian crumples, catching a crushing blow.

"VEAK! Come girl, Volkov. CRUSSHHH!" Volkov taunts, tossing Blackshear aside.

"Com'n, Brian, one high, one low." She whispers, their mistake sending Carla into a rage. Stepping swiftly, slipping Volkov's vicious vice.

"Urgh!" Carla spits, spinning to the floor. Dodging disastrous destruction, the lioness lunges to safety.

"IT'S OVER CHILDRESS!" Wiley wails wildly.

"Take him!" Wiley wrangling a dazed Sam to his feet.

"Don't need em anymore!" Wiley wails, sending Sam sliding to her feet.

"Volkov plane, we're taking off. She'll see it our way!" Wiley winces leaning weakly against the hanger's metal framing.

"I . . . I don't." Jack rises gingerly, readying himself.

"You don't what? . . . Understand?"

"I wasted months under orders preparing you for GYAIA. All I needed was reason enough to be back on campus; those twins were the ticket. You . . . fortunately for me, just couldn't stay out of trouble . . . Oh, yes, I remember the sounds their bones made." Wiley grinning wickedly, leaning heavily on the metal wall pinging as he steadies himself.

"The Shadow in the woods that night . . . was you?" Jack rubs his ribs.

"Who else, Jack? Your flabby friends? Anna? Ohh, sweet Anna? She raised you soft, crawling over their bodies, begging me to stop! Disgusting, that talentless turd Triden was right . . . you're weakness is a weed!" Wiley whips wickedly.

"Could'a killed em. They didn't deserve it." Jack stammers, failing to understand his point.

Walking away, Wiley spits over his shoulder. "Sure they did, so did Triden for being weak!"

"You 'n Triden have that in common. Both couldn't complete a jungle gym!" Jack interrupts, sending Wiley into a rage.

"WHAT WOULD YOU KNOW? Triden's a spoiled brat, and you're just the little orphan that could! I was their prodigy, perfectly positioned to become the first . . . you were adopted into GYAIA! I was bred for it! I was supposed to be ONE! All I ever

463

wanted was to be GAIA's greatest asset, years of expectation eradicated by a single fall! Now they'll anoint the nobody from nowhere!" Wiley evokes enviously.

"Doesn't matter now! Ta ta, maybe I'll give sweet Anna a little visit before we head off!" Wiley's wrathful words working in Jack's favor.

"Imma break you, Wiley!" Jack jolting between Wiley and his escape.

"Ve must go Vildvolf!" Volkov sneaking behind Jack.

"Volkov!" Wiley sneers, securing his case. "Jack, look out!" Carla launching into a kick, stunning the Soviet strongman. Jack jolts, grabbing Wiley's wrist, twisting intensely. "Let go, orphan!" Wiley wails, his feet stumbling on loose gravel below. Reaching into his coat, producing a taser, thrusting it deep into Jack's shoulder.

"Ahh, oomph!" Jack crashes to the ground, a searing pain shooting through his shoulder.

"Stole a few toys from Doc's. Evens the odds, don't ya think?" Wiley kicking Jack viciously out of his way.

"Volkov finish her quickly! GAIA will be upon us soon!" Wiley stunning Brian, ensuring their escape. Wiley shuffling stiffly towards his aircraft.

"Max! Wiley's escaping do you . . . Oomph!" Carla crashes carelessly from a kick from Volkov.

"Visiting good, home better!" The roided rhino roars, running off.

"I got him!" Bray sprinting into the fray, making ground on Wiley.

"Stay down!" Wiley wails, whipping a flash grenade in her direction. "Sh. . .eett AHhh!" Covering her face, flash flooring forward momentum. Stumbling to her feet, sirens searing ears. "Ahh!" Collapsing, clutching her knee shredded by shrapnel, shaken by searing pain.

"BRAY!" Jack roars, running to her side.

"Max, they're getting away, down that bird!" Carla shrieks, sprinting past her companions. Wiley's craft rumbles down the tarmac gaining speed.

"On it! Ok, baby girl, let's ruffle some feathers." Max steadying Soteria over the rising rocket.

"Come on, Max, you got this." Jack steadying Bray to her good leg.

"I got her, Jack. Go check on Sam." Brian taking her weight, attending to the injury.

"Shoot Sam!" Jack sprinting back into the hanger.

Wiley piloting his craft bumping Soteria, rockets off.

"Not so fast, Wildjerk!" Max darts, catching Wiley's craft easily.

"Pudgy one good pilot!" Volkov commends with a click. Comets cascade crackling around Soteria. Max barrels between melting magnesium, shielding his eyes and losing track of his target.

"Ahh! E.V.E. execute emergency landing sequence!" Max moans, hanging his head.

"Sam! . . . Sam!" Jack dodging through aged overturned office furniture.

"Mmmm, mmmm!" A muffled sound meeting his ear.

"Sam! Gotcha, buddy, hold still." Jack soothes, tearing tape from Sam's muzzled mouth.

"Pfff, hfff . . . hfff. Jack?" Sam stammers.

"You didn't report in, always report in!" Jack jests, helping Sam up.

"Always report in, ha!" Sam sniffs, squeezing him tightly.

"All good cadets?" Carla calls. "Yeah, all good. Wiley?" Jack answers, peeling himself from Sam.

"Got away. Dumped an entire payload of flares on Max. Come on!" She retorts, kicking dejectedly.

"Hey, Murphy, keep your head up, cadet." Carla calls, tossing something at Jack. "Anna's keychain!" Grabbing gratefully sharing a knowing nod.

"Payload? Flares on . . . Max's here too?" Sam stumbles, regaining his balance.

"Yeah, dude, he totally piloted Soteria like a madman." Jack steadying his companion. Dejected and defeated, the group assist a still-shaken Bray into Soteria, Sam co-piloting for Max to soar safely home. Solemn silence settling in her cabin, each to their own thoughts. Careening quietly, Soteria settles softly back at GYAIA.

466

"You did well, we got Sam back, and that's what matters."
Brian begins.

"Blackshear?" Jack begins staring out his window, watching
Carla assist his pierced professor into Nurse Jessie's care.

"Brian will do, what's up?" Correcting his cadet.

"Why didn't Sam say anything? Wiley said Sam figured it out
a while ago. Why didn't he say anything?" Jack presses.

"Come on guys, we gotta debrief. Madam Director's waiting."
Carla knocks grimly, gaining their attention.

"She'll be fine, boys. I'll have her patched up in no time." The
nurturing nurse hugs the dynamic duo.

"Matchsticks, debriefing now!" Carla slapping the twin's head
in one strike.

"Matchsticks?" Sam howls, holding his head.

"Oooooo, I'll be your bonfire baby OWWW!" Max shrieks,
tapping his head.

"Alright, Carla, hands to yourself Max." Jack jogs by eying
Brian.

"Oh no, I'm in no rush for this alpha charlie!" Brian backs
down from Jack's challenge.

"Why we always hurt the ones we love?" Max moans, still
rubbing his head.

"Come on, Max, let's get this over with." Sam slapping his
brother's head, sprinting off.

467

CHAPTER THIRTY EIGHT

NEVER DWELL ON WHAT'S LOST

The cool tones glow from fluorescents illuminating indifferent metallic walls adorned with neatly framed pictures of past graduating classes surrounding the room below. "Welcome back, cadets. Please have a seat." Director Stingley calmly commands, waving her hand over a long perfectly polished table with five glowing tablets carefully prepared for the following debrief. A chorus of chair wheels creak filling the cold room with echoes of defeat and melancholy faces as Jack and his companions populate jet black chairs. Sensing setback within her meticulously scripted collaboration, Stingley offers some solace.

"Failing is inevitable, but what makes humans great is that we learn from our mistakes. If one can learn from failure, the result of failing becomes the act of learning. View each loss as a learning opportunity and we will have succeeded another way. Let it hurt tonight and only tonight. We will grow from this team. I will gather Agent Bray's statement after she's recovered from her injuries." Surveying her own stoic face accompanied by five gloom faces reflecting within the perfectly polished tabletop, Stingley alters her approach.

"Cadet Duval, good to see you safe. Cadets take a few minutes to record your accounts; once everyone is complete, we will begin. Blackshear, you were the most senior cadet. When everyone's complete you may begin." Stingley states calmly. Minutes morph into an hour as the companions conclude their comments. Scattered tablets lay quietly upon the perfectly polished tabletop as the conversation continues to reverberate around the room.

"That's not entirely true. I never broke the sound barrier, check the logs, never went above seven fifty, give or take a few mphs. Yes, that's a fact!" Max points in Carla's direction.

"Losing Wiley wasn't my fault? How was I supposed to know he'd free every flare this side the Mississippi?" Max loses his cool, adding more to his statement.

"I'd like to amend my statement to report cadet Childress struck Sam and me upon our return. She also created a hostile work environment for months, leading to tonight's events." Max reaching across Sam for his tablet back. "Gentlemen, I've already spoken to cadet Childress about her actions, and she's expressed unequivocal commitment to remedying them. Cadet Murphy, your silence concerns me. Would you like to conclude recapitulations?" Director Stingley asks.

"Yes, Ma'am. What everyone said is accurate. I share everyone's concerns about Doc's notebook falling into the wrong hands. Hopefully, Doc's encryptions slow Wiley down. I take full responsibility for not apprehending Wiley. I noted in my statement that Wiley became angry when I mentioned his injury, and I also became angry at his treatment of Professor Bray. My emotions compromised the mission. How could someone hide hatred for so long?" Jack noticing Stingley's lips quiver readying a response, he leans closer pausing to listen intuitively.

"Failure affects individuals differently, cadet Murphy. It is my opinion; Wiley sowed his seed of envy long ago. Jack, when you bested the trials, you merely revealed the rot within. We will track down Wiley, but now is no time to dwell on what's lost. Focus on what is. The mission was to retrieve a more important GYAIA asset, I am sure cadet Duval is grateful. The hour is late, cadets. I will review all accounts and inform GAIA of my decision. Given the bureaucratic channels this report must navigate, I have concluded that cadet Murphy's best course of action is return home to rest and recuperate." Directors Stingley states.

"May I? Madam Director Stingley, may I speak freely?" Max stands, raising his hand.

"You may." She directs.

"Sam and I would also like to apply for . . ." Max begins before Stingley cuts him short.

"Granted. Given today's events, I have arranged for all five of you to complete your first official team-building exercise. Cadets Childress, Blackshear mission specs, study and dispose. These three boots are need to know. Get some shuteye, team, you leave 0400." Stingley salutes, dismissing her cadets.

"Team?" Max speaking out of turn, pulled roughly by his tired twin.

"Cadet Murphy, a word . . ." Stingley commands, settling comfortably in her large cushioned seat, motioning him to close the door as his weary companions file out to a much deserved rest.

"Please sit, we have much to discuss."

CHAPTER THIRTY NINE

HOME IS WHERE THE HEART IS

"Guys, ain't this awesome? The home that built the Titan King!" Max muses, staring excitedly out the window.

"Can't wait to meet Ms. Anna. Can we call her Aunt Anna, too? So many trees! Tree! Tree! Tree!" he continues to annoy everyone outside of Jack.

"Does this oxygen thief ever shut up?" Carla kicking his seat in protest.

"Aa, he's just excited. Heck, we haven't seen home in months ourselves. How's it feel, Jack?" Blackshear inquires nudging Jack.

"Feels good, man. It ain't much, but there she is. Home sweet home!" Jack leaning forward in anticipation.

"She's home awesome!" Jack jumps jubilantly.

"Whoa! Where's the rest of it?" Max searching suspiciously.

"Shut it, Max. Looks nice, Jack, very homely." Sam slapping Max's head. "Oww! What?" He mules.

"Come on, guys, let's go." Jack barely allowing Brian to brake. Gravel crunching underfoot, Jack races excitedly. Fighting for position, Sam and Max follow suit.

"First years! You're on duffel duty . . . on the hop!" Carla commands, sending the excited trio to the rear of the black SUV.

"Aww, man, I thought we were on vacation." Max mules.

472

"It's not that much, bro, come on." Sam steering his moaning multiple to their task.

"Jack, grab my duffel; don't want that creep getting any ideas." Carla eyes Max.

"Gotcha. I mean, yes, Ma'am." Jack salutes.

"None of that, Jack. We're undercover act natural." Carla shakes her head, sprinting after Brian.

Steps creek under Brian's bulk, knocking firmly.

"One second . . . just get this cobbler, there you go. Coming!" Aunt Anna's sweet voice echoes warmly.

"Welcome, welcome. Wow, well, aren't you put together, young man. Oh no, we hug around these parts." Anna squeezes gratefully.

"How long has Aunt Anna been single?" Max muses.

"Well, aren't you a southern bell. Childress, right?" Anna hugs Carla, who stammers from her warmth.

"Ye, yes, Ma'am. Carla will do. It's a pleasure." The pair stepping inside, revealing her prized pupil.

"Snff . . . Snff come here you. Fit as always, locks had to go, hehe. How'd this happen?" Anna tugging Jack's chin, eying a pink scar above his eye.

"Snff. I missed you, sweet boy. Oh, how I've missed you."

"Sweet boy, eh?" Max trudges up the steps, tucking taunts away for later.

"I'm good, really, Aunt Anna. I'd like you to meet the twins. Samuel and Maximillian Duval." Jack introduces.

473

"How do you do Ma'lady!" Sam saddled with the bulk of bags settles for a side hug.

"Aunt Anna, you're even prettier than Jack described!" Max dropping his duffel, diving in for an embrace.

"Tehe! Stop it, ya little charmer. You're on a fast track to seconds of my blue ribbon cobbler."

"Blue ribbon cobbler? Jack said nothin bout cobbler!" Max drifts into the kitchen.

"Should've clarified normal." Carla rolling her eyes hard. "Hmm, har, har! Probably so." Brian smirks, snagging their bags.

"Jack, be a dear and show everyone to their rooms; twins in Reginald's room. Carla, take Ari's room straight ahead. Brian will bunk with you, Jack. Supper's almost ready." Anna announces, making her way to the kitchen.

"Out, Casanova, cobbler's ready when it's ready." Anna shoeing Max out.

"This is nice, Jack." Sam patting his companion's shoulder.

"Yeah, com'n, I'll show you Reg's room. He probably left some Dekken Dragon starters somewhere." Jack escorts.

"Double D? Double's the best! Let me at em." Max follows wiggling his fingers.

"Touch me, and I'll break your back." Carla warns, dodging into the hall bathroom.

"Backbreaker? Think Randle has him, Jack?" Max's eyes avert down the hall hastily.

"It's Reginald and I have Backbreaker and his twin sister Spinesmasher! Who be you intruder?" Reggie's voice rings from down the hall baring entry to his sanctuary.

"Reg! Is . . . is it really?" Jack's voice choking slightly sprinting down the hall.

"Okay! Okay! I missed ya too Bud! You look good Jack, better than ever." Reg poking at his friend's ribs. "Stop, stop it. You too Reg, must've lost a few yourself." Jack grins swiping defensively.

"Don't let him fool ya Jack, he's sucking it in. Who's the hottie with ya'll?" Ari's voice cutting through their playful banter.

"Shut up Ari! You're standing up a little straighter too!" Reggie retorts dodging a vicious swipe from Ari. "NO, no Ari not the Earnhardt! Truce, truce! I'm sure miss fit chick likes two-tone hippm m m." Reggie begins before Jack muffles his mouth.

"Well Jack are you going to make introductions? These duffels are not getting any lighter." Sam's voice stabbing through rising tension in the hallway.

"Yeah let's see that Spinesmasher! Ma'am is this Wogglebeast bothering you?" Max motioning to the bedroom, placing another duffle strap on Sam's sinking shoulder.

"I'll show you Wogglebeast. I happen to have "The Herder's Call"; ever seen it in action ya little Slatesnail?" Reggie rockets back in Max's direction.

"Betcha ya don't even know how to use a Slatesnail in battle!" Max muses following Reggie in to his room.

"Well should've expected that honestly!" Jack stifling a smile as he unburdens Sam's shoulders.

"Sam that was Reginald, he prefers Reg and this is Ari. Sam, Ari. Ari, she's Carla and the big guy is Brian. My room's here Sam c'mon." Jack motioning Sam to his room unloading their duffels. Sliding past Ari in the slender hallway Jack and Sam go about their task.

"Ari, pleasure to meet you. Jack where the rest of these go?" Brian politely acknowledging Ari with a crisp smile, sending warmth into her reddening cheeks.

"Yummy, I mean here those can go in here. I believe Aunt Anna said this was your room um, Car, carl, a, ah." Ari stammers at the two picturesque physiques.

"Here's good?" Carla gritting through a smile, cutting past Ari.

"Uhh, yeah, I mean yes. I usually stay in this room. Best mattress in the house. Not sure why I said that, this way." Ari awkwardly shuffles showing Carla where she can unpack.

"I'm going see if Miss Anna would like some help. Ladies, check on the boys in a few." Brian concludes, tossing two duffels on Carla's bed before heading to the kitchen.

"Just rode almost two hours with them clowns. Leave em be for a bit, you wanna do the honors?" Carla cuts nodding at Ari.

"Definitely not. Had to hide with that big lummox while ya'll were driving in. Worst five minutes of my week, I'm sure Miss Anna could use some help with dinner." Ari scoffs as the two share a synchronized smile.

476

With extra efficient hands, supper comes together quickly.

"Boys! Supper's ready!" Anna announces, sending bangs and booms that reverberate down the hall.

"No, no me first!" Max straining past Reg's girth in the doorway.

"No, me first! Ahhh, stronger than you look, your no Slatesnail, ya Dwarfgoblin!" Reggie squeezing past Max.

"I understand you're frustration Jack, but Reg is right. "The Herder's Call" may take spamming your deck with Wogglebeasts, but that card specifically states that four or more Wogglebeasts or any terrestrial herd beasts gain ten percent attack, twenty defense, and fifty spirit points." Sam comforts his conquered companion.

"Whatever man, Max and Reg cheat every time." Jack sulks looking for his opening past Max and Reg.

"Sucks, but them the rules. Our deck needs a Blacksmith's Anvil; d'ya have one? Didn't bring my war maiden deck, and there he goes." Sam inquires as Jack blurs past Reg and Max almost knocking into Carla.

"Knock it off cade. .eht . . ; ehh I mean watch yourself Jack!" Carla cutting herself off, dodging him effortlessly.

The trio tussle for seats near Anna.

"No, Murph, I called this one . . . ya sat by her your whole life!" Max losing easily to Jack.

"Fine, I'll settle for second best." Max seating himself next to Carla, wiggling his eyebrows.

"I'm eating on the roof." Carla excuses herself when Jack jumps up, allowing Max to move.

"I got next." Jack sitting between Max and Carla, saving her the misery as everyone settles in their seats.

"Well, this is nice, let us pray. . ." Anna begins blessing the food. Minutes melt as mouths motoring gratefully.

"Mighty fine, Ms. Anna, mighty fine." Brian polishes off his third helping.

"Thank you, Brian. Hope you're talkin bout the chicken? Tehe." Anna responds, sipping her sweat tea suggestively.

"Did'ya see that Murph, com'n Dude!" Max poking Jack pointing at the two.

"Shh. Max, I swear." Jack whispers, digging fork into femur.

"YEeoow! Cobbler ready?" Max stifling a shriek.

"Not sure if I have any yeow, I do have vanilla ice cream. Jack, be a dear." Anna sweetly asks.

"Yeah, Murph, ice cream sounds goOOOood?" Max jiggling in his seat, Jack pushing down carefully hiding forked fingers.

"Oh, sit, Ms. Anna. The boys can help clear the table. Ari and I'll get the cobbler." Carla offers, nodding towards her and Ari's brief escape.

"Oh yes dishes and dorks are our specialty!" Sam adds.

A tear wells in Anna's eye, the new friends moving swiftly, clearing and setting the table for dessert. Jack directing traffic jovially jabbing at Reggie, Sam and Max. Brian joining in the juvenile jargon much to Ari and Carla's chagrin.

"Let them be boys for a little while longer, Carla. Life requires 'em to be men most of their lives. A boy's life is short." Anna smiling sweetly soaking in their banter.

"And what of the girl?" Carla staring stoically.

"Hmm . . . she goes long before they arrive." Anna whispers for only her to hear. Carla's hands relaxing.

"Who wants cobbler? Sorry, Carla, Ari, excuse my step. Nope, no you'll wait." Brian hosting the award-winning treat high above Max's outstretched arms. Seating themselves, companions sharing stories of trials, and triumphs. Warmth wafting worries away.

"I did, as promised finally washed that dirty ole thing." Anna concludes laughing to tears.

"Not the Eliminator! Betcha Reg cried like a baby! Guys, you don't understand why this thing stunk so badly. Hahaha!" Jack slaps the table, sending laughter circling.

"Ya eliminated the odor!" Sam jokes, sending Max to the floor, bursting with laughter.

"Harty, har, har everyone's a comedian these days." Reggie frowns hiding his hat below the table. "Wasn't that bad!" He exclaims above the chorus of laughter.

"Har, har! Can't imagine." Brian bellows, patting his stuffed stomach. As stories and laughter fade, the new companions clears and cleans dishes with laser-like focus. Carla and Brian excuse themselves to talk specs. Reggie and Max with much help from Sam; convince Ari to play Dekken Dragons till dusk turns to dawn. Anna discovers Jack outside, sitting alone on the old wooden deck like many times before.

"Good group, Jack, seem to get along with Arianna and Reginald well. GYAIA was good for you. What's the matter, Sweetie?" Her soothing voice calming thoughts in his head. "Yeah, it's weird, Aunt Anna . . ." Jack digs in his pocket, producing her keychain.

"You kept it, so what did Jess tell ya?" Taking the trinket, settling beside him.

"Nothing really, ur, you two seemed really close." Jack surmises shooting a look over his shoulder at the sounds of his friend's voices laughing loudly from inside the house.

"We were, we all were. Don't blink too much Sweetie, one day you'll miss the simpler times. Snff . . ." Anna stifles a sniffle, taking the trinket carefully inspecting its memories. Both smile warmly as the pair share an understanding glance. Wishing he'd press Anna about her past, Jack struggles with ruining a fun evening. Silent seconds pass before Jack gathers his thoughts.

"I missed ya'll for sure and I ur, I mean . . . I've learned so much the past six months, but still feels like I know nothing." Jack staring stoically, searching her eyes for answers. Looking down ashamed of her continued silence, Anna sniffs softly hugging him before returning inside. Knowing the boy from nowhere who left months ago now is gone. Replaced by something more, by someone more, someone destined for great and unexpected things.

THE END

JACK MURPHY WILL RETURN. . .

IN SECRETS OF THE SAHARA

www.ingramcontent.com/pod-product-compliance
Lightning Source LLC
Chambersburg PA
CBHW070828260626
47170CB00007B/2296